ACCLAIM FOR RACHEL

"*Murder at the Flamingo* is a dynamite beginning to McMillan's newest series. Both a coming-of-age tale and a twisty case of whodunit, readers will fall in love with her delightfully complicated characters. 1937 Boston leaps to life in vivid detail, while the author's portrayal of anxiety and panic disorder is both heartbreaking and inspiring. I cannot wait to read Hamish and Reggie's next adventure."

—ANNA LEE HUBER, BESTSELLING AUTHOR
OF THE LADY DARBY MYSTERIES

"Rachel McMillan's *Murder at the Flamingo* is an extravaganza of fabulous characters and prose that transported me to 1930s Boston. McMillan has quite a talent for immersing the reader in a profound historical experience. Highly recommended!"

—COLLEEN COBLE, *USA TODAY* BESTSELLING AUTHOR

"In *Murder at the Flamingo*, McMillan, author of the *Herringford and Watts Mysteries*, offers us a new generation of sleuths. And in her skilled hands, 1937 Boston comes to life with rich sensory detail and clever winks to books and films. You'll love the happening and opulent nightclubs, the fast-paced dancing and daring, and especially the two sleuths who will steal your heart."

—KATHERINE REAY, AUTHOR OF *DEAR MR. KNIGHTLEY*
AND *A PORTRAIT OF EMILY PRICE*

"On its surface, *Murder at the Flamingo* is a fun and engrossing pre-war murder mystery that will keep readers turning pages. It's beautifully atmospheric, taking us to late 1930s Boston in such vivid detail you can almost taste the decadent cannoli cream so beloved by McMillan's amateur sleuth protagonists. The pacing is taut without sacrificing development of the endearing cast of characters. But more significant than this, McMillan gives us a story that highlights the struggles of people living with anxiety and panic disorders long before the conditions were properly understood.

Her portrayal of Hamish's challenges is sympathetic and uplifting, and only serves to make his character richer. This delightful series is one I will be following for what I hope is a very long time."

—AIMIE K. RUNYAN, INTERNATIONALLY BESTSELLING AUTHOR OF *DAUGHTERS OF THE NIGHT SKY* AND *PROMISED TO THE CROWN*

"A perfectly-flawed hero and a liberty-seeking lady are the backbone of this delightful and lively mystery novel. Grounded in a city that is no stranger to independence, Hamish and Reggie seek what it means to be free beneath the lights of Boston's glitziest nightclub . . . and a murder that taints its opening night. Fast-paced and at times humorous, the satisfying ending leaves the reader content and anxious for more all at the same time."

—HEIDI CHIAVAROLI, AWARD-WINNING AUTHOR OF *FREEDOM'S RING* AND *THE HIDDEN SIDE*, ON *MURDER AT THE FLAMINGO*

"Adventure—the very thing both of Rachel McMillan's lovable characters seek is exactly what she delivers, sucking the reader back to the '30s with distinctive style. Fans will be clamoring for the next installment!"

—ROSEANNA M. WHITE, BESTSELLING AUTHOR OF THE *SHADOWS OVER ENGLAND* SERIES, ON *MURDER AT THE FLAMINGO*

"Boston comes roaring to life with fullness and flair, a character in its own right. Endearing protagonists carry the tale with wit, charm, and struggles that make them human. Bursting with rhythm, *Murder at the Flamingo* is a toe-tapping, heart-pumping immersion into the world of Reggie and Hamish. A delightful experience."

—JOCELYN GREEN, AWARD-WINNING AUTHOR OF *A REFUGE ASSURED*

"You will want to add Reggie Van Buren and Hamish DeLuca to your circle of friends when you've read this book. This highly original story is a delight. Excellent historical detail and setting."

—MAUREEN JENNINGS, AUTHOR OF THE *DETECTIVE MURDOCH* SERIES, WHICH INSPIRED THE *MURDOCH MYSTERIES* TV SERIES, ON *MURDER AT THE FLAMINGO*

"With a crowded mystery and suspense market, it's hard to stand out from the pack. Rachel McMillan manages to do just this. She revives the classic 1930s-era amateur detective–whodunit set in a gloriously atmospheric Boston nightclub—The Flamingo . . . [*Murder at the Flamingo*] manages to cross the bridge between 'issue fiction' and 'commercial fiction' seamlessly. It's an immensely enjoyable and important read that I can't recommend highly enough. I simply loved this book!"

—TALL POPPY WRITERS

"A delicious mystery chock-full of 1930s charm and romance. I can't wait to find out what Reggie and Hamish get up to next!"

—CHERYL HONIGFORD, AWARD-WINNING AUTHOR OF THE VIV AND CHARLIE MYSTERY SERIES, ON *MURDER AT THE FLAMINGO*

"*Murder at the Flamingo* sweeps the reader into a world of liquid-silk gowns, snazzy gangsters, smoke-filled dance floors, and star-crossed romance. Not to mention a bit of murder. Rachel McMillan breathes life into a cast of characters that defy the clichés of the genre: a rich girl who isn't spoiled, a leading man plagued with anxiety, a mob boss with a heart, and others who bring twists with each turn of the page. McMillan crafts Hamish, Reggie, Luca, and Nate with enough dimension for the reader to inspect each with a slow turn—strengths, flaws, frustrations. Nothing is absolute. The story plays out with the grit and humor of an RKO picture show, with the author's love for the time and place evident with each nod to detail. McMillan gives us a new Nick and Nora, sharing a bicycle and cannoli— and maybe a little bit more."

—ALLISON PITTMAN, AUTHOR OF *LOVING LUTHER*

"Rachel McMillan is a refreshing, talented writer who has created an original and appealing hero in Hamish DeLuca. Enjoy!"

—JULIE KLASSEN, CHRISTY AWARD-WINNING AUTHOR, ON *MURDER AT THE FLAMINGO*

MURDER in the CITY of LIBERTY

Also by Rachel McMillan

Van Buren and DeLuca Mysteries

Murder at the Flamingo

Herringford and Watts Mysteries

A Singular and Whimsical Problem

The Bachelor Girl's Guide to Murder

Of Dubious and Quesionable Memory

A Lesson in Love and Murder

Conductor of Light

The White Feather Murders

The Three Quarter Time Series

Love in Three Quarter Time

Rose in Three Quarter Time

Of Mozart and Magi

MURDER
in the CITY
of LIBERTY

A VAN BUREN AND DELUCA MYSTERY

RACHEL MCMILLAN

THOMAS NELSON
Since 1798

Murder in the City of Liberty

© 2019 by Rachel McMillan

Published in Nashville, Tennessee, by Thomas Nelson. Thomas Nelson is a registered trademark of HarperCollins Christian Publishing, Inc.

Thomas Nelson titles may be purchased in bulk for educational, business, fundraising, or sales promotional use. For information, please email SpecialMarkets@ ThomasNelson.com.

Publisher's Note: This novel is a work of fiction. Names, characters, places, and incidents are either products of the author's imagination or used fictitiously. All characters are fictional, and any similarity to people living or dead is purely coincidental.

Published in association with William K. Jensen Literary Agency, 119 Bampton Court, Eugene, Oregon 97404.

ISBN 978-0-7852-1697-1 (e-book)

Library of Congress Cataloging-in-Publication Data

Names: McMillan, Rachel, 1981- author.
Title: Murder in the City of Liberty / Rachel McMillan.
Description: Nashville, Tennessee : Thomas Nelson, [2019] | Series: A Van Buren and Deluca mystery ; 2
Identifiers: LCCN 2018059446 | ISBN 9780785216964 (paperback)
Subjects: | GSAFD: Mystery fiction.
Classification: LCC PR9199.4.M4555 M88 2019 | DDC 813/.6--dc23 LC record available at https://lccn.loc.gov/2018059446

Printed in the United States of America

19 20 21 22 23 LSC 5 4 3 2 1

To Sonja Spaetzel
Who not only always listens, but also always knows what to say

Through all our history, to the last,
In the hour of darkness and peril and need,
The people will waken and listen to hear
The hurrying hoof-beats of that steed,
And the midnight message of Paul Revere.

—HENRY WADSWORTH LONGFELLOW, "PAUL REVERE'S RIDE"

He therefore turned to mankind only with regret. His cathedral was enough for him. It was peopled with marble figures of kings, saints and bishops who at least did not laugh in his face and looked at him with only tranquillity and benevolence. The other statues, those of monsters and demons, had no hatred for him—he resembled them too closely for that. It was rather the rest of mankind that they jeered at.

—VICTOR HUGO, *THE HUNCHBACK OF NOTRE-DAME*

CHAPTER 1

CHICAGO
MARCH 1940

When Luca Valari was in a room, you had two choices: leave or step aside to await acknowledgment. When Arthur Kent's scuffed shoes clacked the floor of the lakeside-facing warehouse, they took him directly to the left of Luca, leaving the latter with ample room in the middle of the cavernous space, broad doors open to the pre-spring day beyond.

From Luca's vantage, beyond the headline he held up to the light, the Windy City was blue on blue: horizon meeting rippling waters, intersected by men in high-end demi-yachts and sailboats, enjoying the first thaw as the remnants of ice glistened under glaring sun. He folded the page of newspaper back into its neat square and tucked it into his pocket.

Luca smoothed an invisible crease from the double breast of his bespoke jacket. Then turned, obsidian eyes flashing in Kent's direction. "What are you doing here?" Luca was waiting for a man called Phin Murphy.

"I'm in the market—"

"For my shoving you into Lake Michigan?" Luca rarely let anything break his composure, but he hated this man and the

— 1 —

lake was cold and spread before him, wind whistling over the wood slats of the floor and rippling the tarps and sails hung haphazardly on the wall. He could usually coax followers into play, mold them into what he wanted, but he had little respect for men who couldn't keep their loyalties rooted. Sure, Arthur Kent had followed the now-dead Suave around for years, but his next step shouldn't have led him to the man on the opposite side of Suave.

"For business."

"Last I saw you, you were weaseling up to Suave at my Flamingo Club."

"Almost three years is a long time."

"I don't trust you."

"People change."

Luca knew he had a reputation for leniency. A soft touch. Didn't get his hands dirty. He shot a look at Kent and wondered if it was time to break his own rule.

Phin Murphy arrived before Luca gave in to his inclination.

"Well. You two have met?" Phin asked.

Luca tapped his shoe impatiently. Had Salvatore Ferragamo leather ever crossed these ratty boards?

"Heard you had dropped off the face of the earth, Valari." Phin looked him over.

Luca hadn't seen him in years, and the smartly slicked brown hair showed the slightest trace of gray. He kept his voice light. "I don't know if I would refer to Canada as such . . ."

"But they're at war . . ."

Luca raised a shoulder and said lightly, "Doing my bit for the war effort. I am just not sure I want to invest in *that* war effort." He took a nonchalant step in the direction of the open slat that offered a clear view of the sun dimpling Lake Michigan. He dug his hands in his pockets.

"Well, I heard you were sniffing for Beantown again. But finished with nightclubs, perhaps."

Luca kept his face blank. He loved Boston. Had been looking for a way to get back. There were good times there. Good times and pretty girls to be sought in the rhythm of Roy Holliday's band. Good times that smelled like popcorn and beer from the stadium stand at Fenway, that echoed in the laugh of his cousin.

Luca cleared his throat. "I like Boston. There are several smart people there who don't mind looking to creative ways to turn a buck."

Phin grinned. "Munitions."

"Well? People need them, don't they? There are factories, an easy shipping route." Luca didn't fancy smelling fish and gasoline all day, but he wouldn't have to be there.

"It's a well-known fact you never get your hands dirty," Phin said. "That you are never responsible. I figured perhaps since the accident happened . . ." Phin turned his head over his shoulder at Kent, perhaps the first notice the man had warranted since the two other men entered the scene.

"Accident?"

Everybody had a breaking point. Or, as Luca called it, a weakness. Something that turned their head and drove them beyond themselves. Some might think of it as a path to redemption. Luca knew it to be a thorn in his side. One of the few analogies that stuck from church services he had long abandoned attending. He swallowed, taking the words in stride, then inhaled a deep breath and swerved to dagger Phin with his eyes.

"What are you saying?" Luca stole a look to Arthur Kent, who stared at his shoes.

"The surest way to kill a weed is to hack at the source. But there is also virtue in choosing to aim where the bullet will harm the most . . ." Phin paused. "Seems that cousin of yours is still ripe for the picking. Set up a little consultation business in the North End of Boston. Same address as your old office."

A chill tickled over Luca's spine and settled at the back of his neck. It ended in a reflex that grabbed Phin's collar and squeezed tight. "You're right." Luca's teeth were clenched. "I don't get my hands dirty. At least I haven't"—Luca drew a breath—"yet." He enunciated each consonant.

Phin cocked his head to the side. "Interesting." He pulled out a map and returned to their earlier conversation. "Fiske's Wharf." He pointed to an edge on a curve of blue. "You know Boston. It's prime real estate for . . . for what you want to do. But remember what we spoke of on the phone; I am only showing you this because I want in on the cut."

"Show me."

"There are two ways in here. There's an architectural firm: Hyatt and Price. In it for slum housing developments. Highly politicized views."

Luca raised a shoulder. "I don't go in for politics."

"There's also this fellow named Kelly. Rough around the edges. But owns it. Has quite a few men under his thumb too. Including some involved in baseball."

"Baseball?"

Phin lifted a shoulder. "Apparently. The right cops turn an eye. My source says there's one who is a little green. Doesn't get his hands dirty. But he hasn't met anyone with your charm yet."

"You're still here?" Luca flicked a look at Kent.

"I was thinking I might also go to Beantown. I miss it." Kent took a step toward them.

Luca didn't hide the disgust from his face. "I don't trust you."

"Give old Art a chance."

"Art?" Luca had never bothered learning the man's first name. He was just Mark Suave's leech.

"I didn't do anything to you, Mr. Valari."

"Exactly. You didn't *do* anything. You were a shadow."

"Mr. Valari."

Luca jangled the keys in his pocket. "Fine. Go see this Kelly fellow. You can put up with the fish and gasoline. Find out what is happening there. But don't tell him who sent you."

"I'm not—"

"Stupid? Foolish?" Luca stabbed him with a look. "Then go find a Nathaniel Reis in the North End. Housing Development."

"And do what with him?"

"Do *nothing* with him." Luca let annoyance slip into his voice. "Just listen around. Find out what he's doing. What new properties are going up. What he thinks of this new wharf development. If something is happening in the North End, Reis will know about it."

"One of yours?" Phin asked.

"Not yet."

"How will I contact you in Boston?" Phin watched Kent retreat.

"You won't. I'll be in touch." Luca turned to the water ruefully, studied the sun streaming over the little licks of waves. "I lived here as a boy for a few years. I remember it clearly as a man, but there are moments when the light hits the water and it takes me back."

"Luca Valari the sentimentalist."

"I am turning sentimental, aren't I?" He smoothed his face into a look that on some men would have been indifference but on Luca Valari was just guarded charm. "Just means it is time to leave."

CHAPTER 2

BOSTON
APRIL 1940

There really never was a *good* time to drown. But this particular April had been unseasonably cold and promised spring long in coming. The slosh of the Charles River warmed by ribbons of June sun would have been preferable to the crusted sludge of left-over ice rimming the harbor, or so thought Reggie Van Buren as she bobbed up and down like a buoy.

A New Haven Van Buren ought to have perished an old, wealthy woman, tendrils of snow-white hair falling around a satin pillow, comforted in the knowledge that she would be interred in the family plot, her soul destined for paradise—not with water up to her nose, choking as it lapped in and out like a tide over her chattering teeth. But a New Haven Van Buren also might have had the propriety to insist upon the use of her given name and not the "Reggie" she so preferred. The Reggie she was just hearing now in a rather frantic yet familiar voice.

"Reggie!" Hamish DeLuca's panicked voice reached into the hollow dome of her cement cave. "Reggie!"

"I was st-stupid. I s-slipped." She treaded poorly, her arms feeling like gelatin, her form rather lacking the swimming skills she had learned informally alongside her family's schooner on Regatta Day.

Reggie strained to rise above the lapping water. She took turns treading and raising herself as high up on her toes as she could. Rotating and wondering why she failed to complete the ballet classes her parents enrolled her in as a child. Standing on tiptoe might have added inches to her height and allowed her to clear her mouth of the water. As it was, her calf muscles strained. She said something that came out in a series of bubbles before glugging, rising upward, and noticing for the first time how the fog from her icy breath rippled over the water. If she couldn't understand herself, how would he?

"S-slipped," she said again, trying to make him out in shadow. "H-Hamish." She tried again. Funny, usually he was the one with the stutter. Hamish DeLuca with the stutter and the bit of a handshake and that one pesky dimple and those big blue eyes. Her own eyes fluttered. Maybe she would never see him again. She would just slip under the water and rest her heavy eyelids. She blinked until a stream of torchlight buttered the dark walls, crystallizing the percolating water drips around her, and then the figure of her rescuer, whose blue eyes looked even more brilliant than usual in the eerie glow of the flashlight.

Hamish dropped to his knees. "Take my hand."

"This didn't turn out as I expected," she chattered.

"Reggie, we don't have much time." His voice rippled as he looked frantically at her and then over to the grille she had stared at since she got into the mess, watching the water level rise and fall and rise and fall until it made her dizzy. She clung to his hand a moment.

"We should have gone with plan B."

Hamish growled. "We didn't even have a plan A."

"You're my hero, Hamish." She patted his hand with her icy one. "It was so nice of you to come."

"Reggie, just take my hand."

"I'm stuck!"

"What?"

"M-my shoe."

Hamish said something she was altogether certain she had imagined in her half-frozen and very soggy state. And then, of course, he recklessly jumped in to get her.

⁎

For the past two years, nine months, and four days, from the moment Hamish DeLuca awoke, brushed his teeth, and combed his tumbly black hair from his forehead into some semblance of order, he thought of holding Reggie Van Buren. From the moment he bolted back a cup of espresso, passing his roommate in the kitchen, holding her more tightly. Then over a quick stride a few blocks to the Van Buren and DeLuca office on the second floor of a building wedged directly adjacent to the Paul Revere House, the feel of her lips, the eagerness of her touch. He thought of holding Reggie as she hung her coat and hat in the corner before scooting down a flight for her morning bout as a stenographer at Mildred Rue's temporary employment agency. He thought of holding her at lunch when she unwrapped the waxed paper from an egg sandwich. He thought of holding her as she sang along to the song that Jean Arthur and Gary Cooper performed in *Mr. Deeds Goes to Town* in her off-key voice. Something about the Swanee River. He thought of holding her even as he stepped out dancing with pretty Bernice Wong, twirling his dance partner so her skirts lapped up over her knees and brushed his pant leg.

Holding her while they conferred on everything from petty crime to missing siblings to loopholes in employment and housing contracts. Holding her forever. But he hadn't anticipated holding her as she slipped unconsciously into the water, a result of a rather confusing client call leading them down to the harbor.

It was the time of year still somewhat etched in nature's charcoal: smudges of shade and light ruminating over rippled water moody with the eclipse of the dwindling sun behind a hanging cloud. The crocuses in the Common were a tease of spring that disappeared as quickly as the next unexpected bout of sleet and snow.

It all started when Reggie had received an anonymous phone call asking for their expertise on a matter of boat licensing and property law. Hamish, though tired and not usually eager to set off under such vague circumstances, figured Reggie was sick of her stenography work and playing with the radio dial. The bulk of their most recent consultations had been for Hamish's legal expertise alone. Hamish didn't mind. He wasn't necessarily chomping at the bit to set out after a murderer or find himself entangled in the type of enterprise involving people like his cousin, Luca Valari—the reason he had come to Boston in the first place.

Every time they were called out on a vague mystery, he couldn't help but wonder if it was part of Luca's web, a world he still kept on his mental back burner, determined to solve every last unanswered question that his cousin had left behind after a corpse was found at Valari's glittering nightclub.

It had been a routine day. Reggie scribbling something in her journal of independence. Hamish nudging his glasses up his nose as he attempted to unravel a rather convoluted passage of property law. Reggie loved fresh air regardless of season, so the window was open a smidge to usher in the breeze and the symphony of children's laughter and the chatter of tourists from the historic square below, even as Hamish shivered and unrolled the sleeves customarily rolled to his elbows.

"Reg, do you think we should meet someone who won't even give us his name?" he said in response to her enthusiasm to head down to the wharf. It had taken a moment for him to get the sentence out, not because his voice rippled with anxiety, but rather because she was wearing a yellow blouse that perfectly complemented the brown tendrils at the back of her neck.

"Stop thinking of everything that could go wrong." Reggie played with the dial on the wireless. It was almost three o'clock and therefore almost time for *Winchester Molloy: New York Gumshoe* to statically ripple over the airwaves. "Start thinking about everything that could go right! But it's money, Hamish, and an adventure. Did you have plans tonight?" Hamish translated Reggie's exaggerated lift of an eyebrow to mean "with Bernice?" Bernice was his sometime dancing partner. Just as Vaughan Vanderlaan and his shiny car and cologne was her sometime evening companion. Hamish was getting sick of the *sometimes*.

"It's cold and I don't want anyone yanking our chain."

Reggie shook her head. "Something this fellow said about having a business that the city council won't take seriously, and now other people want to use his plot of ocean . . . It was all very hard to understand and punctuated with words that would make Winchester Molloy go to confession. Come! Money is money, Hamish DeLuca." What he read in her tone was *Adventure is adventure.* "Besides, he's our ideal client. A little mystery, lots of injustice. No guaranteed money or actual case." Her laugh wrinkled her nose and its smattering of freckles disappeared. Hamish felt his heart constrict for the eighth time that hour. He moved his forefingers underneath his brace and kept a synchronized rhythm. His panic episodes were fewer in Boston, but the familiar habit made him calmer.

"Money, you say?"

This part was ironic, considering Reggie was would-be heir to a New Haven fortune had she not skipped off to the North End from a high-end garden party on her parents' lawn.

"Money!" She clapped her hands.

"Come on, then." He'd have followed her to the bottom of Mystic River if it secured a night in which she would be with him and not with Vaughan Vanderlaan, rising architect in a posh Washington Street firm, Hyatt and Price. While Hamish was never quite sure of the line between them, it wasn't blurred enough that he couldn't sense the obvious connection tethering them to their past, their parents' money, and their affluence.

Yet in his mind—the same mind that graduated at the top of his class from Osgoode Law School in Toronto and housed a deep and abiding love for Hugo's *The Hunchback of Notre-Dame*—was a grand love story. *Their* great love story. Only problem was one party didn't realize it while the other was Quasimodo aching for the lithe beauty of the Romany girl Esmeralda, whose eyes were turned by the far more dashing Captain Phoebus de Martin. At the pace Hamish was going, he might well end up like the eponymous hunchback in a barren crypt in Paris slowly turning to dust.

So Hamish followed Reggie's buoyant stride out of the office of Van Buren and DeLuca: Consultants in Investigations and Law long before the appointed time and place at Fiske's Wharf and Commercial Street. He lifted his bicycle from its resting spot against the wall and followed Reggie out the door, past the North End Housing Development office of their friend, and Hamish's flatmate, Nathaniel Reis.

"Heading out?" Nate's voice came from the open door. "I mean, I don't blame you. Mrs. Ricci's pet mouse Fluffy hasn't been seen in a week."

Reggie giggled. Hamish rolled his eyes.

"Glad to see we have the serious support of our friends in our business ventures," Hamish said while hopping down the stairs, bicycle over his shoulder.

_⊥_

They could have taken a cab, but Reggie wanted to take Hamish's bike. It was highly improper for a woman of her breeding to hoist herself up on the handlebars of a bicycle pedaled by a young man like himself. But while she reminded him of this several times as they pursued their adventures, she never stopped. Hamish set off, much more used to her weight, propelling the bike with a few kicks of his foot to ramp up speed and rhythm before pedaling. Soon they reached Fiske's Wharf, a barrage of buildings at the end of Commercial Street facing Charlestown across the river. The wind barreled in from the Atlantic, their voices compensating, Hamish's bike swerving with a bit of lost control.

A shadowed figure, collar turned up against the cruel sea breeze, awaited them.

"You came." He watched Reggie slide off the bicycle with her mix of spirit and ladylike charm. "Interesting mode of transportation."

"Were you the one who rang earlier?" Reggie stepped forward, removing her hand from its warm space in her coat pocket to brush back the hair escaping her pins with the whip of the wind. The man didn't answer. Hamish studied his profile—what he could see of it—under a tweed cap.

"I'm Regina Van Buren and this is Hamish DeLuca." She turned her head over her shoulder to smile briefly at Hamish. "Hamish is proficient in legal matters. If you and your associates are worried about some illegal licensing, you could come to the office and we could take a look. It would be much warmer." She rocked slightly on her heels and flashed a smile that brightened the muddy light. It was lost on the man.

"I don't go to offices. People come here to do my business with me." His eyes lingered on Reggie's pinned hair and then over her collarbone. Then slightly down. Even her beige trench, collar tucked up against the elements, couldn't keep her feminine shape from being noticed and appreciated. Hamish stepped up to Reggie so their shoulders brushed. The slight move was testament to how comfortable they had become with each other over the past two years. Reggie remembered their first strides toward friendship. Remembered blue eyes widening in answer to her tugging at his sleeve or the slightest friction between their arms.

The man pushed his hat back on his head, focused on something beyond Reggie for a moment. "Hold on! Kid!" Hamish and Reggie followed his sightline to a lanky black kid in his midteens. "Did you bring it? Paddy send you?"

Hamish couldn't hear the kid's responses even though he wasn't but three feet from them, bordered by their client, muffled by the sound of the wind. Something exchanged hands and the kid set off, tugging his beanie cap low on his ears.

The man swerved back and took in Reggie with a long look, his eyes, steely gray against the canvas of the sky meeting the sea, shifting over Reggie. His Irish accent was light as if it had been churned several times through a ringer and come out American with a few leftover vowels. "So you are familiar with files?" He studied Hamish. "Contracts? A friend said you helped his mother."

"I know the law. Property law, to some extent. Employment law."

"I know your face too. Something about a murder. In that club in Scollay Square. Few years ago now?"

"The murder we solved," Reggie said. "Not quite two years ago. Now we consult on all manner of things from deduction to legal matters. Jacks-of-all-trades."

The man didn't acknowledge Reggie, rather kept his eyes on Hamish. "There's something familiar about you. Ah! Yes. Luca Valari. Bit of an infamous name around here."

Hamish felt an unwelcome spark in his right fingers. He clenched them together and shoved them deep in his pocket to keep them from trembling. "I am quite trustworthy, I assure you. And my associate, Miss Van Buren, is right—we are jacks-of-all-trades.

But it will be much more helpful if we know how to address you. And why we're here."

The man turned, and Reggie and Hamish followed him, Hamish rolling his bike, then leaning it against a large wooden structure darting out to the lapping river. It was a prime spot for water traffic, tugs and freighters chugging in and out from the Atlantic.

"Well . . ." The man spoke barely above a whisper, and something in the cadence struck a familiar chord. Hamish let Reggie set the pace as they followed the man's lead inside. Hamish startled at the door slamming behind him. "You'll see here that my business is being threatened by a motion to turn this property into North End housing."

Hamish's two forefingers were tucked under his suspender, tapping softly.

"Bit fidgety there, Mr. DeLuca?"

"Nervous habit." Hamish looked around. "Not a lot of boats."

Reggie followed his sight line. "What should we call you?" she asked.

Their client hesitated a moment, eyes fixed on Hamish, then cocked his head while his watery blue eyes narrowed slightly in concentration. "Pete Kelly."

Kelly shifted the package the teen had given him, then took a pen and piece of paper out of his pocket and scribbled something with his left hand. Hamish saw the paper showed a map of the wharf and the surrounding area as well as a few notes and lines. He averted his eyes as quickly as Kelly looked up and met his gaze.

"I have had this slice of the harbor for as long as I can remember. We don't have any big frigates here, just sloops that jettison in and out. But this proposal would take the land and give it to Hyatt and Price, the architects. They want to develop here. And I am not sure that they are permitted to."

"You really should be speaking to our friend Nathaniel Reis. He's—"

"I won't deal with his sort," Kelly cut in. "I've heard about him. Around."

Reggie spluttered something while Hamish's forefingers tapped more steadily. "His sort?"

"Fellow like him shouldn't be given that kind of position. Don't trust them. Barely human."

From the corner of his eye, Hamish saw Reggie clench her fists. Her weight was on the balls of her feet and she was this close to throwing herself as a missile in the man's path. Hamish shot her a look. War had already erupted back home, and the national newspaper his father edited covered not only headlines of the battles being fought but the philosophies behind them and the leaders driving their men to war. Sadly, this man's prejudice toward Nate was not unfamiliar to Hamish. But it was still new to the North End, a neighborhood made up mostly of Italian residents who rallied in solidarity with the few Jewish inhabitants who hadn't shifted when the dominant race changed.

"Why did you hire private investigators? Why not just speak to a council member if you won't speak to Mr. Reis?"

"I did. And no one is admitting who signed off on this. Suddenly I've got boats in and out of my area here—surveying—as well as a motion to tear down my entire enterprise. To build housing."

He cursed under his breath, looked up, registered Reggie's eyes on him but didn't apologize. "I have been in this business for two decades. Come over from the Town every day and on Saturdays if it's not snowing. I have never done anything but keep my head down. I hire good men. Some of my own kind. Others all-Americans from all points of Boston. We deal in what we can get at a bargain price. Everything from livestock to handguns."

Hamish assumed his own kind were Irish. So many of the Irish who emigrated, spilling from crude ships when the great famine ravaged their green land, ended up within Boston's perimeters, particularly in Charlestown. Still, the "all-American" term pinged at him. The country was older than his home country of Canada, but not by more than one hundred years, and most of the people he met in the city were first or second generation: a patchwork quilt of all races, religions, and creeds.

Kelly led them through a broad door into an office. It wasn't a lot to look at, but it was neat. There was a pride to his work. Kelly followed Hamish's inspection with a slight smile.

"You approve?"

"You truly take care in what you do." Hamish didn't expound. He knew enough about black-market enterprises: of illegal shipments of weapons and liquor often tied to groups of men determined to cut a buck or two and use violence as a means of wielding power and keeping their enterprises profitable. They were a nightmare for people trying to do honest business in the North End.

"A job worth doing is worth doing well. I accept deliveries from Charlestown. Sure, they could come over the bridge in a van or by train; but if the freighters are about to dock in the harbor farther down, why not send someone over in a little boat to drop things off?" He stretched. "I even have a little black kid from across the river who takes manifests back and forth for me. Fast. His uncle's some kind of baseball player."

"And you wouldn't be getting a child to do anything untoward...," Reggie asked.

"I don't need to share all of my transactions, Miss Van Buren. But legal in the sense that I am owed the right to keep this piece of land. Here." Kelly was on the other side of the desk and clearly prepared for their arrival. He passed Hamish a folder. "I've done some retyping."

Hamish's conscience pricked, but he reasoned that Kelly wasn't expecting them to be a part of his enterprise, just to ensure that those who wanted to build on his property did so legally.

"You rent the building, though?" Hamish leafed through the open folder. "So the land you are on—"

"It's all in there." Kelly nudged his hand at the folder. "Just read the fine print and see if I have a case to stand on."

"You really could have come by the office," Reggie said.

Pete shot her a look. "Why don't I make you useful, show you around, while Mr. DeLuca puts his legal mind to work taking a look at the papers in my office?"

"We work together," Hamish said. "I can look into this later. All of my books are at the office, and I would want to consult with Nate."

"I never know who is in and out." He looked Hamish over. "Or who I can trust."

"You can trust me. But I would rather accompany you and Reggie."

"No, it's fine!" Reggie's smile hit him, wide and assuring. "I'll go and report back." She raised her index finger to her temple in a little salute. "You make sure everything is right here."

"I'll get her back to you in one piece," Kelly said with a skeptical eye over Hamish. "Don't you trust me?"

"Do I have a reason not to?"

⚹

Kelly led Reggie down a narrow hallway that got darker the farther they strolled. Reggie wrinkled her nose at the pungent blend of mold and a blend of gasoline and fish.

"It would be ridiculous to build housing here." Reggie waved a hand toward a percolating stream.

"There we are in agreement, Miss Van Buren."

They walked farther and the chill prickled Reggie through and through. The wind whistled through the building and winnowed through her, and she sensed they were inching closer to the water. She looked back over her shoulder, then studied Kelly before her. "This is a rather empty corridor." She thought she heard footsteps, but they disappeared so quickly, she assumed it was just the echo of Kelly's own shoes.

"Everything important is just ahead," he told her, nudging open a wide door that immediately ushered in another wall of chill from the exposed outside. A kind of boathouse where vessels could easily pull just inside and offload their wares.

There were several reasons Reggie shouldn't have trusted Kelly. Many of which passed through her mind as she struggled to keep from slipping on the sleek stones of the crevice where the boats would tug in to deposit their goods. It was a small, caged half oval. She didn't know why, but she immediately thought of the Traitor's Gate leading up to the Tower of London: a place she had seen in her teenage years when her mother was insistent she have a classical education. That shadow of a life that would never find her trapped in a warehouse on the Boston docks. But Kelly wanted her to see it. To see how the water would make it a poor place to develop housing. Reggie, instead, saw the crates stacked inside. Ammunition. Guns! They should get a gun. For the office. A sleek one like in *The Thin Man*.

"Look! You can go show Mr. DeLuca. This is a poor place for any development other than my own." Reggie refocused on him. His fair fingers were freckled, catching the dull light of the lamp he carried.

Kelly probably didn't mean for the heavy door to shut behind him just as she was inspecting a half-open crate. He was distracted by a voice in the hallway and turned, the intensity of his quick movement startling the door into a slam behind him. Reggie slid over and pulled on the handle.

"Mr. Kelly!" She turned her head over her shoulder, assessing her surroundings. Damp. One dilapidated rudder in the sluicing water that gulped up the slight platform she had. "Mr. Kelly!" she bellowed more loudly, beating at the door with her fist. "I don't think you meant to lock me in here!"

In the end it was the sound of a boat's engine just outside— loud as a shot—that startled her until she slipped and fell sideways. When her mouth—teeth chattering first with shock, then with cold, then with the reverberation of several unladylike sounds— filled with the unwanted water, she kicked and scrambled, and it was then that her foot snagged on the rudder she'd noticed earlier. Panicked, Reggie kicked harder until she remembered a scene from some picture. Darned if she knew which. She supposed that was the first part of her memory to go. All of the stars and plots. *Darn.* But what a stupid way to perish.

⎯ᙅⵊᙅⵊ⎯

For most of Hamish's life, he had focused on the limitations of his nervous disorder. The attacks and quickened heartbeat, the short breaths and panic that drove him from his first court case. He hadn't anticipated that he might have a far greater problem on his trembling hands. Reggie was gone. She was there and then she was gone, and he was stuck in this infernal warehouse as a lob- ster skittered over the floor and a man who had at least a foot on Hamish's medium height walked nearby. Something about the figure, the way he curled his fingers into his fist and the profile cloaked in shadow, clutched at Hamish's chest.

He might have had a second more to determine whether the figure was indeed familiar or whether he was just seeing the past everywhere he went, if the figure hadn't disappeared as quickly as Hamish had made him out.

He called after him, but the man didn't turn around. Hamish heard the slight echo of footsteps and sprang quickly forward. He lunged at the figure but was thrown off with quick ease against the wall. Hamish wheezed a breath the moment the air returned to his lungs and kept going. He didn't know where Reggie was. He didn't know where *he* was. A maze of offices and storage rooms peeked out like dead eyes on either side of dank hallways. The air was suffocated with salt, fish, and mold, and the tinny trill of dripping water punctured his head as he continued to follow what he thought were the footsteps of his attacker. Though he knew it was probably a poor choice, he turned in the direction of a slice of light spilling onto the creaking floorboards around his now soggy spectator shoes. He thought about chasing the man in the dark, but he had nothing to defend himself with.

He peeked inside the office in hopes that Reggie was perhaps in the corner. Maybe with a piece of cloth gagging her mouth. The *Winchester Molloy* serials were rubbing off on him. He took a quick look around, hoping Reggie could fare okay on her own in the interim. She would want the opportunity for adventure. "Do you think Myrna Loy needs William Powell at every turn and corner? I think *not*. She might *want* him there, but she doesn't *need* him there."

The office looked slanted. Hamish assumed it was its uneven position alongside the water, and the piles of papers all around made it look worse. While he supposed the land surrounding and leading up from the wharf must have been prime real estate, the building itself showed little evident value. No one looking around this office could think of it as holding a high price.

He grabbed immediately at a torch on a nearby cabinet. A pamphlet caught his eye, the words *Christian Patriots* printed across the front. A strange group name. If it was a denomination, it wasn't one he had heard of. It didn't sound traditionally Irish either, he decided, after wondering if it was perhaps something from Kelly's home country. He took a closer peek, brow furrowed at what he saw. He had heard of this type of propaganda from his father, who saw a lot of it during the Great War. Hamish grabbed the pamphlet and stuffed it in his pocket. The haphazard state had little to do with someone rifling through the uneven filing system. The office reminded him of the one in the penthouse he shared with Luca when he first moved to Boston in that it seemed to hold little purpose other than for show. But while Luca's office was all sleek mahogany and ornate bookshelves, this one was an eruption of papers. It caught Hamish as funny that it was the polar opposite of the orderly office of his friend Nathaniel Reis of North End Housing Development. He rifled some more, then turned his attention back to the pamphlet in his hand, eyes flickering over a name familiar to him belonging to one of the founding members: Dirk Foster. A man who was momentarily a suspect in the Flamingo murder of two years ago, but far more memorable as one of Reggie's high society friends from home. A close friend of Vaughan Vanderlaan.

Hamish scanned the manifests from some recent shipments. Livestock. Liquor. Cigarettes.

A haphazardly folded paper in jagged handwriting had lines of notes he could just make out. *Erosion. Rising tide.* A few squiggles. *Uneven territory.*

Hamish looked at his feet. This place was uneven, for sure. It looked to be standing, but the hurricane the year before and the rising tides that sluiced in and over the shore had left their mark.

He abandoned his quick survey, tucking the pamphlet safely in his pocket, when a vehicle backfired outside and sent him in faster pursuit of Reggie. The warehouse was a damp labyrinth.

He slid on the water suddenly sloshing over the boards the closer he got to the harbor-facing side of the building. There were no footsteps other than his own. No shadows in the corners. No sound . . . and then a pitiful one. He swerved. *Reggie.*

‒⋏‒

Reggie's shoe was caught in something that he couldn't quite see from the side of the water. So of course he threw off his glasses and dove in. Because she might have been at the bottom of a lava pit and he would have dove in headfirst without thinking. He had long ago decided that if at any point the universe decided to rid itself of Reggie, he wouldn't bat an eyelash before following.

Once the shock of the million stabs of ice shards initially washed over him, he gained enough physical momentum to reach for her leg. Something was coiled around it. He broke the water's surface again and raked his hand through his hair. "Okay, you're stuck." His teeth chattered. "Reggie! Wake up."

Heartbeat, Hamish. It was rather hard to think about his heartbeat when he couldn't *feel* his heartbeat even as the panic of seeing a far-too-inanimate Reggie shuddered through him. He ducked under again and this time wrenched her free, slicing his right finger open in the process. He watched the red stream a moment, then snapped himself into focus, surfaced, caught Reggie in his arms, and propelled them to the edge. He lifted her up and set her on solid ground, then hoisted himself over the edge and retrieved his glasses with a hand shaking uncontrollably—whether from cold or an anxious episode, he couldn't be completely sure.

Somehow in a gray blur, he found his way back to the office with Reggie draped under his arm and the torchlight casting eerie shadows over the walls and rang for a taxicab.

After helping the driver finagle his bike onto the back with a few cables, he slid in beside Reggie and watched her intently. Hamish was colder than he had ever been. Colder than when his dad forgot to pick him up at the ice-skating rink at High Park and his fingers and toes greeted the eventual warmth with daggers. So cold even though Reggie was huddled beside him, her chin on his shoulder, fast asleep. He'd dragged her out of the cave, her wet hair brushing the gap in his damp shirt collar.

Usually Reggie's slightest touch blazed through him, starting at his fingertips, warming through his veins, reddening his ears. Even if it was something as light as the brush of their fingertips as they reached for the radio dial in the office in the North Square. He placed his trembling fingers over her hand, fallen limply on his knee, so close were they together in the back seat of the cab. Ice. Icier still just past the knuckle on her fourth finger. Hamish winced, from more than the pain of the feeling slowly returning to his fingers.

The blurred lights of the city spread over the rain-spattered car window. Hamish's right hand shook slightly, but that kept the blood moving at least. His mind had always loved her since the moment he saw her in the cannoli line at Mrs. Leoni's bakery in the North Square. To distraction. Beyond distraction. He loved her so frantically that his heart jabbed when she even suggested he leave her behind. As if she wasn't half of himself. As if he would know how to wake up and function and greet a day without her.

And it was that love that made him curse the stupid decision to let her out of his sight. She had flashed him a look in which he read her seriousness and capability as she turned to follow the man who lured them there. He'd agreed to let her prove her independence while he puzzled over a few files. From now on he would be more alert and would learn to defend himself—and her.

The cab swerved over as they reached the corner of Battery and Commercial Streets: a line of redbrick tenement-style housing of which Hamish and Nate occupied a town house. The cab parked roughly on the curb, jolting Reggie awake.

"Come on." Hamish held her arm as she slowly roused. He led her half-stumbling to the door of the two-floor flat he shared with Nathaniel Reis.

He maneuvered the unlocked door open with the arm not balancing Reggie, then bellowed inside the lit hallway, the warmth of the house almost overtaking him. "Nate!" He could hardly keep Reggie upright. He ushered her into their small sitting room and laid her out on the couch. Hamish's eyes darted around the room for a quilt or an afghan. Nothing. He hurriedly tucked a pillow under her head. "Reg, I'll be right back. You can't stay in those clothes." If he wasn't half frozen to death or plagued with the thought of her dying of hypothermia, he might have had the grace to blush.

"Reggie!" said Nate the moment he arrived in the doorway. "What happened?"

"I need you to start a fire," Hamish said. "I need you to boil water for tea. I am going to go and find her all the blankets we have. And some clothes."

"Hamish, you don't look so well yourself."

"I'll live. See to Reggie."

Hamish was dizzy ascending the stairs. The feeling in his fingers hadn't completely returned and everything hurt, especially his chest. Thankfully the pulse in the back of his head had dulled. He rummaged through his dresser for anything that she could wear. Settling on pajama pants and a varsity sweater from the University of Toronto and two pairs of socks his Aunt Viola had knit, he quickly changed into dry trousers, a cable-knit sweater, and a hat his adopted home would call a beanie, also knit by his Aunt Viola. He dashed back down, set down the clothes, and lifted her up. Her cheeks were colored again, but dangerously flushed. Her eyes, when they opened, twinkled brown but looked dazed in the glow of the roaring fire.

"Up you get, Reggie." He gently pulled her up. "You need to take your wet clothes off and put these on."

She flopped against him. "Can't move."

"I can't very well undress you myself . . . I . . ." Hamish ran his fingers through his hair. It was still a little damp but mostly dry and lay plastered against his forehead.

Reggie nodded drowsily.

He helped her out of his coat and then her own, stiffly cold. With that bulk removed, he assessed her knit sweater and skirt and tried not to think about what was likely as stiff and cold underneath—right next to her skin. Then he got analytical. It was one thing to be a gentleman. It was another to keep her from catching pneumonia.

"Regina," he whispered. "I want you to know that I am only doing this as a last resort and I respect you and I don't want you to think that I would ever consider overstepping the boundaries of our friendship and—"

"Your lawyer voice, Hamish," Reggie slurred with a smile. Her rich alto was a tad higher with exhaustion and she sounded like a little girl.

"My lawyer voice," he repeated, gritting his chattering teeth.

He centered his hands on either side of her and tried to avert his eyes, fumbling with the ends of her sweater, focusing to get bearings and tug the heavy wool over her head. Her head flopped back a bit with his effort. Hamish tossed the sweater aside and exhaled. *Not so bad,* he blinked into the fire.

Nate crossed the carpet with tea. "Oh," he said, surveying Hamish's predicament.

"I'd call for Mrs. Leoni, but she couldn't get here fast enough." Hamish had ventured a look back at Reggie. With the removal of her sweater, her arms were bare and all that covered her front was the top half of a slip. He reached out a tentative finger to her skin, then reeled back as if burned. "Do people really catch their death from cold water?" Hamish looked up at Nate.

Nate held the steaming cup to Reggie's nose. "Take a sip of this, Reggie," he coaxed gently, holding the cup to her mouth. She sipped tentatively through cracked, ice-blue lips.

"H-hi, Nate."

"Hello, Regina." His voice held a clinical precision. "I want you to know that Hamish and I have no intention of being anything but gentlemen. It is just you are a dear friend. And we would rather you not freeze to death."

Reggie's attempt at a laugh sputtered into a cough. "So pragmatic."

Hamish set back to his task. And somehow with her bottom half covered under the blanket and his placing her hands in the right position they were finally able to get one half of her frozen slip off of her and rapidly pull down the varsity sweater in its place without a flash of anything. Hamish breathed a sigh of relief.

Reggie was a little more animated by this point and was able to handle her garter and stockings while Nate and Hamish studied the fireplace with an intensity Hamish assumed might blind them forever. Then, miraculously, the pajama pants were on and she was tucked under every blanket they owned.

Nate poked at her garments with a fire poker and arranged them into a pile. "Should I send for the doctor?"

"No," Reggie chattered. "You don't need to. I'll be fine."

"Should I send for Vaughan?" Hamish asked quietly.

"No," Reggie repeated.

Hamish looked down to hide his relief and inspected his pruned fingers. Then he looked back to Regina. The blankets were up to her chin, her hair had dried into a thousand tight ringlets—the intensity of curls something he had never quite seen before, even in the dead humid heat of the summer—and her eyes were focused on the flames.

"I have a funny feeling this has nothing to do with boat licensing," Nate said drily, balancing the poker against the brick of the mantel, then leading Hamish to the adjoining kitchen.

Hamish shifted a little in his seat, tugging at a loose thread on the sleeve of his sweater. "It has everything to do with a case."

"Should I be concerned?"

Hamish thought about Kelly and his primitive views. Not only was Nate the best flatmate he could imagine, he was his best friend. Hamish hadn't had a lot of friends. Maisie Forth, sure. She was a police dispatcher back in Toronto. One of his closest friends through childhood thanks to her family's presence in his parents' circle. And Luca his cousin . . . but Luca turned out to be more complicated than any boundaries of friendship should have allowed. Under the slowly burgeoning enterprise of Van Buren and DeLuca, Reggie and Hamish took on clients with every manner of mystery, from lost cats to botched contracts overseen by some of the shadier presences of the North End. In many cases, residents had nowhere else to go and the uneasiness of a looming war overseas, the financial difficulty as America used Roosevelt's series of New Deals to completely recover from the financial depression that had sunk so many so low over the decade just past. And while Reggie and Hamish assisted and occasionally twirled on the wrong side of danger, Nate never pried. He never asked. He merely showed up near daily to listen to *Winchester Molloy* on the wireless, eating his weight in almond cookies and sending clients Hamish's way when they needed advice on employment contracts. He thought about the soggy pamphlet in his trouser pocket.

"He's worried that Hyatt and Price are going to be developing housing where he does his trade. Do you know anything about this?"

Nate studied Hamish a moment, affording Hamish a clear view of his friend's face, most importantly his eyes. "There's always some big Washington Street firms that think we're ripe for the picking. You know this from Schultze and Baskit and some of your cousin Luca's investors."

"You're being evasive, Nate."

"Am I?" Nate looked in the direction of the sitting room. "Can you go make sure that Regina doesn't catch hypothermia on our sofa?"

"You're not going to answer me?"

Hamish waited through a beat of silence before leaving Nate at the table and crossing back to where Reggie lay in front of the fire.

Reggie burrowed down further under the blankets. "It hurts. The feeling is coming back. Ow." She sighed. "We should have had a plan B."

"We never had a plan A. I don't even really know why we were there." He knew he sounded testy. But he was exhausted and she had almost drowned.

She laughed softly. "And you wouldn't leave me, Hamish DeLuca."

"And I never would, Reggie."

She wriggled a little under the covers.

Hamish looked around, hearing Nate. Would she be better situated upstairs in his own bed while he took the couch? But then she would be away from the fireplace. Hamish scratched the back of his neck. Not any more appropriate than disrobing a woman with only one bachelor chaperone. But still . . .

Hamish watched Reggie's lashes sweep the curve of her cheekbones, noticed her freckles stand out like stars in a pale sky.

It had been eons since he first met her at the counter in Mrs. Leoni's in the North Square. Well over a year since they danced, her cranberry silk dress spilling around her like tipped merlot. Well over a year since they had started their business, stitching up a strange patchwork quilt of problems. Hamish employing his quickly learned skills in employment and property law to help residents in the North End who were prey to wealthy landlords. Translating for clients who spoke little English, their first language—Italian—as familiar to him as breathing thanks to his father, who'd ensured that Hamish had a second language as far back as he could remember.

"I guess he got away," Reggie murmured.

Hamish puzzled for a moment, then realization dawned. He had completely forgotten why they were by the infernal harbor in the first place. "I guess he did."

He wondered if he should tell her he thought he had seen

Kent: the silent partner of Mark Suave, the man who had shot Hamish. The man who died by his cousin Luca's hand. And he wanted to tell her even as her breathing was tempered. She would follow him to the ends of the earth, but he wasn't sure if he wanted her to, especially if it meant that he could lose her. Lose her as he had Luca.

"I know what you're thinking, Hamish." Her voice was so quiet he wondered at first if he was imagining it.

"What's that, Reg?" Hamish fixated on embers hopping in the fireplace. He retrieved the papers from under his coat and began hanging them alongside Reggie's clothes and underthings in a strange line.

"How did he find his way back here, and why? Luca . . ."

"So you saw him too?" His voice caught in his throat. His shoulder throbbed and his breath sped up a little bit. If it was who they thought it was . . .

"I thought so." She nodded tiredly. "Kent." She gave a little laugh. "Long time since I heard that name, Cicero."

Hamish watched the fire silently. *Cicero.* Luca's pet name for him. Not one he had heard more than a handful of times in the nearly two years since his cousin left. Maisie Forth, his childhood friend, teased him with it at Christmas on a visit home. He looked up at Reggie: her eyes were fluttering closed. Then he rejoined Nate in the kitchen.

"Cocoa?" Nate inclined an open tin of chocolate powder, pointing at the stove.

Within minutes Hamish stared ruefully into his cocoa. He tugged his knit cap over his ears, eyes settling on a fanned-out page of the *Jewish Advocate*. The serial was as familiar to Hamish as Nate himself. Nate wrote long editorial pieces often contradicted by a fellow named Aaron Leibowitz. There was a comfort in seeing something so familiar.

"I think Reggie's been bored lately," Hamish said. "Most of

our clients have been . . . well . . . the ones you send over. This one wasn't. And she wants adventure. She sits there typing for Mrs. Rue all morning, and then I have her read over legal documents. So I gather when someone called about boat licensing and wanted us to meet at the docks, she flew at the opportunity to get out of the office. A twilight meeting by the harbor. Who knows what she imagined. But when we got there . . ." Hamish squinted into his cocoa a moment. "I thought I saw . . . Sometimes, Nate, I swear I am losing my mind. Mark Suave—"

"The man who shot you," Nate said pointedly.

Hamish nodded. "He had this man with him. At the Flamingo and . . . something or other. I swear I saw him tonight. Suave is long dead and then this man is resurrected?" He shrugged. "We separated. I didn't want to . . . but . . ." Hamish ran his hand over his face, his fingers trembling a little. "I had the funniest feeling that I saw Suave's man, so I chased after him a bit. But I was desperate to find Reggie, and I am glad I did." Hamish flicked a look in the direction of the sitting room.

Nate swallowed a sip of cocoa. "So maybe someone wanted you there instead of where you were?"

"The office?" Did they want something from the office? A file perhaps? "Did you see anyone while we were gone?"

Nate shrugged. "Or this fellow who knew Mark Suave wanted to check in on you."

Hamish shuddered from more than leftover cold. His anxious moments meant that his heart clutched when someone wasn't being completely honest with him. It was funny for the tightening sensation to occur with Nate across from him. His friend was so pragmatic and honest. What you saw was what you got.

Nate turned his spoon over. "Hamish, you know that your cousin is . . . was . . . well, what he was at the very least. There were loose ends when he left."

"Kelly's concerned about a new housing development running

him out. He wanted me to look at the papers. I thought you might be a better person. You know all about the zoning laws. Can they even build that close to the harbor?"

"I do what I can, Hamish, but I cannot control everything that happens."

"The North End Clark Kent," Hamish said fondly, referring to Nate's favorite Action Comic superhero. "Property developer by day, swapping services by night. You need plumbing done at a fraction of the cost of your horrible landlord? No worries, if you can tutor Mrs. Rossini's son in calculus every other Thursday . . ."

"You make too much of it. If it wasn't me, it would be someone else with papers full on their desk."

"Surely you can look through what Kelly gave me and see if at least the zoning laws and building codes are legitimate. I might have a case before they start building. If you see that it isn't up to par."

Nate shrugged. "I can't be responsible for every last slum housing project that men like them want to build in our neighborhood. And I am not sure either of us want to work for a man who leaves Reggie to swim with the fishes. This is more than a legal request."

Hamish convinced himself he was too tired to press on, but he couldn't help it. Something about Nate's answers tingled his fingers. It wasn't a new sensation: Hamish was well versed in being able to tell when people weren't being entirely truthful with him. But Nate had never given him the sensation before. "Well, look through the paperwork with me tomorrow. It's a little damp. I hung it up with her socks."

"I trust your instincts, young DeLuca. And so should you."

Hamish returned to the sitting room while Nate retired upstairs. He was never sure why Nate called him "young"—his friend was only a few years older. For a moment Hamish mulled on the compliment. Nate trusted him to do the right thing. Then his thoughts spiraled to how evasive his friend was being. He decided not to dwell on that. It was late and he was tired, nerves wired. *Trust your instincts.* He focused and exhaled, dropping into the chair adjacent Reggie, feeling the heat and sputter of the fire. If Hamish had trusted his instincts, it wouldn't have taken as long as it did for him to discover the truth about his cousin. Luca Valari had worked his charm to become the center of a network that used illegal means to give protection to men with deep pockets. Hamish tried to accept what it really was and found his mind's eye arrested by several shady men in the pictures Reggie was so eager to line up to see. If Hamish trusted his instincts, he would have known that showing up for a physical the last time he was home in Toronto would have ended with his being turned away from enlisting to fight with his countrymen in the war starting overseas. What was it about a comfortable fire and silence that set his mind raging? Once it started on one thing, it snowballed into every possible thing he couldn't control or had failed at. A flicker of a look at Reggie and he wondered if he had failed her too.

"You're thinking rather loudly, Hamish." Reggie sounded sleepy.

"Sorry if I woke you."

"I was thinking of tonight." Her voice trembled a little like the rest of her.

He reached across and adjusted the blanket covering her feet and legs. "You should rest."

"Hamish, I could just be hallucinating . . ." Her voice cracked a little. "But I could swear that I saw—"

"Suave's man," Hamish said. "Kent."

"Arthur."

"*Arthur?*"

"Not as worthy of a movie villain as Suave, is it?" Reggie adjusted the blanket. "I overheard the police use his full name the night . . ." She waved away *you were shot* from the end of the sentence.

"I was hoping we'd never have to hear of him again—with or without a name."

Reggie stretched and yawned. "Me too," she murmured. "You have good instincts, Hamish. Mine tonight were . . ."

He looked over and she was asleep again, leaving Hamish to watch the sputtering embers in the fire. He rose and stoked it, fixated on one tricky coal that glowered and sparked with the strike of the poker. It settled then toppled onto the rug, seething into an ember. Hamish startled before wrestling it back into the grate. *Good instincts?* Hamish wasn't so sure.

CHAPTER 3

All of the glorious Daughters of the Revolution to which her mother and her mother before her ascribed would have spiraled themselves into a tizzy of apoplexy incurable by any amount of smelling salts: Regina Van Buren slept on a sofa belonging to two bachelors. This was not something listed in her Journal of Independence—but she figured she would scrawl it in with an accompanying check mark to note the occasion. She awoke to the sun peeking through the curtains. The light had exchanged from the last snap and crackle of fluttering embers in the fire grate to the bright morning. Hamish DeLuca's soft breathing in the chair adjacent. His shoulders slumped, head resting on his shoulder, long legs stretched out, a beanie hat still tugged over ears that stuck out a little, covering most of his ebony hair.

Reggie smiled and tried to subdue the sneeze that tickled her nose. She couldn't, and the high hiccup of a squeal stirred Hamish. He blinked. Soon his startling blue eyes, fuzzy with sleep and without the border of his black-rimmed glasses, studied her. Then registered. He startled into an upright position, raked the beanie off his head, and tossed it aside, his hair matted in its shape. His right hand, she noticed, was already shaking a little as if it had not truly found repose in sleep.

"Oh, Reggie, I am so sorry. I should have noticed or stayed awake or found a cab or . . ."

"It's all right." Reggie adjusted the quilts over her, catching a peek of her attire . . . not hers, really. A sweater and cozy trousers and . . . ah! There . . . She focused on her stockings and garter and dress draped haphazardly as a reflector for the last of the fire's shadow. Her face flamed a moment in a realization that sleep had dimmed. "You just did what you had to do to keep me from freezing to death."

Hamish adjusted his collar: buttons of his shirt undone, offering a clear visibility of his collarbone and chest, the scar branded from Suave's bullet. A lady would have immediately recovered herself and turned away. But Reggie allowed herself a moment more, surprised at the feeling that spread over her and warmed her more than the blanket or the hearth expelling the last of its heat.

"May I use your facilities, Hamish?"

"Hmm? Oh! Absolutely. Yes." He ran his hand over his face and then combed his fingers through his matted hair. It stuck up a little with the effort. Reggie rose, keeping the blanket around her, trailing like a makeshift toga, and retrieved her clothes from the line dangling over the fireplace.

When she returned, her clothes wrinkled and her hair (extremely curly from her damp adventure the night before) pinned as best as it would stay, Hamish had changed into his usual white cotton shirt and suspenders, sleeves rolled up to the elbow. His hair was tamed and his glasses were affixed on his nose. He scooped coffee into a jar while the kettle whistled from the stovetop. She tugged it from the stove and handed it to him. The blanket was still draped around her shoulders like the cape worn by the hero in the Action Comic Nate liked so much.

"Thanks." His smile was a little bashful and she didn't blame him. They had been in close quarters all night. The last time she had accidentally spent a night with Hamish DeLuca, they at least had the office door between them.

"I meant to stay awake and check on you." His voice was low in apology.

"You were just as exhausted as I was, Hamish." She stifled a sneeze. "Caught a chill!"

Hamish peered at her concernedly. "We'll get you warmed up. Keep the blanket close." He tugged at its end and a smile creased his cheek, wakening its irregular dimple.

"So if we did see Arthur Kent"—Reggie accepted the steaming mug of coffee with the extra milk he knew she liked—"that might mean he is tying up some of Luca's loose ends."

Hamish brought his own coffee over to the table and they sat. He dunked his spoon in the steaming cup and twirled it around a few times. "Then why not just come right out and threaten us? If he thinks maybe I have something on Luca?"

Reggie sipped her coffee and began a sentence that morphed into a quick greeting to Nate who appeared in the doorway. Surprisingly, he looked less rested than she and Hamish, with dark circles cutting his eyes and the usual glimmer on his face dimmed.

"Morning, you two. Hamish, a large cup of that, would you?"

Nate always took his coffee straight black, and he drank it with little notice to its temperature.

"Nate, did you sleep at all? Hope you weren't worried about little old me." Reggie held up the end of the blanket.

"I figured you'd survive," he said drily. "A lot to tackle this week. Nothing as dangerous as you two, though." He leaned toward Reggie. "You're sure you're okay?" He grasped her hand and squeezed.

"Right as rain, Nathaniel!"

"Perfect! Now Hamish can see if he has learned anything from Rosa Leoni."

"Rosa Leoni?"

"She has been coming by once a week to teach us bachelors how to navigate our way around a kitchen so we can impress gorgeous young ladies like yourself. Go poach an egg or three, young DeLuca." Nate's demand was belied by the fond look on his face. "So, this Kent fellow . . ."

"He was sniffing around the Flamingo two summers ago," Hamish said over his shoulder as he cracked a few eggs into a pan. "And we'll be having scrambled, not poached. Nate, go find a loaf of bread, will you? Your *bubbe* left some of that challah. Some of my aunt Vi's jam should be on the bottom shelf of the icebox." Hamish cracked another egg. Reggie liked watching his long fingers from over the rim of her coffee cup. "Because Luca should have done something with Frank Fulham. We all know what *kind* of something, and he couldn't."

"Luca's a real saint," Reggie said.

"Why not just find Luca, then?" Nate said. "Unless he is somewhere in Boston again. You haven't heard from him?"

"I honestly haven't. I don't know how I would be able to keep something like that from you two."

"And yet I so hoped that Luca had used this second chance to make himself an honest man."

"Don't be facetious, Reggie." Hamish didn't look over his shoulder, scrambling eggs with a wooden spoon.

Nate swallowed his coffee. "This could be something to do with revenge on Luca through you . . ."

"They tried that. Suave shot me. Luca still left. That establishes what kind of relationship we have."

Where there might have been a hint of bitterness in Hamish's tone, he had finessed it into a fact. He might not understand it, but he accepted it, and she knew he still was much fonder of Luca than he let on. Missed him too.

Nate collected the milk and newspaper from the door at the

sound of a knock. He passed the arts section to Reggie with a smile.

A few moments later they tucked into bread with lemon jam, huge glasses of milk, and scrambled eggs seasoned with oregano and Parmesan. Reggie couldn't remember tasting anything so delicious. "I should have more near-death experiences. Because right now, it seems like Hamish DeLuca is a bona fide chef."

Nate laughed and some of the light missing in his eyes took residence. "You must have been very scared indeed!"

"Oh hush, Nate!" Hamish scowled. "More?" He ladled eggs onto his friends' plates.

"Whether this Kent fellow is sniffing around or not, we are all on the same team." Nate raised a nub of challah bread smeared with lemon jam in a makeshift toast.

"And what team is that?" Hamish asked easily, stabbing hungrily at a forkful of eggs. He was still as lanky as the day she had met him in the cannoli line at Mrs. Leoni's bakery, but his appetite had grown. While her growing appetite appeared in a few extra curves around her chest and waist, his was balanced by his constant cycling around the city. And, she supposed, by the fact that even while he was sitting, he was never quite still. Even now, during a short rest from shoveling eggs in his mouth, his right hand shook slightly. She studied him while Nate read the latest from the sports page. The Boston Patriots, a farm team in Charlestown that often provided fodder for the Red Sox scouts, was the second leader in the secondary league. Errol Parker—known as Robin Hood—was the team's intrepid base stealer. When Parker's name was mentioned, both Hamish and Nate spiraled into a language Reggie could not understand. The only thing Reggie knew about baseball was that it sometimes kept Hamish and Nate from concentrating on *Winchester Molloy: New York Gumshoe*.

"If Luca's past is following him and it involves you, then it involves all of us," Reggie said with finality. "All for one." She raised her coffee cup and wrinkled her nose at Nate in the same fashion as Myrna Loy putting William Powell in his place in *The Thin Man*.

"Oh! The *Musketeers* references are starting." Nate rubbed his hands together. "I was waiting for this." He took a dramatic breath. "All for—"

"I bet you were just counting the moments," Hamish said.

"It was inevitable." Nate smiled.

"Wait? Which Musketeer is who? I am *not* Porthos." Reggie sipped her coffee.

"Well, you can't be Athos," Nate said.

"Why not?" she wondered.

"I'm Athos, actually," Hamish said.

"No, you're D'Artagnan. Clearly." Nate looked at him with the same pragmatic precision he loaned his clients at the Housing Development office. "Or maybe . . . wait! Aramis was the pious, convicted one, right? You can be him."

"Oh, enough of this!" Reggie sighed.

"And one for all." Hamish raised his coffee cup with a smile that stretched just wide enough to settle in Reggie's chest and winnow its way down to her toes.

Well, this is more than inconvenient, she thought, with him looking like that. She sank into his smile, letting it linger, erasing the night before so that all that surrounded her were the two faces she held most dear in all the world. She caught herself. *Vaughan.* Of course, Vaughan. Well, *two* of the *three* faces she held most dear. The scent of eggs sprinkled with foreign seasonings, bread twisted and strengthened with the levity of Nate's faith, and she was a part of a makeshift family—more hers because she chose it. Chose it in spite of Hamish's cousin's blight on the independence she had found in their new city and the slow churn toward the profitability of their office.

CHAPTER 4

Reggie seemed to be fully recovered, and the daylight and banter had erased Hamish's sharp panic. Reggie was going to be fine. The weather, too, held promise.

As the days and the fright passed, Hamish repeatedly pondered the Christian Patriots pamphlet he'd tucked into the space between his blotter and his desk at the office. *What?* he thought. And *Why?*

The next time they heard from Pete Kelly, which was over the telephone, it was to see if they had made any headway on keeping property developers from his building. Hamish still didn't know but had asked Nate to find out what shipped in and out. Reggie made a noise that denoted how unimpressed she was at helping a man who had left her to sink soggily in his part of the ocean. She retaliated by refusing to speak to him, handing the phone to Hamish with a look far stronger than any word could convey.

"Is there any reason you just left Reggie and me?" Hamish said after listening to Kelly string together an irritated slew of words about their inefficiency and abandonment. "We come all the way out there, I look through your files, and you take off?"

"Business. Last minute. You're still going to check on the validity of Hyatt and Price?" The reception was scratchy. Hamish assumed this was due to the wind at the harbor.

"I'll try. You know, there is still the very valid option of having my friend Mr. Reis . . ."

But Kelly didn't have time for more discussion. Hamish clicked the receiver. Blew out a breath of air.

"Get anything out of him?" Reggie's smile was bright. They both knew the answer to that. Hamish scrubbed the back of his neck and wished he could be more for her.

"Whoever showed up must have startled him or something. He dropped us as quickly as he did just now, and he took all of that time to get us there in the first place."

"And if that person had been Kent?" She shrugged her answer to her own sentence. Hamish didn't have anything to offer either.

"If he really is concerned about these Hyatt and Price plans, he should go to Nate," Hamish said again.

Nate kept a careful collection of consolidated files and ledgers. He was meticulously organized. Nothing seemed to go on around the North End without Nate's awareness of it.

They'd even found themselves with an ally from the police force. Rob Reid occasionally had a lead for them or called on them on a case. Before Reid, Hamish's introduction to the Boston police force had included those on Luca's payroll, those who were willing and ready to turn a blind eye. Reid was to the letter. It made both Reggie and Hamish feel secure that there was someone on their side. Hamish scrawled a note on his ledger to ask Reid about Kelly.

The investigation part of their business was not as constant as Hamish's need to do discounted legal work and look through contracts for North End inhabitants. While traditional business arrangements would see money exchanged for services, the North End residents knew that the rich got richer and slumlords kept parts of the neighborhood from truly evolving from the tenements that housed its largely immigrant community. As the Depression tapered off and Roosevelt's New Deal gave way to a surge of optimism, the old ways died hard and Nate was at the ready to keep property and development business thriving, while also acting as the middleman in several transactions. He had an ongoing system and file of names, talents, and skills, and the community had been built and sustained through his careful attention and extensive knowledge. Meanwhile, Hamish, a fresh new lawyer, was a quick learner and fastidious student, having spent the better part of his tenure in Boston reading up on property and employment law. Often, it was enough for a client to state that they had legal counsel to scare action into place.

Reggie spent most mornings at Mildred Rue's temporary employment agency, perfecting her steno skills before retreating back to the office for an afternoon of whatever case they were working: from missing hat pins to a lost brother to an unfaithful wife. When there were no cases on hand that required any more than Hamish's legal expertise, *Winchester Molloy* on the wireless kept her occupied.

Hamish, through the lens of his favorite book, *The Hunchback of Notre-Dame*, mentally christened the North End the Court of Miracles the summer he lived with his cousin Luca Valari—and it stuck. The North End's colorful mélange of dialect and nationality—predominantly Jewish and Italian with patriotic flags draped from storefronts, close-hugging brick buildings crisscrossed with fire escapes and dangling white rainbows of hanging laundry—was now as familiar to him as breathing. Fresh bread and molasses and basil and spices mingled from carts and shop windows, and flour puffed out from vents in the streets. Children laughed and men shouted to each other in their first language. Hamish, too, stepped into the other language of his childhood. Speaking Italian allowed him to press through a barrier that kept many North End residents from seeking the fair treatment they should have been afforded. Hamish, who had the propensity to see the world through imaginative perimeters, had immediately thought of the underground community over which Clopin the Gypsy King reigned: where lame beggars retreated far from the magistrate's eyes at night only to find themselves miraculously healed within the cloister of their fellow Romany community—a collective sanctuary far from the solitary one Quasimodo found amidst his bells in the towers of the medieval cathedral.

⋇

So life in Boston was pretty good. Hamish's episodes of panic were far more infrequent than they had been when he was still living in Toronto and climbing his way to the top of his class at Osgoode Law School. The memory of the anxiety that had sped his heartbeat and stolen his breath during his first real court case was a fuzzy frame of humiliation the more he settled into his new life. His parents still worried about him, sure. But he had Reggie and Nate and a purpose. Indeed, most of the time, the only thing that clutched his heart like a slowly squeezing fist was any thought that spun in Luca's direction.

Not only where Luca had been spending the years since he left Hamish alone and bleeding on the floor of the Flamingo, but whether he had finally escaped the world that judged him for his treatment of Frank Fulham. Fulham had been Luca Valari's lawyer in Chicago and the man his cousin was supposed to dispose of. To Luca's minimal credit, he had let the man live and had even helped his wife. Whenever Hamish assumed the worst of his cousin, he tried to anchor himself to this thought. Luca couldn't kill. Hamish never learned all the specifics surrounding Fulham's dealings, though. Indeed, much of Luca's life existed behind a kind of filter where shapes were blurred and lines were fuzzy and nothing ever quite added up. He supposed it was for the best; full knowledge of Luca's dealings could rip everything open again, causing a pain far worse than the sting of the bullet wound he'd received to the chest. Fulham was to blame for what started it all.

The one place Hamish was spared of any anxious thoughts was the dance floor. Years twirling around the monogrammed floor at the Palais Royale with his friend Maisie Forth had given him an authority more legitimate than his black hat. Even as the world changed and the headlines from his father's national newspaper, the *Telegraph*, daily reported of the war in which his home country fought alongside Britain, Boston's dance scene remained the same. Sure, the styles were loose and limber. The Lindy Hop, that dance of swift movement and careful abandon, had been building in popularity for years and had become a mainstay of nights on Boylston and Washington and some of the less glitzy halls in Scollay Square and was, for Hamish, the perfect opportunity to switch off his brain like a light switch.

The world spun and swerved much in the same way his sometime partner Bernice Wong did in his arms with intense immediacy. And as much as he wanted to keep his shoes on the dance floor, the rhythm and the flurry of the music kept him almost an inch off the ground. When the last lines of music trilled to a halt and the stickiness of the dance floor was replaced with the sudden swoosh of fresh air to cool the perspiration on his face, he knew there was a lot of lost magic in his life.

Bernice had been a client, a pretty girl whose ebony hair was always pulled into a ponytail and whose smart brown eyes made him think she probably saw more than her quick smile ever let on, on a night when he was dying to dance and Reggie was unavailable as a partner. The Flamingo Club towered over the square, its emblem and neon sign still trickling light onto the pavement. It was still flushed by the notoriety of a murdered girl and an owner who had shot an assailant—a man with all manner of nefarious connections—in self-defense. Hamish knew it wasn't self-defense. Hamish knew more than he should have about the whole thing. Knew more than he wished he did about his cousin Luca.

Even though Hamish knew that Reggie wore the engraved necklace he'd given her and spent almost every waking hour by his side, it was hard to imagine her stepping away from Vaughan Vanderlaan.

Bernice helped. He was genuinely fond of her. Her lithe figure and inherent athleticism. She was beautiful, tonight especially so, with a new shade of lipstick, its color parting over her teeth—pronounced ivory in the lights of the club. Hamish's hand fit into the slight curve of her tiny waist.

"We should try this joint again." Her voice was all expectation as they crossed that night's crowded floor to the bar. It was casual. Far more casual than the tenders mixing martinis at places like the Dragonfly and the Flamingo. They both had Coca-Colas that fizzed their noses. Bernice wasn't one for fancy cocktails. Not that they were on offer where they were. Mostly straight gin sloshed into squat glasses. A far cry from the flourish and toss of the mixers at the Flamingo.

The band took five then started on the first bars of "Smoke Gets in Your Eyes." Hamish dabbed at the perspiration dripping into his own. So many steps with Bernice. So many nights after a long day at the office, perfecting a twirl and turn, swerving in and out. He didn't feel the same zing and pull that made magic of his time with Reggie. He shrugged off his guilt.

"Hamish DeLuca!" Hamish and Bernice both turned at a voice right over his shoulder. Hamish focused on a face familiar but vague.

"Yes?"

"You have to remember me." The man—who had ruddy cheeks and blond hair that caught the overhead light—pushed the bangs from his forehead and smiled. "You helped my mother last year. They wanted to foreclose on her home and you . . ."

Hamish ducked his head a little bit. He could almost feel the intensity of Bernice's smile beside him. He remembered now. Reggie told him sometimes it was easier to let the cases go so they didn't overtake his brain and crowd it. He could only do as much as he could and couldn't be expected to take on every last issue from every last client even after their consultations had ended. "A pleasure, truly."

"Well, thank you." He extended his hand and Hamish took it. He pumped it enthusiastically, Hamish jolted by the grip.

"How is your mother?"

"She is happy. My sister has moved in. She is expecting. My mother is going to be a grandmother, and she wouldn't have been able to help except for what you did for her."

"I am sure it was nothing," Hamish said, a familiar heat under his collar.

"It was more than nothing."

"That's wonderful."

The man nodded. "And I've helped her find a new place to live. New developments are happening. Not ready yet, but will be. Down in Fiske's Wharf—a new property development on the harbor. I'm involved too."

It was this that struck Hamish's memory chord. *Thomas Greene.*

He hoped his voice sounded nonchalant when he said, "Housing, isn't it? I keep seeing signs around the neighborhood."

"Not for long though." He lifted the crook of his finger in a tentative salute, leaving Hamish to Bernice's wide-eyed adoration. "Building will start and I mean to be in the midst of it."

"You make a difference." She gripped his hand and swung their arms in time as she led them back to the middle of the dance floor. Hamish's brain lit with the mention of Fiske's Wharf. Pete Kelly's building. Suave's man Kent. He tried to shelve it to back of his mind as "Smoke Gets in Your Eyes" was replaced by the frenetic energy of a clarinet solo blasting in the first bars of "Jeepers

Creepers." If he could just forget the words and focus on the music . . . but even though Bernice was close, her jasmine scent in his nostrils, and her pretty eyes holding a charming magnetism, the words to any love song made him think of Reggie. And when he thought of Reggie, it was the strangest mix of sheer panic and utter delight. Worry that if he swept her into his arms and confessed his love, it might end their friendship. But if he didn't, she might decide Vaughan Vanderlaan's long-ago proposal hadn't been such a bad idea after all. There was also the exhilaration of having someone to hop on the handlebars.

Music obliterated all other thought. Later when he was under the streetlights of Boston seeing Bernice home, unsure of how to answer her incessant questions about their relationship, about his meeting her family, he felt queasy. He was raised better than to lead a girl along. Heck, before he moved to Boston, he had never *had* a girl to lead along.

"Bernice." He drew her eyes up to him by finally intersecting her sentences. "You know that I like you as a dance partner. You're really . . . uh . . . you're swell on the dance floor. Best I've seen since my friend Maisie back home."

Bernice's smile widened. "Really?" She tugged at his coat sleeve. They rounded the corner to her street and he watched her jog up the walkway then stop. She turned her head over her shoulder.

"Are you going to come up and kiss me good night, Hamish?"

Hamish didn't have a response. So he slowly joined her, brushed a strand of hair from her forehead, and kissed her cheek lightly. "Good night, Bernice."

He didn't rush home but enjoyed the clear sky spread over Boston like a sparkly blanket. Even the buildings and scenes familiar from the Flamingo incident two years earlier seemed to glimmer under the light of new memories. He had taken a city that had been Luca's and made it his own.

Sure, back home, underneath socks and shirts and a few

letters from Maisie Forth, was a book holding every last clipping and picture from the Flamingo investigation. While most reporters focused on the scandal of the Flamingo, Hamish still wondered if he would find something between the lines. He pretended something in his chest didn't constrict with every flash of Luca's face: either from a staged publicity photo or from the turn of his handsome profile the night he was arrested. But there was still something he needed to solve. Needed to fix. He hadn't told Reggie that the sight of Kent had the opposite effect it should have. It left Hamish hopeful. He hadn't actively pursued Luca. He didn't want anything to do with whatever life his cousin had inevitably found for himself, but he kept hoping the beginning of a trail would stretch to him anyway.

He would defend himself too. In case whatever business might intersect him with Luca again might lead to the same intensity of the injury he sustained at the Flamingo. Even though a doctor in Toronto had deemed him unfit to go to war, he had learned to fire a gun. He had Jasper Forth, a retired constable and as close as an uncle, not only help him choose a small weapon for more dangerous cases but also teach him to shoot. To narrow his eye on a target and focus, to pull his trigger only when necessary.

"Never out of vengeance. Or anger," Jasper reminded him, gripping his shoulder fondly. "Only out of protection."

"Is that what you told Maisie when you taught her?" Hamish said with a knowing smile. There was no way Maisie wouldn't have pestered her father for the same training.

Hamish blinked away the rest of the memory trail and picked up his pace to navigate the last stretch of the North End toward home.

A dog yelped nearby, and a car swerved in the pitch black. Somewhere music spilled over a fire escape and the moon was slick on the cobblestones: the familiar music of his new home. Hamish sped up again and made out another set of footsteps in precise rhythm with his own. He stalled then and turned his head over his shoulder, pressing the fingers of his right hand into his palm, their familiar tremor just starting. It was all right. The gun was in the back of his trouser band.

"Can I help you?" He kept his voice as still and calm as possible. A furtive glance merely gave a view of a deserted road, a streetlight sputtering overhead. Hamish exhaled and quickened his step. He also erected his shoulders and practiced in his mind how he might physically defend himself. Jasper Forth's training was at the tip of his brain.

"Mr. DeLuca."

"Yes." Hamish couldn't dismiss the flicker of satisfaction that his premonition was more than an unfounded prickle on the back of his neck.

"When did you last hear from your cousin?"

Hamish's breath caught. "I-I haven't heard from Luca in quite some time." His eyes swept the street to make out the source of the voice. But it was just shadows and a shrub. Finally, the leaves moved and a figure stepped out.

"Some time?"

Hamish assumed Luca had found his feet again. He always did. *Some people are not easily killed.* "Yes. What do you want?" He clutched the fingers of his right hand together.

The sputtering streetlight lit broad shoulders and height and a shaded face he knew from its strong jawline. When he stepped closer, Hamish made out a figure familiar to him from his first moments in Boston—and beyond. At first, Hamish had been unsure if Phil (he never got a surname) was his cousin's chauffeur or bodyguard—or a bit of both. He assumed the latter.

"Phil, what are you doing here?"

"Luca sent me. I've been keeping an eye on you, you know."

Something caught in Hamish's chest and made its way down through him. A tightness that had clearly also settled in his throat, because when he spoke next it was with effort. "He didn't inform me of his whereabouts." Hamish knew that while he tried to sound casual, his words shook slightly.

Luca's whereabouts may have comforted his aunt Viola when she still had not received word from her son, despite her incessant questioning of Hamish at Christmas. Might have halted his dad's demands as to Luca's whereabouts and why he'd left Boston in the first place. And this . . . this near stranger knew more about his cousin than Hamish did.

"Was he required to inform you of his whereabouts?"

Hamish rolled his eyes up to the slice of moon catching the rooftops. "So you have talked to him? Is he all right?" Of course he was all right. Luca was always all right. "He would want you to tell me. He would—"

Phil raised a restraining hand. "I ask the questions."

Hamish swallowed hard. He hated Luca's life. Never more so than when having to cross an invisible barrier. Luca had eyes and ears everywhere. Luca would always know where Hamish was, but Hamish had gone two years worrying only to learn that Luca was somewhere at home. "Ask away."

"Luca needs to know that you're safe and well."

"You can see I am," Hamish snarled. "I gather Luca wants to stay away from Boston, but he can still get ahold of me. He could call or write, and then I can tell him myself rather than take up more of your valuable time." Everything about Luca annoyed him these days. The timing too. What were the odds of Hamish and Reggie thinking they saw Suave's man, Kent? Now Phil. He'd had a long stretch of nearly two years to separate himself from these people, and here they were all at once. What had Luca got himself into? His slightly shaking fingers tucked into his shirt and found the scar from Suave's bullet. Was Luca back?

"He wants you to be careful." Phil reached into his breast pocket, extracted a piece of paper, and handed it to Hamish.

"This is not for pleasantries. You use this if you need to use it. Not for an Easter card or well wishes."

Hamish blinked up at the man, wondering if the softening in his face welcomed Phil's scrutiny. "And if I rip it up?" Facetiousness was foreign to Hamish's voice. He cleared it from his throat uncomfortably.

"Do what you want, kid. I don't care."

Hamish turned the paper over without truly looking at it under the streetlight, then tucked it in his pocket. He snapped at his brace. "Do you remember Mark Suave, Phil?" Hamish hoped his voice meted a challenge.

"Why do you want to know?"

"Do you or do you not remember him?"

"I try to keep a short memory, DeLuca. It doesn't do to remember too much. In case people ask questions. Nosy kids, for example."

"I'm not a kid. And you came to me."

"I do remember him. Of course I do."

"Do you know what happened to the man who was with him? That night in the Dragonfly?" Hamish left Phil to pick up the pieces first of the two men about to saw off Luca's pinky finger, then to mentally cast out to the dead body of Mary Finn lying at the bottom of the stairwell leading to the Flamingo's well-stocked liquor store, his cousin Luca holding what was later determined to be the murder weapon. And while Luca was innocent of Finn's death, he was far from innocent when it came to acting as the center of an operation that saw the rich getting richer at the expense of the working class across large American cities like Boston and Chicago.

Phil gave a curt headshake before Hamish could recount seeing his cousin Luca in a chair—a man twisting his pinky finger—just before Reggie and Hamish barged through the door to Luca's rescue and Hamish was almost strangled to death. It wasn't until much later Hamish learned that it had been a ruse. A power play. Like so much of Luca's world. His untouchable cousin playing at an ornamented ruse to demonstrate the true power he wielded. "My errand is finished." He gave Hamish a quick, clinical look-over. "You seem well."

"If Luca left me with loose ends . . ." Loose ends that almost drowned Reggie. That found him in the middle of a cold warehouse. Or was he just seeing the shadow his cousin cast over everything? His heartbeat started and thrummed.

"The only loose end is me giving you his contact. *Emergency* contact."

Hamish pulled the slip of paper from his pocket, studied it a moment, then looked up. "And this is where I can find him." His heartbeat pulsed with an acceleration he wasn't sure whether to attribute to nerves or the mention of Luca and the million and one memories that flooded in with the name.

"Don't do anything stupid with it," Phil said by way of farewell.

"His name is Kent! Suave's man! You must know of him. If you talk to Luca, you have to tell him that he's here. In Boston. If you have any contact with him, then warn him. I would, but . . ." Hamish stopped, cleared his throat. "This is not for pleasantries." He emulated Phil's dead voice.

Soon Hamish was stepping into the flat he shared with Nate. The light from the living room funneled into the front hall, and soft strands of music from the radio accompanied the sound of rustling papers.

Hamish yawned, sliding out of his two-toned shoes, lifting them and setting them aside.

"You're up late," he remarked, peeking into the sitting room where Nate sat amidst piles of papers.

Nate blinked up at him. "Well, I find myself pretty occupied these days." He turned back to a file. "You know we're getting closer and closer to the Revere monument!" There were few things about the Revolutionary War Nate didn't know. "Revere's statue will be in the Prado by the year's end." His eyes were incandescent. "Dallin will be there too! Make up for all the tenement housing they destroyed, huh?"

"Sounds wonderful," Hamish said absently.

"Don't get too serious with another dancing partner, young DeLuca. You don't want to break her heart."

Hamish loosened his necktie and shoved the glasses that had fallen down the slope of his nose back on their bridge. "What do you mean by that?"

"Reggie will come around, and you don't want to hurt Bernice in the process."

Phil's appearance had done little to keep his mood light. "Reggie might well be with Vaughan at the moment."

He was being flippant. He knew it wasn't true. What was more, he shouldn't have been short with Nate. Not only was Nate his best friend but he had been nice enough to let him live there rent free for months until money started coming in (albeit slowly) from his joint enterprise with Reggie. "So you work from here now?"

"Sometimes."

"Any reason why?"

"Because I don't have a dancing partner. Need something to while away my lonely bachelor hours. And Aaron Leibowitz, for once, set me only slightly agitated; he's losing his edge."

"Have you seen anyone around the office lately? I mean, after I've left or stepped out? I told you, Suave's man Kent might be around. Kelly might have a man of his own."

"I keep my eyes on the things I can fix. My corner of the world. Some men see in big, broad strokes. They watch the headlines. The war your country is fighting. The philosophies, however ludicrous, coming out of that war. Maybe I bring my work home because I want to keep it close to me."

Hamish didn't believe a word of it. Nate was giving him a small slice of a bigger picture, and his ability to tell when someone was lying to him pricked at his chest. "You can stop it. You can control it!"

"How can I stop anyone, Hamish? I just do what I can to try to get a fair deal for the people in my neighborhood."

"You're much more than that! You know more about the inner workings of the neighborhood than anyone else I have ever met. And I know you are lying to me, Nate—I can tell."

"I keep a lot of secrets to help a lot of people. If these men choose to crowd our neighborhood with more crummy housing, I can't stop it." He exhaled. "I can just ensure that after it happens, when these poor souls are eventually taken advantage of, someone is there to help after. We've been through this." Nate signaled the end of his participation in the conversation by turning back to his papers.

Hamish took the steps two at a time, his mind working at a frantic pace. For one, Nate was never disorderly. For another, Nate had said, "Why bring the office home with you, young DeLuca?" on several occasions when Nate tried to coax him away from his desk so they could take off to a Patriots game or meet up with Reggie to see a picture. He flopped back on his coverlet and removed his glasses, closed his eyes, and pinched them with his fingers. Hamish blew out a long breath and clicked on the lamp beside his bed. He removed Luca's number from his pocket and held it up to the light. What would he do with this? What kind of emergency might he need it for, and what made Luca think Hamish would go to him under any circumstances?

He reached to his nightstand for a notebook.

Hyatt and Price
Pete Kelly
Christian Patriots
Arthur Kent

It was the last name he stuck on. A name he associated with Luca just as Hamish and Reggie investigated a new property development. Luca had been associated with men two years prior who filtered dirty money through nightclubs. It pricked at him that this could be the same type of enterprise.

Suddenly his eyes and brain hurt. He blinked the sting from his eyes and attempted to turn his brain in another direction.

Nate was right. He didn't feel about Bernice the way he did about Reggie. He didn't feel about anyone the way he felt about Reggie. She had popped the cork on something so long bottled inside him that he felt it all the more cleanly, clearly, and deeply than if it had slowly seeped out for years on end. He thought of their banter and chemistry and pizzazz on the dance floor, and the way they shared a laugh as if it were a secret language they'd both learned for the first time.

Hyatt and Price could gain a lot from building on such a horrible plot of land. Sure, they wanted to filter money out of slum housing. And Hamish thought it odd that he'd been seeing more signs than usual indicating new real estate associated with their firm. Or maybe he was just noticing the signs because they bore the name of a firm whose top architects included Vaughan Vanderlaan and Dirk Foster.

Kelly's notes and map included several paragraphs about the density of the land but also the malleability and potential of erosion if they built right there on the river. They placed the housing complex right at the lip . . . not farther up where it would inevitably last longer and withstand all manner of Boston's changeable weather. This winter, for one, had dragged on into spring, tugging it in and out with a frozen tide.

CHAPTER 5

Reggie telephoned Mrs. Rue the night before to say she would miss work the next morning. As most of the work she did was pro bono, she didn't feel complete remorse for the time off. She chose an unwrinkled white dress with a matching hat and applied her makeup with a little more attention than she normally would for a weekday at the office. She even powdered the majority of the freckles from her forehead and nose. Her rose lipstick carefully applied, she fastened a gold bracelet to her wrist. If Hyatt and Price were interested in building on the property at Fiske's Wharf, there was a chance that Dirk and Vaughan were involved, and she meant to get all of the information she could from Vaughan.

As she gripped the handrail on the trolley car for the rumble across the river, she used her free hand to leaf to the back of her Journal of Independence. It had evolved from all of the things she wanted to accomplish to double as an observational notebook. At the back, she had written everything she remembered about Luca's disappearance. Hamish had optimistically assured her that his cousin would drive any ramifications away from him. He seemed to believe in Luca's remorse. Reggie, on the other hand, trusted Luca as far as she could throw him and hated herself for initially thinking he was one of those tall, broad-shouldered Valentino types. She couldn't pitch him but a foot away from her.

She straightened her dress as she stepped off the trolley car and used the walk to Vaughan's firm on Washington Street to check her appearance in the glossy reflection of the buildings. Even though so much of Boston seemed like a portal to the past, striking and modern skyscrapers and deco ornamentation interrupted centuries-old facades.

Reggie found Vaughan's building easily, familiar with the exterior and bronze-rimmed revolving doors, having often waited for Vaughan on the outside. This time she pushed through. The firm of Hyatt and Price was announced with large gold letters under which a secretary sat far more rigidly than Reggie ever did in her own office. The secretary looked up from typing at a word count per minute Reggie envied and studied her with wide blue eyes.

"Good morning. How may I help you?"

"Miss Regina Van Buren for Mr. Vaughan Vanderlaan, please."

The secretary raised a pencil-thin eyebrow. "Is he expecting you?"

"No. But if you could ring him, please."

The secretary lifted the receiver and placed the request. Reggie smiled then stepped away, studying the sheen of the columns and the shine of the white tile.

A moment later she heard a chime from a nearby elevator and Vaughan appeared in a cream-colored suit and spit-shined shoes. He looked surprised but very much pleased to see her.

"I hope I didn't get you out of an important meeting," she said as he approached and gently took her arm.

"Is anything the matter? Your parents?"

"Everything is fine. I needed to talk to you about a few new developments involving your firm."

Vaughan consulted his watch. "Come to my office. I have a few moments before my next appointment." He led her to the elevators and passed the secretary. Reggie smiled but didn't get one in return. She figured this dame was fancy on Vaughan. Most women were.

"Seventeen, please," Vaughan said.

The bellboy ushered them in and they silently ascended several floors, sometimes repositioning themselves to allow for new riders.

"Well, well," Reggie heard the moment she thanked the elevator boy and stepped onto Vaughan's floor. "A reunion. And it isn't even Regatta Day!"

"Hello, Dirk." Reggie didn't even try a smile. "Conveniently, I was also hoping to talk to you."

"Me?" Dirk adjusted his tie. "Golly. Guess I better stick around then, huh?"

Reggie rolled her eyes. "I can't believe you're still friends with him," she said in an aside to Vaughan when Dirk was out of earshot.

"I've known him my whole life." Vaughan stepped aside and waved for her to enter his corner office. "It's not an easy connection to break."

Reggie stepped through the door and into a wash of light. The sun blinked through wide windows and out over the streets below. "I love this view!" No matter how many times Reggie saw the vantage of the city from Vaughan's office, it caught her breath. The Common and the Public Gardens spread below, the snow and slush of the icy spring slowly but surely giving way to the first signs of bloom.

Vaughan smiled and spread his arms out to highlight the sleek sofa in one corner and the black desk by the window. "I've done okay for myself, haven't I, Reg?"

"I never doubted it."

Vaughan wasn't the kind of man who expected wealth. He wanted to earn it. She appreciated that about him. "Take a seat. Tell me why you came all the way here to see me. Shouldn't you be at work?"

"I took the morning off." Reggie smoothed her skirt under her and folded her hands in her lap. Vaughan hopped up on the edge of the desk, facing her. She was glad they didn't have the broad space between them. "I wanted to talk to you alone. And if I told Hamish I was coming, he would want to join me. We're looking into some property development down on Fiske's Wharf. The current owner said that Hyatt and Price intend to build on that land."

"Dirk and I don't always share projects, Reg."

"So you aren't a part of this?"

"No. I would remember if I was asked to work in your neighborhood. Besides, you can see I am up to my ears in a project of my own." He gestured to several rolled-up maps and spread-out blueprints. One etched in great detail on an easel to the right of the desk. "New office suites on Tremont. State of the art! I am still just a junior partner here, but I think Mr. Hyatt thinks I have potential. I honestly thought that Dirk was working it too."

What was Dirk doing with his spare time? "Hamish is worried that we saw someone from his cousin's old set. Which means this development could very well be a way to exploit people into purchasing housing that will make a quick buck. The land that Mr. Kelly, the owner, is on doesn't seem fit for any type of housing at all."

"I can't keep Dirk from doing whatever he's doing."

"I know that. I just came to ask if you could keep a lookout. Hamish and I think that the trouble we ran into—"

"What trouble?"

"Nothing we couldn't handle."

"Regina." Vaughan leaned over, arms folded.

"Hamish and I have invested a lot of time the past two years in trying to help the community there. I love it, Vaughan. It's become home to me. If you hear anything from Dirk or anybody about what they're planning, you have to tell me."

"Because there's trouble?"

"There's a man that could be trouble. Someone involved with Luca Valari in the past. In a . . ." She stalled, hoping to find a way to relieve his obvious anxiety. "Not good way."

"Makes me feel better," he said.

"Vaughan." Reggie gently touched his forearm.

"I promise to let you know. Hey! Means we'll have to set something permanent in the books!" He winked at her as he slid off the edge of the desk and crossed to his date book. "Something in a bit of a routine, huh? So I can transfer information."

"You're impossible." She smiled. "And you're sure Dirk's name is attached to these Tremont plans?"

Vaughan nodded and motioned for her to get up. She stepped over to the easel. At the bottom of the development plans were several names, including "D. Foster."

"You know I wouldn't do anything underhanded, Reg. But I also don't want to get my childhood friend in trouble."

"I think he does a good enough job of getting himself in trouble." Reggie turned to the door.

"I know I'll see you next week, but I was hoping we could see each other before then."

"Vaughan, I don't think we'll need to meet that frequently to discuss— Wait. Next week?"

"Your parents. Dinner. Have you forgotten?"

Reggie blinked. She had seen a picture once where the hero remembered some things while others were locked in a little compartment. She *should* have remembered dinner with her parents. Her mind had another idea. "No. Of course not. Dinner. Thursday, right?"

Vaughan's smile was incandescent. "I'm looking forward to it."

Vaughan directed her to Dirk's office and kindly took his leave. She thought he might stay but was happy to remember that he'd mentioned an appointment, in spite of what he had said earlier about Dirk being a hard connection to put aside. He had known him so long. Reggie didn't want her loyalty to Vaughan seeping through when she questioned his friend.

She said good-bye to Vaughan and joined Dirk in a spacious office but without the view Vaughan's afforded. She figured it bothered him. Dirk seemed to be pitted against Vaughan in a competition of which the latter was less than aware.

"Well, Regina, to what do I owe the pleasure?"

"I am looking into a property development at Fiske's Wharf." She took the seat Dirk offered before he retreated behind his desk.

"Oh?"

Dirk was handsome. Not to the same extent as Vaughan. Vaughan had a natural confidence that highlighted his carriage: the breadth of his shoulders, the way he filled a room. Dirk had all of the right ingredients, sure, but there was something that reeked of insecurity. She measured it more with Hamish DeLuca's influence; Hamish could always sense inauthenticity. Something caught in his chest and started that slight shake in his right hand.

She looked up from her study to find Dirk smirking at her. "A woman with nothing to say. Regina Van Buren with nothing to say." He emphasized every syllable of the last sentence. "Not something I am used to. You either, I imagine."

Reggie widened her eyes to keep them from rolling to the ceiling. "Are you part of a new project in the North End?"

Dirk studied his cuticles. "North End? Gritty. Littered with immigrants. Impoverished."

"I don't recall your being this much of a brute when we were kids. Is it a class you took at Harvard?"

"I want to make money, Regina. There is a war. If you've heard. Rumor is that we might not be out of it for very much longer. I don't want to be left dangling from a cliff when I could be safely nestled on solid ground."

"At the expense of others?"

Dirk's shoulders rose. "What is it they say about the survival of the fittest?"

"Dirk."

"Come on, Reggie. Your own father would be the first person to commend me for my ingenuity."

"Ingenuity?"

"For taking this city in stride. While you're sniffing around playing Nick and Nora Charles with your Italian friend. The shaky one."

Reggie balled her fists, pasted on a smile, crossed her legs. She would take him on. The shaky Italian friend was why she was here. She would share every last nugget with him later. "Vaughan said you're working with him on a project on Tremont. But you're also working on this other one?"

"I can work on more than one thing at the same time. There are some other men involved. They're political affiliations of mine."

"Political?"

"They invited me to this meeting one night." He languorously looked over Reggie, from pinned curls to Spanish heels. "And I loved the idea. Reg, we are in one of the most all-American cities in our country. These men want to keep the American experiment strong. And I don't mind helping these men who have similar convictions to my own. The North End needs more housing. You know that."

"But what kind of housing? Dirk, you and I have had the same privileges our entire life. Some people haven't been so lucky. I've seen it firsthand."

"These people. Our philosophy is that some people were meant for greatness and others better rise to the challenge. Our country has no need for people who are too lazy to grab at its chance."

She imagined a very long pin with which to pop the balloon of his pompous sentences. "If you're working on this project, there is a very good chance you are also working with a dangerous man with connections to a darker cause. And I know you don't want your precious family name slandered in the papers. So work with me. Let me know what's going on. I can investigate."

"Regina." Her name sat in his voice like a parent scolding a toddler on the playground. "I know you like to play at investigation. But leave all of this to the big boys. I'm sure there's some dame whose boyfriend is sending another girl a love letter or a lost puppy that is better suited to your time."

The million and one retorts flooding to the tip of her tongue weighed it down until all that came out was a frustrated squeak. Didn't matter. She would peel through to the end of her Journal of Independence and underline a new section entitled "Things I Would Like to Say to Dirk Foster's Face but I Am Too Much of a Lady to Do So" by Reggie Van Buren. She rose.

"Have you been to the Top Hat yet, Reg?"

"My head is spinning with how fast you are changing the subject. Are you asking me out?"

"I'm taking a friend there tomorrow night."

"Vaughan's rowing night." She lifted an eyebrow.

"Whatever you and Vaughan are to each other these days, it seems you would still be willing to take an innocent turn around the dance floor."

"Why do you want me to meet your friend? I assume it is not you who is desirous of my company?"

"Your tone isn't very ladylike, Regina. If this is about your earlier question, no. I haven't met anyone untoward." He looked pointedly at a rolled-up map in the corner of his office. "I am merely working on firm business. Whatever is happening there with the current owner is none of my business. So. Will you come?" Sometimes Reggie envied Hamish's ability to tell when someone was being dishonest. She couldn't read anything in

Dirk other than his usual smug self-satisfaction. "Vaughan hasn't stopped talking about you, and my friend is interested. I'm trying to make a good impression. I know we're not as chummy, but you're all class, Reg. You doll up like a movie star and take a few spins around the floor. Just laughs, nothing more."

The last thing Reggie wanted to do was go to the Top Hat with Dirk and whatever inevitably snobby friend he was dragging with him. But maybe with a few drinks in him, he might talk. About plans. About developments. About Pete Kelly.

"A few laughs, huh?"

"Wear green, Reg. It does something nice to your eyes."

"Girls' knees start knocking when you roll out the charm, Dirk." She swept her hand across her chest Scarlett O'Hara–style before letting herself out.

─⋇─

Hamish kept Luca's number tucked in his pocket just under fingers that fidgeted over it. It didn't matter if the ink wore off; he had long since memorized it. Stared at it long into the night. It was imprinted in his brain the next morning as he was learning everything he could about the Christian Patriots.

He picked up the phone and dialed Kelly's office.

"I was wondering if you wanted to keep us on retainer," he said after Kelly barked, "What do you want?" through the receiver. *Retainer*, he knew, wasn't the right word. No money had changed hands. Neither had any verbal agreement.

"You aren't on retainer."

"Look, Mr. Kelly. You lured us down there under the guise of hiring us, and my friend almost caught her death of a cold. You just left us there. I saw someone there and I wondered if his showing up made you change your mind about pursuing—"

"I haven't changed my mind," Kelly snapped.

"Then ... where do we stand? Were you threatened? Was it an unwanted guest?"

Or, Hamish thought, *someone who wanted to go into crooked business with you?*

"I've decided that you aren't the best person to be looking into my property at all."

"Listen, I am not interested in working for you anyway. But I am not sure what about our time there changed your opinion about hiring us."

"No *us. You.*"

"Me? Did I say something or—"

"I know who you are."

Hamish chortled inwardly. *An anxious lawyer from Toronto?* "Oh. And who is that?"

"You know. And I know how powerful connections can be."

Hamish felt a quickening in his heartbeat. But he was sure it wasn't a harbinger of an episode, rather just a strange feeling that Kelly was corroborating his theory that it was Kent they saw at the wharf.

He cleared his throat. "Th-then may I ask, Mr. Kelly, why you chose us in the first place? If you don't have such a high opinion of me?"

"I didn't know about you at the time. I had only heard your names around. You helped a friend of my cousin's once. She's often with that lady who runs the bakery."

"Mrs. Leoni."

But Kelly didn't confirm and Hamish heard the receiver click.

Hamish turned the Christian Patriots pamphlet over in his hand. They might not be working for Kelly, but he wasn't about to stop investigating. He put the pamphlet back under his blotter with one hand and called Rob Reid with the other.

"How are you, Hamish?"

The familiar voice allowed Hamish to paint a mental picture

of a sunny disposition, an open countenance, and a few freckles to match the officer's bright red hair.

"I was on a case and discovered a pamphlet from a really radical group."

"It's not a crime to have views," Reid said after Hamish read a few choice paragraphs to him. "As far as I know, these men have been restrained. Their talk is full of hate, but they haven't acted on anything. At least from what I have seen. Mostly high-end, well-to-do gentlemen, perhaps with a little too much time on their hands. Perhaps even an excuse to meet away from their wives."

"So there are no women in the group?"

"A few, perhaps, but not as prominent at meetings. I oversaw one once while I was on duty. Seemed straightforward. Hate listening to them—but what do you do?"

Perhaps it was just a coincidence that some of the supporters were involved with Kelly. "Do you know a man named Arthur Kent?" Hamish asked on a whim.

"No."

Maybe he used a pseudonym? Hamish squeezed his eyes shut and tried to remember if Kent had been in any press during the barrage of names and pictures after the Flamingo Club murder two summers before.

"No Kent. But I have kept an eye on someone who seems to be a blue-collar representative of the movement," Reid said. "Hands out pamphlets over in Charlestown. So far peaceful though."

"Thanks." Hamish signed off and leaned back in his chair a moment, his finger moving over the cotton just above his scar. He'd been told his left shoulder blade might ache at the promise of rain as he got older, but other than that, he was fine and dandy. Hamish was happy to have recovered, but the scar reminded him not only of Mark Suave but of the last time he had seen his cousin.

When noon arrived, he waited for Reggie's appearance from Mrs. Rue's on the floor below.

He waited a half hour, then checked the stairs and through the window of Mrs. Rue's office. He wondered if she was sick. It was unlike her to be late. He was about to worry when someone pushed the slightly ajar door open.

"Are you Mr. DeLuca?"

Hamish rose quickly, almost toppling back his chair. It was Errol Parker, shortstop for the Boston Patriots. Even at close proximity and in civilian clothes, Hamish recognized the figure who so often ensured team victories. He was even taller than Hamish had imagined from seeing him on the field and in photos in the sports section of the newspaper.

"Yes. Please, sit." His voice tripped slightly, not from anxiety but from encountering a man who satiated Nate's desire to find the next Lefty Grove.

Errol lowered into a chair that barely contained him. Strong shoulders stretched a well-worn but pressed collared shirt and a tie slightly shorter than fashionable length. He kept his smartly collared trench coat on.

Parker folded his hat in his lap after shaking Hamish's hand in a strong grip.

"My name is Errol Parker, and I am—"

"You're Robin Hood! I know who you are. You steal bases for the Patriots."

Errol's grin widened. "You're a fan."

Hamish blinked, nodding. "You're the best base stealer I have ever seen."

"Why, thank you." Errol didn't possess any false modesty. He bowed his head politely.

"The Red Sox could use you!"

Errol turned his hat in his hands. "They could use me, Mr. DeLuca, couldn't they? But they won't." He looked at Hamish pointedly and Hamish put the pieces of the puzzle together.

"Their loss," Hamish said, knowing it was the color of the

man's skin and not his prodigious talent that kept him from Fenway even before Errol had to explain. "So many limitations to our city of liberty."

Errol inclined his head. "Exactly. But you say *our*, and forgive me, but you don't sound a thing like a Massachusetts native. No Harvard Yard in your voice, Mr. DeLuca."

Hamish smiled. "Please, my name is Hamish. And I am not from Boston. Toronto, actually. Boston is my appropriated home."

"Toronto! Canada! Great baseball there. The Maple Leafs. Babe Ruth's first professional home run on—"

"Hanlan's Point!" Hamish finished enthusiastically, hoping Errol Parker's reason for calling on him wasn't so drastic it would cut through their growing rapport.

"Exactly. Well, Mr. De . . . Hamish. I am so glad I found you. I thought I had come to the right place."

Hamish cocked his head. Despite Errol's amiable tone, there was something under the surface. Hamish's chest twitched. He hated inauthenticity, wanting to find the quickest way to unearth the problem underneath. "I hope you have."

"Trouble is, I have been everywhere and no one will help me. Not the police. Not any of the private investigators I called on. Don't think it is because you were my last choice. I just didn't know you *were* a choice. But I frequent Mrs. Leoni's when I am on this side of the river—don't tell my trainer, he'd have a thing or two to say about cannoli during spring training—and she sensed something was wrong."

"I'll do what I can."

"I can pay you," Errol said.

"I am not concerned about that. I am more concerned that you haven't been able to find help. My associate—Miss Van Buren—will be along here, but I promise you we will work together and do whatever you need."

"You're a good soul, Hamish. I can tell. I can always tell. And you know your baseball. I know men like me never make the major leagues. But there was a player named Moses Walker who everyone forgets about. It was years ago. I am foolish enough to think I still have a chance. The next Walker. A pipe dream, I suppose, but a chance. You've seen me on the field. I am not trying to brag. I just want you to know I know my skills. I know that I can steal a base and I am the fastest man on the team. My coach is a good man and he has arranged for a few scouts from the Sox to see me. No one has wanted to take the chance. Not yet. No matter how badly they think it could work. Shame, isn't it? Haven't won the pennant in twenty years. I can slug along with the best of them. But I just want to play, Hamish. That's all. And I am not too prideful to harbor any resentment when the news is bad. But lately I get the feeling that someone really doesn't *want* me to play." He fingered the brim of the hat in his lap. "I am used to the jeers and names and the occasional scrawl on my locker. I grew up in Boston. My father was a doctor. A respectable family name. And baseball was always my passion. I can keep a steady pitch when playing an away game with the crowd yelling who knows what in my ear. I am not easily waylaid. I am focused. I have to be if I want to be the next Moses Walker. But lately . . ." Errol took a deep breath. "The pranks have gotten worse. It's no longer names and paint and a spitball."

Hamish was following the story so intently, Reggie's appearance startled his glasses down his nose.

"Oh!" she said as Errol instinctively rose. "We have company." Reggie smiled broadly and extended her hand.

"My name is Errol Parker. Miss Van Buren, I understand."

Reggie shook his hand firmly. "The true Regina Van Buren is turning over in the family plot in New Haven, a relic of the Revolution, so please . . . no misses or Reginas. Call me Reggie."

Errol grinned and the tension of his story dissolved a moment. "Yes, Reggie. A pleasure."

Reggie perched on the end of her desk and crossed her distracting legs distractingly. Hamish blinked and nudged his glasses up his nose and turned his attention back to their client.

"Mr. Parker . . . Errol," Hamish corrected in response to his client's look, "was just starting to tell me about some unfortunate pranks."

"How dreadful."

"Reggie isn't as familiar with baseball, Errol. Reg, Errol Parker is known as Robin Hood, the fastest base stealer in the minor leagues and the toast of the Boston Patriots who play in Southie."

"You exaggerate," Errol complained, but his eyes sparkled nonetheless.

"A baseball player! How exciting."

"I keep trying to teach her," Hamish said.

"I know baseball!" Reggie flashed Hamish a look. "There's bats on a field and a wicket and a bowler and—"

"That's cricket, Reg."

"Well. It all sounds the same to me." She winked at Errol, who returned an easy smile.

"And I was just telling Hamish here that the police didn't listen and no private investigator would take my case. You see, I am used to a certain level of taunting and teasing and pranks and bullying. It's part of the game. Even players from opposing teams who do not possess my color are victim to childishness and initiation, especially in the minor leagues. It's a rite of passage. But lately . . ." Errol swallowed. "Someone put a heart in my locker."

"A-a what?" Reggie gulped.

"A heart. I smelled it, and then the sticky . . ." Errol shook his head. "A true heart. Not a human heart, I learned. A pig heart. Scared the daylights out of me and my mate Jeb Brownling." He looked to Hamish. "First base."

"You reported it to the club?" Hamish asked.

"And they could do nothing. But it wasn't just the . . ." Errol turned his hat over. "Threats are seen as empty. Even stupid horrible pranks. My nephew Toby came to a game and I waited and waited and . . . Toby is just sixteen. Just sixteen. Loves baseball. Works hard too. For someone at the docks. Irish fellow by the name of Kelly. Not the friendliest, but the kid is paid regularly."

Hamish looked from Errol, who had paused, to Reggie to Errol again.

"I couldn't find him for hours. He said he'd wait and we'd grab a bite to eat. But, Hamish, when I found him . . ." Errol shook his head. " I never want to see anything like that again. They had hurt him. His lip and nose were bleeding. He was shivering. Terrified."

Reggie gasped. Hamish felt bile rising in his throat.

"He said *they*?"

"There was more than one. He couldn't make them all out."

"You went to the police?" Reggie was incredulous. "And they did nothing?"

"Yes, and to several private investigators. Jimmy Orlando even. He works in the North End."

Both Reggie and Hamish were familiar with Orlando; he had once occupied office space in their building.

"And no one wants to take it. They think it is just some team rivalry. And that my nephew may have aggravated them or might have been at the wrong place at the wrong time."

"But to harm a child!" Reggie exclaimed, Hamish watching her whiten.

"Team rivalry indeed," Hamish said.

A New Haven Van Buren did not swear—but if one did it most likely would have been Reggie at this moment. Hamish could see the spark in her eyes.

"My locker is always home to graffiti and I can't keep any valuables there. But I never thought it would get violent. That someone would hurt my kid nephew."

Hamish realized he had absently begun tapping a pencil

fervently on the side of his desk, faster and faster until it flew up and crashed to the floor. "It could just be jealousy." He watched it roll into a corner by the radiator. "You are by far the most talented player on the team. Don't believe me? Go next door and ask our friend Nate. He has been following your career since the beginning." Hamish stretched out his arms. "Do you have any enemies?"

Errol laughed bitterly; his tone didn't suit his wide smile and kind eyes. "Several. Several reporters who think the ump's calls are made in my favor, people who want to see me run off the field, a few angry Irish townies who are miffed at us being here in the first place, lazy businessmen who would never wish violence but wish men like me were swept into a discreet corner. That's beyond any rivalry from the game itself." Errol straightened his shoulders.

"This seems far more drastic than baseball rivalry." Reggie recrossed her legs.

"Yes." Errol nodded. "But not more drastic than crimes men of my color have been persecuted with for years. The baseball field has always been a place for as much equality as we can hope for."

Hamish's father's work at the *Telegraph* had offered up years of stories of hate crimes and prejudice. In the first war, his father had been given a card and forced to report as an enemy alien to city hall for months, despite the fact he had no further ties to his home country. But even the persecution and loss of his job were nothing in comparison with what Errol's ancestors had suffered through for centuries. The world's progress was little more than a long train, and while the first-class cars sped into the future, the third class chugged at a slower pace behind.

"It hasn't stopped me from playing and it won't." A sadness crept into Errol's eyes, glistening their kind intensity, and Hamish blinked away at the vulnerable display. "I'm still his hero, Hamish."

Reggie hopped up. "We will do whatever we can. What do you need us to do?"

While Reggie shifted, Hamish rummaged through a pile of

contracts and articles for a fresh piece of paper on which to take notes.

"Can you tell us anything that happened the day that . . . the day that Toby was injured? When you found that awful . . . that heart?"

Errol nodded. Hamish pressed the point of the pencil onto the page.

"It's—what day is it now—the eleventh?"

Hamish nodded.

"The heart was just as we were beginning training for the season. Practices were long and brutal in the rain. Nerves were high. Anxious excitement, as my father would say. There was a fish the next day. Or what was left of a fish. A carcass of a fish that stunk up the entire locker room for a week after." Errol exhaled. "It's a long line of this nonsense in my world—but I don't want anyone to get hurt. I can defend myself, but I don't want to have to, you know?" He shook his head. "It won't help my career to have any blight on my name or reputation. But if I have you two . . . He looked between them. "There's one more thing." He reached into his pocket. "These men have been holding gatherings near the ballpark. Passing out pamphlets. Spreading their viewpoints." He held out a pamphlet. Hamish took it and Reggie stepped over so she could lean in at his shoulder.

"These are frightening views." Hamish frowned. The Christian Patriots leaflet spoke to an all-white American Camelot that would slay the dragon of encroaching war. That sided with the fascism and treatment of Poles and Jews in Germany's war. It quoted the book *The Protocols of the Elders of Zion*, the underlying thesis of the work being a Jewish conspiracy for domination.

Hamish looked up at Reggie. Her nose was scrunched.

"It doesn't speak to me specifically. But I know enough to know that men who will spout these ideas are not the ones who would like black people in the Red Sox."

Hamish looked up from a line about Jewish financiers plotting World War I so they could profit from the shipping on both sides. The paragraph alleged the same thing was happening with the war in Europe. The one Hamish's country was already fighting. Hamish studied Errol a moment, and a slight change in his face unsettled him. His heartbeat thrummed a little more quickly. "There's something you're leaving out."

"I got in a fight. With one of the men who hands out the pamphlets. Name is Bricker." Hamish flicked a look at Reggie, but her face was unreadable. "He dresses all nice but he's uncouth. And a bit of a terrible fighter, truth be told."

"And you think he would be angry enough to do this?"

"I don't know. He seems like the type who likes to be seen. Who wouldn't take the time to do something if he didn't get the credit."

Hamish nodded then looked at his open calendar and rapped a pencil on it. "You play tonight?"

"Yes." Errol flicked a look at his watch. "I really must be going."

"Well, I have tickets tonight." Hamish looked at Reggie. "Nate and I already had tickets."

Errol inclined his homburg at Hamish. "So I can count on you?"

"Sure!"

"Thanks for your time. Honest. I appreciate your doing your best."

After Errol left, Hamish turned to Reggie with a smile. "What a client!"

"A fan, are you?" Reggie laughed.

"You know Nate and I keep a close eye on the Patriots." His smile stretched. "What happened to you? Didn't see you all morning."

Reggie hopped on the side of his desk and swung one leg over the other. Hamish blinked a few times and focused every kernel of energy on keeping his eyes on her face and not on the gams that so perfectly ended in Spanish heels.

"I went to see Vaughan."

Hamish stretched out the knot that tightened his chest. "Oh. Took the whole morning off, eh?"

"It wasn't a social call. I wanted to know what Dirk is up to. Vaughan is working on a project on Tremont, and it seems that Dirk Foster is aiding him."

"Did he mention anything?"

"He mentioned a political party he's a part of."

Hamish held up the pamphlet. "Christian Patriots?"

"Yes."

"Same group that Bricker is part of. I rang over to Reid this morning." Hamish rolled the corner of the pamphlet down with his finger. "And Vaughan knew nothing?"

"Don't sound so suspicious. Vaughan said that he is working on a big project and that Dirk must be doing this on his own. I trust that. Vaughan's not a liar, Hamish."

"I know that . . ."

"Then don't insinuate."

"Reg . . ."

"It's hard enough for me to learn that my childhood friend has turned into . . ." She spread her hands, shook her head. "Whatever he is. The most I can do is stay on top of it in case it has something to do with what we saw at the harbor."

Hamish nodded. "Sorry."

"I don't like Dirk any more than you do. And he was a complete fiend about it. But at the very least Vaughan isn't involved. That's a relief."

Hamish studied her a moment. Vaughan was a page in a closed book he hoped he could open and pry into for a little bit. She looked up at him and he looked away, reached for a pen.

Nate arrived at three o'clock. Hamish watched Reggie beam as their friend strolled in.

"You haven't come for *Winchester* in ages."

Nate smiled and took the bag of almond cookies she pulled from her desk. "I can't stay, Reggie. Swamped this afternoon."

Hamish studied Nate and noticed his focus drift from Reggie to the window. Hamish fingered his brace.

Nate must have sensed Hamish's eyes on him, because he looked down at him with an unreadable expression. Hamish's hand slowly shook and something happened to his heart. Inauthenticity pained him.

"Hey! You'll never guess who was just here . . ." Hamish ironed out his voice. "Errol Parker."

Nate startled. "Robin Hood?"

Hamish smiled. "He hired us."

"Someone's been pranking him." Reggie wound the static out of the radio dial, and the first portentous chords of *Winchester Molloy* pulsed through the speakers.

"You're still coming tonight?" Hamish directed the question to Nate.

"I . . ."

"Nate, come on. We've had these tickets forever. You love spring training games."

"I'm busy right now, Hamish."

"What is making you so busy that you can't spare a few evening hours? I don't—"

"Shhh!" Reggie's voice was louder than the stomp of a foot and the blast shut of a door and the fire of a gun on the serial.

Hamish lowered his voice a decibel. "If you need me to help look over anything, I will."

Nate nodded. "I know." Nate looked over his shoulder. Hamish recognized the movement as a developing habit.

"Are you expecting someone?"

"No. Not really. Though, aren't we always? Should get back."

Nate was always excited about a night at a Patriots game. Sometimes even more so than the nights they spent in the stands at Fenway. "You know I love the Red Sox and those seats at Fenway," he'd say. "But sometimes the best baseball is watching people who could be the next Double X." He meant Jimmie Foxx—"The Beast" as he was sometimes known—who could nail a home run as easily as anyone, even the Babe.

But as much as they loved the energy of Fenway, they also enjoyed the farm leagues. The Boston Patriots played just over the river on the Charlestown side of the city. Tonight's tickets were the first they'd had in weeks. Hamish had taken Bernice Wong once, but she was so fidgety and anxious to graduate to the second promised part of the evening—a Charlestown club—that he didn't really enjoy it to the extent he always did with Nate.

As if she could read his mind, Reggie spoke. "Tomorrow night we should go to the Top Hat."

Hamish looked up quickly and his glasses slid down his nose a little.

"If you could see your face, Hamish! Dirk Foster's taking a friend there, and it is the perfect opportunity to talk to him about Hyatt and Price. I'll bring a girl from the boardinghouse too. So it looks like you just happen to be there."

"I don't know, Reg."

"I might not get everything if I have to play nice with this friend of his. Please. It's also an excuse to take a turn around the floor with a good band. Hamish, your dance card's been full for ages. I want a turn."

Hamish couldn't tell if she was flirting. But he also knew he would never decline her. So he tried to focus on the turned pages of Errol's story the way his father had taught him from years of reporting. Then he turned to some documents Mrs. Leoni's friend had sent over. Her husband was working part-time for a grocer and was docked an inordinate amount of pay for a lost shipment.

A few hours later Reggie disappeared for a picture with a friend and Hamish rapped on Nate's office door.

"Hmm?" Nate barely looked up.

"Nate, we have the game tonight."

"Hamish, I told you ..." His exasperated statement was accompanied by a look Hamish was not used to seeing on his friend. Even when he was drowning in work, Nate's optimism and energy surged through the office, working magic on everyone around.

"Either we go to the game or you tell me what is going on."

"Nothing is—"

"Nonsense! I will sit here and pester you with question after question until you finally spill it."

Nate glared at him. "Some friend you are."

"I am such a friend that I am taking you to see the Patriots. To see Errol Parker! Your favorite player."

Nate exhaled. "Two more minutes. I'll meet you outside."

Hamish followed Nate to the elevated trolley that saw Reggie to and from her boardinghouse to the city every day. He leaned against the windowpane as the Charles River dimpled below them and tried to imagine what Reggie thought of. If she stretched out her legs or set her purse on the empty seat beside her. If she closed her eyes against the glaring bright of the setting sun at the end of the day, running her gloved hand over the back of her neck. He blinked the thoughts away and turned to Nate, who calmly smiled at a passenger on the other side of the car. The man across from them, Hamish noticed, did not return Nate's pleasantry. Rather, he was looking at Nate with a look that bordered on challenge and disgust. Hamish watched him intently as his glassy eyes settled on Nate. He rolled his newspaper but not before gesturing at a headline (though neither Nate nor Hamish could read it) and rapping it on his knee.

Hamish straightened his shoulders and curled his fingers into his palms. Nate must have sensed him stiffen beside him, because he leaned into his ear. "Not worth it, young DeLuca. Angry words. Angry man." He gave Hamish a smile. "No sense in dying on this hill."

They trundled along, Nate distracted and Hamish keeping an eye on the gentleman who seemed to slay Nate with daggers before walking away. Hamish studied his friend in profile a moment. Still that feeling of artifice caused his chest to clutch and his fingers to tremble. But Nate was naturally calm. Hamish had lived with Nate for well over a year and rarely saw his friend in a bad or agitated mood. The only time his feathers were ruffled was in the midst of perceived (and often acute) injustice when Nate felt he could not find a solution. That and his (somewhat comical) agitation at Aaron Leibowitz.

They alighted several blocks before the Bunker Hill Monument: its majestic height drawing nearer as they sauntered toward it, Nate happily sounding off about Joseph Warren and Colonel William Prescott. "Do not fire until you see the whites of their eyes," Nate mimicked. But Hamish was lost to the history lesson. There was something that crept in the incendiary blood orange of evening's first rise. As they ascended the Town's hills, Hamish kept returning to the man on the subway. Clearly the war's shadows and premonitions had crept over the border. His father sent letters and clippings from the *Globe* and the *Telegraph* in Toronto to satiate Hamish's curiosity for news. The war was the first time he had felt torn between two worlds: Boston had become home to him until the nation of his birth requested its young men be available and willing for battle.

"You're quiet, Hamish," Nate said as they settled in the stands.

Hamish gave him a quick smile. "Paying attention." He was watching the dynamic of the players and their interactions with

Errol. Errol wasn't in the dugout laughing with his teammates. Rather, he stayed to the side when he wasn't on the field.

Nate kept jovially companionable but also silent. It was one of the reasons Hamish liked him so much. Nate never felt the need to fill a silence. He studied Nate intently, remembering what his father told him during his home visit about his experience as an immigrant during the war twenty years back. When Hamish was a baby. Ignorance and racism shook Toronto, especially the immigrant communities. Ray DeLuca was seen as an enemy alien and forced to report with a card to city hall every month. Even while the fighting of the Great War exploded an ocean away, its toll of boiled hatred resounded in the death knell of a city's innocence. He had read enough to know that the persecution of Nate's people in Europe echoed in prejudice far from the battlefields. The man on the trolley and his reaction to Nate crept under Hamish's collar, while the only thing ruffling Nate was a perambulatory spring breeze wrinkling his otherwise perfectly pressed cotton shirt.

"Well, don't let what you think you saw on the ride over here bother you. At least not on my account."

"Maybe I'm more sensitive about it than you are." Hamish studied the diamond for a moment. Another *thwack* of the bat, another run for the opposing team.

Soon the next in the lineup for the Patriots saw Errol Parker in his natural habitat—well, almost. He was far more adept sliding between second and third than he was facing off the pitcher, drawing a hasty line in the dirt before swinging the bat over his shoulder and jigging his weight on his right knee.

In the handful of games Hamish had seen with Parker in the lineup, the man nearly flew in an effort to steal base, and in five of the six attempts he succeeded. The urgent grace and immediacy that found him straddling second and third, tricking the pitcher with an eagle-eyed premonition that allowed him to always be a slide ahead of the action of the game, was at complete odds with the man Hamish had met for the first time in his office: polite but nervous. Hamish couldn't keep his eyes off of him.

For the first year of his and Nate's friendship, Hamish shared Luca's season tickets to Fenway. But with his cousin long gone and even with Hamish and Nate's combined incomes, they couldn't keep splurging on expensive Red Sox games. There was something so unassuming about the Patriots games. The crowd settled in without pretension. Wherever you sat you had a close look of the diamond, and people were more willing to get loud and uninhibited. Nate held a theory that the cheap hooch smuggled in all manner of thermoses and jars was responsible for the rowdy language of the crowd.

"I was just thinking of another Coke," Hamish said, rising before a commotion on the field drew his attention.

Nate tugged him back into his seat and they leaned forward to hear words expected from the inebriated spectators around them but echoing from the diamond as a fistfight erupted in the middle of the field—between Errol Parker and one of the players in the same Patriots uniform. Hamish supposed if a fight broke out it would most likely be between players from opposing teams. He had seen several of those before. Skirmishes and congregations over a call. Managers yelling, umps trying to break them up, and spectators booing like an underscore of bass to the rising music of anger on the field. Errol shoving a player was at complete odds with the well-mannered man Hamish had seen in his office earlier, and also with the Errol he had seen on the field a dozen times before. Often just his taking the plate was enough to inspire off-color remarks about the color of his skin. Sometimes heckles from fans of the opposing team. Errol always straightened his shoulders and stared straight ahead.

When the players were pulled apart, Hamish clearly saw that the player he assumed was the instigator was Sam Treadwell, left fielder. Both were expelled for the rest of the game even while the Patriots won with a walk-off in the ninth against a team from Baltimore. Hamish was determined to learn what the fight was about. Perhaps Errol had discovered the culprit behind the recent pranks.

"I find these games more exciting than Fenway," Nate was saying as they meandered through the stands with the rhythm of the crowd. The banter from the bleachers around them was of a very different tone. Nate's conversation seemed almost comical in contrast.

"I can't keep my eyes off Parker. He's so fast. And he seems to know what's going to happen before it happens," Nate said.

Hamish imagined Errol showing up at his locker room the day after contributing to a memorable win, only to find everyone against him. Even more so after a fight.

The moon was gobbled by a cloud, and Hamish realized for the first time that winter was shouting down the earlier tease of spring. The diamond faded behind them, the stadium lights going off, extinguished with a flick like smoke. As they followed the crowd out of the ballpark, a kid was hurrying in, winding by. He ran into Hamish in his hurry.

"Slow down," Hamish said. "Don't kill yourself." He placed a steadying hand on the kid's shoulder. He was tall and lanky and left Hamish with the impression he had seen him before . . . Right. Kelly's messenger. There was a bandage above his eyebrow. Errol's nephew. He smiled and the kid took off with a wave and a "Thanks!"

Soon he saw a face he *was* immediately familiar with. The moment the fresh grass of the diamond gave way to the tarmac and gasoline of busy Charlestown, Hamish registered a height and visage he knew well. Pete Kelly. Of course, the man's presence wasn't surprising. Kelly had told them from the first that he was a resident of the Town. He didn't, however, seem to register Hamish or Nate. Kelly's eyes, hidden by the brim of his tweed cap, were determinedly fixated on the pavement. Hamish was relieved. He didn't want to acknowledge a man who—on first meeting—already had a slur to toss in Nate's direction. Who was so easily distracted by a figure in his building that he left Reggie for dead.

So Hamish and Nate funneled out with the droves onto the same hilly side street in Charlestown that had led them there earlier. The game and the screeching for the Patriots had relieved Hamish of the tension from earlier, and he almost forgot about the man on the trolley. Nate even showed a bit of his usual self. An animated Nate was one of Hamish's favorite things. Hamish brightened listening to him. He was yapping away about the game and the weather and how Howard from the grocer's had a farmer's almanac predicting weather sunny and warm by the weekend. The tension unspooled. Hamish's thoughts weren't pulled in the direction of war or instincts or Luca or Kent. It wasn't until they reached an open area just at the base of Thompson Square Station that Hamish noticed a small group of people milling around in a slow swell.

The noise dissected into distinct sounds, most people separating and trickling onward to the train platforms, when he listened hard enough and narrowed in. And finally the reason for the crowd registered. Speaking of superior races and quoting Darwin and mentioning plans and problems and the Lord's will: familiar phrases strung into an incongruous twist of their original meaning and ending in a maze of strange propaganda. Hamish soured. Then got scared. The half dozen men centered on Nate with intensity and Hamish grabbed Nate's elbow.

"I've read about these demonstrations." Nate's voice was serious in Hamish's ear.

Hamish listened to the filth a little longer until they stepped from the shadow to the line of streetlights bordering the elevated train station. The protesters' voices were undercut by slight slurring, and Hamish wondered if there was even one sober man among the crowd.

It was something in the man's face: beady eyes, quiet smirk, confidence running through the sinews and veins as it might blood in another. Hamish saw in this man's bearing every last thing he lacked in his own. The dissonance empowered him.

"Do you have something to say?" He straightened his shoulders and shoved his trembling hand in his pocket.

"I might. Depends on who is asking." While his words were directed at Hamish, his eyes daggered Nate.

"What is your name?"

"Why does it matter?"

"I want to know." *"You find the name, you find the human,"* his father said. Then they aren't something faceless: whether victim or instigator.

"Bricker. Walt Bricker. You a journalist or something?"

Hamish flexed the fingers of his dominant hand. It couldn't shake with anger or anxiety if it was finding good occupation plowing into Bricker's smug face. In his amateur self-defense lessons, Jasper Forth had told him to never instigate, but he wasn't sure how to remain still with men like this guy. Nate, on the other hand, was expressionless and calm.

"Take a few notes from your friend there." Bricker inclined his chin at Nate in recognition. "Nathaniel Reis." Bricker's voice slithered a few words that pricked at Hamish's neck until he couldn't see anything but the man's smug face.

"You know me." Nate's tone was the same as if he were welcoming a client. "But I haven't had the pleasure."

"You're known to me."

Hamish's eyes settled on the pamphlets in Bricker's outstretched hand while he recalled the conversation with Reid leading him to believe that most of the Christian Patriots were well-dressed businessmen. The fact that Bricker looked like any other man he might see on the street—not overbearing or tall, just a part of the scenery of the city—made him angrier, until the blood in his shaking hand warmed to boiling and bubbled up through his elbow and into the space between his collar and his neck. It flushed his face and darkened his mind. Spots blurred his vision, combining with the shadows cast from the station, and made him blink to focus. He squinted one eye shut, propelled his arm back, and drove his fist into the man's face.

"Hamish!" He thought he heard Nate behind him in a tunnel, but he was focused on the strange tingling sensation that flustered any tremor from his right hand. More noise as Bricker rallied, calmly waving his friends back while dabbing at his bleeding nose. In the half light, Hamish saw a strange light pass over Bricker's face and settle into its not quite handsome features. His left hand was tight on Hamish's forearm. The same hand that had gripped the pamphlets now circled him on the ground.

"I wasn't expecting that of you." Bricker's tone was almost complimentary. "And for that, I am going to give you a pass." He held up his blood-spattered sleeve. "Helps me look a bit of a martyr, doesn't it? Peacefully speaking my truth while this wop kid comes and starts a brawl."

The slur didn't sting. Hamish was too breathless and frustrated to register it. The world buzzed and every last bit of him seemed more alive than it had ever been: pinging through his fingers and surging down to his shoes.

"Hamish!" Nate was repeating. Hamish blinked perspiration from his eyes and finally turned. Nate's face was resolutely set in stone. "We're leaving."

<hr/>

"You're angry at me?" Hamish shook out his fist.

"Of course I'm angry at you!"

"Why? Because I wanted to shove those men onto a train track and rip up their filth?" He kicked at a discarded Christian Patriots leaflet. "Jasper taught me to defend myself back at home, and I'm glad I did."

"So you jump in front of me, and I jump in front of you, and we both end up on the ground in a brawl? I do *not* fight that way. And it's not a very clever way to make it out of protests." Nate sucked in a breath. "There were three of Bricker's friends and two of us, and I couldn't fend off a squirrel. So if you wanted to fly into death, why not just catapult into the Charles and let the fish take care of you?" It was a strange mix of Nate's customary dry humor and a tone unfamiliar to Hamish. "You'll never win a fight flying at a man like that, Hamish. He'll just become a martyr and you'll look stupid and temperamental." Nate's hands clenched with a force Hamish hadn't seen before. "Right now you look stupid and temperamental."

Nate's usual humor underscored Hamish's anger and prickled his nose. The train screeched onto the platform, but Hamish was too angry to board. "I think I'm just going to walk."

"Hamish . . . don't get angry."

Hamish felt Nate's hand on his arm and turned around. "Why aren't *you* angry?"

"There is nothing in my world that would have been better if I fought back." Nate scrubbed the back of his neck "They were all talk, Hamish. I didn't want to play martyr and drag you down with me. It is not worth it. Not for me. Not for you. Come, I'll walk with you."

Despite having paid their fare, they watched the train disappear and set off, their steps taking them away from the platform.

Silence for a few moments as Charlestown fell behind and the familiar rooftops of the North End created a dark, jagged line across the winking river. The Old North steeple the most distinctive, stabbing Hamish with an idea of home. Hamish flexed his right hand before finally shoving it in his pocket. Nate had lived with him long enough for familiarity with his anxious episodes; nonetheless, he hoped the night sky—the moon gobbled up by a gray cloud, the skyline of Boston eerie from the Charlestown side, and the river black ink in its rippled course—would keep his friend's attention away.

"You're going to see more of this, Hamish."

"You know this group?" Hamish didn't want to validate them with a name.

"Of course I do. This has been bubbling beneath the surface here for years. It was bound to rise up. When people are uncertain and afraid and poor, they get complacent. And if the wrong ideas are ripe for the picking in the loudest, most assured voices, then it is easy to follow."

"That doesn't bother you?"

"Of course it bothers me. But I will not draw attention to myself. I don't have that luxury. I can't have these men coming after me or the circle I have created." He stopped in his tracks, the moonlight behind him, framing a face with delicately stenciled lines. He stared up at Hamish a moment but decided against saying anything, and they fell back in step.

Midway across the river, Hamish's eyes fluttered toward Fiske's Wharf. The warehouse jutted out into the harbor, a few boats bopping around it, gutted oblongs silver in the moonlight.

"Let's see that hand of yours, young DeLuca." Nate tugged at Hamish's elbow.

Hamish unfurled his fingers and held out his hand. "Stings a little."

"No!" Nate feigned surprise.

Hamish's smile started slow, tugged softly, and curved up. "But I punched someone! Never done that before."

"Y-yes. You punched someone." Nate walked a few strides ahead, mumbling for Hamish's benefit, "Suppose you'll be expecting some kind of prize for this."

CHAPTER 6

Madison Abbott was named for the town of her birth, and she was up for anything, including playing flirtatious heiress at Dirk Foster's favorite watering hole. She worked at the makeup counter at Gilchrist's: on the bottom story of a towering structure intersecting the fashionable Winter and Washington Streets. It joined rivals Filene's and Jordan Marsh to form a triangle in Downtown Crossing. Its balance of fashionable and financial clientele tugged Reggie into the past. Despite her modest Wisconsin upbringing, there was a scent that lingered on Maddy at the end of her shift that was far more Regina Van Buren heiress than Reggie Van Buren of the North End.

Reggie confirmed the appointed meeting time over the phone, Maddy elated that Hamish was joining them.

"He's cute, isn't he?"

Reggie lowered her voice to compensate for what she didn't want Hamish to hear. Even though he was at his desk and not remotely paying attention.

"He's . . . ," Reggie whispered.

"You said he's a magnificent dancer."

"He is that."

She hung up and Hamish started talking about the night

before. Errol. The conflict on the field. Hamish's own conflict. Reggie's eyes widened at Hamish's recount of his fistfight. Reggie blinked a few times. Something equally proud and sad was warring over his features. She was shocked and inappropriately delighted. He was in that moment the rusty knight she knew him to be. Gary Cooper in *Mr. Deeds Goes to Town*, unlikely champion of the underdog while Jean Arthur watched and waited from the sidelines. No damsel in distress, of course—Reggie had little time for those. But nonetheless in periphery, waiting for the man to step into the potential she felt special for seeing all along.

"It didn't seem as remarkable when I was there," Hamish said in response to her gasping yet again. "And we have to ask Errol about his fight the next time we see him."

"You defended your friend's honor."

"He wasn't that pleased about it."

His blue eyes stayed on hers, the fingers of his right hand tapping their usual rhythm under his brace, the other playing the lip of the homburg still on the edge of his desk like a piano.

She then told him she had put in an order for a tiny ivory-handled pistol. "It's darling. Really."

"You're cooing over a gun, Reg." And he turned back to his papers until it was time for them to change and leave.

Hamish jogged home and Reggie used the communal bathroom at the end of the hall, checking her eyeliner and lipstick in the cracked mirror and then in a coffeepot in their office.

She and Hamish split a cab, which dropped them near the Parker House Hotel so they could walk through Scollay Square to the club.

As the sun swathed over the city like a liberal knife of butter on toast, the Dragonfly came into view under spotlights that had already washed the Flamingo in their passing. Then, finally, the Top Hat.

"The man would attempt to impress a hat stand," Reggie said, referring to Dirk. "And while he's drooling over Maddy, you and I can finally get a dance in."

"Will Vaughan join later?"

"Not if he can spend more time on the river. I know, I know. You can take the man out of Harvard." She overcompensated with an eye-roll.

Behind all of this, she just wanted the opportunity to dance. With him.

The Top Hat was not familiar to Hamish, even though it was in Scollay Square, home to the Dragonfly and the infamous Flamingo and some of the other more elegant clubs attended by Dirk and his set. And Luca Valari, too, when he was still in the city. Still, it had its own charm—mostly in its simplicity. There was no garish spotlight roaming over the dance floor, highlighting the interior's personality, its crisp lines and monogrammed bandstand. It had a large floor and a well-stocked bar but didn't stand on ceremony with all manner of fancy cocktails. The owner, or so the *Herald* reported, was far more interested in using the club money for a band rather than atmosphere.

"People create the atmosphere," Hamish had recalled from the article. "Music creates the atmosphere. It is so dark and smoky in these places, why does anyone need a fake Rembrandt on the wall of the water closet? Or a real one for that matter."

Reggie looked up at Hamish, who had tossed the *Herald* on his desk. Then pursed her lips. "Takes you back, doesn't it?"

His shoulders crept up to his ears. "A little."

"You don't have to be embarrassed. There were some fun times at the Flamingo."

His eyes widened. "Were there?"

"Facetiousness doesn't suit you, Hamish DeLuca."

"There were fun times anticipating the Flamingo," he'd said.

Anticipating. The green dress was a favorite of hers and one her mother never would have approved of for the New Haven set. It had the same backless cut Myrna Loy wore in *After the Thin Man.* The sleeves were thin, and a fake-gold belt gave Reggie the illusion of an hourglass like Jean Harlow's. Her brown hair was longer than usual, and finger waves were a slightly trickier task than they had been with constant trips to a dresser, but with patience she'd created little ripples that would catch the sheen of the club lights.

Hamish, too, had dressed to the nines. The moment she saw him in front of the club, she recognized the ivory suit jacket and bow tie from their first moments at the Flamingo two summers ago. His hair was slicked back, and it made his ears seem to stick out a little. As if signaling something. Alert. She liked the style. It allowed her to see the whole of his features. A half dozen times a day her fingertips tingled to sweep a lock of black hair from his face so she could see him completely.

"Is that your Hamish? Bit sweet, isn't he?"

Reggie had forgotten Maddy was beside her. "Not my Hamish."

Hamish smiled and gave a wave from the doorway.

"Oh, and a dimple!" Maddy cooed. "What a lamb."

"Great dancer too," Reggie said absently.

"Hello." Hamish smiled at Reggie and the smile stretched. Its effect sent Maddy into an immediate demure moment.

"Hi, doll! Reggie has told me so much about you." She squeezed his arm. Reggie watched him blink a few times and tuck his free arm behind his back.

"Hamish DeLuca, Maddy Abbott. She is a fellow boarder."

Hamish shook Maddy's hand. "How do you do, Maddy."

"You'll save me a turn, won't you? Hamish! What a name! I'll never get that from rolling around in my noggin!"

Reggie had chosen Maddy because she was the least annoying

of her housemates, she reminded herself as they entered the club.

Reggie watched Maddy and Hamish dance, standing by the bar. She declined several offers to dance and watched for Dirk. When her eyes did roam Hamish-ward, she squinted to see if anything marked his face. Any sign of Hamish DeLuca in a fight. It still startled her.

He made his way over to her eventually, having spun Maddy away from him into the arms of a tall admirer.

"Fancy a spin?" Hamish asked.

Reggie couldn't recall the last time she'd danced with Hamish. It had been several months. For one, they weren't at clubs together, and for another, it felt more and more that any close proximity made her brain spiral . . . to many places. And her eyes tried too hard to lock with his eyes like an open book and her fingers couldn't help but feel the muscles under the cotton of his shirt and her heart couldn't stop thrumming the way she assumed his did in the middle of one of his panic episodes. But, sure, they were still *friends* when they danced. In the exact same way Jean Harlow and Clark Gable were friends. Right?

Wrong. He was Trouble with a capital *T*. The first time they'd danced at the Dragonfly, Reggie realized she was settling into a new version of herself. In many ways—more than the Journal of Independence—more than throwing her suitcase out the window and scurrying down a tree—it was the first true step toward how free she felt in her new city. She took Hamish's hand and felt every inch of his long fingers over her wrist. He was always careful with her, even when the tug and pull of the music flung them around a floor, lost in a beat. She liked the way it felt when he tightened his grip, his chin just over the top of her head. Just tall enough to be protective.

The spotlight meandered languidly over the crowd, flushing mellow light and outlining each couple on the monogrammed floor. Hamish fell into the rhythm. He knew how to dance. If anything, he was more at his prime than ever, having spent so many hours with Bernice in his arms. But as much as he enjoyed her company and as pretty as she looked with her pink lips and small waist, it was nothing like dancing with Reggie. Nothing like the way the universe slowed with her in his arms as if all of the crowd and the lights and the wordless notes from the band proclaimed, *This. This is what is right. This is what makes sense.*

He could smell her. Taste her, even—so close were the newly shampooed tendrils of her pin curls under his chin. And he was happy (and not for the first time) that he was just a smidgeon taller so that the top of her head could fit perfectly under his chin.

And when they were dancing it was like Vaughan had never existed and there was nothing in the world but the two of them.

"Hamish?"

They both stopped and turned at a voice he immediately recognized.

Just Hamish and Reggie and *Bernice.*

Hamish took a step away from Reggie but couldn't seem to completely let go of her hand.

"Bernice. I don't think you have met Regina Van Buren." This was for Bernice, but his eyes stayed with Reggie. He hoped they had affirmed Bernice wasn't any different than taking Maisie Forth for a spin on New Year's Eve at the Palais Royale.

Reggie dropped Hamish's hand and switched on her charm. "Very nice to meet you, Bernice. That color is lovely on you."

Bernice accepted Reggie's hand. "You are a woman."

Hamish was happy that the spotlight had wandered elsewhere and the club was shrouded in semidarkness. Otherwise the flaming red tips of his ears would have the same subtlety of a fire truck.

Reggie shot Hamish a dagger of a look. "I'm going to see how Maddy is faring."

"We're business partners."

"You certainly don't dance like business partners."

Hamish ran his hand over the back of his neck. "Who are you here with?"

"My friend Alice. Hamish, I really liked you. I thought—"

"Regina and I are not together. Reggie."

"You left out that she was a woman! You left out that you look . . . you *look* at her like *that* when you dance."

"How can you tell?" he said lightly. "My glasses are catching the glare."

"Don't try to be funny."

"Bernice, there is nothing—"

She held up a hand. "Here's the thing, Hamish. You wouldn't intentionally hurt a person. You wouldn't intentionally hurt me." Her voice took on a strange tone, and even though the band had started up and couples spun around them, she stood still. "But you have to realize"—she continued in a lower decibel—"that you don't know the effect you have on a girl. The way we all look at you." She paused.

Hamish cleared his throat. Reggie had said something similar the second time they met.

"Regina is a woman. A woman who looks *like that*."

Hamish followed her eyes beyond the maze of people to where Reggie was slightly rotating the ice in her glass.

"A woman *you* look at like *that*," she said. "I'd best get back, Hamish."

"I'm sorry."

"I know you are. But life is too short to spend it with the wrong dance partner."

⊥

The band's rhythm melted from a fast, brassy set with percussion so heavily punctuated it rippled through his spine to a languid, sonorous piece that drew couples nearer.

He found her at the bar.

"Well, that didn't go well, did it? What is it about women who cannot handle another woman being friends with a man? Happens in the pictures *all* the time."

"Really?" Hamish asked. *The right dance partner. I should just seize the moment. Now. Tell her now.* "Which pictures?"

"*Platinum Blonde,* for one."

"The one with those reporters. And he marries Jean Harlow only to learn he's been in love with his best friend the whole time?"

"Poor example. Take another spin?" She tugged at his sleeve.

"No."

It was dark and hot and she smelled divine, of course, and suddenly he was lowering his mouth to hers. Her eyes, brilliant brown and shining, like congealed starlight (*Rats,* he thought, *I'm even thinking in bad poetry*), almost seemed expectant. The slight curve up of her chin dared him. And the world stopped as he closed his eyes, lowered his face, held her closer, and . . . stopped.

Her eyes were wide when they met his.

He turned on his heel and left the dance floor, fingering his tie, wishing the ground would open up and swallow him whole. It didn't. So he continued.

For someone who stumbled with confidence in so many things, the fact that he found it on the dance floor next to this stunning woman made him love her even more. If he didn't have that certainty, he wasn't sure what would keep his heart beating and the very core of him ticking. She had thrown his world off its axis and now she was moving on while he was left to figure out what to do with its grand shift.

He knew it was ungentlemanly to leave her there, just standing. He resisted the urge to look back, instead shouldering through the crowd loitering by the bar and spilling out of the double doors.

He took a few deep breaths and scratched at the back of his neck to give the fingers of his right hand an occupation other than shaking. He looked out into the light-filled street: neon signs flashing into the square, foot traffic spilling from the direction of the subway like an overturned vessel, billboards guarding buildings shoved into each other like claustrophobic puzzle pieces. There was so much of Luca in this part of the city. And so much of Reggie too.

"Hamish!"

He heard her before he saw her, jogging in his direction, heels clacking on the ground, as she lifted the hem of her silk dress from the pavement and brushed a loose strand of hair from her cheek. "What is the matter with you? Come on. We're just two friends waiting for a very late Dirk and his friend."

"It's not funny." Hamish took his glasses off and studied a small speck in the corner of the right lens. "But we aren't just friends. At least, not from where I am standing."

"You don't want to say anything stupid, Hamish," Reggie said quickly. "Anything that would change our being friends."

He looked away, but he could feel her bright brown eyes, larger with the careful smoky powder and liner she had applied for their night out.

"Do friends dance . . . dance like *that*?" His hand was shaking. He tucked it into his pocket. "Bernice was right. Friends do not dance like that."

"Hamish, let's not make things complicated." Her voice was soft. The throaty alto he loved but in a decibel he rarely heard and suffused with a gentleness so different from her usual spirited straight-shooting. Somehow this affected him more. She was walking on eggshells for him.

"I understand that while I have been unintentionally leading Bernice on—"

"Your lawyer voice, Hamish—"

He ignored her. "You haven't yet settled things with Vaughan Vanderlaan. And I don't want to do anything compromising without . . ."

"Oh come, Hamish!" She punched his shoulder. "You would never do anything compromising."

"But it looks that way, doesn't it? And it isn't right. Not when we're hurting other people."

"Look at me." Hamish didn't turn to her, his shoes very fascinating. "Hamish, look at me."

He finally blinked at her through downcast lashes. "What, Reggie?" Those brown orbs glistened with something surprisingly like tears under the streetlight.

"I don't want things to be this way."

"Then make them another way, Reg." He looked down at her. "I kinda set out all my cards, didn't I?"

"Don't make us into this, Hamish."

"Into what, Reggie?" He shoved his hands deep in his pockets. "We're friends."

"Regina!" The last voice on earth Hamish wanted to hear broke through. "Sorry to keep you. I worked late and Walter here was still over in Charlestown." He stabbed Hamish with a look. "And you're here too."

"It was funny my running into Hamish here," Reggie said. "He was here with a young lady." Hamish watched Reggie scan the faces of a small stream leaving the club as if looking for Bernice even though they both knew she was gone.

The figure beside Dirk Foster stepped into the half-light and Hamish felt his heart drop. Dirk's friend was Walt Bricker.

"Are you finished getting some air?" Dirk asked. "Can't dance out here."

As they shuffled back inside, Bricker, for his part, maintained a level of calm even though the flash in his eyes let Hamish know he was as put off by the meeting as Hamish was. Hamish wasn't of the same set as Regina or Dirk, but even he could tell that the seams on Bricker's suit didn't quite align. That the fabric was off the rack rather than tailored to his measurements. Nonetheless, the pomade in his hair and the way he fingered his tie and mimicked Foster revealed an effort to fit in. Maybe that was why he met Hamish without a trail of leftover conflict. He wanted to play the part.

Last night Bricker had been at the center of the universe, touting his terrible views and foisting his pamphlets on passersby under the shadows of darkness. Here he was Dirk's shadow, his left hand (his dominant hand, Hamish decided, combining his impression of Bricker the night before—the hand distributing leaflets, clutching his sleeve after recoiling from Hamish's fist) drumming a rhythm on the side of the bar. The band was starting again after a short break in the set, and Hamish had trouble hearing whatever words Reggie was exchanging with Dirk. He did, however, make out a request for a round of drinks and mumbled, "Just a Coca-Cola."

The quartet moved to the side, Dirk's hand lightly on Reggie's elbow, Hamish holding on to his soda glass as they moved to a slightly less noisy corner of the club.

"Well"—Dirk turned to Walt Bricker—"Didn't I tell you she was a picture?"

Hamish studied Bricker intently. For the first time his swagger swayed.

"Delighted." Bricker reached for Reggie's free hand; her other manicured nails were wrapped around her lime fizz.

"I've heard your name," Reggie said casually, casting a peripheral glance in Hamish's direction. "How do you know Dirk?" Reggie's mid-Atlantic accent cut through their social classes. Hamish knew Reggie well enough to see she was surprised that Dirk associated with a man like Bricker.

"We attend the same political meetings," Dirk answered for his friend.

"I didn't put you in for the political sort, Dirk." Reggie's sweet tone was caught in her gritted teeth.

The riff of a trombone, a jaunty octave on the piano, and a pulse of drums.

"Can I have this dance, Regina?"

Bricker lured Reggie to the floor while Hamish shoved his hands in his pockets and gave Dirk a side glance.

"Step over to the bar with me?"

Hamish nodded, giving one more glance in Reggie's direction. Bricker was harmless on the dance floor. He wasn't very good, but he was harmless. Hamish appreciated the prospect of air.

"Look, I don't like you."

Hamish chuckled. "What a friendly chat."

"My friend in there doesn't like you."

"The one you meet at your political meetings."

"But *Regina* likes you. And that is a problem. She can play at this all she wants, but you are not of our class."

"Seems like Walt Bricker isn't of your class either."

"It's different. Vaughan is my friend and he isn't ready to give up on Regina quite yet, and you are a distraction."

"Why did you want her to meet Bricker, if you are so concerned about distractions? He's a bit blue collar, isn't he?"

"I owed him a favor."

"What kind of favor would you owe someone like him? You know he spends his nights distributing pamphlets in Charlestown. Getting in fights." *At least inspiring fights.*

"I am working on a new development with some other businessmen. Regina's father for one."

"Housing at Fiske's Wharf?"

"Exactly."

"The Hyatt and Price signs are everywhere."

"Many men in my political organization have a vested interest in seeing this project to its completion."

"Slum housing?"

"Affordable housing that will clear out some of the crowding of the North End."

"The soil around it isn't conducive to building a multistory structure."

"No one says it has to last centuries, DeLuca."

"I guess I am just trying to understand how your political affiliations are involved in housing at the wharf."

"Maybe you don't need to understand." Dirk removed an ivory case and extracted a cigarette that glowed eerily white under the streetlamp. He lit it while scanning the pedestrian traffic in front of them. "Smoke?"

Hamish shook his head. Everything about the conversation puzzled him, but he didn't have time to ask any further questions before Reggie appeared, breathless and looking at Hamish pleadingly.

"Your friend is a horrible dancer and his manners are atrocious," Reggie said.

Hamish scanned her face. "Did he try anything…untoward?"

"He didn't have time. He's in there having a row with a man he doesn't approve of." Reggie crossed her arms. "Something tells me there is a lot he doesn't approve of."

"He's just passionate," Dirk said.

"That's one word for it," countered Reggie.

⎯⋇⎯

Hamish was sulking. He didn't sulk. She had never seen him sulk. Not when he was recovering from the bullet wound to his shoulder. Not when he learned the truth about his cousin Luca. Not when they found themselves in the middle of a case they would never solve. Never. Hamish was many things: Anxious. A little shy. Smart. But he didn't *sulk*. And she had made this new Hamish that she didn't understand. Flexing his right hand in and out, a tall figure still recognizable even as distance separated them.

She was as confused as she assumed he was because she knew he loved her, and, to her great dismay, she loved him in return. But she was still unsure of her connection to a man from her past. And there was everything between Reggie and Hamish in that spark of chemistry, in their easy camaraderie, in their willingness to risk life and limb for each other; but nothing in words. She wondered why it was taking her so long to put her cards on the table and finally just *tell* him. She wasn't being fair to Vaughan or to herself. Especially not on the nights she stared at the ceiling wondering if by keeping Vaughan in the sphere of her friendship she was simply leading him on. She didn't *want* to lead Vaughan on as much as she *wanted* Hamish to kiss her.

She fell back against the cool brick on the outside of the club, the breeze picking up and tugging the scent of alcohol and gasoline from the busy square. She was making this more of a tragedy than it needed to be. She knew that. But she *loved* Hamish. She had for a long time. Probably since that first summer when she was still confused and unsure if it was love or just something stirring with the adventure and their possible future. And then there was a long stretch (and she had the journal entries to prove it) when she couldn't decipher if it was love or the deep friendship and connection that bound them. But she knew friendship. The way she felt for Nate was friendship. The way she felt for Hamish . . . as if she could feel the tremor in his hand and thud of his heartbeat with each escalating episode of nerves. It was more than mere affinity and never more apparent than when they were on the dance floor. They anticipated each other's steps. She could almost *feel* what he would do next: whether it was a twist and turn to a Porter tune or a suggestion spoken in the office, which seemed smaller and smaller every day. She clicked her tongue at herself. Regina Van Buren: strong enough to run away from home, to work on a murder case, to throw herself headfirst into a brave new world as an independent woman, yet unable to screw her head on straight when it came to something as familiar as Hamish. Well, that was to be expected, she supposed. It was easy to screw your head on straight; it was quite another matter to expect your heart to behave in turn.

⁂

Hamish wasn't paying attention to where he was going and barely noticed when he collided with another person.

"Sorry." He backed up and looked into the face of a kid he had seen twice before. Errol's nephew. "Hey! You're Toby Morris."

The kid was wary and didn't smile. He just nodded. "Yes."

"I'm the . . ." Hamish never liked using the word *detective*. He didn't think he was a very good one. *Investigator* didn't work either. "I'm the consultant your uncle hired to look into what's been happening at the ballpark. Like you." Hamish searched the kid's face. Sure enough, a gash on his head was healing. "You were attacked."

Toby relaxed, loosened his shoulders. "I didn't see who it was. Sounds stupid, doesn't it? But it was at night and their hats were pulled down."

"There was more than one?"

"They pulled something over my head. I couldn't see. Then it was just hands."

"What are you doing here at this time of night?"

"Running an errand. Parker House Hotel." He erected his spine a little. "High client."

"Quite a unique way to get to the Parker from Charlestown."

Hamish frowned. A few stragglers from the club were stumbling onto the street. Hamish gently gripped Toby's shoulder and led him to the edge of the square and then beyond. "Do you think they did this to get back at your uncle?"

The kid paused. The speckle of stars pinpricked the clear sky above the line of rooftops and buildings Hamish loved on the Boston side. Hamish fixated on the traffic snaking along Tremont Street. They were just outside King's Chapel, the Parker across the street with its monogrammed awnings and doormen standing sentry. Toby didn't answer right away, but Hamish didn't press. Giving him time to speak in his own time. A trick his father had taught him from years of interviewing sources.

"They warned me. To stay away from what I was doing. I don't really do a lot." Toby shrugged. "Your eyes are really blue. They look pretend."

Hamish adjusted his glasses. "Thanks, I think. They're real. They're my mom's."

"Don't see a lot of blue, blue eyes. Sometimes I see green. I run errands for a fellow over here. He likes to have someone who can get to and from Charlestown while he works."

"Pete Kelly."

"Geez. You *are* some consultant."

"I saw you there one day. I didn't know you were Errol Parker's nephew then."

"He sometimes gives me tram fare too. My mother doesn't think I should be working. But I need something to do. Saving up to follow Uncle Errol on the road. I want to go to Cincinnati."

Hamish knew nothing about American geography. "Is that far?"

Toby nodded. "Would have liked to be a batboy. But they don't have much use for me. My mom would never let me anyway." He scratched at the scab on his forehead and Hamish could sense he was losing him. Kids were only good for a few moments before their minds drifted to something more important, like bubble gum or Coke or comics or a girl—something else Hamish recalled hearing from his dad. None of these things had applied to sixteen-year-old Hamish, however. He never had time for them. Not even girls. Until now. And Reggie—

Toby was saying, "He trusts me. Pete Kelly. With secret safe documents." His eyes flitted toward the Parker. Hamish could tell Toby was warring between the manners his mother obviously taught him and his eagerness to get to the Parker and step into its grand foyer. Hamish wondered if Toby would be turned away.

"He must think you are worth it." Hamish wanted to see these secret safe documents. They certainly avoided him the first night he visited the property.

Hamish rummaged in his pocket. "I'm keeping you. But come, let me walk you inside at least. Those fancy places might have a lot of questions for an errand boy like you." Toby inspected his collar. His clothes were clean but wrinkled from bounding about the city, and clearly secondhand. The hems of his pants sewn and resewn again, Hamish assumed, with every inch he grew. Hamish felt guilty for escorting Toby to a meeting with heaven knew whom. He had already been in one violent skirmish. But he wasn't personally responsible for him, and the kid was safer in the Parker House with its staff and attendants than wandering Tremont Street.

He reached into his pocket for a bill and pressed it into Toby's hand.

"I didn't run you a message," Toby said, inspecting it.

"It's for the subway after. Make sure you get home safe." A smile ticked up Hamish's cheek.

"You're a nice guy. I can see why my uncle chose you."

"Well, I haven't gotten very far in helping yet. Between you and me."

They crossed to the street, just missing a sleek black car of the same make Phil used to drive Luca around in. Hamish led him, adjusting his bow tie and smoothing out a crease in his jacket.

"Who are you meeting?"

"Someone very important. Movie star important, I was told."

Hamish thought of pressing but noticed that Toby was shifting a little. His answers were as carefully evasive as a sixteen-year-old with a big responsibility could conjure.

As soon as they pushed through the revolving doors, Toby's face lit with the grandeur of the dripping chandeliers, the expensive carpets, and the ornamental floral arrangements.

"Excuse me." Hamish addressed a concierge returning from a quick inspection of a bouquet on route back to his desk.

"Yes, sir."

"My young friend here will want to see one of your guests. To deliver a message. You can help him with that?"

"Of course." The concierge smiled at Toby. "Come to the desk and let's see if we can find who you are looking for."

Toby grinned at Hamish and Hamish gave him a rare, full-on smile.

Then he made toward the door. Slowly. Perhaps the man he was here to see would come down to collect him. And Hamish could loiter and see who it was. Keep an eye out. Wait for him. He fingered the brace under his jacket.

But just as a doorman looked at him quizzically, he saw a bellboy collect Toby and lead him in the direction of the elevator.

He took one last look around the grand foyer, smiled at the doorman, and set off into the night.

$$\underset{\sim}{\downarrow}$$

Luca peered through the open windows of his fifth-floor room. He usually stayed on the penthouse floor, but he truly liked a corner suite on this floor. The bells at King's Chapel warred with the ones clanging in Park Street Church at the edge of the nearby Common.

He had already put a deposit on a town house in Beacon Hill. Fashionable and rimming one of those cobbled streets people bought postcards of. Patriotic flags draped from shuttered windows.

The Realtor told him he could still have some control over the fully furnished place he'd requested. Some room for his own art, to exhibit his own taste. Luca liked to step into a place already furnished and decorated. To slip into its deco lines and sprawl on its fancy furniture with a martini from a well-stocked bar. Then slip out as quickly as he had arrived, leaving no imprint of himself.

The Realtor said he could have the place immediately but that the current owners would appreciate having until the first of the month. Luca had a hankering for Boston cream pie and Parker House rolls delivered fresh every morning. So he had Phil drive him to the hotel.

The only remnant of his own mark he had left on this city during his previous stretch here was, according to his vantage from the window, strolling in the direction of School Street. Luca would know Hamish's gait anywhere. Hands in pockets, shoulders slightly raised. Characteristics he could make out from the fifth floor.

He let the curtain fall from his fingers.

It was all about keeping things in play. In baseball you stretched the inning as long as you could. Players rounding each base. Holding on hoping you can fool the pitcher as each play becomes elastic. Luca was always aware of the dream of a setup that allowed him to stay put. His last stint in Boston might have been the perfect stretch, if Suave hadn't followed him and shot his cousin.

Kent was practically useless. His first order of business had been to call on Pete Kelly and stake out his place. Instead he saw Hamish and spooked, telling Kelly that Hamish was Luca's cousin. After that, Kelly would have little to do with him. Kelly wanted to keep his property, Kent said, but if he was going to look for protection and investors, he would rather stay loyal to men of his own kind in Charlestown rather than someone of Luca Valari's stature and reputation.

So Luca, in a slightly benevolent mood lubricated by a few martinis, heard Kent out and sent him to a Christian Patriots meeting where he met a fellow named Walt Bricker who seemed intent on ascertaining the quickest way to rise financially in order to join the set his friend Dirk Foster was part of.

"Dirk Foster knows the Van Burens," Kent had slurred, having downed the drink Luca bought him.

"You don't say."

When it came to Nathaniel Reis, however, Kent was two steps from completely incompetent. Luca was not one given to casual cursing, believing one could give the impression of educated intelligence by carefully selecting replacement words for the ones at the tip of his tongue. He reined himself in as Kent spoke of his great effort in searching Nate Reis's office. He had held up a hand.

"Clearly you won't impress me with anything you may come up with in terms of your association with Reis."

The one slight (very slight) reprieve to Kent's ignorance was his discovery that Pete Kelly used a kid named Toby to run messages and manifests over the bridge from Boston to his home in Charlestown. For safekeeping, Kent theorized. Why use a safe when you had an eager sixteen-year-old kid to store them away?

Luca figured that if the case went to court, Dirk Foster and the Hyatt and Price set would want evidence like Kelly's underhanded manifests as a sure win for their side. If the paperwork disappeared with a kid across the bridge, it would be less likely to be found. And there were dozens of errand boys across the city.

One such errand boy was knocking on his door at the moment; he set his drink down, his reverie cut off with the clink of glass on the marble table.

Luca swished the tie of his silk dressing gown and opened the door.

Toby Morris was scrawny and tall with broad shoulders. Luca welcomed him in and clicked the door shut.

Luca opened his small fridge to put a Coca-Cola on ice for the kid. "Want an ice cream? A burger?"

"No thank you, sir."

"No 'sir.' I'm Luca. You like the room, eh?"

Toby's eyes roamed Luca's broad suite: from the perfectly made bed to the leather sofa to the bar. "Yes."

In the next five minutes, Luca learned that he was an only child, that his uncle had been in two fights on the ball field, that he was failing math, and that he wanted to be a batboy for the Cincinnati Reds. Everything pointed to Cincinnati for this kid. Luca almost peeled off a check and wrote a few zeros to get him there as quickly as possible. The city was growing smaller the longer he sat in this pretty suite waiting for the first of the month and the move into his fancy town house.

"Toby, you're a smart kid. Hard worker too. I like that." Luca handed him his soda. "Sit down. Baseball fan?"

Toby's eyes widened. "My uncle plays for the Boston Patriots."

"Robin Hood, isn't that what they call him? Bit of a baseball fan myself. My cousin and I had season tickets to Fenway. Ever seen the Sox play?"

"Uncle Errol took me once."

"You give me your address and I'll send you and your uncle tickets again."

What Luca liked most about Toby was that while he took in the promise of ball games and started on his second Coke and ate his way through a box of Cracker Jack from a basket on the desk, he knew when to cut off the small talk.

"Your man said you had a proposition."

Luca had sent Phil to the ball game. Phil found Toby shifting from one shoe to the other beneath the bleachers watching the first base line and his uncle parrying between first and second.

Phil had little tolerance for children, but Kent was stupider than them. It was a fine balance.

"Do you know a fellow named Bricker?"

"Angry man. Yells a lot at the subway station. Sometimes at the games."

"Yes. Have you ever seen him with Pete Kelly?"

Toby shook his head. "I thought . . ." He broke off, sipped his Coke.

"Yes?"

"Do you need a message delivered?"

It was past 11:00 p.m. "Where does your mother think you are?"

"My friend Joey's."

"Is there actually a friend named Joey?"

"No."

"So you'll go home, sneak through the window. Or through the front door, saying you got a stomachache while eating candy and doing your homework. I have been sixteen before, you know."

"I just want to deliver the messages. And keep the papers. I don't read them. I don't want to be insta . . . insti . . ."

"Implicated?" This kid had no idea what he was part of.

Toby nodded. "That's how I got this." He pointed to his forehead. "People thought I was a rat."

"Well, I won't make you a rat." And Luca stood and lit a cigarette. Then he smiled down at Toby. "You're a good kid." He used his free hand to reach into his pocket and peel a bill from a sterling silver money clip. "Do you need more for the tram home?" Luca asked.

"A fellow walked me here. He already gave me some." He held up a one-dollar bill.

"A chaperone?"

"Just someone I ran into. Bluest eyes I've ever seen. Don't even seem real."

Luca smiled sadly. He would rather be working with this kid than with Kent. He walked Toby to the door and pointed him in the direction of the elevator, then he fell on the leather sofa near the broad window.

Part of Luca wanted Toby to play messenger again. This time to the North End. To the house that Phil easily found. One Hamish shared with Nate Reis. It wasn't as if he had made a lot of headway with Kent, no matter what the man promised in Chicago.

"I don't know how useful you are going to be to me," Luca had said as he watched Kent down another second-rate lager.

"There's nothing there. He won't talk to me and I went back to his office and there was nothing there. Just books. Tons and tons of books."

"If you can go to an office and just see tons of books, you aren't looking hard enough," Luca had reprimanded. He tucked his fingers into his palm just thinking about it. It annoyed him that someone who had the potential to see so much had seen so little. With Toby, he could get somewhere. The kid had Hamish offering him dollar bills on the side of the street. But then, that was Hamish, dispositioned to do a good turn. Well, Luca had done a good turn too. He paid that Morris kid far more than he'd get from anyone else. He worried several times after Hamish was shot how much of himself had rubbed off on his cousin. In moments like his interaction with Toby, Luca hoped, at the very least, some of Hamish had rubbed off on him.

⫶

Reggie's Journal of Independence proved that you could learn a lot during two years away from your proper upbringing. Perhaps, most importantly, that you could fall in love with a person in little increments. A little bit when it rained and a little bit during the first snowfall. A little bit on a Tuesday and a little bit when he gave you the last piece of cannoli. A little bit on the dance floor and a little bit as *Winchester Molloy* crackled through the wireless. Reggie knew little about baseball. What she knew about it, she knew through Nate and Hamish. During afternoon games on the radio on sticky summer afternoons, *Winchester Molloy* was shelved while an exuberant announcer's inflection rose and fell with the action of the game. Reggie was always outnumbered; she knew she wouldn't win against the two of them and that her favorite serial would have to wait until the next day. But over time, she started forming an image of the action in her mind's eye. And while she had once attended a Fenway game with Vaughan, spending most of her time fanning her cheek with her hat and listening to Dirk's then-paramour talk about dating a Max Factor salesman, she experienced a tinge of excitement at stepping into Errol Parker's world as part of their case.

"You're in my neighborhood!" Reggie bounced a little beside Hamish. They walked up Pleasant Street in the direction of the Bunker Hill Monument: a needle piercing the lemony sky. The smell of freshly cut grass added to a spring symphony of crickets and a lone bird's chirp. This time of year smelled and felt different than any other in the rotating seasons. Late snow, ice, and wind a recent enough memory to inspire constant appreciation of warm weather and blue sky.

"That's my house! That's my window!" Reggie found it odd that Hamish had never seen it before. Perhaps he had walked by it but she had never taken the time to point it out. She saw him more than she saw the circumference of her room or any of the other boarders, but still it was an important part of her life and she was energized by their walking Charlestown together.

When they arrived at the diamond, spectators were beginning to fill the bleachers while the hot dog and pretzel and peanut vendors wheeled their carts to the edge of the field. The overhead lights flickered and filled out, and while the sun still winked down, it would soon disappear, the lights illuminating the players and field.

"Errol!" Reggie turned at Hamish's voice.

Parker wore a smile. He was still dressed in his everyday clothes and there was a tired glaze to his eyes. "Thank you for coming." He shook their hands in turn.

"Do you get nervous before a game?" Reggie asked as they followed him in the direction of the locker room. Several interested fans watched them, some gasping at seeing the great Robin Hood up close.

"More nervous now, I confess." Errol grimaced. "Whoever is doing this is trying to catch me off guard. I need to be in the right headspace before I go out on the field, and whoever is sabotaging me—is doing these pranks—is close enough to know my routine."

"Someone on the team?" Hamish asked. "I was at the game the other night. I saw your fistfight. With Treadwell. Was it about this?"

Errol shook his head. "He thinks Winston shows me favoritism."

"How?" Reggie asked.

"Well, you're here, for one." He smiled at her. "But I let my kid nephew in around the players."

They were nearing the locker room door and Errol motioned for them to keep their voices down. "They know I hired a couple detectives, but I don't want to give anyone anything."

"Is there anyone on your team you *do* trust implicitly? An ally?"

Errol nodded. "The coach. Ed Winston. I wouldn't be here without him. He's also assured me that he has talked to talent scouts about what has been happening here. I don't want to be given an unfair advantage though. I am smart enough to know I will deal with adversity and challenges no matter whether I play here or at Fenway. I can't get rattled."

"You're not sleeping, are you?" Hamish kept his voice low.

"Would you?"

Reggie and Hamish exchanged a look as they followed Errol into the opening of the locker room. It was loud and raucous. Reggie took everything in. A few players were practicing their pitches and swings to the side, halting at her approach. One whistled appreciatively. The other slurred something to Errol that offended Reggie so deeply she wondered if she heard it correctly. Hamish stiffened beside her.

"Well, I hope the other men on your team have slightly better manners." Reggie gritted her teeth.

"Miss Van Buren," Errol said politely, "I am afraid I am going to have to ask you to stay just outside."

"You didn't honestly think you could come inside?" Hamish added.

"I figured we would *all* stay outside and they would come to us." Reggie sighed.

The players who'd aggravated Reggie a moment earlier snickered.

"No comments from the peanut gallery," Reggie snapped.

"These men are not appropriately attired to receive a lady," Errol said. "So, unfortunately, I cannot see them wishing to join you."

He said everything so gently, so eloquently. It clashed with the colorful language funneling from the open door and the jokes from the players beside them.

One exclaimed curse caused Hamish to flinch.

"And obviously the language leaves a lot to be desired," Errol added. "Joe! Joe, can you come over here?"

A short, balding man with a broom under his arm made his way in their direction.

"Will you make sure that none of these louts bother Miss Van Buren if she is to wait here for a moment?"

"Why don't you just go get our seats, Reg?" Hamish asked.

Reggie shook her head and noticed Errol did the same.

"Over there," he whispered, inclining his head to a row of

lockers and a bench Reggie could see through the crack in the door, "is my locker. If I tell Joe here"—he turned to the janitor with a smile—"to keep the door open a smidge for the fresh air, who knows what you might be able to hear while we're talking. From the other players."

Reggie smiled. "I like the way you think." She looked to Hamish. "Why didn't you think of this?"

Hamish tugged at his collar and frowned.

She smiled at Errol. "Keep a few juicy details for me, will you?"

"Next time, I promise we'll meet somewhere a little more inclusive to a lady such as yourself. Now, Joe! You'll be a gentleman, won't you? Guard our fair lady here." Errol's teeth shone brightly.

It took Reggie a few moments to realize that Joe didn't speak at all. He smiled warmly and made sure the door was open more than a slice. Reggie leaned in, making out Errol and Hamish's voices as best she could.

One of the sluggers was still practicing his swings, more fervently the moment a crowd of giggling women peered through the link fence at his activity. He stretched to their advantage, the lines of the muscles in his chest and arms on full display.

He winked at Reggie as he sauntered by her, swinging the bat by his side.

"Move, little man." He sneered at Joe.

She rolled her eyes for Joe's benefit. "What a charmer."

Then she blocked out the sound and swell of the pregame moments as best she could and leaned into the open door to catch Hamish's voice amidst the din.

—⚓—

"Who's this, Parker?"

"A friend."

"You can't just bring friends back here, you know."

"I know, but I have Ed's permission."

"More special treatment, huh, Parker?"

"Not sure it's as much special treatment as my asking nicely, Derek."

Hamish studied Errol's calm demeanor. While the other men threw towels and spouted ribald jokes and used words that were shockingly a noun, adjective, and adverb all at the same time, Errol merely showed him his home space in the locker area. "When we're on the road, we all have our crates and cases. Ed calls it our dunnage because he's obsessed with those big old ships."

Hamish mentally created a roster of possible suspects while Errol unbuttoned his shirt and replaced it with his jersey. He didn't stretch like the others. Nor did he engage with the antics Hamish saw firsthand. Rolled towels flew through the air and stories about conquests ricocheted off the tin lockers. Steam wafted from the nearby showers as a man Hamish recognized as an outfielder splashed his teammates, using his water canteen as a projectile missile.

"You don't warm up?"

"I do everything at home. I usually show up as close to the first pitch as possible." He rolled his shoulders. "I don't belong here, Hamish. I know they don't want me here."

Hamish studied the large gap between Errol's locker near the exit and the commotion and camaraderie of the other team members. He clutched his right hand. The room looked a lot like the playground at school while he was growing up, staying away, doing his homework at home or hiding in the library. But he was smart enough to recognize the difference between his situation and Errol's. Hamish chose to keep to himself, while Errol marginalized himself for the privilege of being a part of this world in any way possible, even from the sidelines.

"I shower at home. I stretch at home. I keep a wide berth." He opened his locker wide and showed Hamish the inside. Hamish figured that was why they needed to go into the locker room and leave Reggie outside. Not that he would hear anything but that he could see the scene. But Errol's locker was bare. No mementos of family or pictures. No rabbit's foot or extra hat. Just a plain bottle of water and an apple. And no evidence of any recent prank. "I keep everything in a knapsack. I don't even carry money on me other than a bill I keep tucked in my shoe. I used to, but even locked, someone always found a way to crowbar in." Hamish shifted at a word he made out on the locker door, murkily smudged with soap as if scrubbed within an inch of its life.

"This, I am used to." Errol followed Hamish's sight line. "That's followed me my whole life, and I knew it was part of the risk I took playing. But the pranks got worse."

The aforementioned bloody heart. A chicken's foot. A decaying fish. Hamish listened intently, his stomach souring, his heart racing at the cruelty of someone—maybe even someone in the batting lineup. Hamish wondered about someone from an opposing team, but it would be too difficult to pin down. He had spent the morning looking through the schedule from the past season and a half, and there wasn't a concrete rhythm to whom they played and when.

"I will change my world by playing this game, Hamish. And maybe I'll change it for a few other people too. My nephew for one." Errol's face changed whenever he spoke of Toby.

"He loves to watch you play?"

"My sister doesn't want him to. She thinks it is a bad example. Toby should focus on school and keep out of a public spotlight."

"She doesn't approve? I think you would be a wonderful role model for Toby."

"I want to invite Toby for a weekend when I get my new place. We'll see a game at Fenway. Eat lobster. We've done it before, but I've always had to get him back. He's a good kid. Hardworking.

But I want to keep an eye on him a little more. Before he gets into a good school."

Hamish smiled. "He wants to get into a good school or your sister wants him to?"

"*He* wants to. He has always had a mind of his own. An enviable work ethic. His father left when he was a baby. But she is so wonderful with him. My parents help, of course." Errol was fingering his towel. "And I do what I can." He paused. "Broke my heart when he was roughed up. Such a good kid." Errol retrieved a picture from his wallet. In other open lockers pictures were proudly on display. Errol didn't even trust leaving a picture of his nephew inside. "Here . . ."

Hamish didn't want Errol to know he had seen Toby. It wasn't his secret to tell that he had seen him with Pete Kelly. Had dropped him off to meet a client at the Parker House.

"Handsome face. I've seen him before."

"Isn't it?" Errol was proud. "Doesn't surprise me you've seen him. Does odd jobs across the river. Gives me something to slug for. Every time I hover between second and third, I conjure up that kid in my head. Remember holding him as a baby. And I can do it." He chuckled.

"Do what?"

"Anything. It's amazing what you can come up with when you know someone is watching you as if you could spread wings and fly."

CHAPTER 7

Hamish handed Reggie a Coke. She switched the carton of popcorn to her other hand to handle the soda.

"The team assumes that the manager gives Errol preferential treatment." Hamish settled into his seat.

Reggie swallowed a kernel of popcorn and extended the box to Hamish. He took a few pieces and tossed them in his mouth. "And what does Errol think?"

"Errol treats people well. Even those Neanderthals we saw outside the locker room. I think if he is shown any preferential treatment it is because of his potential. His friend Mark . . . There—first baseman." He watched Reggie settle her eyes on a large blond man digging his cleat into the dirt. "Said that it's Errol who draws the crowds. And that there's a few scouts from the major leagues who have expressed interest."

Reggie watched the first baseman for a few silent moments, then stood and shuffled as a couple found and moved to the adjacent seats.

"I suppose it's not easy for any scout to make a case for Errol."

"It isn't. And that's why the Red Sox haven't grabbed him yet. Any other player in the world who can play like that . . ." He spread his hands.

"Is he really that good?"

"I've never seen anyone faster on the field. Baseball is a lot about strategy. But it isn't a whip-neck speed of a game. It takes tactics. Errol has both. He is a tactical player. But his instincts . . ." Hamish set his Coke bottle down by his feet and stretched his arms out a moment before folding them with a smile. "For him to be able to anticipate a ball coming from anywhere on the diamond but also to predict what action will happen where." He whistled slowly. "That's why you have to keep your eyes open. Always."

"I hope he does something wonderful tonight," Reggie said, watching Errol to the side of the bullpen swinging his bat in anticipation in the lineup. "For my first time at a baseball game."

"He loves his nephew."

The Patriots battled the Hartford Hurricanes and were already up 3–0 in the second inning. Hamish assumed Nate would be listening through the grainy static of the one radio station that carried the league. As much as he knew his friend would have enjoyed the tour and the proximity to the players, his heart accelerated watching Reggie take in the action around them. She was stepping into the world that was so often his safety zone: the sound of the bat forcefully meeting the ball and sending it far in the air. The collective din of the stands, the squeak of the bleachers, the organ pounding out jingles and ditties and chords to inspire spectator fervor. The shifting scoreboard and communal enthusiasm. The smell of popcorn and beer and, as in tonight's game, the inimitable scent of almost-summer: grass and something in the air that overtook the salt and yeast of the vendors' carts and gave way to the most alluring type of nostalgia.

Reggie watched intently. "Wait! Why is the ump making the call?"

"Because he's not safe."

"Of course he's safe!" She was adorably riled. "I see him!" She pointed with such passion she nearly poked the man in front of them. "He's on the base."

"His foot has to touch the base, Reg. That's why the umpire is looking into it. Sometimes it's really close and a tough judgment call."

The tough judgment call inspired several vehement boos and dissent from the stands, Reggie's voice joining the mounting din. She soon was on her feet, waving her hands around. Hamish chuckled.

"Excuse me." Hamish and Reggie looked a few rows down to a man shuffling to his seat. A second later, the man adjusted his downturned canvas hat and Hamish recognized Walt Bricker. Something crept over the back of Hamish's neck and he lightly held Reggie's elbow, pushing her back so Bricker could shove by.

Reggie forgot about the ump's call, focused on waiting for Bricker to take his seat before exchanging a dark look with Hamish.

Hamish nodded. Bricker was slightly inebriated. If it wasn't clear from his uneven stance, then it was from his scent. Errol crossed to face the pitcher.

He could feel Reggie tense with excitement beside him at the prospect of Errol's swinging in the lineup.

Parker swung at a foul on the first, dug his toe into the plate, and loosened his broad shoulders. There was such intense concentration on his face; Hamish could feel it even from their elevated place in the stands. He was a competent, if unreliable, slugger and he was smart enough to know it. Sure, he had power enough when he hit the ball, but somehow his preternatural ability to anticipate another player's move when he was between bases didn't always translate to the pitcher. Hamish watched the pitcher deftly signal the catcher behind him. Tension was high and escalated when Bricker began yelling obscenities about Parker's race. Errol had taken a moment to regroup with a practice swing, and the action left a silence over the bleachers that Bricker's deep voice could easily surmount.

"Sit down!" Reggie growled, standing and ignoring the looks of the patrons shushing her and asking her to stop blocking them. "Some of us just want to watch a baseball game."

Bricker turned to look up at her in the space between a couple in front of Reggie and Hamish.

"If you like, I will come down there and push you back into your seat."

Hamish tugged at her sleeve. "Reggie, it's not worth it."

"You're a feisty little thing, aren't you? No manners, either. Leaving me the other night."

"The only side I am on is sitting and watching baseball without a cad like you spewing filth that has nothing to do with the game." She sniffed. "You were a fiend the other night and I wasn't going to be party to it."

"Can you lovebirds take your argument elsewhere?" an annoyed patron spat.

Reggie fumed. "Sit down!"

Bricker stiffened and a nerve in his neck twitched. Hamish's first inclination was to rise and take the dispute from Reggie, but he had learned several times in the past few months that she was more than capable of fighting her own battles. More still, she tended to like Hamish more when he stepped aside and let her handle herself. Finally, Bricker sat down, but he didn't even make it through the inning before standing up again and shoving his way again over the bleachers.

"I despise him!" Reggie seethed.

Hamish, though, was focused on Errol. It was clear to Hamish from the player's determined stance and rigid muscles that he heard—and was carefully ignoring—every verbal jab and slur from Bricker's direction. Then the magic happened: the pitcher took a calculated step from the plate and pummeled an underhand toss that sped in a perfect spiral, meeting the sweet spot of Errol's bat with a *thwack*.

After the game they waited for Errol by the locker room door. He was the last to leave.

"No pranks tonight," Errol said with a smile. "I can't decide if that's the calm before the storm or because they know I hired some investigators."

"I'm glad for that. Do you think that your having detectives will be enough to scare the perpetrator?" Reggie asked. It was a word she always was deliciously confused by. Too many *p*'s. Hamish had heard her practice it too.

Errol walked them well in the direction of the subway station, Charlestown becoming more familiar to Hamish: a new friend he was mapping. One of narrow streets and hiccups of hills. Colonial-style housing. Few windows were spared patriotism in a series of stars and stripes. Bunker Hill, the neighborhood's compass—as integral to the character of the place as the Old North's steeple he could just make out across the river as they neared the bridge.

Errol left them, and Reggie and Hamish fell into silence.

"I could walk you home," he said. She had come farther than her residence.

"It's just a few blocks." Nearby a dog barked, skidded over, and circled her leg. Reggie reached down to pet it. The dog loved the touch, tongue lolling. "And I have a guard dog if need be." She laughed. It almost cut the tension that buzzed when it was just the two of them, but not quite.

Hamish nodded. His eyes were on her lips. He blinked away. But she was a magnet drawing him back: to freckles and slightly parted lips and a nose slightly scrunched in delight at the dog's licking her hand. He wanted to brush a curl from her forehead and trace his mouth over her. He wanted to pull her close, uncaring of what Charlestown thought, and keep her with him, as part of him, close and certain, to still his heartbeat, fingers intertwined to stop the slight shudder of his right hand.

"Do you want to talk about what happened at the Top Hat?" Reggie asked.

"Reggie, I need to know that there is some part of you that . . ." He stopped, closed his eyes, searched for a word. His heart said *thrills. Is there some part of you that* thrills *to me?* It was from that song "If I Didn't Care." Then why do I *thrill*? He certainly thrilled around her.

"There's some part of me that never wants to lose my dearest friend." She shifted a little. "I should head home. Busy day learning all about baseball." She tried to lighten her tone, but it didn't work.

In the end she turned and waved and he watched her skip a little before setting off at a jog back to her boardinghouse.

When he turned onto his street, he felt the strangest prickle on his neck. As if someone was behind him.

"Phil?" he mouthed to the darkness. But the shadow he would testify to seeing was taller than Phil. Broader. *Kent?* Hamish clicked his tongue. He was becoming ridiculous, like a jittery criminal in one of Reggie's movies. If Kent was following up for his dearly departed friend Suave, then wouldn't he just find Luca? Luca was the one who spared Frank Fulham. This was his cousin's problem.

Inside, Nate was surrounded by papers, a pencil tucked behind his ear. "Well, young DeLuca." And there was a smile too.

Hamish breathed a sigh of relief. This was far preferable to the Nate who had been preoccupied with constant business lately.

Nate waxed on about Cyrus Dallin. The sculptor had won a contest to create a statue of Revere in his youth in the last century and been offered quite a lot of money for it. Nate knew every last detail. A series of unfortunate happenstances, not to mention Dallin not being given his due either professionally or monetarily. And, of course (Nate's favorite sticking point), the ill-thought scheme to place the Revere statue in Copley Square—far from the North End where the lantern hung in the Old North Church and Revere's trusty steed galloped in the direction of Lexington and Concord on that fateful April night.

"Would you have the patience, young DeLuca? To wait for something for decades—something that you wanted? We want change right away. We want things to happen in our time right when we want them to so we can see the results of our work. I think of the big temples and cathedrals. Like Notre Dame! The sculptors and builders who died before ever seeing their finished product. And poor old Cyrus Dallin . . ." Nate played with a button on his vest.

"It sounds suspiciously like you're talking about yourself, Nate. But you must see what you do immediately. People are always crowding in to thank you and repay you in whatever way they can."

"You don't see everything that happens in my world, Hamish."

Hamish took a deep breath. "What does that mean, Nate? Why are you so cryptic?" He scratched his neck, then used the same hand to emphatically slam the table. Nate being cryptic. Reggie unable to reciprocate what he was feeling. Kent sniffing around. Hamish's nerves had always trumped everything, including anger. Now it was showing up.

"Hey, what's up with you?"

"This." He motioned to his friend. "All of this. There's something so fatalistic in everything about you right now. You talk about Dallin but you won't tell me about your day. Cathedrals? What, you think that whatever project you are working on right now—whatever it is—will outlive you?"

"I don't want to argue with you." Nate disentangled himself from the surroundings of papers and files. "Want to play a game of battleship?" He rose and smoothed his trousers, stretched his shoulders, and made for the pencil and pad they kept on the kitchen table.

They hadn't played their usual chess in several days, Nate was so obsessed with this new game. Before Hamish could protest, Nate dragged him to the kitchen and motioned to a seat. Hamish watched his friend draw neat lines to create the graph. Lines that ran from 1–10 across and A–J on the side, little boxes wherein they would soon mark their strategies.

"It's not ships we're sinking," Nate announced on their first game. "It's U-boats."

Hamish chuckled. Every news reel that week had been focused on U-boats: monstrous oblongs deep in the sea and deadly with their torpedoes and destruction.

Every night they would play a few games, alternating who drew out the graph and who made the cocoa.

Nate insisted they keep all played games.

Hamish silently began to crumple a finished game.

"Tsk-tsk. We can't learn our strategy from the mistakes of the past if we throw those mistakes in the waste bin." Nate smoothed the piece of paper and affixed it on the Frigidaire. "There. Now you can study."

Hamish rolled his eyes. "It's waste."

"It's a memory," Nate said with a laugh.

CHAPTER 8

When Hamish arrived at the office the next morning, he unlocked the door and leaned his bicycle against the wall, only to see the sun catching the prisms like a dozen rainbow diamonds on the floor. He picked up the morning paper and flipped to the sports section. Errol didn't always feature in the coverage of the Patriots. It largely depended on the reporter. But even during games where it was clear he was the catalyst for a win, not every writer was eager to mention him. As if the next morning he could be easily forgotten.

Dirk Foster's views were not rare and not new. Hamish had learned of similar views from entrepreneur Henry Ford. A publication called the *Dearborn Independent* was rife with ideas that crept under Hamish's collar and drove his two forefingers beneath his braces.

He scratched his neck and ripped a page from his legal pad so he had a blank slate. He swallowed and controlled his shaking hand with several circled scrawls from his pen: tracing words over and over with perfunctory precision. In school he was fascinated by Venn diagrams: a visual of a nineteenth-century mathematical principle that discovered the point of intersection. It didn't make sense. The first event that spiraled them into the series of current investigations made no sense. It made no sense that the person who wanted Hamish and Reggie to ensure he was being treated fairly by these new developers would try to kill one of the investigators. But Hamish never saw who put Reggie in that precarious situation, and they both confirmed that Kent had been there.

Kent. Hamish underlined the name within one of the oblongs of the diagram so tersely he finally broke through the paper.

He shoved the paper away. Something stuck about this. Something that reminded him a lot of Luca. He wondered if the premonition was just his being paranoid, imagining he saw his cousin everywhere, fingering over the phantom pain in his chest. He'd make a rotten investigator if every possible mystery was colored by his obsession with his cousin.

You're too trusting. You get these ideas in your head and follow them through. That's your good heart. Your propensity to see the best in everyone . . . Luca had said a version of this to Hamish time and time again.

"Well, Luca," Hamish thought aloud. "Now I don't see the best in anyone. Something, maybe, finally, I inherited from you."

He shook his head, returning to Errol Parker's case. He had written a list of people to telephone for information. One was the announcer for the farm leagues. Len Blaney. The games were carried on a staticky station that he was told picked up a stronger signal in the Town.

According to Errol, Blaney was often the first to arrive and the last to leave, keeping watch over his space and making sure his papers full of stats were at the ready for quick reference. "He spends the days reading all of the national papers and clipping things out," Errol had explained.

He picked up before the first full ring. "Mr. Blaney?"

"Blaney." His voice was eager. He had a strong Massachusetts accent—stronger than what Hamish remembered from the radio— but his voice had a rich resonance and sat in the right octave and pace for gearing up excitement for a game in progress.

"My name is Hamish DeLuca, and I have a few questions about some of the pranks happening to one of the Patriots players."

"You mean Parker? Boys will be boys. What did you say your name was? Are you a reporter?"

"No, sir, private investigator. Mr. Parker employed me and my associate."

"Kid has to have a tougher skin than that if he's gonna hang with the big leagues. You know how it is. I don't say there hasn't been progress in these matters . . . but you can't expect things to change overnight."

"With all those euphemisms, you could have been a diplomat, Mr. Blaney."

"Listen, what did you say your name was? Luca something."

"Something like that . . ."

"I don't pay attention to the players except when they are on that field. My only focus."

"But I heard you're the first at the diamond and the last to leave."

"You think I wanna waste my voice on the minor leagues forever? This job is a stepping-stone, and I need to bring my A-game until someone scouts me for one of the bigger stations."

"That's what Mr. Parker wants."

"What?"

"To be scouted and make it to the big leagues. You have the same ambitions. Surely you want to help him. See, it's not just harmless pranks. It was an animal heart and they beat up his nephew and—"

A broad, delayed laugh filled the receiver. "Errol Parker make the big leagues? Are you kidding? Listen—"

"No, you listen. I know it sounds preposterous to you, but Parker told me about this guy—this Moses Walker—and I think—"

"Moses Walker, huh?"

"Don't you want to help him? Can you tell me if you have seen anything unusual, at least? You're doing your job, I'm doing mine."

Blaney was silent for so long, Hamish wondered if he had disappeared.

"You might want to talk to Quinn."

"Quinn?"

"Quinn runs the corn dog stand. The one that always has those long lines. He's been peddling there for years. You think I'm the first person to come and go? Ask Quinn. Better yet, take him for a pint."

Hamish wrote the name down. He'd be easy to find. He just had to go to the snack stand. Preferably before the crowds arrived. "Thanks. And can you please take my number? In case you think of anything at all?"

"Sure, but I ain't promising that my memory is that long."

Hamish didn't believe him. Not the way he was renowned for pulling stats out of the blue from decades ago. "Thanks, Mr. Blaney. I always love listening to you."

Blaney clicked off.

Hamish exhaled and checked off Blaney's name on his notepad. He yawned and tried a few of the team members with numbers the coach had given him. With little luck and three hang-ups, he decided he needed a stretch and an espresso if he was going to be able to make it through the rest of the morning, and then the inevitable uncomfortableness with Reggie.

He locked the office door and put a sign above the Van Buren and DeLuca letters on the frosted window saying he would return in ten, then stopped by Nate's slightly open door. Nate had been gone long before Hamish woke up that morning, and Hamish didn't want to disturb him but also wanted to be available to run any errands.

He rapped gently. "Hey, Nate?"

"What is it?"

Hamish frowned. That was a tone he wasn't used to hearing from his friend. He creaked the door open slowly. The phone was off the hook and dangling over the side of the desk. The *disorganized* desk. Something wasn't right.

Nate ran his hand over his face. "Rather busy here, Hamish. Can it wait?"

"I was just going to go for coffee. I wanted to see if you wanted anything."

"No." Nate shook his head and ruffled a few papers. "And shut the door, please. Don't know why it was open in the first place."

"Are you mad at me?"

"Mad at you! Why would I . . ." Nate composed himself. Took a deep breath. Said, in a kinder tone, "Listen, it's very nice of you to check in, but I'm a bit over my head and—"

"You're never over your head, Nate. Your world is a perfectly precise chessboard. I need you to tell me if I can—"

Nate raised a restraining hand. "Thanks for the offer."

Hamish slumped down the stairs and into the square. *Great.* Some part of him deep down hoped that Nate would take a break with him. Now he was on poor terms with his two closest friends. Nate was acting very strange and he had made no progress on his open case.

His feet instinctively took the familiar path to Leoni's, but he figured with the way his day was going he might jinx something with Mrs. Leoni and there would go another relationship he couldn't afford to lose. Instead, he made it to Café Vittoria on Hanover Street. He ordered two double espressos and sat in one of the prim white chairs listening to the bustle of midmorning orders and patrons. Somewhat fortified, with caffeine buzzing through his veins, he made his way back to the office, stopping at the delicatessen to pick up almond cookies for Nate. The man couldn't keep him from barging in and setting food down on his desk. While at the counter, he also picked up a copy of the *Jewish Advocate* by the register. He turned to the page of editorial letters looking for the near daily and inevitable exchange between Nate and his nemesis, Aaron Leibowitz. It was an offhand remark by Reggie that the paper being entirely in Hebrew kept it from finding a wider readership that had inspired Nate to talk to the editor. Now, half of the journal was in English. But English or no, there was no Nate in the paper today.

Hamish frowned.

Back at the office, he silently opened Nate's door and found his friend chewing the end of a pen, hair askew and eyes wild.

"I know, I know!" he said in response to Nate's glare. "You don't want to be disturbed. But I brought you almond cookies." He set the package on top of an askew pile of papers. "Because you have to eat at some point, Nate."

"Heaping coals of fire, young DeLuca," Nate said tiredly.

"I also brought you this." He untucked the *Jewish Advocate* from under his arm and put it on the desk. "I leafed through it in the delicatessen line. Looks like Aaron Leibowitz has no contender today." He smiled sadly. "Whatever is going on, Nate, fix it soon. Don't make me go detective on you."

"I know you care. And someday . . ." Nate spread his hands out. "But for now, I am thinking about Cyrus Dallin on his fourth try of the Revere sculpture. But . . ." And here Nate's eyes alighted with just a spark of their usual brightness as he went on about the sculpture. It was an easy way to change the subject: a cover for what was actually preoccupying Nate.

⁂

When Reggie opened the office door just after half past noon, she assumed Hamish would shift in his chair and they would navigate a complicated waltz of avoiding each other.

Instead, Hamish looked up from his desk and the legal document spread across it and seemed halfway glad to see her.

"We need to talk about Nate. I got the *Jewish Advocate* today and it was just Leibowitz. No response." He frowned. "For all the years we've known Nate, he has never not countered that Leibowitz fellow."

"Maybe he just needed a break." Reggie hung the coat draped over her arm onto their coat stand and put her hat atop it.

"Nate Reis taking a break from Aaron Leibowitz is not a Nate Reis I particularly care to know." Hamish rolled his pencil over the desk blotter. "He's gone before I leave in the morning. Our living room is just piles of paper. His desk looks like a tornado blew through it. Something is seriously wrong."

Reggie frowned. "Well, my news won't make you feel any better." Rather than take her seat behind the adjacent desk and fiddle with the wireless dial as was her custom each day before unwrapping the wax paper of her packed sandwich, she hopped onto the side of Hamish's desk just as the phone rang.

"Van Buren and DeLuca. This is Reggie speaking. What? Wait. Slow down." Reggie felt her heart slope in her chest. She closed her eyes a moment, disbelieving what she was hearing on the other end. "And you're sure that it's . . . We'll be there shortly. Thank you."

Reggie didn't bother hanging up the phone. Just left it dangling from her hand as the caller clicked on the other end. "That was Reid. They found a corpse at the diamond."

Hamish felt as if a rug had been pulled out from under him, and though he was seated, the room around him spun. "Wh-who?"

"He thinks it is Parker."

Reggie blanched. "The jersey. Some sort of altercation." She retrieved a handkerchief from her handbag and dabbed at her nose.

Hamish rose sadly as if he was rising through cement. "We'd better get down there."

CHAPTER 9

While every murder-themed investigation of *Winchester Molloy* inspired Reggie to hope for a murder investigation of their own, she knew upon approaching the police cars and reporters outside the Patriots' clubhouse, Hamish silent beside her, that there was nothing exciting about this murder. It devastated her. He'd been so talented and young and so full of ambition.

She conjured his face and voice and smile in her mind's eye as they made the mournful trek, Hamish's right hand under his suspender, counting his breaths with each step nearer the commotion.

Reporters' bulbs flashed as they adjusted their fedoras and flipped their notepads to a fresh page.

Reggie and Hamish's arrival caught their interest and they watched closely.

"Hold up!" A police officer with a thick Irish brogue waylaid them. "What's your business here?"

"Mr. Parker was our client," Hamish said, his voice a slight stutter.

"*Was?*"

"Reid called and said—"

"Then you didn't hear. Mr. Parker is alive and well."

Hamish met Reggie's eyes. "What?" she said. "I got a phone call that said otherwise."

"Someone's dead, kids. But it wasn't Mr. Parker."

"I'm very confused," Hamish said unevenly.

"It was his nephew."

Reggie gasped. "He was just a kid! How . . . Why would . . . What happened?"

The officer turned, leaving Hamish and Reggie to blink stupidly at each other. "Hamish, the man said it was Parker. That it was his jersey that . . . How could he not tell?"

Hamish's fingers picked up speed in their count. "I guess a passing look and—"

"Hamish!" They both turned at Parker's voice. Errol's shoulders sagged and his eyes wildly looked around without settling on anything. "You came."

"We got word that it was you," Reggie said softly. "I'm so sorry."

Errol nodded. "He was with Joe. Or waiting for Joe. I was just replacing my glove. I was in the dugout for five minutes. There was no one around, so Joe said it would be all right if he hung out in the locker room. I had let him wear my spare jersey. He . . ." Errol's voice broke and Hamish put up a stalling hand.

Hamish took a moment. His hand was no longer occupied over his heart but rather trembling by his side. It accelerated and Reggie started to worry. Especially when coupled with the mounting rise and fall of his breathing.

"Hamish," she whispered. "Why don't you go make sure that fiend from the *Herald* knows how to spell our names?"

He looked at her appreciatively and took the opportunity to disappear from their sight line.

Hamish barely made it past the line of police cars before folding over, hands on knees, gulping every bit of air that his flurried heartbeat and blocked airway would allow. Two invisible walls bordered him and crushed closer and closer. He blinked the spots from his eyes and tried to count. To steady his breathing before the uncontrollable tremor in his right hand signaled complete loss of control. He blinked through his frustration. Why did these attacks happen at the most inopportune times? Sometimes he was fine. Gun to his chest at the *Flamingo*—fine. Other times, like now—when he realized that Errol was still alive—not fine.

Hamish spat a curse in Italian—a word his mother always chastised his father for using in his presence. It came out ragged and shaky like his breath. He reined himself in for a moment and studied the grass: a million blades curving in a million un-mowed directions, blurring as his eyes adjusted from blinking at a rapid pace to finally settling as his chest pains subsided and he slowly stilled. He focused on one of the police cars and counted. Slowly. He straightened his spine and erected his shoulders. In Boston, somehow, he could overcome his panic. Before, the fear of being noticed or of never coming out of the pool of dread would have crippled him. Something about the liberty he found in the North End with his new friends and his new life proved the best medicine. He wiped the beads of perspiration from his forehead and collected himself. It was going to be fine. He was going to be fine.

He stuck out his chin a little and nodded as if to assure himself that he had it all under control. Then he sought out Reggie and Errol in the crowd spilling over the lawn near the diamond.

It was in this moment, this phase, that he recalled what Blaney had said about seeking out the corn dog seller. He wondered if the evening's scheduled game would be postponed.

"Absolutely not," one of the uniformed officers said when he casually asked, rejoining the throng. "What good would it do? This poor fellow was disposed of in the locker room—no need to stop an entire franchise because of it. Especially because we have no idea what happened."

Hamish wasn't sure what to think of that. It bothered him, sure. But business was business. After all, his cousin's nightclub opened (to unbelievable crowds) the day after a corpse was discovered.

The fellow's name was Ted Quinn, and he scrubbed at his kiosk. Hamish had seen him several times before. Always protected from the late afternoon sun by an umbrella.

"You see everyone who comes and goes," Hamish said. "Do you remember seeing a tall, redheaded man?"

Ted didn't say anything. Rather, he spent a moment studying Hamish intensely. When he looked to Reggie his eyes softened, but just a bit.

"I see a lot of people," he said evasively. "I'll save my answers for the police."

Reggie and Hamish exchanged a look.

"Are you all right?" she asked after they were out of hearing distance.

Hamish nodded. "As all right as I can be knowing a sixteen-year-old kid was killed in a baseball locker room."

"Hamish!" They both turned at the sound of Rob Reid's voice. "Thanks for coming. Parker is a client of yours. You have every right to come with me."

Reggie turned to Hamish, eyes bright, and they followed the officer to the crime scene.

⚬

Reggie wondered what the ladies served from her mother's silver tea set might think if they knew she was in a men's locker room. The sun slanted through slight windows, the pungent smell of cleats and unlaundered towels tickling Reggie's nostrils. Police officers milled about. One kept an eye on the door as a trickle of reporters streamed to the slightly open doorway. News moved fast, and Reggie could hear the thrum of movement before she saw a conglomeration of figures at the slightly open doorway.

She knew she was studying the commotion over her shoulder

to keep from what was drawing Hamish and Reid nearer. No matter how Reggie hankered after adventure, she would never grow accustomed to murder. She grabbed Hamish's elbow and looked up and over his shoulder at the lifeless figure of Toby. He looked so young—as if he were sleeping and she might shake him awake.

"It was someone who led with their left," Reid was saying. "Judging by the intensity of the blow to his head."

"Reid!" The trio turned at a voice from a cop Reggie didn't recall seeing outside.

"Sir!" The way Reid straightened and responded led Reggie to believe the man facing Reid was of a much higher rank.

"Boys outside say this isn't your jurisdiction. What are you doing across the river?"

"You want the truth, sir?"

"Don't try my patience."

"When I heard word I came because I was worried that some of the men would write it off as an accident. Or just an unfortunate result of a fight."

"And that is what it is." The officer stepped around them and stared at the body. "An unfortunate, tragic waste of life. There was no one at the scene, was there?"

"The boy's uncle found him."

"Parker?" The officer removed his cap. "Temper on that one."

Reggie gripped Hamish's arm to keep herself from lunging at the officer. She could feel the shudder from Hamish's shaking hand even from as far up as his bicep.

"Sir, he was devastated."

"And you let reporters in?"

"They're not reporters. The boy's uncle is their client. They're private investigators."

The cop looked them over. "I thought I knew every investigator in the city by sight."

Reggie removed her grip from Hamish's arm. "Regina Van Buren." She extended a hand, which he did not take. "And this is my partner, Hamish DeLuca."

The officer cocked his head. "That's a familiar name." He studied Hamish intensely. So intensely, he didn't look over when the coroner and a medic arrived and Reid began speaking to them softly. "And a familiar face," the officer continued. "Involved in that business at the Flamingo with Luca Valari, weren't you?"

"Yes. Wrong place at the wrong time. I assure you that everything we investigate is aboveboard." A bit of a ripple in his voice, left over from his earlier episode, stalled Hamish's sentence.

"Mr. Parker has been the victim of a series of unfortunate pranks," Reggie said.

"Well, several fistfights on the field. Some with his own teammates. What do you expect?"

The officer moved past them outside and said over his shoulder, "This was an unfortunate accident. Nothing premeditated." He pushed through the mill of reporters, bulbs ready and flashing through the opening. Reid was leaning over the body and joined them several moments later after removing everything from Toby's trouser pockets before the coroner's initial examination.

Reggie swallowed a sour taste in her mouth. The last time she and Hamish were involved in the death of an innocent person, the police treated it as an unfortunate accident. She knew it wasn't coincidence, but rather that she had stepped into a world where justice had a lot to do with where you came from and what you owned.

"That was Tucker," Reid said, joining them, indicating the officer who had just left. "Maybe I didn't just let you in because Parker's your client." Reid scrubbed his hairline. "Maybe I let you in because I figured that is what would happen. It's why I am here in the first place. Lots of accidents around here." He looked at

Hamish pointedly. "You know that from your time at your cousin's club."

"Murder is a by-the-way when there are so many bigger things at play," Hamish said. "What's that in your hand?"

Reggie followed Hamish's sightline to a piece of paper loosely clutched in Reid's fist. He unfolded it and passed it to Hamish, who turned slightly from Reggie as his eyes wandered over the lines. It looked like an inventory of some sort. She made out just a few words before he refolded it.

Something ending in "-uze" and another word that just read "clus." Writing in the margins, a hand that seemed oddly familiar. In broad strokes. Not completely educated with the skill of a Vaughan Vanderlaan but with the same type of pen Vaughan would use.

"We're going to treat this as a murder investigation," Hamish told Reid, speaking for both of them.

She didn't mind—she was about to say the same thing.

Reid gave a quick nod. "Let's all get out of here, shall we? None of us are here with any jurisdiction."

The officer may have put it on record as an accident, but that didn't stop reporters from asking a dozen hungry questions. They elbowed past them, a small chorus of "No comment" layering the loud and pressing questions.

Reggie stared up at the sun once they left the field and were on the sidewalk, bordered by beautiful, safe houses with the beautiful, safe sounds of almost-evening.

She blinked at its blinding rays and straightened her shoulders. She had found a corpse before at the Flamingo Club. She was an investigator (at least *trying* to be an investigator). Her bottom lip shouldn't wobble (it was); her throat shouldn't scratch with oncoming tears (it did).

A delayed reaction to the lifeless body of a sixteen-year-old boy silenced forever by a brute of a punch.

Reggie shivered. Shivered some more. Reid had left them for his police car. So the world was just her and Hamish and sunlight and houses. They crossed an empty street.

"I'm walking you home," he told her quietly.

CHAPTER 10

Cluster. Fuze. Shell. Carbine. Toby was carrying a manifest for munitions with Luca Valari's handwriting in the margins.

"We'll want to talk to the coach," Reggie said unevenly. "Winston. I heard the men back there talking about him."

"Let's not spiral ahead until tomorrow." Hamish's hands were in his pockets as he examined her. He could see Reggie trying—and failing—to blink the scene from her mind. He wondered if she had gotten a close look at the paper before he folded it up. She would know Luca's handwriting as well as he did from her time as his cousin's secretary. He would have to show it to her eventually as part of their investigation . . . but he wanted a head start.

"The Sons of Liberty used to meet here," Reggie said as they passed the Warren Tavern, sign swinging with the slight breeze, revelers spilling onto the street.

A revolutionary gathering. Men with ideals. Thoughts. Rebellions.

"Reid said whoever killed Toby led with his left." He flicked a look at Reggie, who nodded silently. "Walt Bricker is left-handed. I don't know why I focused on that, but I did. The first night I met him, he was peddling pamphlets with his left hand. When we saw him at the Top Hat, I noted his left hand was his dominant one. I centered in on that."

"Probably to have something to focus on so you wouldn't shove him into a wall?"

"That's me," Hamish said ironically. "Always wanting to shove someone into a wall." He forced a chuckle, then stepped back. "But I wanted to with him. That smug look. His horrible ideas." He fingered the manifest in his pocket. "We should go to one of the Christian Patriots meetings."

That paper. Safe in his pocket. Luca. His cousin had some less-than-savory connections, sure. But Bricker was so crass. So uncouth. Luca would turn up his nose at the man's blue-collar voice and scuffed shoes. Would play friendly but not get involved with him. Walt Bricker within an inch of Luca Valari might rub off on his reputation. But if Bricker killed Toby . . . Toby, the kid who wanted to be a batboy. Toby who wanted to go to Cincinnati. Who was kind and awkward and uneven. Excited to cross the foyer of the Parker House Hotel. Hamish's heart sank.

And if Bricker killed Toby *because* of something to do with Luca, why leave the kid's pockets unturned? Or had he just missed that? Heard someone coming?

Hamish blinked away the rest of the questions uncorked in his mind at the sound of sudden tears beside him.

They passed the tavern and its patrons. Hamish stopped her with his hand alongside a white picket fence.

"Reg?"

And at the small entreaty, a bundle of hiccups and sobs was in his arms. He anchored her a moment, always deliciously finding that his own tremors and shakes stopped when grounded in her.

She fit. Oh, did she *ever* fit. He had never thought much about height until learning that he could tuck her head under his chin. He had never thought much of lips until learning what the stray strands of hair at the top of her head tasted like as he pressed his mouth into them.

She withdrew after a second. A moment. A millennium. Her

watery eyes cocooned in smeared liner looking up at him. She might kiss him. Not on the cheek or the ear or the chin, but *truly* kiss him, as the stars announced their first arrival overhead and another amateur mystery was tucked in their pockets.

She almost (there were too many almosts) did. Her lips were over his jawline and then up over his cheekbone in a soft trace. Part of him knew it was his job to turn his head and the tide and meld their mouths together. But he was too surprised and her touch was too marvelous. He tasted a tang of the salt of her tears.

It had been a horrible day and she had seen a horrible thing.

Hamish DeLuca may not have been bred in her world of fine china and crystal. But he was still raised to be a gentleman. He straightened, cricked his shoulder, and disengaged. The world suddenly a winter morning and him stepping out of bed with no socks on the ice-cold floor.

He saw her to the edge of her boardinghouse. Waited until she jogged up the steps to her door.

⊥⊻

Nate had retired when Hamish walked through their front door a half hour later.

He put the kettle on and retrieved *Notre-Dame*—the copy he kept in the sitting room, an edition in a far more pristine condition (being a recent present from Nate) than the well-loved one on his bedside table. He focused on finding all of his favorite scenes: the one that the film version Reggie spoke of completely ignored. As a detective, and certainly as a lawyer, he was interested in human nature, and he supposed the most he could expect of a night like this—the tragic story of Quasimodo and Esmeralda, outcasts to Paris's elite, clashing with the views he'd heard spouted from Dirk's shared pulpit—was another looking glass into the many complicated and often hate-infused depths of humanity. He leafed through *Notre-Dame*, landing on a page with an underlined quote: "His judgment demonstrates that one can be a genius and understand nothing of an art that is not one's own."

Hamish shut the book. He sprinted toward the front hall telephone. He called the operator and asked to be transferred to the Parker House Hotel.

There was no Valari registered with the hotel when he asked the front desk.

"Has anyone with an Italian surname stayed there recently? Within the past week?" Hamish ran his hand over his face at how stupid the question sounded once out of his mouth.

"Several, sir. I will need you to be more specific. If—"

"A Mr. Hult," Hamish tried, using Luca's Swedish stepfather's name. "Did you have a Mr. Hult there?"

"He checked out two nights ago, sir."

Hamish clicked the receiver. Luca was in Boston.

Luca was back and he had almost kissed Reggie. Again. *Quasimodo . . . Quasi. Almost.* Too many almosts.

Hamish fixed a cup of cocoa quietly and then returned to the sitting room, which currently was an eruption of Nate: in piles of papers.

Nate always treated him with the utmost respect. He figured that pursuing any leads he found in hopes of helping his friend would abolish the guilt of prying. Besides, if Nate truly had things to hide, would he leave them in the sitting room, on the bookshelves and sofa, piled beside the fireplace?

Hamish tiptoed over the carpet and gently lifted a pile of papers. Some were in folders, one glossy and of a larger size than the others in the uniform pile. Hamish carefully pulled it out and smiled. An Action Comic featuring Nate's favorite, Superman. Then, of course, a few longhand ideas for the *Jewish Advocate* in Nate's hard-to-read hand.

He discovered a Christian Patriots pamphlet tucked in among

the other contracts and papers as he worked through the accordion, and he wondered how Nate could stand keeping that filth. Then wondered if there was a reason he needed to. Everyone went to Nate. If men of Dirk's conviction were beginning to sniff around the North End, he would want to be prepared. To know before anyone else what people were up against.

He recalled a conversation he had with one of Mrs. Leoni's friends, trying to help her understand a particularly troublesome contract. *"There are two ways to look at this. One is through the lens of a detective's eye."*

The girl looked up then, eyes sparkling. *"Like Winchester Molloy or Sam Spade?"*

"Exactly. The other is through the eyes of the law. The law is more sure. Detection is all about instinct and a few hunches, but the law draws you back from your hunches so even if you tumble over into something uncertain, you land on solid ground."

Hamish tried to believe what he'd said while looking through Nate's correspondence.

He fingered the edge of a note of thanks from Hal at the Old North. Hamish pieced together the reason for the unending thanks. A couple had been evicted from their flat and Nate ensured they found temporary accommodations. *There is so much of his city I do not see,* Hamish thought.

"You think it is unfair, sure," his father had told him, recalling the backbreaking work he did digging up tracks at the roundhouse in Toronto before he found employment as a muckraking reporter in his youth. "But considering where you came from and the opportunity you still think you will find, you accept it. Without choice. Unions were dangerous. They meant the possibility of a strike. A strike meant you starved. Some of us didn't have the luxury of those kinds of principles. You cannot judge people too harshly, Hamish. They may want to fight against the men controlling them, but they probably want to feed their families more."

Hamish leafed through more papers until his eyes snagged on one. *"E. Parker. March. Job—nephew. Rang Kelly."*

The fireplace crackled its defense. He was happy he had the foresight to toss a match and spark it alive. *"Sometimes,"* his father had always said, *"you need to recognize that life will throw a line drive at you. And you have two choices. You can duck in fear and cower. Or you can hit it straight on. You have the choice to react or to anticipate. Use your power to blast that ball out of the field. Trust me. Anticipate."*

"Hamish! What in . . . Get away from this." Nate was sleepy-eyed, robe sloppily tied around his pajamas. "Honestly."

"This is about Errol Parker. This has to do with my case. You said you knew nothing about it!" Hamish was angry. Too angry. But Toby was dead and Luca was in the city and Nate was standing there looking like the friend he knew while building a larger wall of secrets.

"Hamish, I have my reasons."

"Do you trust me?" Hamish spoke at a lower decibel, tucking his hand behind his back, partly to hide the slight shake.

"Not right now, I don't." Nate kicked at a pile with his slipper. "Fellow comes down for tea because he can't sleep and finds his flatmate going through everything. I left everything in plain sight because I figured if you can't trust Hamish DeLuca . . ."

Hamish wanted to tell Nate that Luca was back. That a kid was dead and he was probably responsible. Well, marginally responsible. If Toby was involved with Luca and had met him at the Parker House that night. *"Movie star important,"* Toby had said.

"Maybe you *can't* trust Hamish DeLuca," he spat. "You're right, Nate." He kicked a small pile with his slipper. "Because look at who his family is."

"Hamish . . . ," Nate said in a tone that sounded remarkably like Nate and not the stranger he kept encountering.

"You don't trust me with whatever secret you are keeping," Hamish said.

"That is not . . . There is no . . ."

"Stop lying to me! I've known you for three years, Nate! Three! I've lived with you for most of that time! And—"

"I don't want to lie to you," Nate said plainly. "But being friends with you comes at a high price."

"What does that mean?" Hamish's voice was louder than he intended. Funny, he had never yelled before that day in his father's office after the panic episode that drove him from his first court case and to Boston. "What high price?"

"Nothing."

"Errol Parker's nephew is dead. You're constantly lying to me! I am clearly a bother to you. Constantly! I can feel it." He splayed a hand over his chest. "I . . ." Hamish shrugged the end of the sentence, pasted on a sad almost-smile. "I won't touch your things again."

He made quick work of the steps separating him and the staircase and bounded to the next level, not bothering to hear or reply to Nate's calling after him.

CHAPTER 11

Reggie hadn't slept all night. And it wasn't just the sight of Toby, either. When one had to face the promise of her parents and Vaughan Vanderlaan while harboring feelings that grew deeper and deeper, one did not always sleep well. She had seen her parents since escaping down the tree outside her bedroom window and catapulting herself into a new life, of course, but never in Boston. At least dinner would be on their turf: the Parker House Hotel dining room, lit with sparkling crystal and pretention. She grabbed her second pillow to smother away the vision of her mother looking at her pointedly—then longingly at Vaughan—then back at her in hopes she would pick up on the equation.

But first she would see Hamish: her still-tingling lips were fully aware of their exploration from the previous night. His breath over her cheek, tasting a little like coffee and a little like the lemon smell he carried with him beyond Mrs. Leoni's cannoli counter.

Hamish DeLuca was the smartest man she had ever met. And the kindest. And the most interesting and . . . Reggie fingered the ribbon at the collar of her nightgown. And maybe—she met her eyes in the mirror—she was in love with him.

Reggie stumbled back. Humming to herself. Nope, nope. Not that song. "Begin the Beguine." They had danced to that at the

Flamingo on the night she learned that dancing was more than the classes that found her perfectly aligned with her breeding's rigidity, a crisp 1-2-3 count, never wholly letting your partner fall into you, following his lead.

With Hamish . . .

The infernal clock by her bed drew morning closer. She closed her eyes, then opened them: a revelation. *She was in shock!* That made sense. Last night! It was shock! So she tucked herself into his warmth and held on to human connection.

The flimsy curtains pulled back completely to usher in the sounds of Pleasant Street. She peered up, the breeze chasing the curtains into retreat, then a slow, ghostly dance. *Shock.*

She reached into the drawer of her bedside table and retrieved her Journal of Independence. She was surprised at how many new entries she had made since arriving in Boston the summer of '37. More surprised still at how many things she had crossed out. She used it as a lexicon, as a list, and for accountability. Sometimes, as in the case of "Learn how to properly make a bed," the entries were left untouched in her perfectly taught cursive. Other times they were scrawled or scratched out with enthusiasm like "Stay up 'til dawn." Which she seemed to be doing now.

"Argh!"

A kid was dead with a piece of paper in his pocket. The piece of paper interrupted by scrawls she knew. But wished she could forget.

The piece of paper . . .

She squeezed her eyes shut and the kid and the paper and the case thrummed away with the clack of the old radiator under the windowsill.

It was not her fault for being confused, she decided.

Dawn was yawning, a slow lemon and pink, waking up the world. Reggie covered the purple under her eyes with Max Factor. She walked briskly as the sun slowly rose and began to thaw the morning chill, the spires and crooked roofs of the North End opening beyond the gentle lap of the river, a few boats chugging in and out. Maybe heading down to Pete Kelly's place. By the time she reached the North Square, candy-striped awnings were being brushed by long brooms, and carts on rickety wheels rumbled over the cobblestones. The world was coming to life. The smell of fresh bread crept under the doors of numerous bakeries, and delivery trucks hugged the curb, their drivers hopping out, milk bottles clinking, soon finding their temporary homes on stoops and steps. The North End had been her home with Hamish for almost three years. Home. Hamish. *Reggie, you need coffee. Straighten your shoulders and fix your lipstick!*

In a rather pathetic attempt to fall back on her upbringing, Reggie took the stairs to the office quickly and deposited her hat and purse before leafing through a neat pile of papers on Hamish's desk and in the adjacent cabinet. Hamish had remarkably neat handwriting . . . with the exception of a few words now and then that betrayed the slight shake in his right hand. And his desk was a study in model precision. She could see how he treated it with the same care as everything in his life. He offered as much attention to a missing kitten as he did to Errol Parker's case. The only personal items were a spare copy of *Notre-Dame* and a framed picture of Hamish with his childhood friend Maisie Forth. He kept it turned toward him, but more than once clients had asked about their relationship. Maisie was striking, with light bobbed hair and bright eyes; there was a trick to her smile too. Hamish looked completely relaxed next to her. Reggie knew Maisie was more like a sister than anything else, but she couldn't help but feel a tug not unlike the one she felt when Bernice crossed the dance floor at the Top Hat.

Reggie resettled at her desk, door open, waiting to hear Nate's key turn in the lock. She picked up a pamphlet and flipped it open, nose wrinkling at the misguided and horrible views she found therein. Then she turned it over. The back was blank save for the stamp denoting the name of the printing house. Her eyes widened at the address: 275 Yonge Street, Toronto.

Reggie picked up the phone and asked the operator to transfer her to the *Toronto Telegraph* office. Once patched through, she upped her high mid-Atlantic accent and lied to a secretary that her call was expected.

She stole a look at her watch. Hamish said his dad kept all hours. Lived at the office. She straightened her back. She was a little nervous. But why shouldn't she find out where Luca was? It *was* his handwriting. If she found Luca, she could meet him. Tell him to stay away from Hamish. Give it a shot.

A moment later: "DeLuca."

"Mr. DeLuca, my name is Regina Van Buren, and I am calling from Boston." She rolled her eyes. Of *course* he knew where she was. Who she was.

"You're Hamish's Regina Van Buren."

She enjoyed the possessive sound of it. "Yes."

"Is Hamish hurt or sick or in trouble?"

"None of the above."

"You're early about it, aren't you?"

"Hamish isn't even in yet."

"I'm listening." His accent was strong. She liked it.

Regina Van Buren, just ask him. "Do you know of a divisive group called the Christian Patriots?" She began to improvise.

"One of my men was on them at a rally a few weeks ago. Dangerous views. Especially here with the war fervor."

"I have one of their pamphlets." Reggie used the hand not holding the receiver to turn it over in the window light. Ironically, she focused on something useful. "And . . . um . . . it reads that it was printed in Toronto. Montgomery's. 275 Yonge Street. Do you know it?"

"Yes. What kind of case are you working on?"

"Not sure yet. It might be linked to a series of devastating pranks on a baseball player, or to some development down by the harbor with . . ." She bit her lip. Improvised some more. She was an actress! Move over, Vivien Leigh. "Nefarious means."

Ray DeLuca chuckled. "I can see why Hamish likes you. *Nefarious.*"

Reggie's cheeks flushed. He had talked about her. "I know that you're pretty busy running a newspaper, but I thought maybe you could send someone. No one important. A junior reporter. I don't want to take up too much of your time with this."

"Okay. Do you have anything specific?" She could hear the scratch of a pen over a piece of paper.

Reggie flushed, caught off guard. She had nothing specific. She was in an elaborate game of make-believe. "N-not precisely."

"Good. Then whatever we find out might be useful. Keep an open mind."

"Yes! That's how I see it. Thank you ever so much."

"So Hamish isn't hurt or sick or in trouble?" he repeated, more lightly this time.

Reggie smiled, hoping it shone in her voice. "No." She took a beat and a breath and felt Hamish's lips over her cheek again in memory and conjured the courage. "Mr. DeLuca, do you know where Luca Valari is?"

There was a long silence on the other end. Then: "And this is about pamphlets?"

"Have you seen him?"

"And Hamish is not in trouble? You are not in trouble?"

Describe trouble, Reggie added mentally. "No."

"I haven't seen him. In a very long time." There was something final in his voice.

"Thank you."

Reggie signed off. Sure, three years later and they weren't an entry in an *Ellery Queen* magazine. But they were trying and they were *getting* there. With Hamish's empathy and instinct and Reggie's penchant for adventure. The last thing she needed was for Luca Valari to show up and scare Hamish away.

Her thoughtfulness turned to an immediate smile when she heard the routine sound of Nate turning the key in his office door. She leapt up and dashed out of the office in his direction, scuffing the side of her oxford shoe as she tripped over a loose board in the hall. She barely steadied herself by grabbing on to the doorjamb. Nate was in front of her in a split second.

"All right there, Reg?" His tone was light but his face was concerned.

"Just eager to see you."

"Come on in."

Reggie stepped into his office. She knew it well, but he still was more likely to be found across from her while *Winchester Molloy* played on their office radio. "I know you keep newspapers. I wondered if you had any on Errol Parker."

"Old Robin Hood, huh?" Nate pulled the chain of the banker's lamp and light spilled over his neat desk.

She lost him a moment as his dark head appeared to rummage through a cabinet. Soon he handled her a file.

"Now, I usually just keep things specific to our little neighborhood here." Reggie accepted the offered copy of the *Globe*, her heart sinking at the deep purple lines under his eyes. "But you know I have a weakness for the Patriots."

Reggie nodded and folded the paper under her arm. "Thanks, Nate."

"You and Hamish have some sort of row?" he asked lightly.

"Why do you say that?"

"Wasn't himself when he got in last night." Nate shrugged. "Maybe it was Bernice."

"Maybe."

Back in her office, Reggie spread the paper. There was a picture of Errol Parker: a professional one. He watched the camera, un-smiling in his jersey, bat poised over his shoulder. The headline spoke to an altercation on the field between innings. Reggie read the fine print. A fistfight. Could someone have wanted Errol off the team? She scrawled some notes before preparing herself for her morning with Mrs. Rue. Later, her parents. Later, Vaughan. Vaughan who had kissed her several times before without ever tattooing himself on her or her memory.

No Vaughan. A dead kid and a pamphlet and a case.

Then it was time to report for her morning with Mrs. Rue. On the landing, she met Hamish, bicycle over his shoulder, a half smile for her that didn't even come near to producing a dimple.

"Hi."

"Oh, hi, Reggie. Feeling better today?"

And Reggie couldn't wait to swing open the door of the tempo-rary employment office and disappear. The feel of his jawline still tingling her lips, the scent of lemon and soap still tingling her nose.

The morning at Mrs. Rue's passed quickly with Reggie sip-ping coffee from a mason jar. It jolted her awake, and rather than fiddle with the typewriter ribbon or study her nails, she concen-trated on dictation and filing. Anything to keep her mind off the evening behind her or the evening with her parents before her.

─⚹─

Hamish parted a sea of journalists on his way back from Café Vittoria for a much-needed espresso. None would live up to his father's staunch standards. To be a real reporter was not to stake out and annoy people, but to so impress them with the need for their story to be told that they wanted to talk to you.

He straightened his shoulders and said, "No comment," sev-eral times. It was worse at Errol's house. He was staying with his sister, who was also on the receiving end.

The phone calls were easily ignored. As were the telegrams. But when people were there, sprawled and talking and casting shadows on the windows and over the stones, it was a different experience altogether.

The only good thing about the noise through the open window once he reached the office was that it helped in his active determination *not* to think about Reggie. He focused intently on a paper Reggie must have procured about Errol. But his eyes fuzzed over the pages. His right hand wasn't stable, but he rapped a pencil on the side of his desktop nonetheless as he went over everything he knew and circled possible scenarios.

He pinched his nose, reading the notes in his slanted handwriting.

He fingered through his drawer and found a folder. It had little in it other than his theory (corroborated by the appearance of Phil) that perhaps Suave's man was just trying to play him. Just trying to let him know that he was there and he had power. Hamish wondered why he felt the need to assert that power, that unexpected influence.

After a while he called Coach Ed Winston, the name and contact easily procured from an earlier call to Reid, in hopes of setting up a meeting to talk about what happened.

"No press. No police," he said.

"Listen. I like Parker. He's a good player. But I am with the police on this. It was an unfortunate accident."

"On top of the pranks . . . ?" Hamish was certain it wasn't so.

But he got the same initial response from every teammate he dialed thereafter. Including Treadwell.

"The only good thing to come out of this"—he smacked his gum—"is that I overheard Parker say he is playing in the kid's honor. So maybe he won't come after me anymore mid-inning, huh?"

Hamish cradled the phone on its hook, pressed his hair back

from his forehead, and wondered if worrying about Reggie wasn't the better option.

⁎

Vaughan was to meet her at the front of his office so they could walk together to the dinner meeting with her parents. She willed the hours to stretch and keep dinner at bay. Hamish hadn't said two words to her since she arrived from her shift, and she studied his profile.

This afternoon for the first time in ages she was pricked with a memory: *she and Vaughan motoring over New Haven in the fresh air, the slight chill coaxing a cardigan over her shoulders, the scarf she wound around her hair soon tangled in her curls.*

Her parents, of course, were delighted that they arrived together. Her mother on the lawn, hand raised to visor her face from the sun. Her father striding forward to Vaughan, pumping his hand and calling him son.

Cocktails were at five. Dinner a black-tie affair. Her mother admonishing her softly for her high-waisted trousers while her father proudly showed Vaughan the progress on his model of the Mayflower.

Reggie changed in the communal washroom at the office. She had chosen a dress that scooped just so in the front and left little to the imagination at the back. She painted her lips, used her finger to smooth her eyebrows into place, and stepped into the past. But not before passing Hamish and his bicycle on the stairwell.

"You look lovely." He gave her a half-moon smile.

"Thank you. My parents."

He nodded. "Sorry if . . ." His shoulders crept up to his ears a little.

"Not my idea of a lark, Hamish. Especially not now. The world keeps turning even though poor Toby . . ." She couldn't finish the sentence. He gave her an empathetic smile.

Make Hamish happy. It was a line she had scribbled so often in her Journal of Independence that it took precedence over kissing in the moonlight, being caught out in the rain without a driver, ordering something that fit from the Sears and Roebuck catalog based on measurements she took herself.

But Vaughan... He was the only man from her parents' set she could remotely tolerate, and they had always been good friends. He had established himself well in Boston and was making new friends with his easy charm. But she was playing a dangerous game and she was not the kind of woman who would toy with any man's affections. Yet wasn't that what her unsure heart was doing?

When she and Vaughan arrived at the Parker House, she sucked in her stomach and straightened her shoulders and stepped into the world to which she had been conditioned.

Vaughan placed a reassuring hand on Reggie's wrist in private, or so he thought, before Patricia Van Buren's bright smile drew everyone's attention away from their assorted sweetmeats. Reggie hated sweetmeats and found little to do with them other than make an interesting pattern with her fork. Her parents wanted to hear about Vaughan's business but nothing of her own. A lady simply did not talk about making her own bread. Reggie gave it a good shot nevertheless.

"Hamish and I are working on a related case that might tie some underhanded property development to Dirk Foster. Not to mention a kid was murdered."

Patricia Van Buren drew back. "Dinner conversation, Regina."

"You must not speak ill of a dear family friend, Regina." Her father swished wine as red as the blood trail from his rare steak, apparently having missed the latter part of her statement. "The Fosters are longtime acquaintances of ours. And the Vanderlaans. Whatever young Dirk is doing, I am sure it is for the betterment of the firm."

Reggie rolled her eyes in Vaughan's direction. He just smiled.

Vaughan was tugged into the archaic tradition of cigars and brandy in the next-door pub while Reggie's mother insisted they remain with the tea service.

"I must commend you, Regina."

Reggie smoothed her skirt beneath her and picked at the russet armrest of her chair. In the teapot's reflection, she could make out bow-tied waiters scuttling about with regal trays, their posture reminding her of the waitstaff at home. Reggie didn't miss it at all. Not the perfumed air. Not even clothes pressed and hung by a hand other than her own and awaiting her each morning. She liked changing lightbulbs and burning toast and finagling nickels into the radiator of her boardinghouse.

"What are you commending me on?"

"That you still have sense." Patricia Van Buren sipped her tea gingerly then raised a hand. "Cold. Honestly, you would think the service here would be up to par considering its name and history."

Reggie, who fondly remembered how quickly the servant assisted her in her running away to Boston and who more than once turned a blind eye while Reggie snuck out the window at night to meet Vaughan and his friends, took the gesture with a small smile and a look of deference when her eyes met those of the waiter who overapologetically set down a new pot.

Once he left with a slight bow, Patricia Van Buren sighed, then gave Reggie a look intersecting expectation and disappointment.

"What sense do I still have, Mother?" Reggie blew the steam from her tea.

"That even though you are doing heaven knows what for that Rue woman—"

"Stenography."

"—and living in that odious place in Charlestown—"

"A respectable ladies-only boardinghouse."

"—and keeping company with that young man, that . . ." A word was inserted here that blew steam out of Reggie's ears.

"Mother!" Reggie cut off the slur in her mother's crisp voice and set her tea down so quickly it sloshed over the side. "How can it be you raised me one way and you speak in another? If you are referring to Hamish, he is my friend and colleague, and he owns half of the business we run."

"Owns? Regina, I know your father sank some of his hard-earned money into keeping his princess happy. Lord knows I tried to stop him."

"We are helping people. Hamish is a lawyer, Mother."

"Truly? I have never seen him associated with a firm."

"You know that's because he is working with me."

"I don't want to argue with you, Regina."

"Then don't use words like *that* regarding people I care about!"

Patricia smoothed a strand of chestnut hair—the same color as Reggie's—away from her high forehead. "I don't expect that you with your carefree ways and your new liberal life will under-stand how women in our positions, of our blood, are forced to make sacrifices."

Reggie ran her index finger over the stray drops of tea on her saucer. "What kind of sacrifices?"

But with the way her mother shifted in her chair and stole a furtive glance over her shoulder as if there wasn't a foyer and parlor separating them from where her father and Vaughan were inhaling expensive Cuban cigars, Reggie had a premonition about where the conversation was headed. And try as she might, she couldn't swerve from its course.

CHAPTER 12

J ust because Father made bad investments doesn't mean that I should be sold like cattle."

"Regina, you are being overdramatic."

"I have to *marry* to save the estate? That's like something out of an Edith Wharton novel, where the heroine subscribes to the conformity of marriage or ends up in a millinery somewhere drinking a sleeping draught into oblivion." She couldn't imagine her parents without money. It was the backbone of all that they were, their value system, their golden calf. But being forced to marry? She felt ill. She had seen this play out in the pictures, but it was quite different watching it happen to a heroine she knew would end up with the love of her life by the end of the film. "I can't marry him, Mother. I love Vaughan, but not enough to marry him. I have a new life in Boston."

"Do you want us to lose our home? Our fine things? Your legacy?"

"You can't ask me to marry a man I don't love. And I want a different legacy than a bunch of cold money and . . ." *And a man whose entire body and soul would never stir me half as much as the slight brush of a hand over my shoulder.*

"You are *fond* of Vaughan. That is enough. He is a good match for you. He lives in Boston now and you would be able to stay in the city. It is not so much of a sacrifice. People marry for various reasons all the time. And you would be doing this for your family. For your father."

Reggie blinked tears away. "But I . . . There's . . ."

"There's someone else?" Patricia's right eyebrow became a familiar comma. They both knew who she meant.

Reggie trod carefully. "I just think there's a possibility I could marry someone I truly love. Don't you want that for me? To be happy?"

"Vaughan is in total agreement." Her mother carried on as if she hadn't spoken. "The man loves you. How much of a burden would it be to marry a man who worships the ground you walk on while doing this slight favor for us? You would live comfortably. We could keep our house."

"You mean Vaughan knows?" Her voice went up with the question. "You talked to him before me? So when he proposes, I will know it is some kind of arrangement?"

"He loves you. He asked before with no discussion. Without even asking your father! Like you—impetuous! Before you slapped him in front of all our guests."

Reggie felt two large walls closing in to suffocate her. Vaughan. She enjoyed his company. He was sturdy and safe and a far better shot than most of the suitors her parents might have thrown in her path. But while her brain could easily wrap around the possibility of Vaughan, her heart . . .

"Never listen to your heart, Regina," her mother had told her often enough when she was a girl. *"The heart will wander in the woods with no inkling of security or a future. Your brain will map a certain course."* Now her brain was supposed to latch onto duty: the certain course that saw her family through any ripples in their otherwise smooth journey.

"What type of investments?"

"Property."

"Property? Father is in insurance."

"A trusted colleague opened him up to a new opportunity, and it seems to be failing. Everyone takes a bad turn. We need you to be our certain course. To make up for your father's lack of judgment."

Reggie wasn't someone who ever felt comfortable with a certain course. The wind picked up and her sails didn't stay on course. Instead, they flapped and fluttered. *Property. A trusted colleague.* Her stomach turned. *Dirk?* No. She wouldn't go down that path. She took a mental swerve back to Vaughan.

I don't love him. Even though she *should* love him. Even though he was worthy of love. She didn't love him. Not in the way a woman should love the man she was to marry. Vaughan was such a part of her past. But was he part of her future?

Of course, he would let her work for a while, she assumed. But then he would want her to be on his arm, draped like a gilded ornament to show off at cocktail parties. Then he would want an heir, and Reggie knew she would never relegate a child of hers to be foisted off to nannies and treated like another bauble or family heirloom. So she would be trapped while keeping her mother in the season's finest and her father in brandy and cigars.

"I don't think you quite understand how dire our circumstances are. And what if America becomes involved in this useless war? We were lucky to make it through the last one. Your father made some bad decisions. You can make the right one. Ah!" Patricia looked up. Reggie followed her mother's glance over the white-linen-draped tables spread with sparkling silverware to the sentry palms on either side of the restaurant's path back to the hotel.

Reggie didn't want to look at Vaughan, who doubtless knew what they had been talking about. Why had she worn this dress? It was the color of claret, which Vaughan loved, and when he ushered her to the table earlier in the evening, she could sense it was taking every ounce of his considerable restraint to keep his eyes on her face.

She might have given him the wrong idea without meaning to. Sighing, she conjured a smile. Whatever game her parents were throwing her into, Vaughan was a good friend and, what's more, a good man. "I'll think about it."

"You should do more than think about it. You could be set up for life." Her mother reached over and fingered the glossy sleeve of Reggie's dress. It was, Reggie supposed, an almost sign of affection. The closest she supposed she would get from her ice sculpture of a mother.

Reggie's father settled the bill presented on the silver tray and they walked out to the large foyer, a white-gloved attendant helping the women with their wraps.

"You must have a lot to talk about," Patricia said pointedly, with a lingering smile to Vaughan.

Outside, a newsstand was closing for the night, the doors latching over headlines pulsing with ammunition and warfare, shots of a world so far away as Boston settled into its nightlife of late bands and popped champagne fountains, a city uncorked in clubs and dazzle.

Reggie was surprised Vaughan hadn't spoken yet. She took a deep breath, thought of speaking, and stopped.

"It's a nice night." She fingered her wrap.

"I'll see you home, if you like. Want to get a taxi?"

Reggie shook her head. "I can take the trolley."

Vaughan frowned. "I don't like you crossing the river when it's this dark."

"I'm a self-sufficient woman. I've crossed it off in my Journal of Independence hundreds of times."

"Your journal of *what*?"

How did he not know? Hamish knew. "I keep this little book. Since the day I left home. Of all the things that are helping me become the woman I am supposed to be."

Vaughan's kind eyes were on her profile. "What woman is that?"

"One who boils an egg and crosses the river to Charlestown at night and changes a lightbulb . . ." Reggie brushed a comma of hair from her forehead. "I need to think."

Vaughan pulled her close and trailed a kiss from her ear to her chin. "Reggie, you know I love you. I would give you anything. I will help your family. This wasn't my idea. But you know I love you. And I think you should consider what your mother talked to you about tonight."

"I'd far rather consider something you came out and asked me."

"The last time I proposed, you slapped my face and ran away from home."

Reggie winced. "See? Nothing to worry about. Safe as houses with me."

"It isn't funny."

"But it is, Vaughan. My mother as good as proposed for you when you weren't in the room."

"Your father has made some mistakes. Bad investments. I think he stands to lose a lot. I don't want to frighten you, but, Reggie, I could ensure that you and your family are taken care of. I will never ask you to give up your investigations. At least until we start a family of our own, and then you might find you want to have a different priority."

Reggie's head spun. "You are jumping so many steps ahead of me. A family . . ."

Vaughan's hand on her shoulder was gentle. "This isn't a transaction, Reggie. No matter what your mother said. And I know . . . I *know* you are afraid of becoming your mother. Your parents didn't marry for love. But I *love* you. We're already ahead of the game, darling."

"I know that." She could feel the pulse of his heart through his fancy suit jacket.

"I don't want to cage you, Reggie. Think of the freedom you

would have with me. You would help your family and I would let you be *you*."

Reggie blinked a tear away. She didn't want to hurt him. She gently pulled from him. "I just don't like marrying for this reason."

"Reg, I would have kept asking you until you said yes anyway. I truly love you. I always have."

"You're very persistent." She didn't pull away this time when he enfolded her and pressed his lips over her own. Didn't pull back when he moved his arms over her back. She loved how he smelled, his strong varsity rower's shoulders, how he could hold her tightly but gently at once. Protective.

And he would save her family.

When the need for a deep breath kept him from deepening his kiss and lightening her head even more, she closed her eyes, swallowed, and made a decision. What other choice did she have? Mooning over Hamish DeLuca in the office every day? Fielding phone calls from her mother underscored with the tragic inhales of martyrdom because her thankless daughter chose a North End investigative firm over her own parents' happiness?

Reggie and Vaughan crossed the street from the Parker House. She peered through the gate of the Granary Burying Ground, the headstone of Franklin towering above little tombstones crowding into each other like too many teeth in a gapping mouth.

"And we would live in Boston?" she said.

"And we would live in Boston." She could feel Vaughan rise beside her as if he had grown a few inches.

"Might as well put that ring on my finger, Vaughan Vanderlaan. I figure you have it with you."

Vaughan's face broke like a dam. His happiness sparkled under streetlights and the shaft of moonlight. "I can't properly put this ring on your finger in front of the tombstones," he said. "Come."

A few strides later they were in the Common, the moon set

amidst the tossed diamonds of stars scattered in the sky. He reached behind his breast pocket and extracted a small box.

He opened it and Reggie sighed. Let him think it was a reaction of love. Really it was her resignedly staring at a cluster of diamonds she would have to turn into her palm every time she crossed into the North End.

"If it's too much. They reminded me of you. Strong on the outside, see"—he pointed over three diamonds in a circle—"and much more delicate within." In the middle the most precious one: a small yellow crystal that prismed light.

"It's beautiful. And thoughtful."

"The jeweler had nothing perfect. I had it made."

"And . . . and how long have you walked around with this in your pocket?" Her voice was coated.

"A long time." He slid the ring on her finger, then interwove her fingers with his and clasped her tight. "An exceptional girl—no, an exceptional *woman* needs something extraordinary."

He kissed her then, and everything in him was in the caress on the back of her neck and the soft pressure of his lips over hers. Hovering tentatively at first before giving in. She even heard the soft intake of his breath as he deepened the kiss. She kissed him back, but her mind was elsewhere. *You are playing a stupid game, Regina. You know he is not marrying you to save your father.* When they disengaged, her face was wet.

Vaughan misinterpreted. "I know I'll make you happy. A bit overwhelming, isn't it?"

Reggie nodded. She wondered if she'd regret it: this weight on her finger, this perfect gentleman on her arm.

Most of all when she opened the door of their office and saw someone sitting behind a desk, ebony hair falling over his forehead, brushing the tops of the frames of the black rimmed glasses that magnified alarmingly big blue eyes. Another prospect. A preposterous suitor to her parents: one who fit in the margins of stutters and shakes, measured heartbeats and fingers crooked under braces in an endless count.

Reggie felt her heart speed up. Dizzyingly. Her forehead sheened with sweat and she folded her fingers into a slight clutch. *Oh.* Was this what he felt like all the time? She held her ring finger out to the moonlight, wondering if her nerves would calm and her breath would steady the moment it was off.

CHAPTER 13

Hamish could tell when Reggie was lying. So he knew when she said that Mrs. Rue kept her for extra paperwork, she was being less than truthful. Also, he had left for Vittoria Café at noon and Mrs. Rue's door was locked, light switched off. Reggie had been elsewhere, even as the sun crept over the rooftops and the children in line for the Revere House disappeared from the cobblestones. The music of the North End was a crescendo in certain moments—especially around noon—but sauntered legato in the middling hours between high afternoon and evening.

But she was here now, shaking out her curls, stifling a yawn. "Long morning. Anything happen here?"

"I made some phone calls."

Reggie's eyes were on him now and he could see the dark circles under them. Her hands were tucked deeply in the pockets of her high-waisted pants, and she rocked a little on her oxfords. She hung her hat and her handbag on the stand, then sank into her chair just as the telephone rang. Hamish watched her reach for it and with the familiar gesture noticed something catch the sparkle of the sun slicing through the window. He blinked and focused, blinked and focused, then swerved in his chair. Heart sinking, breath caught. His heartbeat sped and his breath came in pulses of staccato. The prism that caught the light was a diamond.

But no. It couldn't be! Hamish felt his stomach turn over and lurch. He knew what the glow meant, winking expensively in the streams of sunlight like crystal on fire. But wouldn't she have told him if she was planning to take that next step away from him? Wouldn't she have been a little less eager to show up every morning and let her head fall against his shoulder when he carried her soaking wet from the wharf?

The first time he tried her name it stuck in the back of his throat. He tried it again and his voice rippled a little on the R. Then, in a voice he didn't recognize, "Reg . . ."

"Oh. Right." She tucked her hand behind her back. "Well. Turns out I'm engaged."

"Congratulations." His voice rippled on every consonant.

"Only you could make congratulations sound like I've contracted Spanish influenza."

"I wasn't expecting it."

"Neither was I."

What was that tone? It was clipped and elusive like one of the heroines in the pictures she liked when confronted with a beau from the past. Hamish studied the floor. Tears were harrowingly close to forming in his eyes and his hand was shaking something fierce. Every nerve and jitter and quake was suddenly very alive and aware and awake. He was going to get the girl. He figured he had time. He saw her every day. They solved puzzles and people together. She had become a constant. He looked up only to see the sun streaming through the wind slice over the pendant at her collarbone. The necklace he had given her. *Spira, Spera.*

"Anything more on Toby?" Reggie said for the second time before he heard it.

"No."

"Well . . ." Her tone was casual now—too casual—as she hoisted herself on the edge of her desk. Darned if that ring didn't flash in the transition. Clearly expensive, blinding diamonds—one yellow—bright like the sun over the North Square or lemon can-noli or her smile.

How fortunate you are that somebody loves you. Hamish mentally quoted Quasimodo telling Phoebus, the golden-haired soldier, that the object of his affection, Esmeralda, pined for him.

⤞

Reggie could make out that dimple in his cheek. He brushed a truant strand of hair from his forehead. She watched his profile when he turned away. Slight comma of ebony hair, strong profile, chin that jutted out, just a little, ears he most likely grew into in adulthood, unfathomably blue eyes magnified by black-rimmed glasses.

"I made things strange between us, didn't I?" Reggie asked, using the voice her mother taught her to use to apologize for breaking the Pellers' floral heirloom vase, even though it was her schoolmate Jenny Wyatt's fault.

"I don't know that you did, Reg. Maybe they were always meant to . . ." He was searching for a word, eyes darting to all four corners of the office. When he couldn't pull it from the ceiling, he exhaled and shifted. His long legs stretched before him, ending in his customary two-toned shoes, scuffed a little at the edges from his fervent cycling.

Then he crossed his feet one over the other and reached for a pen, simultaneously extracting a folder from a drawer. He tucked the pen behind his ear. It stuck out, just a little, always alert. Hamish was someone she had trouble imagining in complete repose.

"Hamish, I don't want you to think that . . ." Could she say *anything* without saying *everything*? "That I haven't considered that you and I . . ."

His head shot up, sending his glasses halfway down his nose. He readjusted them, a look of surprised expectation on his face.

Reggie wondered if her face mirrored the melting endearment streaming through her. "I am very fond of you. We have this . . ." She stalled, crooking her mouth pensively. "Connection."

Why did the word have such an air of finality to it? Hamish's eyelashes flicked over his cheekbones a few times. He remained silent.

Connection. Was that the best she could do? Reggie inspected her nails: a little chipped at the tips from her last self-manicure. She studied the radio at the edge of her desk, then reached out and fiddled with the dial.

Soon enough, the distinctive minor scale ushering in Winchester Molloy's case du jour waffled through the speakers. Reggie turned up the volume, hoping the triad of chords undercutting the first muted conversation between Winchester and the femme fatale Veronica would draw Hamish's attention up from contemplating the edge of his desk blotter. Reggie's voice eventually did.

"There's more to this story than you know," she said sadly, hoping he didn't notice her fingers play delicately with the necklace tucked under her collar. *Spira, Spera.* The necklace he gave her on the roof of the Old North Church in thanks for the pearls she pawned to secure their office.

"I don't like not knowing just a bit of a story." Hamish shrugged. "I guess it's the lawyer in me." He took a breath that was almost indistinguishable from the crackle of the radio. "Or maybe it's the romantic." And if she hadn't been straining to hear and if she hadn't been studying him, she might not have seen a flicker that showed his heart. She might have doubted he said it at all.

"Hamish, why can't we be just friends!"

"Are you asking me or yourself?"

"I-I don't know! I don't want to ruin anything."

"So . . ." He rolled his pencil across the desk and caught it. "We'll be friends."

"Don't say it like that."

"I can't be dishonest. Not with you. If I start talking, I will start *talking,* and then I won't be able to stop any words. So I think"—the pencil rolled and he shoved it up again—"we should . . ." He flicked the pencil again and it made a farther trail before returning.

Reggie flinched. "Stop rolling that infernal pencil!"

"There's a Christian Patriots meeting tonight," Hamish said, his voice drained of color. "If you can attend unchaperoned with me."

Reggie soured. "Vaughan is willing to make a lot of exceptions for me, Hamish. Because he wants us to be friends."

"Well, we'll go make it work."

⭥

At the strike of noon, with a slight nod to Reggie and a polite smile for Hamish, a man lowered himself into the seat across from Hamish. Not just any man. Joe from the baseball field. The team was on the road and Joe had time on his hands. Reggie rose and leaned against the wall, just under the window, one shoe crossed over the other at the hem of her light cotton, high-waist trousers.

"How may we help you?" asked Hamish. Then, clearly recalling that the man didn't say much the day they visited the ballpark to question Errol about the pranks, Hamish retrieved a pencil and legal pad from his desk.

Joe nodded and moved to sit in front of Reggie's desk. Reggie slid into the seat Joe vacated on the other side of Hamish's desk. She studied Hamish's scrawl on a fresh legal pad.

He raised an eyebrow, sliding the paper to her side of the desk. *Does he seem at all guilty to you? Wouldn't he have seen what had happened?* Hamish had jotted.

Reggie read Hamish's neat, slanted writing and looked furtively at Joe. He was taking careful consideration, at least according to his body language.

Reggie looked at Hamish and filled the lines under his questions. *I don't know. But he knows more than he lets on. He observes.*

She slid the paper back. Joe looked up and Hamish quickly grabbed a folder, innocently looking through it.

Reggie laughed. In his quick movement Hamish had knocked over another folder. He scrambled to pick up the papers, his glasses sliding down his nose.

Joe motioned to leave, and Reggie and Hamish stood at attention. Reggie walked him to the door with a broad smile, and Hamish tried to focus on his desk rather than studying the way her hips moved while the sun through the window lightened her hair.

When he resettled into his chair, he gave her a comical look. Maybe things could tick on. Maybe they could be work colleagues. Reggie wound a strand of hair so tightly around her index finger it almost cut off circulation.

Hamish was studying Joe's comments.

"What do you see?"

"He thinks he saw the man who attacked Toby Morris." Hamish worked his lip with his teeth. "The first time." Hamish squinted over the writing. "Toby told me it was several men who pulled something over his head. Truthfully, I thought it might be Bricker and the men I saw at the train station that night. But Joe disagrees. He said it was only one. The same one who has been attending several games and hanging around too often."

"Bricker?"

Hamish just shrugged. "My guess."

"Well, who else?"

The rest of the afternoon was slow. Rosa Leoni dropped by and batted her eyelashes at Hamish, having him look over an employment contract for a cousin Reggie suspected did not exist. Then they tied up the last ends of a case they had been working on before Errol, even before Pete Kelly. Hamish was called as witness to a court case, and they were both finishing the paperwork and statements to close it for good.

─ ⋎ ─

"I wish we could go to the movies instead of to some silly political meeting." Reggie tried to keep her voice light, but Hamish could read through it. "It's my turn to buy the popcorn. You bought the last three times. Besides, you seemed bored at *Prisoner of Zenda*, and I owe you something you'll enjoy."

"I wasn't bored," he told her. No one could be bored with Reggie's running commentary on Ronald Colman's virtues intermingled with questions about how Madeleine Carroll's blonde curls kept so perfectly in place.

"Well, not completely bored." Reggie collected her hat and handbag. "Too much sword fighting for that. And with all that derring-do, Madeleine Carroll's hair was always perfect. Always perfect. She was escaping death and it looked as if she had just stepped out of the salon!"

"There must be something just *as* exciting about a political group with hateful views entangled in property development."

"My mother said something about my father being in property now."

Hamish's eyebrow rose. "Here in Boston?"

Reggie shrugged and began to collect her things so they could go to the rally.

He watched her ruefully as she attended to smoothing her pants and piling her papers in neat order for the next morning. "If you were my fiancée, I wouldn't want you to step out with another man. Not even on a case."

"Step out with another man?" Reggie's nose wrinkled with a spurt of laughter. "You are not *another man*. You're Hamish!"

Hamish warred with feeling relieved and confused. And a little hurt. He was Hamish. Good old Hamish! He gripped the handlebars of his bicycle and maneuvered it out of the office into the hallway. Then he hoisted it over his shoulder and walked it down the staircase, Reggie right behind him. She fit well on the front of the bike now, due to their practice. It was natural to him, too, to feel the extra weight. The night was calm and warm as he navigated the North End over Cross Street and into downtown Boston.

Once they reached Washington, she hopped off the handlebars.

"I don't think Vaughan Vanderlaan would enjoy your being on the front of a man's bike."

"Well, he'd better get used to it," she said. Shifting.

"Reggie." Hamish sighed.

"Why are there monsters and gargoyles? In *Notre-Dame*?"

It was a less than graceful way to swerve the subject. But he humored her. "They protect the cathedral from evil spirits. They guard the saints."

Reggie looked up at Hamish, eyes bright as they passed under a streetlamp. "And Quasimodo thinks they're his friends?"

"He talks to them." Hamish was surprised at how easily he explained it. A book that was as much of his makeup as the cells and blood and valves and ticking heartbeat. "And they hear him. He can't hear because he has always rung the bells and they are loud and burst his eardrum."

"Like your dad?"

Hamish's mouth twitched. "Sort of. He can still hear in one ear."

"I leafed through your copy one day. When you were out. Started reading it. It's so sad. There was something about it that made me feel . . . small . . . trapped." She shrugged.

He remembered telling her on one of their first meetings how imagining the stones and crevices, the parapets and turrets, even the bells made him feel safe from the world. Yes, his nerves clanged and his heartbeat thudded; but Quasimodo's safe sanctuary was something he would mentally retreat to.

She fingered her necklace. *Spira, Spera.* She looked up at him.

They passed newsboys bellowing the evening edition's headlines in a raucous competition: Roosevelt's Moral Embargo urging American companies to refrain from business with the Soviet Union. The sinking of the German U-Boat U-36.

They hadn't really talked about the war. It dominated all of the letters from his father and the *Telegraph* just the same.

"Do you have friends over there?" Reggie asked while Hamish rolled the bike.

Hamish nodded. "A lot of boys I went to school with."

"I'm sorry." She squeezed his arm.

"Me too."

The artificial light of Washington Street drenched the pavement. Reggie nodded at the Bijou: "Vaughan took me to *Gone with the Wind* at the Bijou. Clark Gable sweeps Vivien Leigh into no less than three end-of-the-world kisses. One while Atlanta burns around them."

Her eyes flicked up to Hamish's, which were suddenly the color of the Charles after a storm and not their usual light blue like the sky above the Common. His lashes flickered downward, his mouth turned up. She wondered what it would taste like to press her lips against his, kiss that crescent moon of a smile away. They reached Bromfield, which reminded Reggie of the first job she was offered when she came to the city. The memory put an end to the dangerous waters of end-of-the-world kisses.

She described the man who wanted her for more than her less-than-perfunctory skills. "He was a lecherous oaf of a man." She wrinkled her nose. "And then I found your cousin and he was all moonlight and Valentino."

Hamish laughed. "And then you got to know him."

"And *then* I got to know him."

"Regina!" They turned at a familiar voice.

"Dirk." Reggie said the name like a word that a New Haven Van Buren wouldn't use in polite company.

He flicked a look at Hamish briefly but without a smile or recognition. He offered his hand, but Reggie kept her own hidden. Finally, he leaned forward, his cologne tickling her nose, and kissed her on both cheeks. "Fancy meeting you here."

"We're here for the Christian Patriots meeting."

"The one I am speaking at!" he said pointedly.

"Still surprised you are interested in politics, Dirk. Trying to place when—"

"Since we're at war." Dirk didn't stop the annoyance from creeping into his voice. "Well. Humankind is at war."

"Since when are you interested in human—"

Dirk silenced her with his sleek gloved hand. "Reggie, you will find I have spent some time getting my head on straight. We're young. Idealistic. We will be the ones to make this nation great." He turned and truly looked at Hamish for the first time. "Your countrymen are already over there, aren't they? Britain snaps its fingers and—"

Reggie rolled her eyes and tugged Hamish's coat sleeve. "We don't have time for this. If you're just going to be condescending."

"Tsk-tsk, Reggie. Keep an open mind. It's time for us to step out and decide what we believe. Beyond our parents and our heritage."

Reggie cocked her head. "What we believe?"

"Just follow me," he said. "And try to remember you're a Van Buren." He stabbed Reggie with a look.

Reggie raised an eyebrow. "Last time I heard you speak was at your commencement. You were quite fond of quoting W. H. Auden, if I recall. And in the most surprising contexts."

"I made Mark write that for me. You remember little Mark

Talbot? Scrawny freckled boy whose parents delivered our groceries?"

"Such a charmer, Dirk." They let him get ahead. He took them down Winter in the direction of the Common, the Park Street Church steeple just under the swath of stars. Reggie's eyes followed Hamish's to the apartment building he'd shared with Luca Valari two summers before. It was easy to find: the shiny windows of the penthouse catching the glow from the streetlights and the thumbnail of moon. "Why go chasing the case when the case might come to us?" she whispered as Dirk led them through an open door, light ribboning out to the street.

"I do agree that we'll have to decide things for ourselves beyond our parents and heritage," Hamish said. "I don't come from the same heritage, but I only know war through what my parents lived through, and I would like to understand this one better."

"You're a diplomat," Reggie said thoughtfully. "You should have been a politician."

⚜

They settled into their seats. The speakers were adamant that the war in Europe was doing one thing very well: assessing the inhabitants of certain races and tracing the downfall of economies and militaries based on racial profiles. It nearly (nearly) erased Reggie's proximity from Hamish's mind.

When the speaker's ideals became too uncomfortable, he watched Reggie shift, then cross her legs. Then uncross them. Then she flinched. Then she blinked. Then she seethed. Then her mouth gaped and a small sound that almost became a word formed in the back of her throat. Hamish tugged at his collar. It was almost as cold over the tiles and in the hard wooden chairs as it was outside, but something inflamed him. As if even just hearing the misguided words in these ignorant, hateful voices could burn. It was the wrong kind of incendiary. A directed passion pointed in a direction that shocked and sickened him. He stared at his shoes. He felt guilty even for being in the same space as these words. The only thing that kept him there—beside Reggie, who was obviously equally troubled—was what his father always said: that every viewpoint, even the most appalling ones, helped one form a well-rounded view of human nature. What if a man who subscribed to the same point of view as Dirk and his political friends were to knock on their office door? What if Nate heard this nonsense spewed at his office?

The Christian Patriots were inspired by the Dudley Silver Shirts of the Great War and those in Hitler's Nazi Party on the other side of the world. But while Hitler's brand of national socialism was deeply grounded in the working class, Dirk's sect spewed a philosophy to attract those who were decidedly not of the working class. The elite. The upper crust, who Hamish decided were at core afraid that the Jewish American population would somehow take the wealth from their pockets. They were susceptible to a patchwork quilt of ideas that when sewn together found a root cause they could rally behind with self-righteous indignation, filtered through words and slurs ill-suited to their Brahmin accents.

The most arresting of the night's speakers was a former journalist and lay politician, Leonard Tucker. Hamish mulled over the name. The officer they'd encountered at Toby's murder scene was Tucker. Never mind. It was a common name. His take on Christian Patriots took the best of what America's founding fathers stood for and twisted it to ensure that it spoke only to some of the nation's residents, leaving little room for the inhabitants of the North End. What chilled Hamish the most was how the words sat in such a cold, calculated, and articulate tone. There was scientific reason, Tucker believed, to why some men were created superior to others. It was here that Hamish lost completely the track of Christian

Patriotism (if, indeed, he had found it at all). Then a man named Walter Norman next took the podium to speak to his loss in the first war and to the crippling depression that saw his Aryan ancestors on his mother's side in Frankfurt under the oppression of what he called "the Jewish Problem." Eventually, just "the Problem." As if there was one singular problem in the current political climate of the world and one race solely responsible.

Walter Norman cleared his throat and rasped his way through a reading from the *Dearborn*, a newspaper attributed to Henry Ford from several decades before. Hamish studied Reggie a moment: she was pinching the fabric of her light cotton pants and trying to look anywhere but at the speaker. Hamish followed suit, studying the men and women intently taking in the ridiculous views. He studied to see if any of them looked as uncomfortable as he was sure he and Reggie did. Barely able to sit still, looking over their shoulders to the clock and the doorway. But most looked like the kind of people Hamish would find on the street in passing. Nothing singled them out other than the fact that most of their clothes were well cut, their status more of Reggie's world than Hamish's. Men in perfectly tailored suits and women in fashionable hats. Hamish didn't know much about clothes, but he knew enough from the film magazines Reggie kept around the office to decipher what was modern.

"This would infuriate Vaughan," Reggie whispered. "I wonder if he even knows what Dirk is doing. They work together, sure, but I don't hear him mention his name as often outside of his office talk."

"This would infuriate anyone," Hamish said. When his lips lowered to her ear, he could almost taste her shampoo with her hair just a breath from his lips. It was a nice distraction from the tempered theses of hate he was hearing in the level voices of these besuited men.

He was sick of the Christian Patriots, thinking of their leaflets at the train station in Charlestown, the pamphlet on the desk at Pete Kelly's building.

"You know what Nate always says." Reggie tried to lighten the mood.

"If you're not informed, you don't have the luxury of an opinion."

"Exactly!" Reggie's voice was a little too loud on the exclamation, and a woman turned and shushed her with a sneer. Reggie stuck out her tongue. "I want the luxury of an opinion."

⋆

Scraping over her childhood with a fine-toothed comb, Reggie was hesitant to admit that Dirk might have come by his belief system honestly. He never had to work. He never had to see a person who didn't mimic his background and bearing in any role but that of a servant. Nonetheless, his speech addled her nearly into Hamish's lap. She could not sit still.

When the meeting was finally over and they loitered for the purpose of their investigation, she could say little but, "You're a boor, Dirk. Oh! And speaking of boor." Reggie felt the luxury of taking her time on every last consonant in a line of perfect, derisive articulation as Walt Bricker stepped into view.

"Miss Van Buren." He nodded. He didn't nod at Hamish. He didn't see or acknowledge Hamish.

"Some of our funding comes from the development of housing in the Boston area," Dirk said. "Funding from appropriate men who align their wallets with their political ideals."

"I can just imagine," Hamish said. "Properties like Pete Kelly's?"

"You think that what is happening in the world is just a by-the-way?" Dirk raised his chin. "There is always a source. You are obtuse and it is getting us no closer to coming to the root of the problem. Our cause needs well-bred and intelligent men and women. Like me and Reggie here. And even you."

Hamish raised his hands. "I am not here to talk politics . . ."

"Our close friend and colleague Nate Reis is the face of what you are trying to destroy," Reggie said vehemently, choosing to settle her ire on Bricker with a narrowed glare. "He is part of the glue that keeps our neighborhood together." She turned back to Dirk. "And you have the gall to sit here on your high horse and spew this nonsense? What do you or any of these people know about hard work? About community? Dirk, you have always had things handed to you on a silver platter. You speak of the Depression, but you know nothing about it! You strolled through life as you always do, except maybe your tailor took a little extra time in getting the fancy Indian silk you wanted for your ties. So you're speaking about things you never experienced and appropriating a view to combat a battle you never fought."

Dirk ignored her, coolly turning to Hamish. "And you? You're smart enough. Your countrymen are fighting already, and what are they fighting for? We have branches in Canada, you know." He looked Hamish over. "You're not our *usual* candidate." His eyes narrowed on Hamish's face. "But you can't help one-half of you, can you?"

Hamish bristled and tucked his fingers into his palm. He had a million things to say, but it wasn't worth it. They would jumble in his brain, taking up space the moment he left the building, but if he did say them, they would fall ignored on the linoleum anyway. "Mr. Foster, a sixteen-year-old boy was murdered at a ballpark in Charlestown. Do you know anything about that?"

"Never was a baseball fan, myself."

Reggie stepped in. "He ran messages for Pete Kelly down on Fiske's Wharf. The very property you're trying to build on."

When Dirk said nothing, Hamish turned to Bricker. "Do you know anything about this?"

"Why would I kill a kid?"

"We've seen you there before," Reggie said.

Dirk silenced Bricker with a slight grip on his elbow as the last lingering attendees from their meeting pushed through the open door. Once they had a pocket of privacy to themselves, Hamish continued. "Toby was a messenger. He ran errands for Pete Kelly."

"Kelly will be out of there soon enough."

"At the price of a kid," Reggie added dramatically. Too dramatically, perhaps, because Hamish and Dirk and Bricker turned to her quickly.

Hamish prolonged the silence, watching Dirk and Bricker. The latter was turning over a leaflet in his left hand. The former, merely staring at Hamish. Hamish had won a grade school spelling bee once, on the word *derision*—its meaning quite evident on Dirk's face.

"So neither of you knew Toby Morris at all?" Reggie asked.

"I know him to see him," Bricker said. "But I'm not in the mood of killing people."

"He died from a forceful blow to his head. A punch," Hamish said pointedly. Studying Bricker. Then assuming he was on uneven ground with Dirk. Yes, Dirk was very much the leader, both in stature and in bearing. Luca always said some men were just followers. But how far would Bricker follow?

"I think it is time to call it a night," Dirk said. "Neither of us were anywhere near the ballpark when that unfortunate death happened. You can check with Hyatt and Price and . . . Bricker here." Dirk looked at Bricker, only the slightest doubt flashing in his eyes. "Bricker here will find you an airtight alibi, won't you?"

"Of course," Bricker said.

Once outside, the two of them free of the rally and well up Washington Street, Reggie rolled her shoulders. "Well, that was horrifying."

"I guess at the very least it helps us understand some of what is going on in the world," Hamish said. "That there are these ideologies."

"And now with the war that's already started there . . ." Reggie didn't finish her sentence, and they kept a ruminative silence as they walked down Washington Street, Hamish rolling his bicycle beside him while studying his spectator shoes.

"The reason I didn't pass the medical had nothing to do with my eyesight, Reggie."

"What?"

"You know. When I went home."

Reggie stopped abruptly. "You were going to enlist?"

"I wear glasses for reading. I don't have great eyesight, but that was not the primary reason."

"Then what was—? Oh." Reggie blinked. "I didn't think that—"

"But there is a doctor in Canada—and of course my dad found him, because he *would* find him—of course he found him—who was doing studies on men like me going to war."

Reggie grabbed his arm. "He was just trying to protect you."

"My dad didn't even go to war. So our family just doesn't fight for Canada? I live here now, but I am Canadian. It is my heritage. My identity. What have we contributed? And now, hearing this man with his ideas, and I could have done something to stop it." He shoved his hands deep in his pockets. "But I can't because I am prone to nerves."

"Hamish."

"I don't know why I am telling you. Other than I wanted to fight . . . fight for a place where whatever they were spewing off tonight would never be part of the conversation."

"I understand."

"You'd miss me if I went to war, wouldn't you?" he said after a long silence, one in which he conjured a pretty clear image of Reggie waiting for him at a train station amidst a mill of people, pressing into him and kissing him tightly before he disappeared in a sea of khaki. Writing him while he was away. The things he would do to make the world better for her upon his return.

From the corner of his eye, he could see her focus on the street before her, hands in pockets, eyes covered by curled lashes, nose and chin a little impish in the way they curved out to the night. "I'd miss you if you went anywhere," she said lightly.

⁎

Reggie met Vaughan in the foyer of the Hyatt and Price firm. She'd assured Hamish she would get home safely, but detoured, knowing Vaughan would be working late. His eyes were bleary with tiredness and his usually bright smile was dulled with exhaustion. Reggie didn't stand on ceremony.

"I just came from one of Dirk's political meetings."

Vaughan frowned. "He's caught up in a few things."

"That's an understatement. Were you able to find out anything about the project he is working on? From your end?"

"Do you want to have a late supper?" Vaughan fingered her collar gently. "We could go to this little place over on School Street. They have the most amazing mushroom tartlets. I was telling your father. I—"

"You were talking to my father?"

Vaughan nodded. "He is in some sort of business venture with Dirk. They have mutual investors or something. You know I was never much into playing the market. Your dad has a far more savvy head for those things."

"Indeed." Reggie smiled at Vaughan and gently removed his

arm. "Supper sounds fine. But what sounds even better is picking a lock."

"Reg . . ."

"Do you remember when we were kids and your uncle wouldn't let us take the propeller boat out so we broke that lock and did it anyway?" Reggie widened her eyes. She knew Vaughan loved it when she bounced a little on the balls of her feet and looked up at him entreatingly.

"I don't know, Regina."

"Is there security here?"

"The cleaning ladies come in"—he consulted his Rolex—"twenty-five minutes."

"More than enough time! Come on."

Vaughan explained that only one elevator functioned after 10:00 p.m. It was quite normal for the executives to work late over glasses of bourbon in the dying light. But with the staff mostly gone, it was seen prudent to conserve as much electricity as possible.

Vaughan used the privacy of an elevator without an attendant to try for a kiss. Just a butterfly one in the delicate space below her ear.

"You're already feeling quite spontaneous," Reggie said, the sensation making her laugh rather than filling her to the brim.

"You smell divine. Like lemon, I think. Clean."

Reggie stepped away. Lemon equaled proximity to Hamish DeLuca: in a darkened theater, pressed against his shoulder in the sticky confines of a meeting that soured her stomach with its base words and views.

They reached Vaughan's floor.

"You're skittish tonight," Vaughan remarked. The lights were dimmed.

"Excited for our covert break-in." She flashed him a smile. "How many times have you told me you wanted to be a fly on the wall of one of my investigations with Hamish?"

"I don't have a key." They stood outside Dirk's office.

Reggie thought for a second, then brightened with an idea. She extracted the pin from her hair so a fringe of brown curls fell over her forehead. The look in Vaughan's eyes at the motion stopped her heart: not with returned affection, but rather guilt. She needed to make up her mind. But there was time for that later. For now, she straightened out the metal loop of the pin's end and smoothed the wire into a straight line. She gently shoved Vaughan out of the way, bending over so the top of her head was in line with the key hole. She curled her right knee and took a deep breath and slid the pin into the lock. "I've seen Hamish do this with a paper clip. Something he learned from his mother. She was a lady investigator. Actually, I think she still is. Can you imagine?" A Van Buren lady did *not* ramble, her brain reminded her while her words flooded out. She wasn't sure what it was about tonight that made her so uneasy around Vaughan. She supposed it had something to do with gargoyles and Romany girls turned to dust and talk of end-of-the-world kisses as a soft evening breeze tossed a strand of Hamish's hair across his forehead.

The makeshift key clicked and Reggie smiled at the shift in weight. She could feel it in place. "There."

"That's a useful skill," Vaughan said.

Reggie straightened. "If you had heard what Dirk was saying tonight you would have no qualms about what we're doing, Vaughan."

Vaughan followed at her shoulder. She could feel the cotton of his shirt against her arm. Vaughan flicked the light switch and Reggie scanned the room. It was neat with few visible papers. "You display your blueprints. On your easel," Reggie recalled. "Dirk doesn't."

"Maybe he wants to keep his ideas to himself."

"A man like Dirk wants everyone to see what he's accomplishing. He would want a bird who happened to settle on the ledge

there to peek in and see his brilliance. Don't give me that look—
that man is a sponge for attention." Her fingernail scaled over a pile
of papers on his desk. She tried the first drawer of the mahogany
desk. It didn't budge. She tugged the chain on the green-shaded
banker's lamp and put her makeshift pin key to good use.

"Here we go!" She beamed, handing Vaughan receipts for services rendered and a folded blueprint sketch.

Vaughan studied what he held. "Looks like they have early
buyers for these properties. Renters."

"Is that common? It is still Pete Kelly's building."

Vaughan nodded. "People want early investors but also guaranteed tenants when they can get them."

"May I?" Reggie scanned the names on the loose sheets. A few
names she recognized as the men who spoke at Dirk's political
meeting. Or, at least, were listed in the program she had ripped to
shreds to keep from rising and upturning her chair.

MacMillan. She figured this was Brian MacMillan, another
leftover from the Flamingo Club. She had danced with him. He
was kinder than the others. She went cross-eyed looking for
the name Kent. Then figured a man like that wouldn't want his
name anywhere. There was, however, another name of interest
added in pencil below the carefully typed list: *E. Parker.*

"What is it? Breakthrough, Reg? You just gasped."

Reggie ripped a piece of paper from a nearby notebook and
copied exactly what she saw in exactly the same order. "Vaughan,
you darling." She lifted up and kissed him on the cheek, enjoying
the scent of him, the slight brush of the sideburn sloping along his
cheek. "We make a good team."

Vaughan had manicured hands. Well looked after. Used to
folding idly over blueprints or spreading out to emphasize a
vision in a presentation. His fingers weren't long like Hamish's.
Or bruised from whatever he got himself into. There were none
of the scars that Hamish's right hand bore: from years of digging

his nails into the skin in anxious moments. Vaughan noticed her study and tightened his hold. "I know what you're worried about."

"What's that?" She lifted her eyes and met his blue ones with her own.

"That after we're married I will expect you to turn into some version of your mother, running those DAR meetings and keeping house. I know that you will want to continue what you started here, Regina. I only ask one thing."

Here it starts. Reggie swallowed. She owed him this conversation, even as her mind snagged on the case she would rather have been pursuing. She straightened her shoulders, pasted on a coy smile. "What's the one thing?"

"That you'll hire a secretary. I know you'll still want to help Mrs. Rue. I mean, I don't see that as any different than the charitable work your mother and mine do with all of those church teas and quilting circles. But—"

"A secretary, Vaughan? We don't have the money, and it's ridiculous to think we need the extra help with the middling business and . . . oh . . . oh, you mean a *chaperone*."

"I know that Hamish is a good man. I just have enough on my hands explaining why you spend most of your day in the North End, and it will help, Reggie. It will make things easier for both of us."

"Vaughan, you said things could stay as much the same as possible. We don't have the money or the need for a secretary."

"I thought that lady from the bakery . . . Mrs. Leoni. She has a daughter in college, right? Maybe hire her part-time for the time being and . . ."

Reggie had her mouth open to speak but sighed instead.

"We should spend more time together. Get to know each other a little bit better."

"Vaughan, I have known you longer than most people in my life."

"But I don't know if I truly know you at all. There's this new side of you that's exciting and flourishing and adventurous, and I just want in."

"Vaughan, you know you can change your mind at any time. Before we start with this party. Before—"

"Reg, you know how I feel about you. And I am willing to wait until you feel the same way. There are so many reasons people get married. Many happy marriages are based on even less than what we already have."

But what about love? What about fixing your hair the way someone likes it or thinking about them in season and out? What about remembering the way they feel close to you and wanting to step into their brain and walk around a little so you know every last detail? What about the kind of love that William Powell and Myrna Loy had, finishing each other's thoughts and sentences? Or the passion with which Quasimodo ached for Esmeralda? Reggie shook her head. She couldn't let her thoughts stray toward that last example. It was too dangerously close to . . . Why did her parents have to get themselves into financial trouble?

"Reggie, I'm not asking for anything that you can't live with, and I never will. Just think about it."

Reggie nodded. "Let's set a date, shall we? Before the Parker House books up?"

A date. They were setting a date. Vaughan retrieved a small diary from his jacket pocket while Reggie kept her heart from pounding through her blouse. Now it was just a date for a party. A social announcement. Soon . . . it would be a date from which she could never look back.

CHAPTER 14

The first time Hamish noticed he was different was when he would shudder in the corner at school recess. He would tremble all over if there was a new kid in class or the teacher called on him, and the answer on the top of his mind would stall on his tongue. If it eventually found its way out, it was through a rippled stutter. Soon he stopped trying to talk at all.

The chest pains that would spring up and latch on like claws scraping under his ribs developed a bit later and assured him he was dying. The fear, of course, catching his breath so that it was stuck in his windpipe, coming out in gulps and gasps. The scars on his hands from digging his fingernails in. The rumored treatment of frontal lobe surgery and electric shocks that would eliminate his anxious episodes forever.

It was only since he moved to Boston that he learned his father had protected him from the worst at the expense of Hamish's understanding that he was seen as *less than*.

He couldn't be *less than* tonight. He couldn't have Luca's influence or his limitations around him.

Hamish hadn't touched the clothes fitted and made for him by Luca's tailor since that fateful first summer in Boston. He fumbled in his dresser for the silk bow tie he knew was tucked somewhere between balled socks.

Finally feeling it, he pinched the edge of it with his fingers and tugged it out, slamming the drawer so vehemently it shook the pictures and bottle of aftershave on top. One framed picture of him and Maisie Forth in their New Year's best before a night he well remembered at the glamorous Palais Royale on Lake Ontario. Luca had snapped the pic. Another of his parents. His mom's striking blue eyes looking out at him as if she were right there.

He straightened the frames and took to getting ready. He combed his fingers through his hair and studied himself in the mirror a moment. Frowning. He had to look the part tonight. He had to conjure up some of the flair Luca had summoned for the opening of his club. He jogged out of his room and through Nate's open door. Surely Nate had pomade somewhere. Nate was about as interested in fashionable things as Hamish was, but he remembered Nate saying his mother insisted he tame his hair for schul.

"Sorry, Nate," he whispered to the dark room, finding a jar at the back of the top of his dresser. "Desperate times." Besides, Nate owed him. He wouldn't be half as nervous if Nate were joining him, but Nate, as usual in recent weeks, had to work late. "I could use you. I could really use you." Use him as he stepped into a world in which he was losing Reggie forever.

As much as his conscience pricked over their slow strides to find Toby's killer, he couldn't see beyond the wall of Reggie being lost to him forever.

To his credit, Nate had looked genuinely remorseful but nevertheless declined. Once again in front of his mirror, Hamish took a deep breath, rubbed some of the gel-like substance on his hands, and attempted to tame his ebony locks. The look always made him a little self-conscious about his ears, but Luca had inspired him not to care. Luca. Hamish recalled the folded-up piece of paper with Luca's number in his trouser pocket. He didn't want the aura of Luca surrounding him when he had spent a long bike ride mentally listing all of the things he had done to stand on his own two feet. He slipped it out of his pocket and placed it at the back of his top sock drawer. Beneath the hose and garters, tucked under a slat of wood.

Next, he tried his look: bow tie and suspenders, white jacket with black lapels. Houndstooth pocket square. He squinted at himself in the mirror, turning a little. Then tried a bit of a smile, wide enough so that his dimple appeared. Bernice was not the first girl to tell him about his smile. It was something that Reggie mentioned on several occasions. When he fully smiled, apparently it transformed his face. He tried it. Nah. His smile was too crooked. He scratched his nose and nudged his glasses higher. Maybe he should keep them on. He would look smarter that way. Professional. Like the lawyer he was. He used his now nervously shaking right hand to remove them for a moment, studying his face without them in the reflection, and decided he had enough to worry about without minimalized vision.

Worry. So much worry. Because he knew what people expected. He knew what the A-B-C plot of a *Winchester Molloy* serial promised. He had thrown himself into the investigative business without the first clue how to make good on the amateur profession. Three years of having a good inkling of human nature and more than a dose of empathy. But it was still three years with part of his brain cast out to perceived expectation. The way a murder *should* be solved. The amount of crime one should *anticipate* in a case. But the same mental reel would reveal his expectation of Reggie in his arms at the climax of the plot, and that was just one more thing he couldn't guarantee.

He thought about splurging on a cab so he arrived in pristine condition, but a quick assessment of his heartbeat, tempered with his two forefingers, inspired him to tuck his long pant legs into his gartered socks and cycle. He would need the fresh air and the time. He smudged on a little more pomade to keep his hair in place and told himself he would be careful.

He tucked a stray strand of hair into place and inspected his polished two-toned shoes one last time. Then he collected his bicycle from its usual place in the front hall and wheeled it out the front door. He swung his leg over the crossbar and pushed off with momentum, leaning over the handlebars, soon pedaling and swerving over the uneven streets in the direction of Cross Street. The setting sun courted the familiar skyline of Boston's most familiar buildings well. Hamish picked up speed, flicking a look up at the Custom House's familiar clock tower, then over the matching columned structures of the North and South buildings of Quincy Market. Ahead, the Old State House looked as he assumed it had when the Declaration of Independence was announced from its east balcony that warm and jubilant day.

Beyond, the sun snagged on the shadow of its steeple, the site of the Boston Massacre: one of the many catapulting moments toward Revolution. Finally, on School Street, just past Old City Hall, the Parker House Hotel towered. Hamish wheeled his bike to a uniformed man beside a revolving door who maneuvered it inside for safekeeping, pocketing the bill Hamish handed him, while Hamish made his way toward the side entrance. He used the time to roll down his pant legs and inspect for any pedal scuffs on the sides of his shoes. He used the reflection of a chauffeured car to inspect his hair, which, thankfully, had withstood the bicycle ride.

"Heartbeat, Hamish," he whispered, feeling his breath snag a little as the doorman stood aside and he stepped into the grand, chandeliered lobby.

An easel sign indicated the events of the evening, and Hamish swerved past the famous restaurant to ascend to the second floor. Nearby men and women dressed to the nines in hats, satin, and fur stoles, which must have been for presentation rather than necessity in the warming temperatures, made their way to the lobby's many elevators. Hamish wanted to avoid the din a few moments longer.

This was Luca's world, he thought. Never more so than when he reached the mouth of the grand ballroom, a quartet plucking out the perambulatory bars of a Bach composition while waiters with silver trays full of hors d'oeuvres and champagne turned in an elaborate waltz amidst a stretch of strangers. This was Reggie's world, too, he admitted. At least the world from which Reggie had sprung. Not the Reggie he knew who liked *brutti boni* and seeing the same picture several times until she could quote her favorite lines. Not the Reggie who liked to sit for hours and make up new *Winchester Molloy* plots with Nate. Who wrinkled her nose so that the freckles disappeared and crossed off things as delightful as "Change a lightbulb" and "Kiss in the rain" (the latter he had only learned one evening in pursuit of a missing kitten when she was so sleepy she murmured it before falling asleep on his shoulder in Boston Common) in her Journal of Independence. Reggie who colored his world and made him see life in a way that was constantly new. Reggie who made him want to learn more and see more and be more just for the privilege of keeping near. Reggie who fit perfectly on the handlebars of his bike and also in his arms on the dance floor. Reggie who was marrying another man was being celebrated in a lush gathering at which he didn't even remotely belong.

A woman with bleached blonde hair and a dark bow for lips sidled past Hamish, studying him appreciatively. He watched her join her friend, the back of her dress dipping suggestively low with nothing underneath, and soon her companion with russet red hair and heavily lined eyes was looking back at him. He supposed it was an engagement party and women from any set would be interested in their own prospects while love was in the air.

Love. Hamish tugged his bow tie. This was a disaster.

"This is a disaster." The voice he most wanted to hear was at his ear, brushing just over his collar.

"You look . . ." Hamish couldn't finish the sentence if he tried. He couldn't remember his own name in direct line of Reggie, who was wearing a dress he had never seen before. A dress *no one* had seen before. Even if it was the most popular fashion in this upper set, it would never spill over anyone else the way it did her. He was used to seeing Reggie in cranberry and green, and she had a preference for yellow in the summer months. But this dress was a sleek ivory that dipped low over her neck and down to the floor, hugging places he knew his eyes shouldn't be dwelling on. Her lips were russet red and matched her painted nails. The locket Hamish had given her with the inscription *Spira, Spera* was missing, but in its place a simple gold chain danced in the light. Hamish swallowed, his fingers finding home under the fold of his jacket.

"You clean up swell." For the first time in the relentless moment stretching between them, he noticed she had been studying him as intently as he had her.

"You look beautiful, Reggie," he finally said.

"This is a nightmare and I feel like I could scream," was her response to the compliment. "See those girls over there?" She discreetly pointed toward the women who had been assessing him earlier. "Watch out. They'll prey on you." She crooked her blood-red fingers into claws with a teasing hiss. "And her?" She inclined her head to the side. "Ten o'clock." Hamish followed her direction. A bubbly brunette was exchanging an empty champagne flute for one overfull with bubbly amber liquid. "You will want to dance with her eventually, just for the stories later. In fact"—Reggie leaned forward and straightened the bow tie that had become crooked with Hamish's earlier fidgeting—"I insist you dance with her so you can tell me all about it later, Hamish Cicero." She laughed and he joined her briefly, both recalling some of the women of Luca's set back when they were exploring the Scollay Square clubs.

"You're the only girl I want to dance with, Reggie," he said, disappointed that his voice rasped a little as he said it. He knew that wouldn't be an option. She would dance with Vaughan, of course, and her father and a cousin and perhaps an attached old friend from the Harvard rowing set. But he didn't belong here.

"I know," she said, with surprising tenderness and understanding. "But..." She shook her head. "I just..."

The mirrored glare of one of the champagne trays caught the expensive light and Reggie grabbed two glasses. "Still your nerves," she said, passing one to him, knowing he wasn't fond of the taste or feeling. "At least have something for your right hand to do." She looked left and right and, determining that no one was closely watching her movement, reached into the fold of his coat and grabbed his hand. His trembling fingers sparked with the feel of her hand over his. Intimately hidden by his suit jacket.

"Here." She placed the glass in his right hand and ensured that it was steady even if it shook a little when she removed her grip. "Now. I am warning you ahead of time that whatever you hear tonight and whatever anyone says to you . . . They're just jealous and confused, Hamish. Of you. It will have nothing to do with you. And nothing you might hear or experience will ever match what I think of you." She searched his face with nervous vulnerability. She held tightly to his sleeve with the hand not holding her champagne glass. "And I won't ever be leaving us, Hamish. No matter what you hear tonight. Take it all with a tiny, tiny grain of salt. The tiniest." She sipped her champagne and stepped back, her head cocked at an angle that slightly swerved her careful updo. "Besides, Nick and Nora find themselves at insufferable parties all of the time."

It was in that last sentence that he noticed the transformation: her elocution was cut glass with a Boston Brahmin twist and her body language changed. She was going to play this role and she would play it well. In the way her spine elongated and her free hand found the curve of her waist. It fascinated and terrified him.

But it was part of her too. When she turned away, he switched his champagne glass to his left hand so that his right hand could find its safe spot behind his suspender, tucked away.

CHAPTER 15

M other, I swear. If you say anything to him, if you treat him like a bug to be squashed, I will storm out of here and throw Vaughan's ring on the floor and you will never see me again."

"Regina, you're being overdramatic."

Rather like your ensemble. Her mother's regally long purple cape accented the flourished ripple of an expensive dress. And an even more expensive frosting of jewelry. Reggie's mother intended to be not only seen but remembered.

"At least you chose a suitable color for the occasion." She ran her manicured nail over a flounce in Reggie's scooped neckline. "You look quite pretty."

"You sound surprised."

"Well, you haven't had your hair properly set in heaven knows how long, and I can see quite clearly that you have forsaken your calisthenics."

"I walk to and from the North End to Charlestown almost every day." Reggie shifted her dress over her hips. "That is calisthenics enough for me."

"Well, Regina." Her father appeared, a glass of whiskey in his hand and on his breath as he leaned in to kiss a bit of the powder from her cheek. "You sure know how to draw a crowd."

"It's not because they care a fig about Vaughan and me, Daddy."
Reggie surveyed the room. "It's because they're curious about
this girl sleuth who keeps an office in the North Square and ends
up in headlines."

Reggie's mother made a noise that Reggie wasn't sure could
be described in any dictionary. "Come on, then. Let's get this
over with," she said out of the side of her mouth. "You must meet
him eventually." She felt her pulse quicken at the thought of it.
"Behave, Mother. And Daddy, remember I am doing all of this for
you. So you *will* be kind to my friend."

It wasn't hard to find Hamish. He was carefully smiling at
one of the young women she had pointed out to him earlier. The
champagne glass was long gone and his hand was inside his jacket
pocket until . . . He looked up and saw her, straightened his shoulders, adjusted his tie, and removed his hand from his jacket.

Reggie caught his eye to steady him through it, but he was
already gently excusing himself from his one-sided conversation
and stepping toward her. She mouthed an apology that she covered with her hand and an exaggerated cough when she felt her
mother's piercing gaze on the side of her face.

Then something that Reggie would bottle and keep for the rest
of her life happened. Hamish strode confidently forward, shoulders fitting the tailored lines of his suit, extended his hand, and
stretched his smile so magnificently wide it not only pressed that
full dimple in his cheek but lit his eyes behind his glasses. Reggie's
heart stopped a moment.

"It is so nice to meet you, finally, Mr. Van Buren." Hamish
shook her father's hand firmly, then turned to her mother, and the
smile stretched a little more. Reggie watched her mother intently,
noting that the smile's effect was astounding. "And now I know
where Regina inherited her beauty," he said, accepting the hand
that her mother tried to extend but really just dangled and lifting
it to lips still spread with that smile. Where was that smile from?

He beamed, and she was shocked it didn't spark light like a bulb and illuminate the whole of the dimly lit hall. "It is quite an honor to meet you, Mrs. Van Buren." He backed up but kept a slight bow before straightening.

"DeLuca, is it?" Her father drew his attention back.

"Yes, sir."

"I understand your father is a newspaperman." Hamish's smile didn't falter, but he did subdue it slightly, and only Reggie would have noticed the care he took in tucking his right hand into his pocket. But he was performing magnificently; her mother couldn't take her eyes off him, and Reggie wanted the moment of her parents being thrown off-kilter by this man to last a lifetime.

"Indeed, sir. He is the chief editor of the *Toronto Telegraph*."

Her father was impressed. "That's a national paper."

"Largest in Canada."

"It is?" Reggie asked. He'd never said as much to her. She supposed it was because he kept anything but his natural humility tucked into his pocket where his right hand currently hid.

"Yes, Regina." His eyes were soft on her.

"But you were in the law?"

"I still am. I consult on all matters of employment and contract law." Hamish's voice was smooth, free of any ripple. He was choosing his pace and consonance carefully. And while she could detect the slow, methodical care he was taking, her parents would only think they had found a man who was too smart to rush to speak.

"Alma mater?" Her father was insufferable.

"Osgoode Hall. Most prestigious law school in Canada."

"Good grades?"

"Graduated summa cum laude. Top of my class, sir."

"And your firm?"

"Well, while I was still there, Winslow, Winslow and Smythe. Prime barristers in Toronto."

Reggie's father studied Hamish as intently as one of the treasured bottles of scotch whiskey he so enjoyed collecting. "Hmm. And tell me, young man." He nudged at Hamish with his glass. "Your fellow countrymen are at war. You didn't want to enlist?" Her father's bushy eyebrows rose.

"I cannot, sir, on account of my eyesight." He used his left hand to straighten his glasses. "But I assure you I did return home for my medical exam. I tried."

Her father looked at Hamish studiously, then raised his glass slightly. "Good for you. Say, you've nothing to drink. Come. Come. I'll get you a glass of this, huh?" He smiled at Reggie. "Show your young Canadian friend the best New England whiskey."

Hamish turned and smiled at Reggie. Then he bowed shortly in excuse to her mother and disappeared. Leaving Reggie absolutely smitten and her mother still speechless.

"Well, Mother." Reggie snapped a canapé from a passing tray. "See? He's not some gutter rat from the wilds of Canada."

Her mother shot Reggie a dark look, her old composure returning and the ice resettling in her eyes. "I'll grant you he has some wonderful manners."

"His mother, as I recall, is from a family as prestigious as ours—though on a slightly more Canadian-sized scale." She popped the canapé in her mouth and chewed. She knew she should be finding Vaughan. Last she'd seen he was with a few school chums on the roof nodding to his waning bachelorhood with a case of Cuban cigars.

"He's handsome all right. If you like that dark complexion."

"Even you have a dark complexion under these lights," Reggie said, ignoring the condescension.

"Quite the smile on that one. He's a charmer, Reggie. You never mentioned that."

"Well, you didn't want to hear anything about him." Her mind was associating *Hamish* and *charmer* in the same sentence. She'd always identified a kind of charm in him, but it was far from the type lauded by her mother's usual set.

"That smile." Her mother was still at it. To Reggie's infinite amusement.

"Like a lightbulb."

"Still, Regina. No matter who his father is or what his class standing was. He is an Italian."

"I don't fancy the way you say that, Mother. I don't fancy—"

"And he shares lodgings with a Jew."

"I don't fancy the way you say that either." Reggie pursed her lips. "You've a pretty small world, don't you, Mother? Well, mine has expanded. And we had a deal. A deal that I am honoring even having this stupid party in the first place."

"I'll have your father fetch Vaughan," her mother said, turning. "It's ill form for him not to be on your arm receiving your guests. Don't be seen with DeLuca too often."

"He's my friend and associate."

"I don't care if he's Clark Gable. This is a night for our closest friends and family to become accustomed to you as a set."

"We sound like golf clubs."

"And keep your snide remarks to yourself, young lady. I never thought I would say this, but your young Italian friend could teach you a thing or two about common manners."

CHAPTER 16

Hamish saw Vaughan for the first time that evening with his arm looped around Dirk Foster's shoulders.

"DeLuca!" he said, interrupting a sentence wherein he was chiding Dirk for missing the first quarter of the party.

The confidence Hamish had conjured for his meeting with Reggie's parents dissolved.

Hamish adjusted his bow tie. He knew Vaughan was as genuine as Dirk was falsely sincere.

"Always last-minute business. Hard to find assistance," Dirk said. At his elbow was someone too familiar to Hamish.

"I can imagine. Especially in your line of work." Hamish kept his voice in check as best he could as his eyes moved between Foster and Bricker. Nevertheless, it rippled a little when he said, "Mr. Bricker. I wasn't expecting to see you."

Vaughan broke the tension with a laugh. "Right? I keep telling him to screw his head on straight. Life's too short to take things so seriously." Vaughan looked to Bricker. "And to let me know when a friend will be arriving unannounced to my party."

Dirk started to say something just as Vaughan tightened his grip on his friend's shoulder. "Tonight we are leaving our separate politics at home. You're *finally* here—you can come and help toast me and my beautiful new fiancée." Vaughan gave Hamish a polite smile.

It didn't help that Vaughan was such a decent fellow. More than making up for his tardy friends, Foster and Bricker. Hamish watched Vaughan's broad frame and rower's shoulders turn in the direction of Reggie and her parents. Bricker was there, too, combing his gelled hair back.

"Night off from handing out garbage in Charlestown?" Hamish said.

If there had been some underlying tension, some conflict or adversity, maybe he would be able to feel that Vaughan was an opponent, rather than a nice man from Reggie's past who, through no fault of his own, was getting everything Hamish wanted. He couldn't blame Vaughan for loving her (it was as natural to Hamish as breathing). He couldn't fault Vaughan for where he was born and his family's proximity to Reggie growing up, nor their status.

Speeches were starting, after which there would be dancing. The chamber quartet was replaced with a band of Vaughan's choosing: its leader a Harvard alumnus like Vaughan and most of his circle. The older set would move to another more private room in the hotel for brandy and civilized conversation, and the young people could rip up the dance floor.

Hamish wasn't sure how long Reggie expected him to stay.

Soon the emcee, a man Hamish didn't recognize but who seemed to have a lot of inside jokes that sparked Vaughan Vanderlaan's deep laugh, took to a small podium and lifted his champagne glass.

Hamish studied Reggie, standing to the side of the makeshift podium and stage, staring at her own glass: the bubbles caught the spotlights, as did the sparkle of her elaborate diamond ring.

Hamish watched Reggie through a line of speeches, more from Vaughan's acquaintances than Reggie's. It seemed that those who did speak about her—a few young women Hamish had never seen before and didn't recall Reggie mentioning—spoke in broad strokes. Nothing that painted an intimate portrait. Nothing that conjured the details of the Reggie he knew by heart. Like the Gershwin song: the way she sipped her tea and held her knife, her raucous singing and the way the sun caught just a bit of light in her brown hair in the summertime. These people didn't know Reggie at all. Just the shell.

When it came to Vaughan, it was guffaws and back slaps and best wishes at securing a pretty girl from a grand family.

Hamish kept near the door; it was slightly open to let in fresh air from the hallway. He raised his glass with everyone at the end of each speech. And he genuinely wanted her to be happy. But it was clear to him (so clear he wondered how the rest of the people at the party couldn't so plainly see it) that she wasn't happy. She was swimming through a tight current.

Luckily, no one gave Dirk the platform. Hamish wasn't sure his pasted-on pleasantry could survive that. He had promised a few women a dance or two after the speeches, and he thought at the very least it would feel good to be out on the floor, moving fluidly to what he was certain, given the caliber of the event, was a good band.

Rippling applause at the end of another toast kept Hamish from hearing a voice beside him. He turned to see one of the hotel staff looking up at him. "Are you Mr. DeLuca?" he repeated. "The lady over there said she thought you might be."

"Yes."

"I have an urgent message, sir. If you'll come with me."

Hamish's heart thudded. He nodded silently and followed the man out to the front lobby.

"Ah. Mr. DeLuca? A young woman here to see you." The concierge nodded in the direction of the door where Mrs. Leoni's daughter stood wringing her hands.

Her mother. Hamish shook a little and closed the three strides between them. "Rosa. What's the matter?"

"Hamish, I am so sorry to . . ." She sniffed.

"It doesn't matter. Tell me what's wrong. Is it your mother . . . Is it . . . ?"

Rosa shook her head. "Hamish"—and until the moment he died he would never forget how the next part of the sentence punched him in the gut—"it's Nathaniel."

⎯⎰⎯

Hamish didn't care if it was Reggie's sham of an engagement party. And he certainly didn't care that Rosa tugged at his sleeve. His shaking fingers put a bill in her hand—the only money he had on him—then he turned and dashed up the flight of stairs to the party. He frantically moved through the guests until he found Reggie, affixed to Vaughan's arm. Rosa said Nate was still at the office being attended to, and Hamish meant to get there as quickly as he could.

"Reggie, we have to go." His voice was hard to find and, once found, skipped out like a stone on a choppy ocean. He tugged at her arm.

She swerved to face him. "Hamish." Her voice was an emphatic whisper. "I'm sort of in the—"

"Reggie . . ." He gulped a breath, but his voice cracked anyway. "It's Nate."

Reggie dropped Vaughan's arm. "I have to go, Vaughan. It's Nathaniel."

Vaughan swerved to her and excused himself from his conversation. "Is it serious?"

He looked to Hamish.

"He didn't . . . There was . . . Yes, it's serious." Hamish nodded. "Rosa came." Hamish's hand was shaking fiercely now and he tucked two fingers beneath his suspender. "He might . . ." Hamish couldn't finish the sentence, though the look Reggie gave him told him she understood everything.

"I'm sorry, Vaughan," Reggie said.

"Reg, what will I say?"

Reggie sniffed and straightened her shoulders, then stopped trying. "I don't care, Vaughan. Make something up."

"Are you sure that Hamish can't look after this himself? Until . . ." Vaughan's voice was soft.

"Look after *this*?" Reggie spat. "*This* is Nathaniel. So, no. Hamish cannot look after *this*. It's Nate . . ." Saying his name set off her waterworks and wrenched Hamish's heart even further.

"Come on." Reggie gripped Hamish's hand and the two of them moved at rocket speed out of the party, without looking at or acknowledging any of the people who tried to catch Regina's attention in their wake.

⁎

"We'll cycle faster than a car would take us," Hamish said resolutely. Reggie agreed, thinking of the after-theater traffic from School Street and the night just beginning to fill Scollay Square. He collected his bicycle from a doorman and soon she was in her familiar position on the handlebars, Hamish pushing off. She saw his right hand was gripping the handlebar with white-knuckled intensity to squeeze away the tremor.

Her heart was a hundred types of shattered, and she blinked back the tears that were trickling at odd angles on account of the bike's velocity and the pressure of the breeze. Though she knew her extra weight added to the strenuous task of pedaling them at the pace Hamish was moving, she couldn't hear his breathing. Or anything. He was completely silent. She knew that he was as traumatized by the news as she was. She could see it in his eyes: frantic and sad. The last time she had seen the same emotion was when Luca was taken away by the police the night he was detained for a murder in his club.

Of course they drew attention. A woman wearing a dress like hers, its skirt now possessed of a jagged slit from her less than graceful attempt to keep her feet stable and fastened above the spokes. She wasn't interested in the catcalls. She barely heard them after the first inspired her to look upward. Reggie . . . well, Reggie wasn't sure what she would do. It was too unfathomable. She didn't care a fig anymore for the high social world she had just come from.

Finally, after a lifetime—the familiar route seeming to take hours longer than usual—they disembarked at the North End. Reggie hopped off the handlebars with an ease that had taken months of steady practice. Hamish quickly leaned the bike against the side of the office, in the slight space that separated the building from the Revere House. She followed him through the front door and up the stairs to the second floor where police officers were still looking in and around the circumference of Nate's office. Reggie reached ahead and gripped Hamish's hand. She could tell herself it was to desist its uncontrollable shaking, or she could accept it for what it really was: an instant and potent need for a connection that would set her at ease.

"You can't be up here," an officer said from the top of the staircase.

"We need to know what happened," Reggie said. "We heard that Mr. Reis—" She swallowed. "We occupy the office just next door and he's a dear . . . dear . . ."

"Is he dead?" Hamish asked.

"Do I look like a doctor?"

Reggie's voice surged with anger. "Excuse me. We are gravely concerned and were called here urgently. We want to ensure that our friend is alive and well."

Reid stepped out from Nate's office. "Not sure if he's well, but he's alive."

"H-how did you find him?" Hamish asked.

"He must have called Mrs. Leoni. She called us."

"Maybe we should have gone straight to the hospital," Reggie whispered to Hamish.

"They might not let us in anyway." Hamish turned back to Reid. "Has someone notified his family?"

"I did."

"Thank you." Better Reid than the other surly officer who was impatiently tapping his shoe. Hamish straightened his shoulders and brushed gently past Reggie, ascending the final step to the second floor in a direct line to Nate's open door. "We'll take a look now."

The officer they first encountered stood strong. "I don't know . . ."

"I swear to you we work in this building. We are private investigators and Nate is a dear friend!" Reggie pleaded. "Reid?"

"I'll vouch for them," Reid said. "Come on, they're not going to touch anything. Are you?"

"No. If anything, I can help," Hamish said, tripping only slightly over his consonants. "I could see if anything is missing."

The officer finally consented with a murmur that suggested it was against his better judgment.

Reggie didn't even realize she was holding tightly to Hamish's arm until he disengaged himself to flick the light switch. Then he took an infinitesimal step back in invitation for her to hold tightly again. She gripped his arm and pressed close, their sides touching, the light of Nate's office catching the glimmer of her ring. She scrunched her nose and willed away the events of the night up to when she left with Hamish. Vaughan probably had to sweet-talk his way out of the horror of his absent fiancée.

A muttered under-his-breath Italian word from Hamish didn't need translation. That's when Reggie saw it. A streak of blood. Nate's. In the corner by the desk. Reggie shivered and squeezed Hamish's arm.

"Oh, Hamish."

He was a study in attempted calm. She could make out his Adam's apple bobbing in the slight light spilling from the hallway.

Hamish's fingers were under his suspender. He had left his fancy coat with his bicycle and rolled up his sleeves. His bow tie was a relaxed comma around his neck. All of the sparkle and attention of the night was gone. "I bet it was Bricker. I bet it was. He was late to the engagement party. Why he was invited at all is beyond me." Hamish's blue eyes flashed black. "Why would you let your fiancé let that man into your party?"

"Don't take your anger out on me," Reggie said gently. "Nate has been secretive lately. You've said so yourself. Who knows what enemies he makes just from doing his best every day?"

"Do you have a handkerchief?" he asked Reggie.

She reached into her small purse and passed it to him. He unfolded the expensive silk and used it to open a few desk drawers. Lift a few files.

"We have to get going," the officer said from the doorway. Reggie had forgotten he was there. "So I can't chaperone this much longer. Have you seen what you need to see?"

"Was anyone here when you were called in?" Hamish asked, nearing the door.

"Just the lady from across the square."

"That's where we're going next," Hamish said to Reggie as they sidled past the officers to the staircase.

There was something grim about the night that contrasted the bustle and light Reggie loved of the North Square. It was as if the street was an imposter. Shaded with unfamiliar tones and colors and a sound that was worse than no sound at all. Rather the sound of a place trying to be quiet. She followed Hamish, her heels catching in the cobblestones.

Mrs. Leoni's sign read Closed and the flower stands that stood sentry on either side of her open door during the day were gone. But the lights burned low through the windows. Hamish rapped three times and she appeared.

She reached up on her toes and pulled Hamish's head down, one hand on either side of his face. She kissed him on each cheek before drawing him into a brief hug. Then she turned to Reggie and performed the same.

"You look very beautiful," she said to Reggie in Italian.

"My engagement party." Reggie smiled. Had she told Mrs. Leoni she was engaged? She hadn't exactly been yelling it from the rooftops.

Mrs. Leoni looked puzzled and then swiftly looked to Hamish. Then back to Reggie, tugging her inside.

"Rosa has just gone to bed. Thank you for seeing to her safety, Hamish. You must come and I will make tea."

"We don't have time for tea, Mrs. Leoni. We were just at the office where Nathaniel . . ." He didn't finish the sentence. Mrs. Leoni's face crumpled.

"He is such a nice boy. Nathaniel." She muttered in Italian. Crossed herself, then pulled her arms tightly around her ample chest.

"He called you. When it . . . when it happened?" Reggie said, shifting her weight to the other uncomfortable foot.

Mrs. Leoni nodded. "He was here so late. I thought it was late. I saw a second-floor light on in the office as I was bringing the plants in."

"Had anyone been around today? A stranger? Someone unusual? Maybe watching the office."

Mrs. Leoni shook her head. "I should pay better attention."

"No. No," said Hamish. "Not your fault."

"I did see that baseball player."

Hamish and Reggie startled straight. "Which player?"

"Mr. Parker. I knew his face from the papers."

Hamish went far away for a moment. His blue eyes staring at nothing, his right hand slowly shaking. Reggie could hear his heartbeat from where she stood.

"Thank you, Mrs. Leoni." Hamish squeezed her shoulder. "But Reggie and I have to go to the hospital and see how Nate is doing."

Mrs. Leoni nodded then turned in the direction of her display counters. Empty. She prided herself on making each delicacy fresh for every morning. Reggie shuddered to imagine what time the lady was up in the morning. "You wait here."

She disappeared despite Hamish and Reggie's protests and returned with a white box. "Cannoli. I know Nathaniel is your friend. And I will pray he will be all right."

She pressed her hand into Reggie's, and they let themselves out to the sound of Mrs. Leoni clicking the door shut.

⁕

Hamish sat silently next to Reggie on the hospital steps. Something in Nate's office was off. It wasn't something Hamish could pinpoint beyond instinct. But it wasn't because of whoever attacked Nate. Nate's office was almost unrecognizable to those who knew him best. First, the desk was a mess of papers. Second, the bookshelf was almost empty. Hamish assumed most of its contents had been moved with the work that seemed to pile higher and higher around their flat. The office was just a noiseless space now. Hamish scratched the back of his neck. He should have been five steps ahead of this. Should have anticipated disaster. He *knew* something was wrong. Why would he leave Nate alone? Now Errol? Had Errol gone to the office looking for them and found himself in an altercation with Nate? It didn't make sense.

"A penny for your thoughts? All the pennies? Truly, Hamish, if you could see your face."

"Why was Errol in the North End?"

"He is renting that property from Kelly. When all of the construction is complete and the development is built. He could have been here on business for that. Was there a baseball game tonight?"

Hamish shook his head. "No. Maybe he was looking for us."

"You don't think he has something to do with Nate?"

Hamish wiped his face with his sleeve. It was hot all of a sudden. Everything felt small and close. He ignored the mounting pain in his chest and the heartbeat that thudded like an anvil. "No. Unless he was provoked unintentionally? I mean, he just lost his nephew. He's been the victim of pranks. Maybe he broke." But even as the words left his mouth, he realized how ridiculous they sounded.

"I don't believe that. You're right. Errol wouldn't attack Nate. There was blood. There . . ." Reggie reached to touch her absent *Spira, Spera* necklace and Hamish followed the gesture to her collarbone. "My parents will be furious." Reggie now picked at the ripped satin of her dress, which floated around her on the steps outside the hospital.

They hadn't been permitted to see Nate, who was in serious but somewhat stable condition. They weren't family. Not to the hospital staff. Reggie started into a diatribe about what constituted family in the first place but ended up trailing off when she didn't get a rise—or even a look—from Hamish's direction.

"Nothing was as important as Nate."

"Funny." Reggie mulled a moment.

"What?"

"When I first met you, you would have apologized. Even if I knew that in your soul you didn't mean it."

"Nate is more important than any party."

"Still . . ." Reggie smoothed her skirt again. It was beyond salvageable.

Hamish studied a scuff on his shoes. Had it only been a few hours since he had pedaled over after stealing some of Nate's pomade, determined to put forth the best impression he could? It seemed like several lifetimes or several chapters of a long book.

"You were brilliant with my parents tonight, Hamish."

"You sound surprised."

"I have never seen you like that. I've heard your lawyer voice." She nudged him with her elbow. "But you charmed them. My mother was speechless—and my mother is never speechless."

Hamish knew it was reckless, but he looked at her anyway, just as she was raising her chin and their eyes met. Hers were tired, the carefully applied makeup smudged. "I knew how important it was to you," he said.

"I saw Luca's handwriting."

"What?"

"On the paper Reid retrieved from Toby's pocket. Is he back?"

Hamish shook his head. "I don't know."

"But if he is back, you'd tell me, right?" Her eyes were round and sheened with almost-tears, searching his face.

"You can't choose your family," he said sharply.

Reggie grabbed his hand. "Yes, you can."

─ः/─

Hamish turned the key and stepped into the dense quiet. He flipped on the light and blinked away the scene of Nate's office, the smell of Reggie's hair under his chin as she tugged hard at his sleeve, the stiff opulence of the whiskey he'd sampled with Reggie's father contrasting the devastation of the rest of the night and the realization that she had left with him. She could have asked him to report later and clung to Vaughan's arm and social propriety.

The keys jangled in his shaking right hand, so he tossed them on the table in the front room. He stared a moment into the empty fire grate. It had to be Bricker, of course. Or one of his men. Or maybe even Dirk Foster . . . Hamish scrubbed his neck. But Dirk was at the party. He saw him. His mind rifled through the evening. But they had arrived late, hadn't they?

Hamish pinched his nose as if to contain the many thoughts spiraling in several directions and dropped onto the sofa and angrily swatted a pile of papers Nate had left there; they fanned on the floor. Hamish nudged at one with his shoe. Nate had never been untidy—until recently. Bringing everything from the office home every night as if the building might go up in flames and leave him without anything. Maybe he was worried it would.

Hamish leaned down and gently picked up the papers. He flicked his eyes over them, recognizing a few names but not many. Feeling guilty for prying into Nate's business. Besides, as much as he hated to admit it to himself, there was a pretty good chance Nate's attack had nothing at all to do with business.

The room buzzed with a quiet that rang in his ears. He was so used to coming home to a light in the sitting room or the rustle of mug and kettle in the kitchen. The latter he could remedy. He filled the kettle and put it on the stove. Then he wiped the crumbs from the table. A half loaf of bread sat open on a wooden cutting board. Nate must have been in a hurry. But he also must have been home between the time Hamish saw him at the office and the attack: the bread hadn't been there earlier.

He opened the Frigidaire in pursuit of the last of the morning's milk. As he closed the door, his eyes settled on their most recent game of battleship. Nate affixed them proudly around the house.

"*We will learn and be better.*" They saved all of them.

Hamish ripped it from the icebox and tore it up. "Stupid game!" It was just another reminder of how much Nate had changed. No more chess. Battleship. Little dots instead of *x*'s. Papers in the hallway and in the living room and all over. He was too exhausted to mount the stairs and perform his usual nighttime routine. He found a leaflet for one of Nate's neighborhood safety meetings. Sometimes he came up with excuses to miss them. Now he thought he would give anything to listen to Nate's terrible puns and reminders for people to lock their doors and keep their trash bins roped so that rats and critters didn't multiply in their housing units.

He fell backward on the lumpy sofa, ripped his bow tie completely off, undid another two buttons of his shirt, and threw his arm over his eyes, hoping the extra darkness would speed what he prayed was a dreamless, imageless, Nate-less sleep.

He awoke to the sound of the telephone, sat up, and hoped it was about Nate.

"Hello!" he said urgently.

"Hamish! Are you all right? Is Miss Van Buren?"

Hamish blinked and ran his hand over his face. "Dad? Yes. Why? . . . Oh. Something in the papers there already?"

"A violent attack at your North End office. MacDonald, you remember him? From the *Herald*? He rang when you were here at Christmas. Anyway, he rang over. He got it and nearly went mad when he saw the address. Not as mad as I did."

"It was a friend of mine." Hamish barely kept his voice intact.

"Does this have anything to do with the pamphlets that Miss Van Buren rang me about?"

That woke him up. "Reggie called you?"

"She had me look into some pamphlets from the Christian Patriots. They were requisitioned here by a D. Foster."

"No. Not exactly."

"She also asked if I had heard from Luca." There was a long pause. A significant pause. A pause that made the chiming grandfather clock in the hallway take on the solemnity of a death knell. "Have you heard from Luca?"

Hamish reached for his glasses and slid them on his nose. He knew he wouldn't get back to sleep now. "You always told me that a story kept in confidence required a measure of grace."

"Are you quoting me to evade talking about your cousin?"

"You also told me that not everyone's story is ours to tell."

"I taught you too well, it would seem."

"I appreciate your concern."

"And I appreciate not having to find out from the newspapers that my only son was shot in an altercation involving his cousin and—"

"Three years." Hamish pinched his nose. "It's been almost three years and you knew the whole time and you are *just* talking about it now." His dad and he had crossed mountains when it came to Hamish's episodes of panic, his hiding his hand behind his back in intense moments, his ironing out his stutter, and yet . . .

"A story kept in confidence requires a measure of grace."

Hamish let out a sound that hovered between a frustrated growl and a submissive yelp. "I give up."

"Just tell me if you hear from Luca."

Hamish said good-bye without promising anything. His heartbeat was thrumming and beads of sweat were forming at his hairline. Both familiar sensations that ebbed on the shore of a familiar episode.

But why shouldn't he panic?

Someone *had* to be accountable for Nate. For the terrible views in the Christian Patriots pamphlets. For men like Bricker! Pete Kelly and his obvious black market. Errol Parker was subjected to inhumane pranks, and Dirk Foster was building his own house of cards that would only make those around him topple. And on top of it the city called Toby's death an accident. A punch in the head. No, someone had to be accountable—it was how the world turned and how justice was served. Without accountability there was nothing. The war at home would last forever . . . and the people responsible for very possibly maiming his best friend would be free. He could just imagine Nate sliding back into the office and refusing to give up the name of his attacker out of some sense of forgiveness and reparation.

Hamish focused on his sanctuary. Like Quasimodo. Here he could be himself. He could speak in his second language and sip espresso and taste Mrs. Leoni's lemon cannoli as the bells clanged and the world was fresh and new. People knew him here, sure, but just as Hamish DeLuca, the kid with a penchant for contracts and legal matters. Nothing of the moon-shaped scars on his hands or his parents' expectations followed him over the stones or draped from the tenement-style houses. He didn't want anyone to take away his freedom.

Through the open slice of window, a dog barked. A siren moaned. Familiar sounds. He gulped through a few breaths then snatched at a thought buzzing at the back of his brain. Hamish opened his sock drawer and reached under a flap of fake wood, withdrawing the scrap of paper bearing Luca's number, worn from being in his pocket. The number was imprinted in his brain, but it gave his long fingers something to do.

Luca's writing was on a manifest found in a dead kid's pocket, and Luca's thumbprint was all over the new initiatives for shipping munitions on the same manifest.

But Hamish was just a stuttering kid on a bike.

A stuttering kid who at this moment felt his heartbeat mounting and an all-too-familiar pang in his chest. The walls seemed closer and the room drained of air. The same way it felt when Dr. Gillies told him he wouldn't be able to fight for his country.

"When men come back from war, they feel unwhole. It takes the people around them so they can feel whole. I think of you as one of those men, Hamish. You sit there and there is a part of you that is not whole. A part that is broken. A space that you can fill with friends and family. People who truly appreciate and care for you. You are not any

different than patients who have an injury or a missing limb. There is a doctor here in the city who believes we should be doing a better job at deciding what young men we send over—and then we might be able to welcome them home on the other side ready to be citizens again. Look at you. You're—"

"Uneven? H-hopeless?"

"Shaky." Dr. Gillies lifted Hamish's arm. "Look. You can't fire a gun. Or call an order." He gently released his grip. "Men over there cave under pressure. I saw it dozens of times in my unit. But I have the opportunity to stop you. Your eyesight isn't perfect."

"But you would have signed me off."

"I am not just thinking of you, Hamish. I'm thinking of the other men in your unit. I'm saving their lives as well as your own. You're not fit."

Not fit. Hopeless. So if he was so hopeless, why shouldn't he call Luca? Choose a different side. Who would fight for Toby? Who would stop Bricker? The police wouldn't. Reid had no jurisdiction. Hamish and Reggie only played at detective. But Hamish had a lifeline. Luca inspired great loyalty. But he also gave it. To Hamish.

Hamish let his hand flop to his side. Why count his heartbeat? It was already thrumming at several times its natural pace. He splayed his palm on his chest: not to count but to feel. The breaths were more painful now: sharp and stabbing. He swallowed reason away and logic too. In moments like these he could focus on little. He sometimes couldn't get past his own name.

Tonight was different. It linked his current panic to the past in a chain tightening around him. He couldn't patch up everything: the world, his inability to enlist, Reggie, Nate . . .

Nate. His brain snagged on that name over and over. (Later, Hamish would rationally work through other solutions. His brain would easily conjure a list of steps taken again and again, never once landing on the option that found him reaching for the telephone.)

A few ticks. Static. Finally, the operator patched him through. On the other end, a voice he hadn't heard in almost two years.

"Hello."

"One drop of wine is enough to redden an entire glass of water." He had been playing the quote in his head over the ripple of silence. He hadn't expected he would say it aloud.

"Interesting greeting, Cicero," his cousin said drily. "Am I correct in assuming it is something from *The Hunchback of Notre-Dame*?"

"Luca, I need your help." If he could fix *one* thing, then maybe everything else would domino into place.

The voice on the other end was quiet, then said softly, "Are you in trouble?"

Luca sounded so far. But Hamish knew he was close. The Parker House Hotel. A man who registered under the name Hult. None of it mattered now. "I'm not in trouble. But my friend Nate is." Silence. Hamish waited several beats. Then said with urgency, "Luca, someone almost killed Nate. In his office. He's in the hospital."

Luca exhaled, then said gravely, "Tell me everything, Cicero. I'll take care of it. See? I knew that number would serve you well someday."

CHAPTER 17

Reggie was surrounded by balled sheets of paper. She was trying—and failing miserably—to write three letters at the same time. One (and most importantly) to Nate's bubbe expressing her condolences. Another to Vaughan's parents attempting to explain why she committed the unpardonable sin of ruining their engagement party by running off on her groom-to-be. And the third to her own parents. Or maybe she should just call. Or maybe she should write because words on a page meant she would buy some time with the distance and the post before they could send their response. Then again, they could telegraph their response. *Bite the bullet, Regina!*

Hamish was at his desk mapping out something and mumbling about Hugo's "point of intersection": another obscure *Notre-Dame* mention. Really, it was almost a perfectly normal day.

She reached for the telephone when it clanged. Listened. Inspector Reid.

"Bricker's dead!" Reggie let the phone fall without clicking it on the receiver. She turned to Hamish.

"H-how did he die?"

"He was found outside a pub in Charlestown. Hamish, do you need a glass of water? You didn't like the man and now you look like you're about to fall over." His fingers were underneath his brace. Her initial diagnosis was shock. "You said yourself he had it coming."

Hamish nodded before the words came out. "I didn't want him to die."

"I know that. He had a lot of enemies. Reid said it looks like it was a fight. He probably let his mouth run off." She paused. "Guess we can cross off one suspect for Toby's murder. One *living* suspect. Oh! That sounded rather cold, didn't it. My mother would remind me that he was someone's son, too, and . . . Hamish! Heavens! Are you all right?"

Hamish blinked several times quickly and his breath caught in his chest. Reggie was accustomed to Hamish's bouts of anxiety, but never used to them. But she was used to Hamish. Which is why his reaction pricked at her.

"You know something."

"I . . ."

"You're not the only person who can tell when they're being lied to."

"I know that."

"So tell me."

"I called Luca."

It was Reggie's turn to fall back. "You what?"

"I called Luca last night. I went home, Reg, and it was so empty. And I couldn't figure anything out and I called Luca and told him what happened. That Nate was hurt. What was happening. I told him everything."

"How did you even get his phone number?" She held her hand over her chest.

"Philip. His driver? You remember him. He slid me his number ages ago. Said Luca was looking out for me."

Reggie blinked at the face she thought she knew: thoughtfully etched contours and lines, bright blue eyes and slightly longish nose. Dear to her in the way no other face in the world was. "The Hamish DeLuca I know wouldn't call in a hit from his cousin."

"A hit? It wasn't like that. It was . . ."

Hamish's right hand was uncontrollable and every word came choppily like a boat on mounting waves. But she couldn't recall being that angry before. Not after Vaughan's ill-timed proposal at her parents' garden party, not even to this extent during her employment with Luca Valari. But now. She saw red. The nerves in her arms tingled and tightened.

"I wanted him to get one of his men . . . his people to threaten him. To show Bricker he wasn't invincible. That he couldn't get away with terrorizing half of the city with his stupid views. That even Dirk Foster couldn't protect him. I told him not to go too far."

"You couldn't," she seethed, jabbing her index finger into his chest. "Because *you're* Hamish DeLuca and you always believe in right over wrong." She shook her head. "You didn't do it."

"I did, Reggie. I called Luca." He tried stoicism, but she saw something flicker in his eyes: an uncertainty taking residence there. He gulped a breath and sank forward against the desk.

Reggie slammed her palm down on the desk, jostling the radio, telephone, and typewriter. "Do you really think that Luca could solve anything? Bricker is dead! Did we really need another murder? We would already know our first suspect!"

"Luca promised me he wouldn't kill anyone. Those weren't his words. But the gist was there. We're partners, Reggie. You should support me on this."

"I can't believe you thought this was the answer. You knew what Luca would do!" She knew her voice sounded shrill; it certainly hurt to speak. "He left you. Shot and bleeding on the floor of his stupid club. Do *not* give me that look! I had to stay and answer the questions and move that horrible gun into your hand. You think he cares one iota about helping your friend? Evening a score is more like it. That's not the kind of loyalty you want, Hamish. And it's not the kind of loyalty Nate would want."

"I know there must be more to this, because Luca said he wouldn't go too far."

"Hamish! Luca doesn't know how to do anything *but* go too far. He feels he owes you because of what happened at the Flamingo. You know he would overcompensate for his own guilt. The first request his beloved little cousin has asked of him and Luca will..." Reggie spread her hands to finish the sentence. "I didn't think it could get any worse, and there you are—making it worse."

"I was going mad, Reggie. Someone has to be accountable for Nate. No one is even close to solving what happened to Toby, and Nate is our friend. You do what you can for your friends."

"I met him first," she sobbed. "Before you! He was the first true friend I made outside of my stupid family. He gave me a lifeline here in Boston. He's my friend too. And my heart is broken and now—you broke it even more."

She blinked a film of tears from her eyes and caught his own. Hamish was breathing heavily and he blinked several times at her, probably trying to see through his own tears. They stared silently a moment, Reggie almost unable to keep their eyes locked, watching the hurt behind his. How could she love him so much and hate what he did so passionately at the same time?

"I'm sorry Reggie," Hamish said unevenly. "I am sorry that you don't see why I felt I had to do this, but since I did, I guess we are at an impasse."

"Where is Luca, Hamish?"

"I don't know."

"Yes, you do. And our seeing Kent was *not* an accident. He wasn't some ghost. *That* past has followed us here. All along I thought that perhaps we were solving Errol's mystery, when really you have just dragged us into Luca's domain again!"

"If he were here, he would come and see me! He wouldn't

send Phil, who came to me and gave me his number and said Luca is looking out for me!"

"Luca only looks out for himself! Hamish! You are *better* than your cousin! I will not follow you into his world. Getting out of his world got you shot!"

"Reg…"

"You might think, Hamish, that your biggest limitation is the fact that sometimes your heartbeat speeds up and sometimes you take a moment to catch your breath. It's not. It's him."

"I had to do something before it was too late."

"It's already too late."

Reggie wanted to scream. Of course, Van Burens did *not* scream. Van Burens weathered everything with a calm demeanor. She twisted the ring on her finger and took a breath and looked at the stranger who had suddenly stepped into the man she saw before her. And her heart clutched tightly and threatened to splice and splinter. *How can I possibly weather the future I am stepping into if you are not my constant?* her heart shouted. The world was shifting on its axis. Nate, of course. Hamish … *Her* Hamish. She cocked her head and looked at him so intently she wondered if she could stare completely through him. Her head told her that he was broken and worried and had acted impulsively. Kind Hamish with his almost-smile and big blue eyes. Hadn't she acted impulsively when she slapped Vaughan and ran away from home? But her impulsive actions wouldn't see violent results. She had no doubt that Luca would take things to the extreme. Luca lived in extremes. She couldn't let Hamish hover under his cousin's shadow.

Reggie's heartbeat mounted and she wondered if in this moment she was finally understanding what rippled through Hamish every day of his life. "I didn't recognize you, Hamish. Not when you called your cousin. I didn't recognize the Hamish who would do that—for whatever reason." His eyes met hers.

She wavered a moment, reaching out, clutching the desk to keep steady. "And I hate that." Her voice was low. "It frightens me."

"We have a case to solve."

"Hamish, you might be dragging us into something that we cannot get out of. Not just one case. Not just a mystery here and there with your human empathy and my gumption. It's *Luca*!"

"Reggie, there is a very, very good chance Bricker was responsible for Toby's death. He—he's left-handed! He hated the kid! He hates Parker! In which case I did nothing more than jump-start justice."

Reggie wiped her hand over her face. "Are you listening to yourself?"

"I am sounding pretty rational."

"I repeat: you're not the only one who can tell when someone is lying."

"Perhaps not. Wish I could have been there when you accepted Vaughan Vanderlaan's proposal!"

Reggie shook her head vehemently. "No. No. I won't let this continue. Because the Hamish DeLuca I know doesn't even possess that tone of voice. Would never *think* of saying things like that. Would never cut or hurt with words. You need to go back to being the Hamish DeLuca that *I* need. And if that means ending this conversation, then—"

"Is that what these three years have been to you, Regina? Me being the Hamish that *you* need? Do I just live and breathe and act for *you* while you go and slide another man's ring on your finger?"

Hamish's own long fingers were a perfect triangle around a pencil where he was working through a diagram tying the tapestry of the spring and summer together.

"I didn't mean it like that." Reggie coaxed her voice through the black tunnel it seemed to be happy lodging in.

They fell apart a moment. Then together when Reggie peered over the blotter on his desk.

When Reggie saw Dirk's name scrawled in Hamish's bold, slanted hand, the past snuck up and tapped her on the shoulder. Men with rower's shoulders and sun-kissed hair, the glisten of daylight on water, one young man teasing her for her freckles before Vaughan stepped in and stalled him.

"I don't think Dirk is capable of killing anyone," Reggie said.

"Is he left-handed?"

Reggie couldn't remember. Reid said that the driving blow was from the left side, but could Dirk be competent in strength from both sides? She knew he fenced and boxed. What might men of his station and training pull off in a moment? "I don't know..."

"Is he capable of truly hurting someone? Someone like Nate? Maybe you should ask Vaughan."

"Hamish!" Reggie said.

Hamish's pencil was over the diagram, eyes intense. He used his lawyer voice, free of any tremor or ripple, hands solidly stretched to balance his weight across the desk as he studied his notes, always more than what he thought he was.

"I think men like Dirk—at least from what I have seen—so take that for what it's worth—try to find a web. In this web, there are people who will lift them up. Dirk needs to have the upper hand."

"I suppose . . ." Reggie started a sentence she didn't know how to finish. Her mind was a flood of fancy cocktail parties and revelries after football skirmishes. Was she justifying Dirk? He was one of her own, wasn't he? And she *was* marrying Vaughan. Hamish and Reggie had sat in this office a thousand times before, but the four walls had never closed so tightly.

"Dirk could play the system," Hamish said plainly. There was an undercut tension in his voice, bubbling like a volcano to the surface. "And men like him are always looking for the next large paycheck, which means the people we work with are an easy target for the next Big Person strolling into the North End promising a cut."

The intensity pricked the dimple in his cheek. Maybe she had held him up too high, thinking he could be completely removed from mistakes. That he was always innocent. That he would never steer off the course she set for him. It was unfair. She hated when expectations were placed on her.

Parker was the missing piece. If it were sheer prejudice, that would make it a separate case altogether. Reggie blinked, inspected her manicure. "I know they're connected. I can read it in your eyes."

Hamish startled a moment, his breath sharp. "I don't know. Two men were left-handed. Bricker and Kelly."

Had she listened to too many serials? Had he read too many books? Were mysteries meant to be solved by two people with overactive imaginations?

Would Kelly kill a kid for a manifest? Didn't he have his own manifests? Black-market goods she spent far too long studying as icy water threatened to claim her whole?

The bells in the North Square chimed. Pealed from the Old North through the Prado over the space waiting to be filled by Dallin's statue. This was her world. But it seemed new nonetheless.

She kept a passive tone. "Dirk isn't the only one sounding off those Christian Patriots ideas. The first time Errol was here he mentioned it."

Reggie closed her eyes a moment. When she opened them, the office was the same. Not, as was her futile hope, a blank slate where Hamish had not walked in and looped his name and bad judgment with his cousin's.

She drifted into a long reverie, unaware that such a long stretch of time had passed until the bells from nearby St. Stephen's announced the hour.

Hamish's glasses were on top of black hair in need of a trim, his long fingers drumming the desk. She wasn't certain his fidgeting was anxiety; he could have just been deep in thought. Shouldn't she be able to decipher between the two at this point in their relationship?

"And does it surprise you that the coach favors Parker?" Hamish said.

"Favors? Tolerates."

"I mean clearly he is the best player on the team, but there has to be some difficulty in featuring a man of his color in a sport that is very old-fashioned in its ways. Treadwell. They did get in a fistfight."

"Do you think Winston is pretending when it comes to Errol? But how could he be? They're the best in the league."

"But you heard what Errol said. That there have been scouts. Maybe he holds it against him that he could leave and take his talent with him."

"And is he uncouth enough to shove a pig's heart in the man's locker?"

"If Luca taught us anything, it's that it is easy to find someone who can do work for you."

"How likely, Hamish, is it that one of the scouts from the Red Sox would take a chance on Errol? We're still too far behind."

It was almost like a game of tennis at her mother's country club. Back and forth and back and forth. Posture and poise. Remember your training.

"All I do know is that it is easy to have limited views." She remembered Dirk Foster at a fancy dinner during their first investigation involving the Flamingo Club. Dirk was prejudiced toward the unemployed and destitute. The same hardworking, down-on-their-luck people who funneled out of the temporary employment agency every day. Errol Parker had the color of his skin working against him. And Reggie was certain that would inspire far more vehement retaliation than men out of work.

"I need something happy," she said. "I'm going to Leoni's."

"Then I'm coming with you." He took a beat, watched her. She felt exposed under the study of his blue eyes. They weren't magnified as they had been behind his lenses, but somehow he was the microscope and she the specimen on the plate. It unnerved her and she twisted the ring on her finger. Which drew his attention downward a moment.

"Reggie, we have to work through this. I know you hate me for what I did. I hate myself. But I can't . . . I can't . . ." He stopped, swallowed, and she knew he was evening out his stutter, rolling his tongue in his mouth, attempting to keep it from tripping over what came next. It pricked at her. *She* was doing this to him, throwing him off. The tips of his ears were red, exposing his humiliation. He blinked several times and tapped under his brace. Reggie found a place on the wall just behind his left shoulder to focus on. His breathing was coming more quickly. "It's too strange here. With you . . . j-judging me like that."

"Something you said earlier. About a threat. Luca threatening Bricker. What if the threats toward Errol were something to do with his altercation . . . the one in the paper?"

The phone jangled. It was Reid again. Apologizing.

Reggie clicked off and looked at Hamish. "Reid thinks that perhaps we were missing something about Nate. That maybe he was helping the development at Kelly's place."

"That's ridiculous! Reggie!" Hamish had been sitting but was up again, out from his desk, standing, tapping a pencil against the side in an incessant rhythm. "The police cannot think that about Nate."

"I know it's ridiculous."

"But you saw him taking piles of paper home every night. He wasn't talking to me anymore—definitely wasn't talking to you."

"We know that, Hamish. I am not disagreeing with you. But it *looks* a certain way. Reid is giving us a notice. He was there the night you met Toby at the ball game."

"What motive would Nate have to kill a teenager!"

"You're shouting at me! I am just the messenger!"

"How can you stand there and even entertain these ideas?"

"I am not entertaining *anything*. I am just reciting what the police told me." She gestured to the phone.

"Reggie, I can't listen to this." Hamish's hands raked through each side of his hair, teasing the black waves up a little.

"This is a line of police questioning. We have to entertain it. Think like them as we continue to figure out everything that is happening. You already tried to take things into your own hands. Now we're two steps back because they're looking for a concrete reason that Bricker would attack Nate and then die."

"Because he was prejudiced! Because he had horrible views that would lead many people to violence!" Hamish slammed his hand on the side of the desk. The pencil broke in half with the force.

Reggie's breath caught in surprise. "You don't have to yell at me about it!"

"No . . . you have enough to worry about. Picking out a wedding dress. Nice veil. Cake testing."

"You're not being fair. Wish you had taken the phone call. You could have gotten angry with Reid and spared me. *He's* being helpful. He's telling us some things about our friend so that we can be aware. We should use this as an opportunity."

Hamish nodded under her glare. They stood off a moment silently, Reggie wondering if the city had changed him. She wanted Hamish to crawl out of his turtle shell, to stand up for himself. But she didn't recognize his tone or the darkness in his light blue eyes.

"I should go."

Reggie held up her wrist. "It's still lunchtime. What are you doing?"

His hand was shaking a little and he flexed his fingers. He noticed her watching him and tucked it in his pocket. "I need a w-walk."

"You're all right? Do you want me to come with you?"

"I'll be back."

He left the door open. She listened to his footfalls fade in the hallway. She retrieved her Journal of Independence from her top drawer.

She had boiled an egg and changed a lightbulb and stayed out after midnight. She had opened her own bank account and written a check, and she even owned property (well, *half* owned her property with Hamish in their office and bought with help from her father). But she knew there was a line somewhere. Impressed with pencil from many nights when the summer wind tousled the blinds and the starlight was a mural for the Bunker Hill Monument she could view from her open window.

Make Hamish happy. She wove her fingernail around it. That shy, stuttering Canadian kid who showed up with suave Luca Valari and was tossed into a life of betrayal and crime.

Reggie thought she could make him happy. He made *her* happy. That goodness about him and the innocent way he saw people and not their status or the figures attached to their names.

Reggie returned the journal to the desk. She worked the ring on her finger midway to the knuckle, then finally off for a moment, holding it to the light through the window. It was beautiful, sure. But her hand felt lighter without it. She studied the groove it had made from its near constant wear. She set it down on the desktop a moment, her hand moving toward the pendant at her neck. *Spira, Spera.*

"You need to make a decision, Reggie," she whispered amidst the familiar sounds funneling through the window, ticking the clock of her routine. Amidst the nagging anger that tied Hamish to his cousin. She picked up the ring and put it back on her finger, then opened the file of their case notes, tucked a curl behind her ear, and got back to the matter at hand.

No wonder Hugo idolized the architecture of Notre-Dame, the breadth and grandeur of Paris's buildings, the cornerstones of the city. For while the streets he loved ran rampant with the blood of a student revolution he witnessed every day in his pursuit of his favorite scenes, so did the city stand strong. Hamish thought there was no firmer foundation than the brick of the Old North, no sentinel that more anchored the North End—and, indeed, the whole of Boston proper—than its steeple. He couldn't think of it without thinking of Nate's ties to revolution.

Revolution. Familiar to Hugo too.

It was among the saints and monsters and stones that Quasimodo found the community saving him from the horrors of the outside world. And, for Hamish, the Old North Church signified a place of peace barred from the ugliness of the outside world. His nation's mounting war, a city that revered Revere while some of its residents targeted men like Errol Parker and Nate. For as long as there was the Old North Church, there was an immediate quiet.

The church was open to everyone during the day. A reprieve from daily life. He didn't need Hal, a church caretaker and long-time client of Nate's, for admittance. It was for everyone at this time of day. He didn't want to creep up to the top on the circular stairs that wound his heartbeat to a frantic pace and quickened his pulse. Sure, from up in the tower amidst the change-ringing bells (the same bells that had lived in Notre-Dame in Paris, or so Nate told him), he could see the entire city, its people colorful dots. He creaked the small door open and slid over on the slick wood, staring up at the arched windows and dripping chandeliers. His father told him that when he first arrived in Toronto from Italy, St. James Cathedral held the pieces of his heart that the back-breaking, knuckle-splitting work at the roundhouse threatened. The light he thought might be extinguished, the constant anxiety of learning a second language evaporated in the grand sanctuary in a pew over which bellowing organ pipes stood sentry high in their rafters.

It was Nate who told him that the same change-ringing bells in residence at Notre-Dame and in the Old North Church could also be found in Toronto at St. James. Hamish scrunched his eyes shut and recalled the latter's clear peal over King Street's foot and trolley traffic.

When he opened them, a shaft of sunlight had spread like an outstretched hand over the nave to the transept, setting the windows ablaze with sunlight. Hamish blinked three times, adjusted his shoulders, tucked his slightly trembling fingers into his palm, and *thought*. Sure, his brain could betray him when the anxiety that crept over its edges filled it with a million worries large and small. Worries uncontained and grand, imagined scenarios that had little root in reality but seemed to Hamish's vulnerable brain like a wave of a burdened certainty.

Hamish rubbed his temples.

Was Nate's secrecy because he felt guilty and responsible for what was happening in his neighborhood—housing touted to be affordable that was being carelessly constructed? Why would Hyatt and Price allow one of their top architects to align themselves with the project, even if in a roundabout way?

He wondered if it was sacrilegious to think about these things in God's house. His dad would tell him anything to do with justice for the least of these was God's business: in His house and everywhere.

Nate always said there were secrets that were his to keep. But he was always for the underdog. The North End Robin Hood who bartered services under the noses of the wealthy.

He had put off peeking behind the curtain of Nate's office since his hospitalization, even though he showed up at Nate's room every night and pulled a chair across the linoleum. Hamish kept his friend appraised of everything happening in the North

End: from the grocer's almanac to the rise in cannoli prices. The nurse often told Hamish that Nate was unconscious on account of his head injury and probably couldn't hear, but Hamish ignored her. The night of Nate's attack, Reid had done them the favor of taking their word that there was nothing of interest left at Nate's office. He wondered why Reid was so accommodating: first letting them into the office, then giving Reggie updates on the investigation. He scanned his brain and decided the officer fancied her. There was no other reason he would let them carry on the investigation.

Hamish looked down at the right hand resting on his knee. It was stable for the moment. He remembered how Nate withstood Bricker's words, calm and even. Not letting anyone see him rattled.

He left the church, standing to the side of the front door as a couple, smiling, strolled in.

Hamish assumed they were pursuing the history and not the silence.

Maybe both.

He ran into Rosa Leoni steps from the office.

"My friend took your advice and isn't moving to the new place." They had run into him in passing the week before, and Hamish worried he had been too hasty in his response, but apparently it had set in.

Hamish smiled. It was something he hoped to hear after telling her in no uncertain terms that she should stay clear away. "Good. Thanks for trusting me." He would make it his mission to ensure everyone knew what he did about Hyatt and Price's intended property.

"She's moving away, Hamish. Out of the North End. To Jamaica Plain."

"I'm sorry."

"There's nothing here. Nowhere for her to live." Rosa's eyes were wide and dewy looking up at him. "I told her that would change. That you and Nate would make it change."

"I don't know if I can make it change. Or Nate."

"Mother went to see him this morning. He just lies there. Doesn't say anything. She said the worst part is his eyes aren't *scintillante*. You know the way you look at Nate and he is always, always full of light?"

Scintillante. Sparkling.

"I will be by later. To check on him. He'll be all right, you know."

"Anyway, I wanted you to know that I appreciate your trying." She reached out and stole Hamish's hand. He startled at the sudden gesture. "You do so much for us. Mama is so fond of you. *I* am so fond of you."

Hamish squeezed Rosa's hand and offered her a half-moon smile. "Thanks, Rosa. That means a lot. Your mother really welcomed me to the city when I first moved here." Moved here. To the North End. To Nate. He was always at the office. Gave everything to the neighborhood. It was his livelihood, sure, but it was also his heartbeat.

"I was thinking maybe some night you might want to go dancing."

He thought about Nate and Mrs. Leoni: his teasing her that her kitchen wasn't kosher. Informing her that it was more than ingredients. She would need to have a rabbi bless the stove and the counters and the dishes and the flour and the sink.

"I . . . Look, Rosa. I have to get back to the office." He looked down at his wrist in a show of checking the time.

"You're not wearing a watch." Rosa laughed, but her black eyes shaded with disappointment.

"Ha! You're quick. I . . . I've got to go." He gently let go of her hand and jogged the rest of the way, past the Pierce-Hichborn House and the Revere House on his rambling old square. Taking the flight of stairs two steps at a time and landing in sight line of Reggie.

"Do you want to hear something stupid?"

"Always," Reggie said.

"The night we first went to Fiske's Wharf."

"The night I almost drowned?" Reggie raised an eyebrow, a signal they were on temporarily sure footing.

"I didn't want to bring up an unpleasant—"

"Where I was bobbing up and down like a fish?"

"Well, yes, but—"

Reggie's smile was tentative. "Where my foot was caught and I struggled like an agitated eel?"

Hamish grinned. "Yes. That. An eel. Something or someone got us out of the office."

"A distraction?"

Hamish nodded. "And Nate would have gone home by then. That was before he was living and breathing his files and folders."

"So someone knew that with all of us cleared out they might have free rein in his office space?"

Hamish shrugged. "A long shot, but a thought."

Reggie was up from behind the desk and dashing past him in the direction of the open office door. "What?" she said without looking back at him. "You were the one to teach me how to pick a lock. I picked Dirk Foster's. Darling Nate won't mind."

⼃⼂

A hairpin click later, they were inside Nate's office. Reggie looked around the medium-sized space. There was so much of their friend in the neat surfaces of his desk and blotter. Reggie decided whether they found anything or not she would break in again and again to ensure that every surface was wiped spotless for his eventual return. Because he would return. She knew he would.

There was a Red Sox pennant on the wall and a picture of Nate and his bubbe on his desk, Nate squinting into the sun. Framed on the opposite side of his typewriter and telephone was a sketch of a man on a horse: tri-corner hat and queue, horse bounding into the night, muscles rippling with careful deft precision in plaster. Paul Revere. The statue that Nate believed would someday honor the Prado, that large space behind the Old North Church, cloistered by redbrick walls, once home to tenement buildings torn down to allow for public space.

Hamish leafed through files, his long fingers working paper like the grooves of an accordion. "There's so much here and yet *nothing*. Something's been bothering Nate. His aversion to talking about Pete Kelly's development cannot be his involvement in it. But he had to know something we don't."

Hamish paused a moment as Reggie ran her finger reverently over the framed print of Revere.

"I've lived with the man for a long time," Hamish continued. "He anticipates everything. Down to an empty milk jug. I've noticed him shaking a canister of Ovaltine to ensure that it doesn't reach below the half point before he replenishes it. And he never forgets a birthday. Even his third cousin. He is so precise in everything."

Reggie followed Hamish's line of sight around the office. "Not like Luca with his long memory."

Hamish shook his head, looked at her straight on. "Nate leaves notes. He has two calendars: one in the kitchen, one in the sitting room. I am sure he has one in his bedroom too. And if someone found . . ." Hamish paused, eyes turning intently to a file in his hand. Reggie grimaced. He was trying to hide it, but Reggie had known him long enough to anticipate an episode. He continued to navigate paper trails with his left hand while his right hand trembled softly at his side. He was blinking several times a minute and breathing in a calculated meter. Every moment or so, he would leave the file on the edge of the desk, affix two fingers under his suspender and count.

"But he wouldn't want anyone to find anything," Reggie said. "He needs to be the middleman. People trust him. If anyone was ever in need of the secretary Vaughan wants me to hire for our office, it's Nate."

Hamish looked up, his glasses over the bridge of his nose. "What?"

"Oh. Yes. Vaughan thinks we should get a secretary. To make everything look proper. Don't worry. I'll talk him out of it."

Hamish blew a long string of breath. "They must have told Nate what was happening and he refused to listen because he didn't want to be a part of it. Because Nate would never be involved in this. There are so many files at home, Reg. He has been bringing his work home. Maybe he thought . . . You've heard his rants about the Prado and how they destroyed housing. He's really sensitive about bad housing for the residents here. Pete Kelly's property is a nightmare."

"So Pete Kelly was the lesser of two evils. Sure, he moved things in and out of the black market, but at least the families in the North End wouldn't be subjected to unsafe conditions?"

Hamish was leafing through a book. "His appointments book. Look." He slid it across the desk. "Look. Nothing! There is absolutely nothing here!" Hamish's kneecap hit the desk.

"So you're going to break his furniture?"

"Shhh! Reggie! Listen!" Hamish jostled his knee again.

"I don't hear anything."

But Hamish clearly did. He leaned down and opened a drawer he hadn't seen before. Reggie squinted: it looked very much like it was decorative, but it wasn't. "This has to be it. His system for keeping track of all of the services people do for each other in the North End!" Hamish was gleeful.

He untied a string from the packet of papers and smoothed

them across on the desk between them. It wasn't what Hamish thought.

"P.K." Reggie frowned. "He has P.K. listed in here several times. I had never seen that man in my life before he hired us to look into his business. And yet it looks like Nate saw him regularly." She shook her head. "But Pete Kelly said he would never consult Nate. Unless Nate was consulted by someone else. One of the many property development people *against* Pete Kelly."

"Nate was *never* here. Did you notice that? He went from occupying his office before we arrived to well after we left each day." Reggie straightened, brushing her skirt. "Even when he *was* here, he was so distracted he may as well not have been here at all."

Hamish cricked his neck. "Yes, changed," he repeated. This time his voice was intense. Purposeful. "Look at this." Hamish held up a slip of paper. He was reading intently when she joined him—shoulder to shoulder—their gazes running over the print in unison.

Insurance papers. A quote for the property Kelly owned. Nate knew about it—somehow. And either he filed it away like the rest of his work or he was hospitalized before he could do anything about it.

Hamish's look reminded her of the way he looked the first time she danced with him. Vulnerable. Hand outstretched. As if he were a partner less than what she would have settled for had she been Irene Dunne. His not understanding Nate's motives shoved him into a corner and drained him of his confidence. Hamish needed a sure thing.

He looked up at her all puppy-dog eyes and almost-smile. He was trying, but she wasn't going to play ball. This was who they were . . . at least for now. He rang his cousin to solve problems, and she would have shuffled the cards a different way.

"So what's our next step?" she said after a silence she convinced herself was comfortable but judging by his face was anything but.

"Ball game tonight?" he asked, long fingers exploring the blotter on Nate's desk. "I mean, if you can stand my company for three hours."

If he went low, she would go high. She pinched color into her cheeks and smoothed her skirt, the artful cluster of diamonds in her ring spinning sunlight into prisms. With the ball players and interviews, she was sure to be momentarily spared the silence hanging heavy and low between her and Hamish.

At home, much later, she affixed a straw hat at a jaunty angle and swished her skirt out the door and onto Pleasant Street. In the fifteen minutes at a brisk pace it took her to reach the diamond, she imagined cornering the men who harassed Parker. Pointing a finger with the aplomb of Rosalind Russell, her eyes as vague as Garbo's.

In actuality, the moment she crossed the field, noting the empty space to be later occupied by the corn dog stand, she was less sure. Debutante Regina with her shiny ring and ideas about how others should behave. Her Journal of Independence never anticipated being shrouded with judgment toward others. Especially the press. And not from the society pages. The same leeches that had slowly disengaged from the North Square reappeared at the edge of the field in dwindling pockets. The last stragglers hoping for a story about the shortstop's nephew. The big papers, of course, didn't care. Toby wasn't a headline. He wasn't the right color or station. He didn't have the right education. Parker might have been a heck of a shortstop, but that didn't earn front-page space for his nephew.

She pushed through this sea of second-rate reporters.

Toward Hamish . . . of all people.

Then suddenly he was there: profile in view, hands in pockets. Her eyes brushed over him, stopped at the side of his trousers, trying to see if she could make out the slight movement of his hand shake in his pocket. How could you love someone so much yet be so befuddled by them at the same time? In the same instant that her heart clutched in anger at his calling Luca—*Luca!*—her breath hinged in anticipation of closing the last bit of space parting them.

He merely led her to the back. Not a smile. They wouldn't try the locker room, he told her, merely wait for Errol's teammates to step outside it and answer their questions under the big blue sky. Coach had told them to watch their language around a lady too.

Some of Errol's teammates gave themselves away in tone. They weren't expecting a man of Errol's color on their team and they wouldn't make excuses for it. And they certainly had nothing to do with his kid nephew. Wouldn't tame or temper their disdain that someone was asking questions. Still, Reggie had to wonder if they would care enough to take action. Those who were the most put out by Errol's appearance in the lineup seemed the least likely to spend the energy to remove him. Prejudice left a wide berth for inaction. If anything, the teammates they interviewed were too indifferent to do anything of their own volition other than talk.

"The pen is mightier than the sword." Reggie remembered Hamish quoting his dad. And it seemed like any jabs or steps toward violence with this lot were purely in colorful verbs.

"I was tossing the ball off the wall and back. In my own little world. Bit worse for wear from the night before," said one.

Reggie and Hamish moved from him to Thornton: he was the star of the team, at least in looks and publicity potential for the papers, if not in sheer talent. Golden-haired, sun-licked, broad-shouldered, and suited to the uniform. If the papers took the time to snap a photo of the Patriots, it was with him as the emblem: cleft in his chin, sparkle in his blue eyes, all-American kid. He had the wholesome milk-and-cookie accent too. From the South. Florida, to be exact. Reggie listened to him go on about the orange trees in his mama's yard before breaking into the questions. Each answer somehow looped back to him like a boomerang. Throughout the tedious emittance of hot air, Reggie wished she and Hamish were in one of their dances of perfect rapport. She wanted desperately to throw him a look to catch and volley, a glimmer that said, "I see you. I'm with you. This man is about as deep as the puddle I crossed to get here."

Instead, she stood sentry at his side, rocking a little on her oxfords and too aware of his obvious stillness. Stiff and subdued, about to blend into the backdrop. She might not have known he was alive had he not coughed and posited the first question to the next player.

Stevenson. He held a rather egotistical grudge against new Soxer Ted Williams merely for being better than himself. Of course, in Stevenson's viewpoint, it was the talent scouts' fault for only watching Parker. Yes, it was quite obvious the scouts were enamored by Parker. Stevenson was adamant (so adamant his opinion was bookended by rather creative cursing) that Parker was a waste of time. Still, his anger didn't result in a vehemence that would suggest a bullet meant for Errol's head.

Reggie verified her assessment by glancing at Hamish in periphery. Were Stevenson lying, Hamish's fingers would have lodged under his brace in a quick succession of counts. Instead, his brow was furrowed, dimple and mouth evened into a straight line. He almost looked like the shy, vulnerable man she met in the pastry line at Mrs. Leoni's. She could imagine him like that. Almost. Until the pinging of her memory conjured up the same blue eyes, same full mouth that told her he had taken justice into his own hands. Maybe Bricker was dead because of it.

Reggie blinked back toward Stevenson just as he was explaining how he could never tell Toby and his uncle apart from a distance.

"They look the same. They *all* look the same."

At first, Reggie was irked with the brush that painted everyone of Errol's race together. Then something tickled her nose and tingled her fingers. It could have been a terrible mistake.

"I don't think any of them did it." Hamish's right hand was deep in his pocket. He was addled by something—she could tell by his dozen different ways of hiding a shaking hand—but she also knew that when he was counting over his heartbeat, it was more serious.

"I overheard some fellow talking to Joe about a kid. Toby, I assume."

Hamish and Reggie exchanged a glance. "What were they talking about?"

"Just that it wasn't working. That it wasn't worth the effort."

"The pranks weren't worth the effort?" Hamish translated.

"I don't know."

Reggie tugged him away from the ball players. Hamish dug in the grass with the toe of his shoe.

"We can keep doing this. But my instinct says we're off base here."

"A pun?" Reggie raised an eyebrow.

"There's something bigger at play."

"Another pun?" Now both of Reggie's eyebrows reached to her hairline.

"I have instincts. It was what made me a good . . . no . . . what *theoretically* would have made me a good lawyer. My instinct is that we can question every ball player until the cows come home but there is not enough jealousy or vengeance to lead to a dead nephew." Hamish adjusted his glasses. "Reggie. These guys play every game for a break. Would they really waste it for the prospect of a jail cell? Sure, they might rough Errol up or toss a few things in his locker, but kill a kid?"

"In the heat of the moment?"

Hamish looked in the direction of the locker room, then over the bleachers and stands. Then in the direction of the kiosks shaded by umbrellas striped like candy canes. "My instinct tells me no."

"Your instinct also called Luca Valari," Reggie muttered.

Hamish ignored her. "When Esmeralda is awaiting trial and execution for the attempted murder she didn't commit, it's like a storm cloud is hovering over her wherever she goes."

"Thank you, Hamish. You're so uplifting these days."

"I am just expressing my mood."

"I miss the days when you did everything you could to cheer me up."

"Did I?" he asked, his eyes blue and bright like stars.

She nodded. "You did."

"I might need to pick a happier book," he said.

"Might."

They were silent the rest of the stroll to the field, stopping at the corn dog stand only to see it occupied.

—※—

"Uncle's off." The lanky kid smacked gum while tending to a customer. "Too many reporters with questions."

Reggie bought two Cokes and told him to keep the change.

Hamish accepted the drink she offered him. Soon they were in their seats and the first of the lineup began taking the plate.

Errol Parker strolled and swung at nothing.

"Sad," Hamish said after another swallow. "Errol would have loved to have the cameras snap in his face for the moment he was signed for the Red Sox. Like a regular Ted Williams: spirited to the field in the blink of an eye."

Reggie played with the condensation on her Coke bottle.

The camera bulbs flickered and flashed. Passersby yelled their retorts, and not too far away, just a slight, savory jaunt in the warm sunshine, Hamish figured the Christian Patriots were nearby, doling out ivory pamphlets like precious flowers, smiles wide and eyes glistening. He was going through the motions without passion or drive.

Hamish and Reggie watched from just behind home plate, leaning forward from the first bleacher. Errol's sister would not find time to find her way to the office, they'd learned, even though Reggie assumed she would have appreciated the privacy. Instead, Errol sent word that she would meet them at the game. That even though Errol would be preoccupied on the field, she would benefit from having a familiar face near.

When a figure slid next to him in dark glasses with a hat pulled over her face, Hamish felt a wave of compassion.

"Mrs. Morris?" he asked.

She gave a quick nod and slowly sat beside Reggie.

"I am so sorry about your loss," Hamish heard Reggie say.

"You try your best to raise a child right. And you cannot help when they turn in a different direction." The woman folded her hands in her lap.

Hamish couldn't see her face, and because he hadn't turned to greet or speak to her, due to Reggie's warning hand on his knee, Reggie listened carefully and silently for a break in the woman's voice, but it was plain and cut through the bustle of the stands with intensity rather than volume. Reggie spoke softly, but not so softly Hamish couldn't hear. "I feel horrible for what happened."

"He aims too high."

Hamish took in Jean Morris's posture from his seat over: shoulders raised like armor, feet firmly planted on the ground. "Your son found him a wonderful role model."

"To return day after day to be ridiculed and humiliated?" Jean shook her head slightly. "Why not choose a safe occupation? Not draw attention to yourself. Not set yourself up for failure."

Reggie picked at her skirt. "You don't blame him." It hovered between a question and a statement.

Hamish leaned over Reggie's shoulder in an attempt to hear more clearly.

"I wonder if my son would have thought he *had* to work for those men. He talked about Cincinnati, but I thought that was a dream he would grow out of. He wanted Errol to pay attention to him. And Errol did. But I can't help wondering if all of this might have been avoided if Errol had chosen a respectable job. A working man's job."

It was clear the boy's mother had little evidence or understanding about her son's job with Kelly.

⤜

After the game, Hamish walked silently beside her as they left, plenty of space between them and the exits of other attendees. Reggie turned her head over her shoulder to see Errol join his sister.

She wanted to look up and talk to Hamish. But she flicked her eyes away. *We all do stupid things when we're upset,* she reminded herself, then wondered why she held him to a different standard. He was *too* human.

Maybe that was what bothered her so much. That he couldn't be expected to hold to everything she expected of him. That he couldn't be her conscience because for all of his inherent goodness, he was just a man. As fallible as she was.

Beside her, he was muttering something.

"Speak up, Hamish."

"'He took great pains to conceal his deafness from the general notice and normally succeeded so well that he had even come to deceive himself. Which is, as it happens, easier than one might think. All hunchbacks hold their heads high, all stammerers make speeches, all deaf people talk quietly.' It's a quote."

"What does it have to do with anything?"

"You can make yourself believe a great many things about the choices you make, Reggie."

She wasn't sure if it was an apology. Or if she wanted it to be. Or if his reciting quotes meant he was drawing away from her. He didn't see her far on Pleasant Street. Rather, he let her go. She resisted the urge to check and see if he was watching her, and soon the lilacs near the fence and the crickets hiding in the long grass and the lure of her comfortable screen door were all she saw.

CHAPTER 18

Hamish's father told him more than once in his childhood that news could turn a man's stomach. Not just the facts, but the position.

"Every paper has a bias, Hamish. We try to be balanced. But the scales tip and we cannot remove the perspective."

Hamish knew his father, especially when he traded in the title of reporter to be an editor, attempted to allow all voices to be heard. He wondered, fingers shaking as he lifted the Christian Patriots pamphlet, how his father could sift through so many lines of hate and imbalance and still keep a level head. For his father had told him countless times about similar societies during the Great War. When Hamish was a baby. When his father still had to report to Toronto City Hall as an immigrant alien.

People will always want a scapegoat. An enemy. Another tidbit from his father he learned spending life with newsprint on his fingertips, trying to make sense of the columns from a world he hid from. Hamish pinched his fingers over his nose. The war at home luring his school chums and changing the shifting face of his country had to be so much more political than a few insidious pamphlets.

Hamish studied the pamphlet again. It had been read intently. Hamish wasn't sure if Nate had been studying it or internalizing it.

He seemed too smart for the latter. He was never one to take things personally, but rather to assess the situation and look through a lens of balance and logic.

The end table lamp made Hamish's tossed coat shimmer like liquid and the books on the opposite table look like a leviathan in shadow. Hamish ran his finger over the pamphlet, watching the slight shudder of his fingers, then set it aside. He couldn't imagine Luca being prejudiced. Luca didn't have time. He wanted to stay ahead in the life to which he was accustomed. Luca would entertain batting for the Yankees before he would affiliate with a political party.

Hamish rose, letting the pamphlet fall between the sofa cushions. The part of his brain that normally wondered about Reggie's reaction to a next step was conveniently turned off.

He retreated to the kitchen and picked up one of the battleship games he and Nate had played. He pulled out a piece of paper and a pencil and drew a new grid himself. Might need to practice so when Nate was better they could play at the hospital. Letters down and numbers across. Nate's little dots. Very precise too. Hamish squinted at a sequence of marks in one of the grid boxes. He nudged his glasses up his nose and stared.

Then he retrieved an old grid he had crumpled from the side table and smoothed it. Nate had a pattern of playing the same moves, but always with a meticulous strategy for the placement of his little dots. The time he took to play the game always annoyed Hamish. At first he figured Nate put the same careful strategy into it as he did into his chess games. Then something fizzed like the nearly burnt-out bulb in the kitchen lamp.

Nate didn't leave any paper trail as to the transactions he made in the North End. But he might have made another kind of trail. Hamish made a cup of tea, pulled some leftover lemon cannoli from the fridge, and began to crack a code while part of his brain ran over the following: Kent was at Pete Kelly's; Nate was alone at the office and someone wanted something Nate had—badly. Hamish nibbled at a piece of cannoli. Phil had been in contact with Luca. Luca had given Hamish a phone number. It was from New York but could always be patched to somewhere else. He put Luca and Nate together a moment in his mind and hated where it led him: to similarities. Both respected men who never told everything about their enterprises. That inspired fierce loyalty. Nate was the center of the North End, knowing everyone, matching people with services so they could bypass crooked landlords and property owners. Luca had the same magnetic ability to build a world around him.

One side of the world, Hamish knew from newsreels and papers, was fighting a war. The other side was inching toward that war. His country was already wrapped up in it, but his adopted home was not. But what might people do for this world? First, he smoothed the manifest found in Toby's pocket over the table. *Cluster. Fuze. Shell. Carbine.* Munitions. His father had lost his hearing in a case involving black-market shipments between Toronto and Chicago. But that case had been during the last war with anarchists at the helm. But what might people do nowadays for munitions? To make a buck? Were they simply invested in the war overseas—or the war that might meet them any day?

Hamish swallowed the last bite of cannoli and threw the wax paper away.

☆

When Reggie arrived at the Van Buren and DeLuca office, she stopped and ran her fingernail over her name. Hamish's too. She had been so proud. The office rent had been purchased by her grandmother's pearls, thus Reggie's insistence that her name be listed above Hamish's. A stupidly childish whim. She looped the V with her finger while putting herself in his shoes and wondered if she wouldn't have done the same thing. Something drastic when the rug was pulled out from under her. She fingered the locket she wore daily. Its translation meant "Breathe. Hope." A gift he had given her when they opened their office.

Inside the office, he was not alone. Mrs. Leoni's daughter was with him, a young woman who had a huge crush on him. It had deepened when Hamish was able to stop her mother's landlord from jacking up the rent price so she could afford to keep baking and selling the best cannoli in the North End at the intersection of the North Square and Prince Street. He wasn't giving Rosa a full smile. She hadn't seen one of Hamish's full smiles since the night of her disastrous engagement party.

Reggie crossed the floor and greeted Rosa. She was a sunny-faced, pleasant-looking young woman. Reggie got the impression she was seeing a carbon copy of Mrs. Leoni several years before in Rosa's bright black eyes and luscious dark hair. She was twisting a strand of it around her finger with all the flirtatious subtlety of Claudette Colbert stopping a car in the road with a hiked-up skirt in *It Happened One Night*.

This act was completely lost on Hamish: glasses halfway down his nose, studying papers, rapping a pencil in his absent way. "This makes absolutely no sense." He nudged his glasses higher with the crook of his finger. "I confess, Rosa, that I only started learning property law when I moved here. But there are neighborhood jurisdictions." He didn't seem to register Reggie, squinting at the fine print on whatever Rosa was showing him. Reggie knew in her soul it was made up. Hamish had already helped advise her mother.

This was what her nana's pawned pearls had purchased: an erstwhile stream of damsels in distress to counter the occasional almost-drowning adventure. Reggie showed her teeth in a smile, inspected her careful self-manicure and the russet half-moon design on her fingernails. Rosa left and Hamish waved her over.

"I think I figured something out last night." He reached into his satchel and produced several finished games of battleship.

"I don't want to play right now." She was tired. Annoyed.

"I know. I don't want to ever play again. But this is where Nate was hiding his information. The papers we could never find. The connections."

"What?"

"Every letter here . . . See? A surname." Hamish took out another piece of paper. He pointed at the letter portions of the grid with his pencil. "Reggie, Nate was scared of something. Acting strange. And part of that strangeness was his moving everything from his office to our home. The one thing I did find from him was a list of all of the family names he usually works with. We've been here long enough to be able to fill that. Now look. It's here." He pointed to a few dots. "It's the last letters of surnames aligned with the numbers of an address. It's a crude system, but I think it is *a* system. The best he had to keep anyone from seeing where people connected. The services he helped trade."

"But how would we know who was matched with who?" Reggie had played the game a few times but was by no means an expert.

Hamish gave her a half-moon smile. "I think it is in the position. On the grid." He chuckled. "In *Hunchback*, Quasimodo can see all of Paris's streets from above. All the people and houses tiny specks below. He has a view of Paris no one else has. Nate has a view of the North End no one else has."

"This is a crazy theory."

"But it might be right."

Reggie sighed. "Who do you think he was keeping this from?"

"Kent, for one."

"Kent."

"What?"

"What do you mean *what*?"

"You have a look."

"Oh, come on, Hamish, not all my thoughts are yours."

"So you have thoughts."

Reggie sighed. "You keep forgetting I am angry with you. Well . . ." She spread her hands. "*Some*what angry with you. Truth be told, I sometimes forget to hold my grudge."

"Reggie . . ." Hamish's voice darkened.

"Why does it have to be Kent? I know someone who would love control of the North End. Someone who might figure enough time had passed for him to pick up where he left off."

Reggie didn't expect an immediate response, and she found it disconcerting to watch Hamish's train of thought behind his eyes, no doubt aligning with her own. "But Nate. He wouldn't . . ."

"Wouldn't what? Get his way? He has you exactly where he wants you. Again. *Still!* You think your weakness is your hand or your anxious episodes or your tripping on words. It's not your heartbeat, Hamish! That's not your weakness. *He* is still your weakness!"

"He is not! He has no influence over me!"

"You called him! Bricker! Bricker was his influence!"

Hamish raked his fingers through his hair. "I was trying to do something right."

"I know! But it's not up to you to pick fights and fix the world. Just because you can step into a corner of the world doesn't mean it is your space. Hamish, Nate's misfortune had nothing to do with who he is . . . It was *what* he does."

Hamish was silent long enough for Reggie to feel the pulse of the ticking clock through the rapping of her fingers. "If you're right, then I killed Bricker."

"What?"

"Because I called Luca . . ."

"Hamish."

"Reggie!"

Reggie swallowed. "You didn't kill him," she said softly.

"You told me I did! You're changing your mind?" She supposed he wanted the words to be forceful, but the pleading in his eyes belied anything but fear.

"You made a stupid mistake, Hamish."

"One that I won't forgive myself for."

Reggie studied him a moment. His eyes were on his long fingers, the ones on his right hand shaking slightly. "But you will. Eventually. You will have to. So . . ." She inhaled. "Why don't I forgive you first, and then you at least have some forgiveness until you can catch up, huh?"

⧊

It was strange not having Nate to call on. For any reason—battleship codes or Hamish's guilt. Reggie knew he would have pointed them in the right direction after a few wry asides. Instead, they visited Thomas Greene. Reggie remembered him vaguely from a case last year involving his mother. She supposed it didn't immediately spring to mind because she hadn't been central to solving his problem. Rather, he had needed Hamish to ensure his mother was treated fairly.

His insurance office wasn't in the North End, where he lived, but on Hadassah Street near the Park Plaza. It was small but costly. He said he paid the rent not for the space but for the location, to try to accumulate higher quality clientele. Reggie sauntered past Hamish with a look he read as her giving him an extra few beats before he would have to smooth the worry from his face.

"And Pete Kelly has been here?" she said brightly.

"Just once."

At this, Reggie looked to Hamish.

Hamish studied the paperwork and assured her it was legitimate. There were a few addendums he puzzled over, but Thomas waved them off.

"I have been in the insurance business since I graduated. These are usual protocols."

Hamish took a copy nonetheless, thanking Thomas profusely. He laid it on a little thick as they left his office and stepped into the sunshine.

"What are you thinking?" Reggie asked, a question posited as much to satiate her own curiosity as to solve their mystery.

"Hyatt and Price have no intention for this property development and housing to be a success."

"What makes you say that?" Reggie asked as Hamish steered them toward the Common. The black wrought-iron fence framing a span of green and centuries spread before them. Reggie kept his pace on the sidewalk rimming the park.

"Greene. He couldn't even find his mother a home. Had to come to us. I know—I *know* that sounds crass. But it's true. A true Realtor, a *proper* Realtor for a firm of Hyatt and Price's caliber, would want the best in the city."

"So they want their project to fail?"

Hamish shook his head, then drew a line with his pinky finger, slicing the air between them. "On both sides of this we have sheer stupidity. No! Don't look at me like that. I won't stand on ceremony. Stupidity!" He smiled. "On one side we have Kelly: he stands to earn on the black market, more so as the prospect of entering the war becomes nearer. Across the border, people will want what is scarce. Nylons. Liquor. Who knows? He stands to make a buck, especially with his prime waterfront property. Boats easily move in and out." Hamish took a beat, blue eyes roaming from Boylston Street to the steeple of Arlington Church: a breath away in their sight lines. "On the other side we have Hyatt and Price. A firm host to views that are at their core very antiwar. War, to them, and according to the pamphlets, is a conspiracy. They quote *The Protocols of the Elders of Zion*. One treatise of many that believes there is some form of Jewish conspiracy. But they don't stop there. They prey on any group of people they think are lesser than themselves. War, to them, just gives their inferiors power."

"So munitions?"

"If they found out that Kelly's property was being used to transport munitions? Like we found on Toby's manifest? They would think it was their duty to stop it. This is more than slum housing. Though the slum housing was two birds with one stone. The uneven ground and obvious disarray would hopefully drive out any unwanteds while still keeping Kelly from his enterprise."

Reggie fell back on the heels of her oxfords. "And Toby?"

"Toby was an errand boy."

"Yes, but—"

"Something intersected. Someone may have been using Toby to work for both sides. The side that wanted the cheap housing, the side that wanted Kelly to keep his shipments."

"So what you are saying is . . ." Reggie put her index finger to her stained lips.

"Yes?"

"None of this has anything to do with baseball."

They took a taxi back to the North End to decide what to do next. It was around lunchtime.

They bought sandwiches to go from Leoni's and retreated to the Prado. The sun was scorching, but the breeze tickling the rambling trees and over the red bricks was a nice reprieve.

Reggie and Hamish were mostly silent while eating. Reggie felt as if a yardstick dangled between them, keeping them at a safe distance. Sure, he was animated under the spell of solving a problem. But he also tried to be a gentleman next to an engaged lady. Reggie folded the paper from her sandwich.

They reclined, a large stretch of fountain between them, watching the water spray. Reggie couldn't sink into the moment like a comfortable old sweater—her ring caught the rainbow in the water. She folded her arms.

Hamish was far away for a moment. He nudged his glasses up with the crook of his index finger, his gaze lost in the color of the Prado. The trees weeping down over the red brick. The pedestrians spilling between the bordering churches at either end.

Reggie saw an intensity in his eyes, but also a sadness. She slid over slightly and nudged him with her elbow. "You're thinking of Nate."

Hamish shrugged. "Or maybe I am just thinking that I don't want this place to change."

The stroll to the office was silent, punctuated by the familiar sounds of a North End afternoon: shoppers bartering with grocers under striped awnings; a car horn a street over; tourists playing with their bulky Kodak cameras, the click of the button immortalizing historic tableaux Hamish snapped in his mind as they made their way back to the office.

Several moments later, so deep in thought, Hamish didn't even look up when the phone rang. Reggie voiced her usual greeting, excitement rising in her voice so that she had to check herself and smooth her skirt. "How?" she asked, covering the mouthpiece and murmuring, "Officer Reid," to Hamish.

"That hot dog vendor. Had a crisis of conscience when his nephew was in a fight. Pete had apparently slipped him some money. From what I know about Pete, that seems to be a common thing."

Reggie signed off and looked up excitedly at Hamish.

Hamish's eyes were wide behind his glasses. "And?"

Here Reggie bounced a little in her chair. "And!"

"Stop the jack-in-the-box routine, Reggie, and tell me."

"Pete Kelly had a few people at the ball game working for him. To say the least."

Reggie and Hamish rang Errol for his sister's address, then wasted no time finding it.

When they arrived, Errol answered the door.

"Is your sister here?"

Errol nodded. "Jean's in the kitchen."

The house was simple but immaculate. All furniture and spaces had been dusted. From the front of the house, Reggie's nose made out the kitchen.

"The church ladies are going above and beyond," Errol said. "Smell that? Roast chicken and potatoes and bean salads and casseroles to feed dozens. My sister hasn't had an appetite. Can't blame her." He turned to Hamish. "Did you listen to the game last night? No amount of roast chicken could change the way I've been playing."

"Maybe you should take time off. It can't be easy to focus on the game."

Errol motioned for Reggie and Hamish to take a seat in the sitting room. "If you want anything to eat, there's lemon pie . . ."

They both declined. But Reggie accepted the offer of two Cokes straight from the icebox.

Errol returned and handed the bottles across the couch, his sister not far behind him. While Errol was chatty, Jean was not. "I don't know how I'm still waking up, you know? When something cuts your knees out from under you. I guess I just keep myself going forward. I think it's because I still want to prove that I can do it. For him. For my sister too."

"Do you want anything to eat?" She looked tired but prim. Starched collar and ironed skirt as if anticipating company, falling back on manners that seemingly exhausted her.

"We're fine," Reggie said. "Thank you."

Reggie tried not to look at her. It went against every last inch of her upbringing. She knew she was being rude, but she wasn't sure what her eyes would betray. This woman had seen countless officers. Had seen her brother's and nephew's names in the paper. Had to live with the blown-out wick of the candle of a kid who wanted to go to Cincinnati. Who was young and energetic and hardworking, probably determined to raise his mother from this crooked sofa (with one wonky leg) and the slight crack in the clean front window. To live up to his uncle.

"May we take a look at his room?" Hamish asked moments later, after taking a long slug of Coke. "When we're finished here?" Hamish felt like a smart and determined kid who had become the go-between for men who both had a desire and claim on Kelly's property.

Toby's mother nodded. Hamish was drawing circles on the table with his thumb.

"Hard for me to go in, you understand," Errol said. "But if you think it might help, then please go ahead."

Silence. Reggie and Hamish exchanged a look. Reggie remembered the first night she saw Errol on the field, the way he stepped to the plate and owned the field, drowning out the sounds from the stands, planting his shoes on either side of the plate and swinging the bat as if it were an extension of his body. The same Errol, in front of her, seemed small and deflated: shoulders hunched, staring at folded hands on a shiny-clean wooden table.

"Are you still planning on moving into Mr. Kelly's property?" Hamish asked after a moment.

"No. I haven't decided what I am going to do now."

"Any scouts come yet?" Reggie asked, to lighten the tone but also because she remembered how much of an influence it seemed to have in their first conversations about his prankers.

Errol shook his head. "And there won't be if I keep playing like this." He spread his hands. "But I will keep playing, you know. And I am happy that I took the time to seek you out."

Their Coke bottles finished, Jean collected them with a smile before retreating to the back room, leaving Errol to point them upstairs. The banister was dark wood and each step covered with worn carpet. On the next floor, first door to the right, they would find what had been Toby's bower.

Bower was the word Errol used, and as soon as Hamish and Reggie crossed through, she could see why. It was a sanctuary. The door had a sign—Please Knock—written in careful calligraphy. Each wall featured banners and pennants from the Boston Patriots. Errol told them he always offered to pay for Toby's tickets, but Toby wanted to earn his frequent attendance. Reggie figured this was why he ran errands and messages for Pete Kelly.

On the mirrored dressing cabinet, Reggie found a pile of ticket stubs. Toby didn't want to forget a moment. Each game a relic.

Otherwise, the room was a study of an average boy. At least from what Reggie could see from corduroy comforter to print curtains.

Dust speckles appeared with the slice of light from the window. A few building blocks rested on the hardwood floor. From long before. A lifetime before. Reggie approached Toby's desk. Her breath caught at the pile of half-finished homework. The boy's pencil scrawl beginning a thesis on the fall of Rome. Pennants from the Reds and maps of Cincinnati littered the walls.

Reggie's eyes stung.

Meanwhile, Hamish studiously inspected every inch and corner. This room was a life. A mausoleum. All that remained of a vibrant human cut off before he was able to fulfill his potential.

Reggie carefully, gingerly, explored the other papers in careful piles. Most was homework. Another sheet—peeking out—was something else entirely. Reggie removed it.

"Hamish!" Her eyes didn't leave the fine print and insignia she immediately recognized.

"Eh?"

"I think I found something."

Hamish joined her and they studied the paper together. "There's far more on this than should be allowed at some little warehouse on the wharf." Hamish looked over lines and lines of goods. "Imagine this! Fish. Pigs."

Reggie startled. "What?"

"Someone could easily play some horrible pranks after receiving some of these goods."

Reggie scanned another piece of paper while Hamish continued with the fine print. "Guns. Ammunition."

Hamish stole a look over her shoulder. "Were there guns and ammunition when you were there, Reg? That you saw? When we were first at Kelly's?"

Reggie nodded. "I think so." She squinted. Flummoxed. Reaching for memory. "I was trying to notice, Hamish. Just like Nora Charles would. But then I fell into the water and—"

"Because all I saw was alcohol and cigarettes. Weapons are something new. And something that would mean a lot. You know this, Reg. From the night we were at the Christian Patriots meeting."

He took the paper from her. "Let me see this. I don't think this has anything to do with Kelly going quietly. I think this has something to do with a man still desperate to make a buck even though he knows he is cornered. They're bigger than he is."

Hamish's mind churned over everything that had happened and somehow rested on Toby. A kid who would do anything for a buck. From either side of two parties invested in a property. For completely different purposes.

"I'm going to think out loud."

"What? Again?" Reggie's voice was light.

"I was thinking about a trial."

"Pleasant time to think about a trial!" Reggie chortled.

"In school. It was on one of our exams. In the example, a fellow was standing trial for sabotaging his own property. He stood to gain more by destroying his property than by selling it. The insurance."

"Oh." Reggie rolled a corner of the paper between two fingers.

"What do we know so far, Reggie?"

"That when we go find Kelly he will be accepting his last

shipment and working very hard to make his property disappear? I wonder."

Hamish tucked a requisition into his suit jacket. "We know that Kelly really wants to keep his property. When I was there, I saw several pamphlets from the Christian Patriots. This is a man who knows to keep an eye out for prospective rivals."

Reggie sank onto Toby's bedspread. Her eyes flitted around the room, and she almost rose again, worried that she had gotten too comfortable and desecrated a sacred space. The wallpaper. The sweater haphazardly hung on a hook behind the door. As if Toby might barge through the door any moment.

"The Christian Patriots are pacifists." Hamish lowered his voice as if someone might be around and would hear them. His eyes sought all four corners of the small room. "At least they have tricked themselves into believing they are pacifists. The war my country is fighting is, to them, a distraction from their cause. False. Fake. Why would they stand by and let someone capitalize on weapons and ammunitions for what they think is a fake and organized war? We talked about this!"

"So . . ."

"They think there is some virtue in stopping what is happening in my country and overseas from coming here. And any money they would make—perhaps at the expense of the very people they want to eliminate from their perfect world—could help spread their philosophy."

"Money! People who would jump at the chance to live in the new building might be the perfect bait for their rallies and pamphlets." She warmed to his theme, face animated. "But also someone who wants the opposite. Whose sole gain is to make a buck."

"Precisely."

She looked over Hamish's shoulder. "Toby would keep Kelly from getting that money."

Hamish nodded. "But the kid playing both sides? He was smart, but he was just a kid."

"You think someone else was at the helm?"

Hamish didn't answer. Reggie rose, smoothed over the blanket on Toby's bed. Took one last look around a room that stung her with nostalgia for a childhood she had never lived. A childhood of the scent of apple pie drifting from downstairs (as it was now) and sun streams buttering a homemade bedspread (as they were now).

Reggie was a little overwhelmed. But happy at the same time.

⎽⍒⎽

Reggie insisted she return to the office to collect the office gun before they confronted Pete, miffed that she hadn't thought to bring it in the first place. Hamish wanted to cycle over immediately and get a head start. Gun or no gun.

"You sure you can protect yourself?" Reggie asked. Logically. More logically than Hamish responded when he answered in the affirmative.

Hamish nodded. He wanted to buy time in case someone showed up. As his tires skidded into the white signs marking Hyatt and Price's development a half hour later, he made out Kelly at the side of the building.

"Mr. Kelly!" Hamish called, hopping off his bicycle and walking toward the open door.

"Mr. DeLuca."

"Miss Van Buren and I couldn't figure out what player would play horrible pranks. Not only that, but get the means to. A fish. A chicken. A pig's heart. Gruesome."

"I have no idea what you're talking about."

Hamish nodded. "You do. And you had the means to do it. Joe. The janitor. He's a connection of yours. A customer. You had someone to help you."

"What would I care about a baseball player?"

"You needed to distract him. You had Errol's kid nephew doing all sorts of things. Figuring things out. What's more, you didn't like the idea of someone like Errol playing for any league: farm league or no. And to add insult to injury, he was the first investor to rent. People are always shipping stuff through here. Boats coming and going, you could have easily taken what you wanted. A gun. I do think you went to the ballpark that night to confront Errol. To see if you could bribe him. Or taunt him. Joe would tell you when he would be around. And he was that night." Hamish took a breath. "And then you found out that Toby wasn't *just* working for you."

Kelly turned from Hamish. "You might want to collect that bicycle of yours and go back to where you came from."

"Toby met someone playing *both* sides. Someone way out of your league."

Kelly blinked. "You're wasting my time."

"You got scared when my cousin was back in town. You're scared now, which is why you think you can still find a way to make a buck. You'll light fire to this building and turn a profit. Keep Hyatt and Price from ever getting to it. But it won't work. Because they have high-priced lawyers—the same lawyers they probably came and spooked you with before you found me. They will find a way to take all of it. You won't get the insurance. You won't—"

"I am on a bit of a deadline." Kelly cut Hamish off, his face unchanged. He turned into the door and Hamish followed him, though he couldn't see in the middling dark what Kelly was reaching down to pick up.

It became ultimately clear at the flick of Kelly's torch.

"You're setting this place on fire! For the insurance. Act of God. Can't be much of an act of God if they find the match and the gasoline can. And a witness."

Kelly shoved Hamish against the wall and ran outside. Hamish found his balance and followed him. He sloshed gasoline around his shoes then made a dripping trail.

Hamish pounced, wrestling Kelly, and the can toppled, a steady pungent stream spilling onto the grass.

Kelly was strong, but Hamish was fast. Reflexes compensated for every sudden movement.

Hamish ducked at Kelly's swing then leveled a few of his own. He whipped his glasses off and tucked them in his pocket. They were so closely engaged, he could make out the heavy breath and perspiration and ire on his opponent's face.

"I didn't mean for the kid to be killed."

Hamish blinked fury from his eyes. They stung with sweat and now with something else. Something split between hoping Reggie would arrive with a gun and hoping she would stay clear away.

"I've had quite the business offer of late. Kid would have gotten in my way." Kelly panted, repositioning himself. Falling back. "So much for my good deed. Thought the kid would be quiet. Out of respect to his uncle. Started sending his uncle things. But then someone made me a huge offer and I couldn't have my mistake of a clumsy teenager be the one thing that kept me from it."

"Who!" Hamish bellowed. "Who showed up?" He knew the answer.

Kelly started to reach into his pocket, but Hamish was faster, clutching both of Kelly's forearms. Hamish gritted through his teeth. "The police are coming, you know. And you just gave me a confession."

"Confession!" Kelly laughed. "I don't think you'll be around to report it." Kelly showed him a packet of matches.

Hamish's eyes widened and he wrestled him down. Kelly squirmed until he had enough momentum to throw Hamish off, then landed a careful blow to his nose. Hamish's world buzzed a moment; he held his face and rolled back. When he blinked the blurriness away, Kelly was holding up a match, making a show of striking it on his shoe. "You'll have to be quicker."

Hamish's quickening heartbeat startled the breath from him as the slow flame flickered then licked and snaked over the gasoline-ravaged grass. Hamish leapt to his feet in pursuit of Kelly as the fire raced. There was a sound to it too. A sudden, sickening roar. Hamish blinked as it crawled up the sides of the warehouse.

He tackled Kelly from behind. But the fire was too close. Kelly swerved and landed another blow to Hamish's face. Hamish coughed and took it, rallying enough to return the same. Kelly fell back and Hamish lost him like a shadow, the smoke stinging his eyes and turning his vision into a wall of blurriness.

He blinked it away and panted a moment. He needed to breathe. But couldn't. The smoke was suffocating. But he needed to. The longer he worried about not being able to, the faster his heartbeat thudded and his nerves snapped.

He slipped his hand beneath his right suspender a moment, finally finding Kelly in shadow. He reached out to pull him up. Tough him. Grip him. But Kelly had a weapon Hamish didn't have.

The gasoline can.

And Hamish's world went black.

⚕

Reggie was with Reid, of all people. She had headed straight back to the office after their visit to Jean's, and Reid was waiting.

"I'm here for a gun," Reggie said.

"And I'm here because after weeks and weeks of waiting I finally have a warrant for Kelly."

"What? How?"

Reid nodded enthusiastically. "Some small infraction. Minuscule. But enough. And even in my jurisdiction."

"I need to find Hamish. He was going to confront him."

"Ride with me?"

Reggie was enjoying the stint in a police car. Smoothing her skirt and laughing at Reid's attempts at humor. It wasn't until they neared Fiske's Wharf that she started to feel uneasy . . . unsure . . . panicked.

Smoke swirled as Reggie and Reid inspected the looming fire from the car windows.

Reid tried to calm her. "I see your ring there." He nodded from the driver's seat. "You're engaged. Congratulations."

Reggie tried to speak but instead just squeaked and nodded. They parked far away from the smoke. Gray and billowing.

"You stay here," Reid said firmly, placing a restraining hand on her shoulder. "Stay here. I am going to see if I can help."

Reggie looked out the gritty window. The firemen and ambulance were just arriving. The smoke was overpowering, crawling through the door Reid quickly opened and stealing her breath.

"You promise you'll stay here? Don't make me handcuff you."

Reggie coughed, nodded. Lied.

She waited until he was out of sight. Which wasn't long considering the black cloud was spreading. She fingered her ring. She couldn't bring her hand to her necklace. *Breathe. Hope.* It was hard to do either when everything before her was an inferno.

She opened the car door and stepped into the murky gray. *Well, it's preferable to water,* she lied to herself as her eyes began to sting and the atmosphere swelled and closed in, choking her.

A fireman grabbed her arm. It took her a moment before she saw him, blinking, but she shoved him off.

‑�ᴪ‑

At the very least, when he imagined dying, he hoped it would be in the middle of an adventure. Quasimodo protected his saints and his monsters of stone from Frollo's men and the Parisian guards and even Clopin, king of the Romany people, and his willing followers. He protected what was his from the raging smoke. Hamish was light-headed, probably a bit delirious too. For once he entertained a few *Hunchback of Notre-Dame* comparisons, thinking of the battlefields far, far away. His mouth was dry. He tasted grit and everything around him was closing in like a wall.

He tried standing up but his bones felt like gelatin and he lay down again. He didn't know where Pete was. If he had gotten away. He didn't know. He was slowly getting sleepy, his eyes fluttering shut. He should put on his glasses so they could identify him. But then, just as his eyelids were railing against the gray, he thought he saw something. Sunshine. A splash of yellow. His eyes widened.

Reggie wore yellow. Reggie had been wearing yellow. Earlier when they had Cokes at Errol's place. Yellow like her engagement ring. He slumped a little and decided to just sleep it off . . . forever if needed. Until she called his name.

⸸

The outfit would be ruined. It was expensive too. One she kept from her time as a Van Buren debutante. Sartorially impressive. It contrasted nicely against her chestnut hair. A dozen times she thought she'd found him, pressing through the haze with her arm, tainting her dress. And then she did. It had to be him. Even with black hair and black, sooty clothing, she saw him. Just a moment. A flash of unbelievably blue eyes through the fog.

Reggie dashed over, pulled him up with strength she didn't know she had, the muscles in her arms feeling like they were being ripped out, her arms from their sockets too.

"Don't you dare, Hamish!"

His stiff form beside her straightened and suddenly he was

helping her. Moving on his own. Away, away from the smoke, through the waterfall spray of water hoses and in the direction of the river.

She could see him. The curtain of dark parted and a wide slice of moonlight made its place beyond the fire and dark.

He was coughing, spluttering. Wiping the grime from his face. He looked at her a moment, squinting. She wasn't sure he completely saw her. Then he fell back, coughing again.

Reggie looked at him, scrunched and smeared and singed. Then back toward the building alive with eerie flames, barely controlled by the firemen, and her mind made a connection of *That was too close* while her heart had another idea altogether.

So her fingers were entangled in the back of his hair and her lips were on his. Claiming him again and again—over his lips and then over the ash smudged on his cheekbones and the smoky line of hair at each temple. She kissed him and kissed him and she was sure the tears trailing from her eyes stung his dry lips, but he kissed her back. Still. She was shaking. Her mouth tasted like ash and dust. But she didn't care. *He* had almost died and she hadn't spared two ticks of a thought before racing to go with him.

When they fell apart, hands still holding on for dear life, he sought her surprised eyes underneath the ratty light.

"You shouldn't have come after me, Reggie." His thumb ran over her cheek, catching a strand of hair.

But she had to. *Her* Hamish with his glasses and his long nose and his beautiful eyes. He tugged the sun into her sky in the moments she saw him every day. She wanted to fall into him and keep him safe and navigate a twisting road less traveled with him at her side. She was sorry they had spent any time navigating around each other and a few misunderstandings and her own anger at his decisions. Love was imperfect. And so was he. But she loved him all the same.

Hamish's glasses sat askew at a dilapidated angle, a strange contrast to his face: a hybrid of red and gray smog. While he held her, she stole a moment to look down at the muted twinkle of her diamond ring, filmed by soot. She brushed it against her skirt until she was certain it shone again. Brushed and brushed again and again until it hurt. Everything hurt.

Her brain backpedaled, the cloud of smoke and passion and the eternity of their kiss clearing into cold reality. There was Vaughan and her father's bankbook beyond the tumbledown hair of this man before her: his soft touch and big eyes, drinking her deftly in. *Who* was she? Reggie was rebellious but not unfaithful. She knew what her commitment to Vaughan meant.

She took a moment and pulled away, rubbing at her forearms. *Where* was she? Away from smoke and danger, away from the tight pull of his arms, the wavering passion in his kiss, the uncertain yet desperate tangle of his arms.

"I'm sorry," she tried to say steadily, knowing his own tremulous voice in a moment of intense fear or passion would never match the steadiness in her own. "The lack of oxygen has gone to my brain."

Even in the dark and smoke, rippled through by the blare of sirens, she could see his heartbreak, and then she felt it with an intensity that caught in her throat.

"O-of course," he stuttered. And it had been so warm and wanting to be with him, near him. *Reggie, you* stupid *girl*.

"I'm engaged," she said lamely, as if it could possibly patch up the rift in their friendship their pressed closeness had spliced. She would tell herself it was the intensity of a near-death experience. She would tell herself. She would . . . Oh, there were a million things she would do later, and they would all lead to her biting her self-manicured nails at the web she had tangled around her heart.

"I know." Hamish's voice was hollow as if a rug had been pulled out from it and he had fallen. "I wasn't much of a gentleman." His right hand was shaking, and as headlights pulled in near, she saw a garish red slice across it.

"Hamish, you're hurt!"

"Reggie, I love you."

"I know." She licked her dry lips and regretted it because the motion took a little bit of him from her.

"And that's it?" His voice splintered.

She realized she wasn't absently rubbing her engagement ring, but rather tugging at the locket he'd given her. *Spira, Spera.* Well, the *breathe* part was nearly impossible with the leftover swirls of smoke and the air she was just beginning to replenish after kissing him again and again and again. But *hope*? "It was an end-of-the-world kiss."

He scrubbed his hair, dull gray with matted soot. Reggie's eyes turned away from him to the skeleton of the building still consumed by smoke and fire in the hazy moonlight. She had made such a mess. Her eyes pricked with tears she hoped were camouflaged by smoke. "When you think it is the end of your life and everything is scary and falling apart and you are relieved to see the one person who . . . matters the most."

Hamish was impossible to read after that moment. She had confused him and given in to the stupidest impulse of her life.

"Do you need to see a medic?" he rasped.

"*You* need to see the medic," she said.

Voices milled and the volume mounted, and soon Reggie and Hamish were bordered by two police cars, a fire truck that had roared in from Haymarket Square, and a medic's van. Hamish insisted Reggie see a doctor even though she countered that he was the one with the injured hand. He ignored her. The headlights and torchlights illuminated him: sooty shirt open at the collar, hair a disaster, long, sinewy limbs dragging, blue eyes electric against the smoky dark.

Hamish was pretty certain he was dreaming. Otherwise, he couldn't imagine recalling Reggie in his arms and kissing him. The type of sweet, unexpected, knee-buckling kiss that would drive him into a burning building again. And again.

The firemen had controlled the fire. Pete wasn't found. At least that was what he made out from snippets of comments. His ear was ringing. Then he saw someone he knew.

"Errol!"

"I came to confront him. After you left," Errol said, spreading his hands. "When I arrived, well . . ."

"How did you know to come?"

"I found a letter in our mailbox. Just after you left. Returned to sender. It was a letter from Toby addressed to Mr. Kent. Telling him he didn't want to be a part of it anymore. I came to confront him."

"Your nephew had something that Kelly would kill for. Something a much more powerful man wanted. It was how we ended up in his world to begin with."

"It was a mess." Errol shook his head.

"You can't feel guilty," Hamish said. "You can't lighten it. That was a part of it and it's not selfish to acknowledge it."

"What kind of influence would I have been on my nephew then—if he were still with us? If I go off and defend Pete Kelly stupidly? That's no kind of legacy. At least not the kind of legacy I would want to leave."

"It's unforgivable." He watched Errol turn the weight of the world over in his mind.

Errol shook his head. "Nothing is unforgivable, Hamish. Forgiveness is freedom. True freedom. I don't want to be shackled with this man's hatred. I don't want to be bound to the hate of this injustice. But I will always be shackled to it."

Hamish opened his mouth to speak, but nothing came out. Behind his eyes a film reel of Reggie and Nate and fire and anger unfurled.

"You're thinking about your friend." Errol's voice rumbled low over the bricks and debris.

"You're perceptive. No wonder you can see a fly ball a mile away."

"You want to take on the world. Just like me, huh? You're angry and it fills you and you need some way to let that anger out."

"'Anger is the least interesting emotion,'" Hamish recited, his smile a slight comma up his cheek. "Something my mother used to tell me. From a book she read."

Errol chuckled. "There you are, then. Fighting battles out of responsive anger might get an immediate response. Or change a slight part of a bigger problem. But I am not going to fight just for the near future. If I fight, I want to do so for a marathon. For something that will last long after I am gone and beyond my problems to something bigger. And I think once I wash this grime off my face and get back into the field, I can fight with my gift. All of this . . ." Errol's eyes roamed over the wreckage and jagged beams that looked like errant limbs. "This is unfortunate. But this is not my fight." He squeezed Hamish's shoulder. "Go find your young woman."

Reggie. At that, Hamish was lost. He nodded and twisted a string trailing from the bandage wound around his palm.

⚓

Then it was as if all of the moments Hamish had ever experienced with Reggie had flitted up in the smoke of the warehouse. The curtain drew on Vaughan pulling her in and sweeping back her hair, and while Hamish couldn't see Vaughan's face from his vantage point, he assumed his eyes were two shimmering pools of concern. Over Vaughan's shoulder Reggie looked at him, and he should have been able to read a million things on her open-book face, but on this night he needed translation.

CHAPTER 19

It was an end-of-the-world kiss. But it was a start-of-a-world kiss too.

Reggie saw this Hamish again, the one she knew by heart. The fire purged her anger at his calling Luca. But what sat in its place was far more dangerous—though both incendiary fusions felt similar. The heat of anger and disappointment, the blood-flushed cheeks of her loving him again. Now having something to hook that love onto—like a clothesline draped with the feel of his fingers and the taste of his lips, the light of his eyes breaking through a smoky night.

Love meant accepting the lowest of a person. The parts that made you tingle and shrug. Love saw through every fight and stilled every fear and weathered every doubt. Love meant pushing past perceptions and surmounting expectations and accepting that someone would never always live up to the ideals you placed on them. And she loved Hamish. She had known it for a long, long time. At least her heart had. And because she loved him, she saw him through his shadow and back to himself.

Reggie passed him a note with a name familiar to them both.

"Aaron Leibowitz." He studied the handwriting on the envelope. "I know next to nothing about Aaron Leibowitz—but I wasn't expecting this handwriting." He tilted the envelope to Reggie. Leibowitz had a delicate hand.

"I was saving it for you. I thought we could open it together."

"We can't open Nate's mail."

"We have to. I don't want it to be anything that would distress him. He might be more sensitive."

"He loves this feud. It's his favorite thing."

"I don't know what kind of mood he will be in. I think we should take a peek."

"Okay." Hamish opened the envelope and slid out a piece of paper.

Reggie squinted, leaning into Hamish to study the note. He backed up slightly. She ignored it, this measured line between them.

They read it concurrently then looked up, eyes meeting.

"Oh," they said at the same time.

⎯⎯⎯ ⭑ ⎯⎯⎯

Aaron Liebowitz—also known as Sarah Abrams—was a lovely and soft-spoken woman with a direct, intelligent gaze.

"You don't have to stand in the doorway," Reggie said warmly. "We don't bite."

She took a tentative step and eventually sat in the chair Reggie gestured to.

"I was so worried about him. I've never met him, but I feel I know him. If the *Advocate* hadn't posted a notice . . . Tell me, is he going to be all right?"

Hamish smiled. "I cannot believe you're a woman. Nate talks about Aaron Leibowitz constantly."

"I use the *Advocate* as a way to work out some of my questions about faith and what I am learning," Sarah explained, picking at a thread on her skirt. "My father is very conservative and does not feel a woman should pursue theological questions. But when I write to Nate, the passion with which he writes back . . ."

Reggie clapped her hands together. She was sitting on the edge of her desk, legs swinging easily. "You realize you are a household name around here?"

"I am so worried about him. I know I don't really know him other than through the newspaper."

"Oh, you know him," Hamish said. "He pours his heart into those letters."

"And he has a very big heart," Reggie said.

"What's he like?"

"He's one in a million," Reggie said without missing a beat, her eyes flicking to Hamish a moment. "There is no other human like Nate on the planet. He is warm and funny and he cares about everyone. He loves the North End. He loves its history. He is obsessed with the statue of Paul Revere they are erecting in the Prado. He treats every person who crosses his path as if they are the King of England."

Sarah watched her a moment then turned to Hamish.

"He's my best friend. We share a flat. He is probably the best person I know."

"He will feel so betrayed if he learns I am a woman," Sarah said with a pleading look to Reggie. "I just really wanted to know he was going to be all right. You probably think that is strange. A man I don't know."

Reggie giggled. "He is going to love that you are a woman. It will delight him." She lingered on Sarah's face a moment, and something crossed her mind. Something she would tuck into her pocket for the moment.

Later Reggie declined a walk with Hamish, with the intention of finding Vaughan at the office and somehow untangling the mess she had roped around them. She left Hamish at the street-light at the end of his street and swerved in the direction of Cross

Street. She didn't get far before she felt someone behind her. She swerved on her heel and investigated the spill of streetlight, the sounds of the shadows.

She continued. Then stopped again. "I have a gun in my trouser pocket and I haven't slept well in a fortnight. So you might want to choose another lady to pursue."

A low voice laughed. A laugh she recognized too well. Her breath caught.

"I never want to see you again." She barely kept her voice from rippling. "I won't even look at you." She tilted her chin up and squeezed her eyes shut to keep them from curiosity.

"It's very unladylike to hold a grudge, Regina Van Buren. Especially for the man who gave you your first real employment."

"What do you want, *Mister* Valari?"

"There's that voice. Those manners. That Clara Bow accent."

Reggie slowly turned and found Luca there. Dressed to the nines, black hair purple under a streetlight.

"You and Cicero have been sniffing around Toby Morris's house."

"For a case," Reggie said, hating that her voice wavered.

Luca nodded with a patronizing raise of his eyebrow. His hands were tucked deeply in his pockets, and his whole body seemed a study in leisure: cavalier, as if he were just out for a stroll.

"I need you to give me anything you found there. Papers. Are they at the office? We can just duck back there."

Reggie shook her head. "No. Get out of my life."

"I'm in your life, Reggie, because you are in my cousin's life. Bit of a circle we have going."

"Did you kill Walt Bricker?"

Luca waved his hand. "I don't kill people, Regina."

"No. You just make other people do it. Were you behind Kelly killing Toby?"

"What use would a boy's corpse be to me?" He started walking as the lights of Haymarket Square winked over them, and Reggie, through some force she couldn't describe, fell into step. His magnetism, she supposed. He drew her. She hated him for it. And for a million other things. "What people do out of a sense of loyalty to me, however misguided, is on them and not me."

Reggie wondered if he included his cousin in that statement. "That would make a good epitaph for you," she said. "I don't have anything from that case. We saw some orders in his bedroom when we investigated, then Hamish took them to Kelly's where he was almost burned alive." She said the last part emphatically, hoping to stir some reaction from Luca. It worked. The only redeeming thing about this man was his obvious love for his cousin. Luca's impeccable stature faltered with the slightest tug at his collar.

"Is he hurt?"

"What are you doing here, Luca?"

"Is Hamish hurt?"

"Tell me!"

"I tried and failed to get Nate Reis. That man has a working knowledge of a neighborhood I found myself missing. Not much use for nightclubs if we all go on bully beef rations if the war comes here. I have some business prospects at the docks here. War, Regina. You've heard of it, right? If your country is stepping in that direction, we'll need a contingency plan. Is my cousin all right?"

"Did you hurt Nate?"

"No. Kent did."

Reggie was surprised Luca was so straightforward.

"I had nothing to do with it," Luca said. "He thought if he could lure him to my cause, I would appreciate it. Rather ironic, isn't it? Like that fellow at my old nightclub. Kent will not be allowed near any enterprise or endeavor of mine. I don't condone brutes beating up Hamish's friends. How is Hamish?"

"He's fine. Not like when someone allowed him to be riddled with Suave's bullet."

Luca chuckled through his exhaled relief. "Well, I miss him. But I didn't come here to shoot the breeze. I came because I had a rather interesting phone call from Schultze telling me that a Mr. William Van Buren thought he might like to pursue property development. Fiske's Wharf to be exact. I was, of course, surprised. The Van Burens were always insurance people, I thought. But times are tough and people are constantly making bad investments."

Reggie's shoulders straightened. "I-I don't really speak to my parents. I don't know what business Father is part of. I . . ."

Luca reached over and lifted her ring to the halo of a street-lamp. "Bet my little cousin loved seeing this on you. It's gorgeous. You could pawn it and buy a yacht."

He dropped her hand, but Reggie could still feel the creep of his touch. She tucked her hand behind her. "What do you want?"

"I want you to keep an eye on that development. I told you. I am interested in the area. The geography. Pete Kelly took a few stupid turns, but I know you won't. You're smarter than that, Regina."

"You have to speak English, Mr. Valari. Despite my penchant for mob pictures, I am not completely fluent in gangster speak."

Luca smiled but his eyes were dark. Pitch dark. Darker than the sky around them. "Hamish has my number, but you'll do best to reach me here." He handed her a calling card with a fancy Beacon Hill address on it. "Got tired of the modern amenities. Thought I'd invest in one of those rambling old houses."

"I *won't* need to reach you."

"Regina, William Van Buren has quite the name for himself. Quite the set. And now quite the loan. Yes, a few bad investments here and there can easily be wiped away." His eyes flitted to her ring. "And people find that the right money can unfetter them from some hasty choices."

Reggie felt her cheeks heat as if she had been slapped. "I don't want that."

"I want Hamish to be happy. This is one way we all get what

we want. You can end your sham of an engagement, your father can find a thriving business world, and my little cousin can finally get his girl."

"No. I don't want you near my family. I don't want you near Vaughan. My engagement has nothing to do with you, Luca!"

He raised his finger to his temple in a makeshift salute and turned. "Wonderful to be back, Regina. Always loved Beantown."

CHAPTER 20

Errol Parker was on the road with the Patriots and Nate was back in his office.

Hamish was thrilled to step through the open door and find its desk occupied.

"Just discharged. Came right here. Don't want that fool Liebowitz getting any further ahead." His eyes were light as he looked around his desk.

"Nonsense. You couldn't bear to spend another day without checking up on your neighborhood."

Hamish watched Nate and his heartbeat started up a little. There was a part of the puzzle Nate was leaving out. "If I hadn't introduced you to Luca . . ." Hamish shifted in the chair across from Nate's desk.

"He wanted me to work for him. I'd be a horrible mobster, you know."

Hamish winced. "I'm so sorry."

"Oh, please. Don't take attention away from my predicament by stealing the blame." He winked at Hamish, who smiled in turn. "I was always meant to intersect with Luca. It was part of life's plan. Everyone is threaded together. A tapestry. If I didn't have Luca, I wouldn't have his cousin. So I'll take the trade-off." Nate sipped a glass of water. "You weren't really worried about me, were you?" Nate's eyes were glossy, but they held a bit of their usual twinkle. A tired twinkle.

"I was a little worried." He cleared his throat. "About having to pay the entire rent check myself."

"Right. So worried about the rent you slid into a horrifically uncomfortable plastic chair and talked my ear off while I was trying to be a good comatose patient?"

"What can I say?" Hamish kept his voice light. "Times are tough. Are you . . . I never learned . . ."

"About how crippled I am?"

"Nate . . . I . . ."

Nate held up a restraining hand. Then reached for a walking stick, holding it up for Hamish's inspection. He still looked tired and his eyes had aged, but he was back to his good humor. There were slight bruises on his cheek and a bandage under his hairline, ensuring the stitches healed properly.

"Makes me look sophisticated." Nate gestured to the stick.

"Is it forever?"

Nate shrugged. "I don't know. Let's hope not, huh?"

"Nate. All of those times you brought work home . . ."

"I don't have your cousin Luca's memory, Hamish. I like paper and files. Keeps me organized. I am my own secretary. Good job at keeping my office clean, by the way. I assume that this is you and Reggie." He inspected under the blotter and swiped a patch of dust away. "But it became harder and harder when I knew that people were finding ways to sneak around here. Like Errol Parker's locker. I didn't have anything so gruesome happen to me, but I have a responsibility to keep the secrets of the neighborhood."

Hamish scraped the chair opposite the desk close to its rim. "This is why you started bringing everything home . . ."

"And keeping it in seemingly disorganized piles all over the house? Yes." Nate scratched at the edge of the blotter. "I should have told you more, Hamish. It's not that I didn't trust you. It's that I didn't ever want you to be put on the spot. If you didn't know, I thought you would be safer. Especially when I understood that your cousin was involved."

"I'm not afraid of danger." Hamish mimicked Winchester Molloy's gravelly voice.

Nate laughed. "You aren't, are you? I created a code system. It took me hours and hours. That is why I was always working. I had a hunch . . . an inkling that something might happen to me. I am lucky to be alive, Hamish, I know that." He reached into his desk and took out a file. Hal Simpson's: the fellow from the Old North Church. He slid it across the desk and reached for a pen.

"So you're going to show me your code system?" Hamish said lightly.

Nate passed him the pen. "*You're* going to show me my code system. I knew if something happened to me it needed to be left with the person I trust most in all the world."

Hamish laughed away Nate's compliment. "I suppose this means we can go back to playing chess." But Hamish accepted the notebook and the pen and began drawing the familiar grid. Ten numbers across, ten letters down. A million possibilities intersecting. "Each letter formula is an address. So it's not just x's."

Nate beamed. "Circumnavigating the globe."

"Exactly." Hamish concentrated, flexed his fingers, and put what he had deciphered to good use. "And I knew the names because I had all of your papers around. Not only that, this is our neighborhood." He lingered on the latter part of the sentence with a fond look. "The numbers became a code for the services they do for each other . . ."

"Hamish . . ." Nate's eyes shimmered. "Really . . . I knew . . ."

"I was right." A half-moon smile crested Hamish's cheek. "It was easy enough to find your clients' names."

"How long did it take you to figure it out?" Pride undercut

Nate's voice. Pride in Hamish, he assumed, but also pride in himself for taking a course of action that worked.

"Two days. I was so angry, Nate. And I was about to throw the cocoa tin across the kitchen when my eye caught the side of one of our unfinished games. And then I was even angrier with you. Irrationally, I guess. For always playing the same scheme. I looked through the games you made me keep, and then I figured it out. You always used the same moves and you taught Reggie too. Made her keep the games. Then I wondered why as soon as you finished with the files for the night you always wanted to head to the kitchen. Even if I was in the middle of a book. And . . . then I thought about how careful you are. That, sure, you keep paperwork all filed and neat. But how you would need another system. You would always need another system." He smiled despite himself. "Battleship."

"You can't tell anyone."

Hamish rolled his eyes with mock exaggeration. "Cross my heart."

Nate adjusted his kippah and took back the pen Hamish extended to him. "I know what you did, Hamish. About Bricker."

Something drained out of the room and settled between the two of them. "How did you know?"

"You came and blabbed it to me at the hospital."

"You were asleep!"

"Not *that* asleep. I could still hear you. You meant it well. I know that. But, Hamish, I don't seek revenge or vengeance. Every year I celebrate Yom Kippur. It is a day of forgiveness. The only way I can see through the bleakness of this world is to forgive."

"That man who . . . who crippled you. He . . ." Hamish immediately regretted the intensity of his tone. He promised himself Nate would never hear him say the word, and here he was the one who uttered it.

"I do, Hamish. Because I have to. I believe that forgiveness is the only thing that unfetters us. I am just grateful to be here."

"You even forgive Luca who wanted you to work with him. Without him this never would have happened."

"Yes."

"You knew he wouldn't break into your house when he would risk my seeing him."

"That man's only redeeming quality seems to be sitting across from me."

"You should have told me. I would have gotten him to stop. It makes my calling him—"

"Ironic? Isn't it just?" Nate smiled sadly. "You don't need him in your life, Hamish. I could handle him."

"You should have told me." Hamish was bowled over, and not for the first time, at Nate's act of grace. He plucked at the fabric on his trousers to keep his hand from shaking so fiercely as to coax concern from his friend.

"I didn't want that part of your past in your life anymore," Nate said brightly. "I stayed late at the office. I knew when you would be gone. I agreed to meet him only because he was your family. But I don't know why he thought I would do anything for him. Other than his idea that it would be profitable. For my residents. And they wouldn't be deeply enough involved in his scheme to be held legally accountable." He stopped. Shrugged. "Well. Seems Mr. Kent wasn't too fond of my declining. Even though Luca for his part did stay away. Mrs. Leoni was around. She had a rabbi in to bless her kitchen. She says she will make it completely kosher. I even got flowers from the *Advocate*. I . . ." Nate stopped. Took a beat. Took in the office with his eyes. "I love this neighborhood, Hamish."

Something crossed Nate's face. Hamish, unused to this shadow, felt his heartbeat speed up and his fingers tremble a little. He tucked his hand under his brace. "I love this neighborhood," Nate continued, "and I will do everything I can to protect it. The biggest mistake that someone can make is assuming that I can be played. I will protect *my* North End with everything I have."

Hamish nodded at the challenge in Nate's eyes. "I know. I respect you for it."

"Let's leave your past in your past," Nate repeated with a strong look. "Because I have renewed determination. Your cousin drew a line in the sand, and I am on the other side. I listened to him out of my affection for you, but the North End is my first love and I will not shy away from fighting back. And not just with battleship games."

"I know."

Nate nodded, his face somber. "Sooner or later, Hamish DeLuca, you're going to have to take a side. And it might mean never seeing your cousin again. It might mean surrendering him."

Hamish flinched. "I know."

"Do you?"

"I met Aaron Leibowitz," Hamish said calmly, the name lightening him and, he hoped, the conversation. "When Reggie and I were trying to figure out who hurt you."

Nate's walking stick clanged on the ground. He didn't pick it up, giving Hamish his rapt attention. "That is the first truly interesting thing you have said," he said. "What was he like?"

Hamish shrugged. "I think you'll have to see for yourself. Come 'round the office in about half an hour? Reggie has gone shopping for sandwiches and tea. We'll have a little party."

"I confess I am excited. I never thought I would actually meet the fellow face-to-face. But it's a new perspective now, isn't it? I might actually be able to sit and have a cordial tea with the man. New leaf! Or will it be? Maybe he'll say something and I'll have to—"

"Nate." Hamish held up a hand.

"No, no. You are right. I am grateful for my chance at life. I am even grateful for this Leibowitz fiend." He rubbed his hands together. "I can't wait to see what he's like. What he looks like. What does he look like, Hamish?"

"You'll see for yourself."

"I wonder if he's devastatingly handsome. That would annoy me, maybe. But only a little."

"I can tell you"—Hamish chose his phrase carefully—"Leibowitz has always wondered the same about you."

<hr>

Reggie was still beside herself with excitement at the revelation that Aaron Leibowitz was actually a *she*. Sarah showed up at the given time and looked softly pretty. Her bobbed hair was fastened with a ribbon and her gingham dress was modest but still flowed and flounced in feminine places. Reggie reached into her handbag and extracted a Max Factor tube. "Lipstick."

"I never!"

"Just a bit of color. This lovely peach," Reggie said. "It will bring out your complexion."

Sarah accepted the tube reluctantly and pressed it to her lips. Reggie loaned her a compact. "Do I look okay?"

"You look beautiful." Reggie delighted in the young woman's soft glow.

"Knock, knock," said Nate with his customary habit, leaning on his walking stick. Reggie took the office in two quick strides and gave him a gentle hug and a kiss on the cheek. "Sight for sore eyes, Nate. I missed you something fierce."

Nate disengaged from Reggie, squeezing her shoulder with the hand not balancing his cane. There was a lifetime of friendship in his eyes. "Oh, my apologies." He noticed Sarah. "I didn't know you had company, Reg. Might not have stood on ceremony anyway, but would have tried."

Sarah rose slowly, a flush of pink spreading across her cheeks as she saw Nate for the first time. Reggie reveled in Sarah's obvious attraction to what she saw.

"Nathaniel," Hamish said from the doorway. "This is Sarah Abrams."

"A pleasure." Nate used his good hand to take Sarah's. Reggie kept her eyes on Nate's face and surmised the lipstick was working. *Everything* was working. Her heart clutched seeing the immediate rapport between them. She just hoped it lasted through Sarah's revelation.

"I am Aaron Leibowitz," Sarah blurted.

"Pardon?"

"A woman should not study the Torah. A woman should not write to newspapers. My family is very conservative, but the first time I read one of your editorials, I knew I had found a mind like my own. So I baited you. And . . . and . . . debated with you."

Nate blinked. Reggie was sure he was reconciling the million and one names he'd used to describe his epistolary nemesis with the pretty girl before him. "You're a woman."

"I must have shocked you. I—"

"You're a woman!" Nate repeated, Reggie unable to read the tone—just that it was loud and he was obviously surprised. "Is this a joke?" He looked to Reggie and Hamish in turn.

Sarah responded, "I know, and I am sure you think the worst of me, but when I heard that you were ill . . . I just . . . I always wanted to meet you. I always looked at you as sort of a friend and . . . I suppose you must hate me." Sarah reached for her handbag. "Your beliefs are very valuable to you and you must think I am a disgrace and . . ." She broke off.

Nate blinked over her a few times. Then looked over his shoulder again to Hamish and then to Reggie, who did nothing but smile at him. "You're a beautiful girl! You're a smart and frustrating and beautiful girl!"

Reggie was delighted at the anticipated reaction. Her eyes glistened. Sarah laughed uncertainly, then it evened out to a line of music.

"I feel like I've known you for years," Sarah was saying.

"You're a beautiful girl! See, Hamish! See! She's a beautiful, smart, and strong girl. Sarah, is it? Sarah, I am Nathaniel Reis, though heaven knows no one calls me that. It's Nate. Only Nate. And that handsome fellow over there who looks like a bit of a blue-eyed puppy dog is my flatmate, Hamish DeLuca, and . . . oh. So used to connecting people. But you have already met? I'm rambling. Nervous, perhaps, because you are a smart and beautiful girl. I would like to know what you are doing for Shabbat dinner. And then for the rest of your life." Nate stopped, looked at Hamish, then at Reggie, then out the window where the bells and steeples and roofs collided and everything in his life lined up and made sense. He took a long breath, and even though Reggie could see his eyes were tired, the familiar twinkle was there. He looked out with love to his city and it loved him back. "Welcome to my neighborhood."

⊹

"That had the desired effect." Hamish watched Nate and Sarah disappear, leaving Reggie and Hamish with lemonade glasses to wash and crumb-laden plates to brush off.

He was sorry to see them go. He knew they needed time to talk—to truly get to know each other beyond Hamish and Reggie—but Hamish wasn't sure how much longer he could sidestep the elephant in the room. Reggie had kissed him. And it wasn't just any kiss. Not a kiss born of a moment of reckless gratitude. Not a magnanimous Scarlett and Rhett kiss like she told him. He tasted a future in that kiss. Dreams and ideas and passion wrapped with a tight bow. She loved him. He knew it when her lips shuddered against his. She *loved* him. Maybe not to the same exponential extent that he loved her. That would be an almost impossibility. But she loved him nonetheless.

Reggie wrapped the leftover cannoli, twisting the ring on her finger. She was thinking about it too.

"Reg, we have to talk." He fingered his brace. His fingers were shaking slightly. Shaking with the ripples of doubt: he didn't deserve her. Quasimodo waiting through the toll of the bells.

"Hamish . . . I can't—"

"What do you mean you can't!" Hamish crossed and shut the office door. "What do you mean you can't?" he repeated in a lower voice. "Reggie, you love me. I tasted it. You tasted it! That sounds like a line from a film. But I felt it. I felt it. And you did too."

"I am engaged."

"Reggie, please. You don't truly love Vaughan Vanderlaan. He is the last thing binding you to your parents' expectation."

"My father has poured so much money into our office, Hamish."

Hamish dashed to her and gripped her arms. "And we will pay him back. I will pay him back. I would do anything . . . Reggie. I have loved you since the moment I saw you. At Mrs. Leoni's. I loved you. Immediately. I loved you. I *love* you. More now than even then. You're all I think about. Day and night. You make me more than I thought possible. I can do anything if I am with you."

Reggie blinked tears. "I can't . . ."

Hamish swallowed. "Look me in the eye, Regina, and tell me you don't love me."

Reggie shook her head and tugged her arms from Hamish's grip. "I can't."

"You don't love me?"

"I don't know!" She threw up her hands. "I mean, I know that—"

"Reggie." Hamish's voice was just above a whisper. "If you break my heart, I will never pick up the pieces again."

"Hamish, my parents will lose everything. They need me to marry Vaughan so they can keep their estate!"

Hamish stopped in his tracks. "What?"

"I promised because it will save my family. I know it sounds horrible—especially to someone like you. But my mother doesn't know how to live without her parties and her friends. My father made a few bad investments."

"And this . . . This is why you said yes?" His heart turned over.

Reggie nodded, her eyes a film of tears. "You must have a dozen words for me on the tip of your tongue. Hamish DeLuca! So straitlaced. From a good family." She tried a smile. "What is it about you that makes me cry so? Myrna Loy *never* would. And I didn't before I met you. No. You *can't* look at me like that." She sniffed. "Hamish, your eyes. They're so big. I am only human! I am shattered thinking I've hurt you, Hamish, but we are products of our environment. And the three years I have known you have been the best of my life. Maybe I am weak, but I cannot completely shut my past from my life. Vaughan is my past."

"But you don't love him." There wasn't a ripple or tremor in his hand or his voice. It startled Reggie, this certainty.

"In a way I do, Hamish. That's something you have never quite understood, I think."

"He'll keep you from everything you love. You've put it off for so long. Polishing silver and hosting teas. Please, Reggie. You're not going to go through with it."

‑‑‑⋇‑‑‑

Reggie was at a crossroads. She twisted the ring on her finger so hard she broke skin. If she didn't marry Vaughan, then Luca had the desired effect. But if she did, it would now be not to save her family but to spite Luca Valari.

Well, it might have ended up here all along. Love in Reggie's upbringing was synonymous with transaction: a bartering price, a chip to be played with the right hand. But really love was the taste of lemon on someone's lips or the feel of their finger pads over the back of your neck, just as the tendrils whispered over your cotton collar. It was the silly things you remembered to fill a room they had left. Love dazzled away the money and contracts, softened the corners and blighted the business voices. Love made your right shoe rise slowly in the middle of a world-ending kiss and made you cry for no reason and ink-spotted the pages of your journal.

She twirled her ring. Vaughan had rung over to take a stroll and she agreed to meet him at the cusp of the Common. She arrived as the sun hovered directly over the Massachusetts State House, setting its gold dome on fire.

She looked behind and saw the friendly steeple of the Park Street Church. Her eyes flickered to her ring. It was around here that he put it on her.

She would tell him tonight, she decided. Tell him she had kissed Hamish. And see what he said.

When Vaughan arrived, his hair was somewhat out of order from his combing his fingers through it, and his top two buttons were undone, tie loose. This was not a Vaughan she recognized.

"Anything wrong?"

"Your father was in some pretty dire straits," he said. "As you know."

Reggie turned. Vaughan was embarrassed. "Yes."

"And so Dirk Foster offered him an opportunity to invest in some properties he was working on as an alongside to his usual business with Hyatt and Price."

"Oh."

"I think you know the rest. I'm sorry, Reggie. I have myself to blame. I wasn't paying attention. From the start."

"You have nothing to reproach yourself for, Vaughan. You are not Dirk's keeper." Reggie picked at a scab on her elbow. Tattooed from her night at the burning warehouse. Her mother would scold her for ruining her perfect skin. She found a faraway star to fix her eye on for a moment. *But my skin has never been perfect. I've always had these freckles.*

"You're wrinkling your nose," Vaughan said.

"Thinking. Scabbing my elbow. Getting into one scrape after another. What man would want to marry me?" she said lightly.

Silence fell like a curtain. Vaughan started to say something then stopped. Reggie wished the ground would open up and choke her through. It didn't.

"I'll make sure your father is advised wisely from here on in. A lawyer friend is going to help him sort this out." Vaughan chuckled darkly. "I suppose you have your own lawyer friend."

Something shifted. Reggie felt something hop in her heart. There was a chance. There was . . .

"It's very kind of you, Vaughan. Very much appreciated." She stopped a moment. "I kissed Hamish."

Vaughan's face was shadowed, unreadable. "That can't have been an easy secret to keep." His voice gruffly diplomatic.

"No. And I apologize. It was one of those 'I thought you were dead' moments. That doesn't excuse it, but it was a momentous moment."

"A momentous moment." Vaughan let lightness tinge his voice.

Suddenly Vaughan's mouth was on hers. He tilted her chin up with the crook of his thumb, and in that kiss she tasted his loss and her past. Everything he would never say to her and every touch and caress and plan he had. And she tasted a tear in that kiss, unsure if it was his or her own. And she felt his curve of a smile. She returned it, deeply. Enjoying the feel of his hair in her fingers for one last time. Enjoying the breadth of his shoulders in starched, perfect cotton against the light frothy gauze of her dress.

"It's lovely," he said, voice thick. "You're still that sixteen-year-old girl who wanted a ride in my car."

Vaughan's lips traced over her collarbone while his forefingers played at the butterfly collar of her cotton dress. His fingers marked and mapped over her shoulder blade and stopped in the groove of her neck.

"Distracting." He nudged at her *Spira, Spera* necklace with the crook of his index finger. "Gets in the trail of your neck."

Reggie's heart thrummed. And the same slip of guilt that always found its way through her did so at that moment. She exhaled and Vaughan gently pulled away. Tears pricked her eyes when she recognized herself in the moment of inevitability.

Vaughan's eyes brushed over her face, from forehead to liquid eyes, down over her lips. He gently let the necklace fall from his loose grip.

"It's time I take my ring back, Reggie. A gentleman does not wed a young woman whose heart is tied to another. I'll still help your father. But I think we should call a spade a spade."

Reggie swallowed. Not trusting her voice at hearing the decision she never would have made, she settled for steadying his shoulder with one hand while letting the other explore the back of his hairline: cut with precision like every other perfect line that made him Vaughan. That recalled the world she was from and the promise she was breaking.

"Vaughan. I never wanted to hurt you. I made so many mistakes when it came to your heart. When it came to my own. It's unforgivable, but I am truly sorry."

Vaughan traced the circumference of her face like it was a portrait in a gallery. Committing it to memory, she supposed. But he must have already, as she had so often been cartographer of his own contours: smile lines and bright blue eyes, the blond framing close-set ears. The blond stubble that evaded his razor. He must not have made an appointment with his barber this week. She knew his scent and collar and the light pressure of his hands. And for a moment, Reggie, eyes still meeting Vaughan's, was back in her childhood bedroom of ruffle and lace and the dead glassy stare of porcelain dolls imagining the feel of Vaughan's lips on hers while he pulled her tight against him.

"You could lose yourself in a man like that," her friend Katherine once said, speaking to Vaughan's easy protective bearing and broad shoulders. So different from Hamish's wiry form. But the heart was stupid and the heart didn't listen. And the heart couldn't tell east from west—it charted its own territory and made its own path. It trundled along even as its owner tried to stop it, bounded ahead no matter who bore the brunt of its indecision. Reggie brushed her hand over his cheekbone and down over his shoulder.

"I won't be responsible for holding you to something you don't want," he said. "I sometimes wish that I hadn't let you go from your parents' the night I first proposed to you. That if I had somehow kept you in my sight line . . . But would that really have done anything?" Vaughan swallowed. "I would do anything to make you happy, Reggie. But a gentleman knows when to step aside. And a gentleman knows when he can take a bit of a lady's burden."

Reggie blinked up at him. "What burden?"

"Your father is keeping some pretty interesting company. Never thought I'd hear wind of that nightclub owner again."

Reggie felt the breath leave her lungs in one long deflation. She reached out and clutched his arm. "Vaughan, do not get involved. Not for my sake. Not for my father's sake. Please. Oh please, Vaughan." She released his arm and began to turn his ring around her finger absently. Turning and turning until its diamonds glistened, catching a prism of light. She felt its weight as she worked it over her knuckle, felt a strange lightness when she placed it in Vaughan's outstretched palm. But at what cost?

"We go to great extremes for love, don't we? We barter and beg. We marry Frank Kennedy." Vaughan's voice was low.

At the mention of Scarlett O'Hara's ill-suited second husband, Reggie snorted. "She did that out of love for Tara."

"It's still love."

Love filled his eyes, softening his face. It was thrilling and uncomfortable at the same time.

"And you forgive me?"

"I have to, don't I?" Vaughan said. "Because that's what love would do." The ring in his hand seemed to burn him, and he transferred it to his pocket, slowly turning away.

"Please take care of yourself, Vaughan."

"I would do a lot more for you, Regina," he said without turning his head over his shoulder.

The tears pricking Reggie's eyes sloshed over her cheeks as he disappeared. She fell against the Park Street Church and gulped for breath. She couldn't repay him for this. *Luca.* Her teeth clenched. She would ban him from her life. From her world. From Vaughan and Nate and Hamish and everyone she loved.

You need to forgive yourself, she thought.

Reggie had forgiven her mother and father. Had forgiven Vaughan for the impromptu proposal that catapulted her to Boston and her new life. Had forgiven Hamish. But herself?

Finally, Reggie nodded, eyes blurry and throat tingling. She would let herself off the hook. Deep breath, eyes to the future. Exhale.

Regina Van Buren had already climbed the mountains needed to find herself on a path of independence. The last stretch would be a cinch. With the grace of Vivien Leigh and the panache of Irene Dunne, she would weather the last stretch, shoulders back and lips curved in a smile, her brown eyes twinkling at the prize ahead.

For if she was the heroine in the picture of her mind—camera panning, adventure unfurling—then Hamish was the hero at the helm.

CHAPTER 21

Light spilled from the slat in the curtained window when Hamish arrived home that night. His brow furrowed. He didn't remember leaving the lamp on, and Nate was still at his bubbe's where Hamish had left him, having lost several hands of cards.

He moved to put the key in the door, but it was slightly ajar. Hamish took a breath and nudged it open with the crook of his finger.

"Hello?" he called to the empty hallway, switching on the light. He felt in the back of his trousers and retrieved the handgun. His hand shook a little around the steel. He locked his elbow in hopes of stilling his nerves.

He stepped quietly, stopping at the sitting room. A familiar smell, a smell that had not crossed his nostrils in many months, met him. Cologne. Expensive cologne. Trademark cologne. "Luca," he said, slowly turning.

His cousin was sitting in the armchair Nate usually occupied, taking a long drag of a cigarette lodged in a sleek holder. He was dressed impeccably. Black hair slicked with pomade. Smile bright but never reaching his obsidian eyes.

"Hamish DeLuca with a gun!" Luca made a quiet sound, almost a whistle, as Hamish lowered the weapon. He breathed a sigh of relief, leaving it on the side table. Not just that he wouldn't have to fire but that a split second of instinct had found him moving all of Nate's papers to a safe in Nate's room that morning.

"How did you get in?"

Luca just tilted his head. "Please."

"What are you doing here?" Hamish set down his coat but couldn't seem to make himself move any further in his cousin's direction. "You choose this moment to seek me out?"

Luca's lips twitched. He reached for a glass half filled with port he had helped himself to. "This isn't bad. Can't be yours. Nate Reis's, isn't it?" Luca shifted and set the glass down after a long sip. Hamish wondered if he was going to rise and embrace him in his old Luca way. With the same fluid ease he did everything and the same telltale cup of his hand at the back of Hamish's neck.

"Suave's man," Hamish said shortly. "The Flamingo. Frank Fulham. The entire business I got shot for? His name is Kent. And he was sniffing around Boston for you, wasn't he?"

Something crossed Luca's face and settled in his eyes. Guilt? Annoyance? "That's history, Cicero. I've been looking out for you. Making sure you're safe and well."

"A postcard would suffice." Hamish dropped onto the ottoman.

Luca crossed his legs. "My kind of people." He reached into his jacket pocket and extracted a folded piece of paper.

Hamish's heart thudded. He placed his two forefingers under his suspender to count its beat. Seeing Luca took him back to a smoky club and the rise and fall of Roy Holliday's band trilling through a barrage of upbeat numbers while the cold steel of a gun was pressed to his chest. Took him to the moment the world swirled and stalled and the pain exploded in his shoulder and he took the blame so that Luca could get away. Seeing Luca was something he assumed was eventually inevitable but also something he would never be prepared for. Not even now while his cousin watched him.

"You don't look happy to see me."

"Bricker. He's dead. I asked you not to go too far."

"You're not angry about that," Luca said coolly. "You're angry that I left you there. At the club."

Hamish sighed. "It's history, as you said. I wanted you to get away. I wanted you to be safe. I don't regret . . ." Hamish shrugged.

"Always doing the right thing. Being someone's conscience."

"I don't think so."

Luca chuckled softly. "I do." It sounded anything like a compliment. "Is that Reis fellow going to be all right?"

"He will be. Yes."

"Shame what happened to him. A lot is happening to people who don't deserve it."

Hamish's heart was racing. Luca was keeping something. Hamish could feel it in the tremor of his right fingers and the stabs at his chest. "Luca, did you seriously come here for a chat? Because if so, I will put on the kettle. My mom sent some lemon jam. I could—"

"Cic—"

"You wanted to use Nate!" Hamish barked. "For whatever nonsense you wanted."

"Aren't you quick on the uptake."

"I can't believe you would do that. He's *my* friend."

"He is talented."

"Kent?"

"Kent wants to work for me. Bit of a leech. He's a follower. When Suave died, Kent needed someone else to tug on to. Some people are followers. You whistle, they'll jump without thinking. He's been on my radar since my Chicago days."

"And he couldn't get to Nate."

"Well, can't blame him for trying."

"And Toby? He was in the middle."

"Toby?"

"Luca! Toby went to visit you at the Parker House Hotel. Errol Parker's nephew. You saw a way in. To play *both* sides. One side was Pete Kelly. Dumb, sure, with his stupid shipments. The other a group of supposed patriots who wanted to make a buck while ending the war—as if they could—and providing crummy housing." Hamish stared at the gun.

When Luca spoke, it was as if he hadn't registered one word Hamish had said. "It's my fault, isn't it, that Kent was angry with Nate. I should have known he would be capable of roughing him up." Luca's eyes softened. Hamish couldn't tell if it was affection or guilt or something else entirely. "And he was your friend. My loyalty is still to you, Cic. I had nothing to do with Kent."

"I don't believe that. Your loyalty is to you."

"I don't know if that's true." Luca paused. "I do like where that Pete Kelly was set up." He had a faraway look in his obsidian eyes. "The river. In and out. The war is bringing a lot of opportunity. For shipping. Munitions. Textiles and materials. Would benefit a lot of people here. I could use someone with a head for contracts and good North End connections." He looked pointedly at Hamish.

"You're unbelievable. You truly are." Hamish threw his arms up. He blinked the fury from his eyes. "So you're back in Boston, then?" He reached out his flat palms and worked them over the back of the chair he stood behind.

Luca shrugged. "Don't fancy going back to Toronto and enlisting. Don't want those Patriots around either."

"Why are you telling me this?"

Luca raised a shoulder. "You know I am not just going to sit around and volunteer at a soup kitchen."

"Luca, we're on opposite sides."

"I don't call all my own shots."

"Is this still to do with Fulham and his supposed death?"

Luca had apparently said all he was going to say.

Hamish tugged his collar with the hand not leaning over the armchair. Racketeering? Luca could commandeer a fortune.

"Your father said you tried to enlist. Brave of you."

"He feels guilty for not going," Hamish said absently. He saw Luca so differently now, and yet his cousin looked the same. Sounded the same. It tugged him into the past a moment and forced his fingers into his palm. This was a trip he didn't want to take.

"Yes. That case in Chicago. Lost his hearing with one of those anarchist bombs. Funny, all those stories we heard as kids. And I could never tell which ones were real or not. A Mountie. Roosevelt."

"They were all real. There are records. In the papers."

Luca rolled the paper he had extracted and rapped it on his kneecap. "I always loved Chicago. Felt that it tied me to my past somehow, you know? I lived there when I was a little boy."

Hamish was too agitated to play this game. "I am not in the mood for a trip down memory lane, Luca. I still don't know why you're here. You used Nate. He was hospitalized, probably because of you. If you're trying to get me to soften toward you, I'm not . . . I'm not . . ." He swallowed, evened out his tongue as best he could to avoid a stutter. "I don't know if I am ready."

"That is what your father used to say anytime anyone wanted to tell you about this." He rose and handed Hamish the folded piece of paper before sinking back down and reaching for his port, glass raised to his lips, eyes expectant on Hamish.

Hamish's right hand was shaking a little as he unfolded a full-spread page of newspaper. The date was from 1912. Which corroborated the story he was always told about his parents working on a case involving anarchist bombings. His eyes tripped over the headline: "Altercation Between Toronto Reporter and Criminal Valari Results in Death in Botched Bank Robbery."

Hamish looked at Luca, his hand now shaking fiercely, then

back to the article. *"Heritage Trust Bank: Ray DeLuca, a reporter for Toronto's* Hogtown Herald, *killed criminal Tony Valari in an altercation for the apparent defense of a police constable out of jurisdiction. DeLuca, 31, admitted to . . ."* Hamish couldn't read any more. His hand was shaking fiercely now.

"I never heard this before." Hamish shook his head. "This isn't true, Luca. My father couldn't kill someone. He couldn't kill his brother-in-law. He loved Tony. He . . ."

Luca drained the port. Hamish tried to catch his eyes in the half light, but they were completely unreadable. "Oh, it's true. But we couldn't tell precious Hamish. We had to protect Hamish. He couldn't handle it. He got some stories but not others. He was never ready. Well, *you* have a gun and *you* are a grown man and deserve for someone to finally show you some respect."

"Luca . . ." Hamish blinked at the headline until it blurred. "I'm . . ."

"It isn't *your* fault. You can't help who your father is, and I couldn't help who mine is. And here we are."

"I thought he died in the same explosion that hurt my dad's ear." Hamish was bowled over.

"And no one ever corrected that. It's true, of course. Call up Jasper Forth and ask him straight out. Or your father." Luca chuckled darkly. "Yes, call your father. He wouldn't lie if you asked him straight out."

Hamish crumpled the paper and threw it in the direction of the empty fire grate. It missed by several feet. "Why are you telling me this?" He clenched and unclenched his fingers.

"Because you're not the only one who needed protection, Hamish! But you got it. I got nothing! You sit there and judge me and think that I am trying to destroy everything you love, that I left you there at the Flamingo, whereas really, Cic, I knew that Reggie would care for you far more than I ever could, if I didn't break and leave you. If I didn't leave you with your new friends, you would still be following me around. Seeing you there with Suave's gun pressed to your chest slapped me in the face." The control that always leveled Luca's voice floundered. "We're more alike than you think."

Hamish couldn't find words. He studied Luca a moment as if he were showing a side of himself here that might fade away forever. And for all that, the veil had been tugged back so that Hamish saw, for the first time, the many truths about his cousin. He didn't want Luca to hate him. He needed Luca. He couldn't lose him. Funny, he hadn't thought about Luca as something he could lose for a long time. Maybe because he assumed Luca was already lost.

"Please leave Nate alone," Hamish finally said. "Luca, please. For me." He took a breath. "M-maybe . . . Maybe I don't have the right to . . ."

Luca didn't answer, just pulled his hat on with his inimitable flair, rose from the armchair, and sauntered past Hamish, who followed closely. Luca clutched the door handle, then turned on his heel and extended his hand to Hamish.

"I'll see you around." Gravity undercut his carefree statement. Hamish studied Luca's hand a moment. Unmoving. Then he met Luca's expectant eyes. "You won't even shake hands with me anymore, Cicero?" Luca's voice was coated in hurt that he tried—but failed—to lighten.

Hamish stepped forward and threw his arms around Luca's neck, holding tight, surprising his cousin before Luca recovered and cupped the back of Hamish's neck with that customary gesture of affection.

Luca squeezed Hamish's shoulder. "You're such a good kid." He adjusted the brim of his expensive hat. "You're the best person I know, Hamish DeLuca. Don't ever—ever—let anyone change even one ounce of who you are. Not even me."

"We're long beyond your having any kind of influence on

me." Hamish tried to keep his voice light, wondering if it was true.

"Good."

"And if we f-find ourselves on opposite sides?" Hamish said, his stutter flaring.

"You should still call me. For anything. That doesn't change, Hamish." The door clicked closed behind him.

Hamish lingered a moment, then returned to the sitting room, sinking into the armchair by the window that Luca had occupied, peering through the curtains to the street. His eyes avoided the crumpled newspaper as his heartbeat sped up, his breath coming in jagged gasps as if everything he had been able to counter with Luca there was now unfettered.

He didn't move save for the rise and fall of his shoulders and the drop of his head to his knees until the telephone jangled in the kitchen. Hamish debated answering; his mind was reeling, heart thudding, world off-kilter.

"Hamish DeLuca?"

"Yes."

"I probably shouldn't be calling you, but the papers will be out soon enough." It was Reid. "I have some news on Walt Bricker."

Hamish rubbed at the space around his heart; it had, if possible, constricted even more with the sound of Bricker's name.

"A witness has come forward."

Hamish listened to the rest of Reid's sentence as if in a fog. Hearing a few words through a spinning brain. Piecing together the entirety of the puzzle only when Reid signed off. An altercation was seen between Kelly and Bricker, resulting in the latter's death. The former had a history of drunk and violent behavior. Though Kelly was adamant that Bricker had been dealt quite a few blows before he got there and assumed he could get away with just finishing the job. Hamish felt all of the air leave his lungs in a delicious deflation. *I am not responsible.* For a brief moment the world wasn't tilted on its axis. Hamish felt absolved. Reggie would surely forgive him, and the thoughts that plagued his brain in the dark moments just before sleep finally arrived would be a thing of the past.

Hamish stood stone-still in the kitchen, unbalanced. For the millionth time, he wished he heard Nate's footsteps overhead. Why would Luca accept the blame for something he wasn't responsible for? Because Hamish helped him get away before? Because he wanted to prove he was invincible?

"Because he wants me to still believe in his power," Hamish said to the empty kitchen, to the thrum and buzz of the icebox, to the vehicle backfiring out the window, to the slow and steady tick of the clock in the front room. "That he would do something magnanimous for me. He needs me to believe in him."

For the first time in his life, Hamish felt something for Luca he hadn't before. It knotted his chest and turned his stomach a little, sheened his forehead with perspiration and started his hand trembling. It wasn't love or pride or anger or hatred or misunderstanding. It was far worse. Belittling. *Pity.*

Hamish's hand hovered over the telephone. He took a breath and began to dial a number that his fingers knew before his brain even caught up. Then stopped.

What was the point? Just to remind his father what he lived with every day? Hamish couldn't fathom the burden of carrying someone's death with him, like a millstone. Especially not the death of a family member. He breathed in deeply. Empathy. His father wrote of it often as the greatest gift. The least Hamish could do was offer some.

He dialed another number instead.

"Station One," said a female voice on the line.

"Hamish DeLuca for Maisie Forth."

A second later, a bright voice funneled through the wire. "Cracker Jacks, DeLuca. Calling me at my place of work. The other girls think you're my boyfriend. Which you are not. Rich

Halbot asked me out again last night. Took me to the Royal York for cocktails and—"

"Maisie, I need a favor." He smiled. Cut her off.

"Sure thing, kiddo."

"Your dad keeps all his case files still, eh?"

"Piles and piles."

"I need you to look into my uncle. Tony Valari. Find out what happened in Chicago. Summer 1912. Who he was working for. If the same . . . operation or what have you . . . is still in existence."

The other end of the line was quiet. "You're finally going there, huh?"

He twirled the telephone cord around his finger. "I need to understand Luca a little better."

SEPTEMBER 1940

The Court of Miracles was a study in jubilant tranquility. The racket came from applause and thundering footsteps as hundreds crowded into the Prado until the churchyard spilled like an over-turned vessel. Banners draped low and light in Hanover Street. But it was peaceful. The fountain jumped and pranced in the prism of September light. The sun was kind enough to settle just above the steeple of the Old North Church, its rays snagging on the tower where the fateful lantern hung to signal the arrival of the British. Today Hamish felt even the sunshine had a smell, contributing to the potpourri of basil and bread, oil and gasoline, and coffee.

The sculptor, Cyrus Dallin, was given a finite moment to speak of the artistry that consumed most of his life. A moment in a languorous symphony of speeches. Hamish would have been caught up in the excitement of the moment even if he didn't know every last thing about Dallin and the statue's history from Nate's unending enthusiasm.

Nate leaned on his walking stick, Sarah Abrams affixed to his other arm, straining to see over the sea of people to Dallin himself. The statue was still shrouded in its covering, and Hamish enjoyed his friends' excitement. Nate was looking beyond the gift-wrapped emblem of liberty to its creator. Dallin had a pointed white beard and an intelligent gaze—an interesting face.

"I almost didn't live to see this," Nate said somberly, turning from Sarah without loosening his grip on his cane or her elbow. "Can you imagine?"

It was one of the few times Hamish had heard his friend speak morbidly. Hamish imagined a city of freedom that had found a darkness underneath. While people applauded and alighted at this symbol of Revere's magnificent trail to liberty, so many were still shackled. Hamish tugged at his collar, thinking of Errol.

The sky was turquoise in a parade of autumn light. Hamish thought the North End courted all seasons well, but there was something about the crisp blessing of autumn winds and the slight chill that matched the red brick and cobblestones better than any other time of year. Now, the Prado—that eruption of space cloistered between the bells of St. Stephen's and the Old North Church—would display a grand emblem of liberty.

Hamish scratched under his collar. Liberty. This Revere statue and the pomp and circumstance of officials and politicians droning on in monotones the crowd could barely hear.

Hamish couldn't fit into this liberty, though he promised himself he would stand through the endless processions for Nate and his palpable excitement. Nate's new love was at his side and the world was shimmering around him.

More speeches and words that fell on deafening applause. No Reggie though. She should be here: her freckled nose squinting in the sun, her profile upturned intelligently. Her little asides. Just like the one he was giving Nate. He hadn't seen her in two months. She had gone home to spend time with her mother, to help her father with his books. They talked on the phone, and something about her voice was always just out of reach. Something evading him that he couldn't place his finger on. But he was determined to learn what it was. To erase any last lines between them. Not seeing Reggie was becoming harder and harder. There were no little mysteries in the office. Just contracts and legal paperwork and the headlines that tugged the war closer and closer even as it rampaged in Europe and pulled men from Toronto by the hundreds.

"He worked his whole life," Nate was saying, breaking Hamish's thought. "And he was given but a moment."

Hamish faltered as Nate clutched his stick in one hand and clasped Sarah Abram's hand with the other. Nate was immortal in his incessant need to speak and write and be the conscience of an entire neighborhood. A blip or notch on a long line of time. A moment. They were all given but a moment . . . to snatch and keep or hold tight.

The cover was pulled back and the life-sized statue was resplendent, catching the lacy pattern of the shadow of the leaves as the sun filtered through them. Revere with the aura of a knight fighting for his new world, hat draped in hand, dashing in the direction of Charlestown to round up the farmers of Lexington and Concord and start a revolution. Every detail was deft, shadowed by sunlight highlighting the crevices of Dallin's mastery: the muscled flanks of the horse's thighs and hoofs, the blacksmith's boots in the stirrups. Hamish could spend a lifetime gaping up at this artistry and never see the entirety of its sculptor's intent.

Your great cathedrals. Their architects never saw the end of their labors. They went to their graves never seeing their final product. Boston was in itself a cathedral: towering, bells pealing, attempting through history and humanity and light to reach heaven on merit and folklore and legend.

Cyrus Dallin saw the fruits of his labor. Poorer. Older. Hamish wasn't sure if he was wiser. But he lived to see his legacy.

Ascending to the top of a church. Pulling back the curtain on a crime. Or, in Nate's case, holding out his arms to the whole of a historic neighborhood and tugging it into him.

Then the crowd dispersed. Hamish left Nate and Sarah to explore the statue and catch another look at the sculptor.

Hamish was happy life was finding its usual rhythm of Nate and history, cobblestones and cannoli. There was just one thing missing under the span of blue sky.

He smiled, sidestepping inhabitants he knew well. Neighbors whose names were imprinted on his mind. Who once looked like tiny dots in a battleship game but now flourished in real, beating life.

And in the middle of the commotion and the symphony of North End sounds—the bells tolling and the carts rolling across the uneven stones, the whistles and layered languages of the world, the music spilling from somewhere high above a flower box—he focused on a figure in yellow.

Bright as the sunshine and the catch of the window light on Vaughan's ring.

The clack of Reggie's Spanish heels on the stones echoed the nearer he came. Revere was alive now, and every time he crossed over that slip of a courtyard he knew by heart he would take a moment and stall and wonder. The redbrick Prado with its fountain, wedged between two churches, their bells pealing jubilantly as if for him . . . and her, of course.

"Regina!" Hamish caught her elbow, turning her so her dress spun around her bare legs.

She was crying in the middle of the sunlight while the rest of the city was a smile.

"Reggie, what's the matter?"

She looped her arms around his neck and held him tight. He could feel a stream of tears trickle onto his neck. He tightened his grip and let his long fingers fall into the curls at the back of her neck. "Reggie?"

She mumbled something into the space between his cheek and earlobe, damp with tears and breath.

"I'm sorry?" he gently disentangled her and searched her face.

"I missed you, Hamish."

Hamish smiled, loving the feel and smell and nearness of her. "I wasn't even half of myself without you, Reg."

⎯⋇⎯

Reggie loved him, of course. With every breath and every thought and every pulse of adventure. She loved him beyond reason. Loved him enough to tug him out of his bell tower and into the sun-dappled North End even as the world blasted its uncertainty over the wireless and in the newsreels. She wanted to throw her lot in with his until she couldn't tell where she ended and he began: insecurity and episodes and shaking fingers and hiccupped breaths. She wanted to breathe something into him. Something pristine and new—just like the statue erected in the corner of the world as familiar to them as their collective heartbeats. And she needed him to be a center for her as she navigated the choices she saw around her. Her father. Vaughan. The world she so long held tightly to slipping through her fingers, and not on account of her running away.

Hamish was expectant. Watching her through lenses reflecting the sunlight, blinking his wide blue eyes into focus on her, then painting over her face, his gaze like a brush. Then they were in the North Square, having stolen through an alley crisscrossed with fire escapes and stones nudged close together, a slice of secret in the rambling bricks of the North End. The North Square was a burst of lemony light. Mrs. Leoni's awning at one end ushering in Prince Street, the familiar schoolchildren ignoring their teacher's guidance before the wood-slatted Revere House.

She lightened her voice for him, turned on the switch that

allowed her to straighten her shoulders and tuck the hurt and insecurity inside.

He walked calmly beside her, the swing of her skirt brushing his pant leg. One minute he looked like a kid at Christmas: knowing there was a stocking full of wrapped toys but unsure when would be the appropriate moment to dive in and explore. The next, his eyes were on her profile and something was turning over in his mind. His hand shook slightly to prove it.

"So you see, Hamish DeLuca," she said, keeping her eyes on her shoes, her tears drying, the uncertainty of the future and her father's choices and Luca falling with the stream of sunshine pooling on the stones. "I am a silly girl who spends too much time in her mind and gets too excited about the prospect of murder. But I love you. Truly, wholly love you. And I always, always will. And so I think . . ." She looked up at him. Then said, "No! Don't open your mouth! Don't you dare think of speaking. Van Buren comes before DeLuca, remember? It's there on the front of the door. I practiced in my head. Everything I was going to say." His eyes were bright and glistening, his cheeks flushed with surprise. His two forefingers crooked underneath his suspender. A measured count.

She reached up on her oxfords and brushed a comma of black hair from an ear that stuck out just a little—not too much—the perfect amount, settling her fingertips in the crook of his neck. Her Journal of Independence opened across the space of her imagination. *Make Hamish happy,* she had written over and over again. Hamish. Here he was. Right before her. She would fling herself smack dab into the middle of loving him with his short breaths and panic episodes, his tremors and stutters and shakes. "Your heartbeat," she whispered, treasuring the slight reverberation in her throat, sure that her voice would tickle in his earlobe. His breath was jagged. She was breaking something and settling in the cracks within. Too close. Just right. Squeezing the breath and the inhibition and her heritage from her. She spoke again in an uneven whisper. "So, as I said, I was practicing . . ."

"You're lying to me, Regina." His voice was steady. "But you're here and I'll protect you. Whatever it is. Do you understand? I would do anything for you. *My* Reggie."

"I love you."

"I know."

He pulled her in and she was surprised that someone could be so firm and gentle at the same time. He kissed her first at her temples, just a soft brush, then over her cheeks, and then, before making his way down to her lips (too slowly, for her taste), he ripped off his glasses and folded them into his pocket. Now there wasn't an inch between them. She eagerly opened her mouth so that she could return everything. Every last thing! And he kissed her very senseless, while the colors of their neighborhood exploded and the bells continued to chime.

A NOTE FROM THE AUTHOR

While *Murder in the City of Liberty* draws greatly on the political and sociocultural climate of 1940 Boston, I did take fictional liberties to heighten the atmosphere and tension of Hamish and Reggie's world in an accessible way.

As a voracious reader of historical fiction, I am most invested in stories that are suffused with enough historical ambience and detail that I am inspired to read more about their settings and time periods, and I sincerely hope readers feel the same.

While the Christian Patriots were a fictional organization, many anti-Semitic and racist groups were rampant in large cities across the United States and many of the viewpoints aligned with Henry Ford's *Dearborn Independent* became popularized as the war rampaged overseas.

All of the baseball teams and players are fictional, but I did find Ken Burns's *Baseball: An Illustrated History* a remarkable snapshot of the racial tensions experienced by players of color in Major League Baseball during the first half of the century.

During the beginning years of World War II in Canada, there were many shifts in the view of psychological evaluation for men enlisting. Psychology was still met with skepticism, but within the higher ranks of personnel selection, greater attention was being placed on determining the psychiatric competence of men fit or unfit for duty. I find it likely that a Canadian doctor would—beyond the censure of his colleagues in the medical field—posit that men with anxiety with episodes and visible symptoms such as Hamish would be seen unfit for duty overseas. After all, many of the men on these committees served themselves in the Great War.

The Cyrus Dallin Museum in Arlington, Massachusetts, was an incredible place to learn more about the man behind the iconic statue in the Prado behind the Old North Church. I highly recommend reading more about the nearly half century it took for the statue to find its rightful place and for Dallin to fulfill his promised commission. As well as on-site research, I found Rell G. Francis's *Cyrus Dallin: Let Justice Be Done* a fantastic pictorial guide to this remarkable man and his work.

I did rely on the Massachusetts Historical Society's impressive range of 1930s maps to attempt to recreate the Boston Reggie and Hamish would have cycled and strolled. All errors in the presentation of history are completely my own.

However, what is wholly accurate is my passion for Boston, its people, its heritage, and its culture.

While I conducted extensive research into how Hamish's illness would be viewed through the lens of 1930s medicine, I required no research in presenting his symptoms. I have suffered from a panic and anxiety disorder my entire life and am determined to normalize it in the fictional community. I encourage readers to engage with me on social media using the hashtag #FictionForEmpowerment to continue the discussion.

DISCUSSION QUESTIONS

1. While Reggie continually acknowledges her desire to "make Hamish happy" she is not completely free from her tie to Vaughan Vanderlaan. Vaughan binds Reggie to her past and her parents' expectations. Do you think it is possible for someone to be attracted to a person not for who they are but for the life and history they represent?

2. At its core, the Van Buren and DeLuca series is about an anxious young lawyer who innocently enters his cousin's world and learns more than he ever wanted to. In *Murder at the Flamingo*, Nate says that Hamish has "loyalty cataracts" when it comes to Luca and what he is involved in. How do you see Hamish's opinion and his loyalty to his cousin shifting in *Murder in the City of Liberty*?

3. Boston plays a starring role in Hamish and Reggie's lives. Both feel their adopted city is a major part in their development and in their happiness. Is there a place that you have felt an immediate attachment to?

4. While the Van Buren and DeLuca series features murder mysteries, a large part of the mystery is that surrounding Hamish's cousin, Luca, and the truths he learns about the dark world of Boston as he familiarizes himself with his

adoptive home. Part of this dark world includes the vast divide between those with money, power, and influence and those with little means to defend themselves. Can you think of other genre fiction where a deeper message such as social justice is explored? Why do you think it is is helpful to explore issues through artistic forms of entertainment such as fiction?

5. Nate tells Hamish that if the wrong voices are ripe for the picking in the loudest, most assured voices, they are easiest to follow. Can you think of such voices either in recent years or history that prove Nate's statement to be true? Why do you think people are so susceptible to being swayed by these types of opinions and how do you keep from falling into their trap as you navigate your own values and beliefs?

6. When Hamish learns his father was responsible for Luca's father's death, he withstands the temptation to telephone and confront his dad, feeling that he should act with a sense of empathy, as he still feels responsible for Bricker's death. Is there a moment in your life when you have held back from a difficult conversation due to a sense of compassion or empathy despite the importance of the topic to you?

7. As in the first book of the series, Hamish's anxiety and panic disorder is a constant hurdle but also an incredible strength in that it allows him a sense of unique empathy and the rare ability to tell when someone is being inauthentic or lying to him. Can you think of something in your life that you always thought of as a weakness or drawback that might actually be a strength?

8. Hamish's country is at war and yet his adopted country is not. While Hamish knows he cannot go to war, he still feels guilty for not joining the action and being a true

patriot. In what ways does Hamish try to fight the war in his own way in Boston even while he is unable to do so overseas?

9. Throughout *Murder in the City of Liberty*, the lead characters are put in situations that require them to act one way even though their conscience pricks at them. Reggie agrees to marry Vaughan to help her family, Nate Reis meets with Luca Valari, and Hamish calls Luca for help when Nate is hurt. Even though you might not necessarily agree with their choices, each has their own reason for acting the way they did. Have you ever had to justify something you have done for the right reason but in the wrong way?

10. When Hamish calls Luca with his suspicions about Walt Bricker and the attack on Nate, it is because he is tired of others getting away without being held accountable for their actions. Can you think of a time when you would have done anything to ensure justice for a wrongdoing?

11. Both Nate Reis and Errol Parker teach Hamish invaluable lessons about forgiveness. Hamish has to learn to forgive himself for calling Luca about Walt Bricker and Reggie has to learn to forgive herself for her treatment of Vaughan. Can you think of a time when it was far easier to forgive someone else but not yourself?

ACKNOWLEDGMENTS

Allison Pittman: for being my constant. I love being half of our team. *I love you, Bucko.*

I am so delighted to work with the team at Thomas Nelson. Thanks to Allison Carter and Dave Knox who continually find me interesting and exciting new places to talk about my books. Also thanks to the amazing editorial eye of Laura Wheeler and Lauren Schneider, *Murder in the City of Liberty* looks good! Thanks! Thanks! for making me look smarter than I am.

Kim Carlton: thanks for listening and supporting me and putting up with my emails. Mostly, thanks for being an all-around delightful human.

Jamie Chavez: I loved my experience with you on this book and I learned so much. Thanks for believing in my characters and their journey and for having not only a keen editorial eye but incredible wisdom.

Jared and Leah: I know you read every word I write and it is incredible to have that support. But mostly I am just happy that we are all (at least for the moment) in the same country (and the same continent) and can laugh our heads off together #SiblingSunday.

Ruth Samsel and Bill Jensen: I am so lucky to have you in my corner! Thank you for everything!

Kat: I have come to the conclusion that without you I just

wouldn't be able to write books. Thanks for being Kat. You save my spirit on so many occasions.

Annette: knowing you makes me an immediate winner. Whatever team you are on, I choose that one.

Gerry and Kathleen McMillan: with every book I learn more and more what an anomaly you are. The unconditional support. The undying belief in me even when things change or get a little uneven. You always recognized that what I thought was my greatest weakness was actually my greatest strength. So, again, I gifted Hamish DeLuca with all of the symptoms that might have been a plague or a millstone but rather, thanks to you, instill a deep sense of empathy that—when coupled with our family's unique brand of humor, grace, and aplomb—make me indefatigable.

DON'T MISS THE MYSTERY THAT STARTED IT ALL!

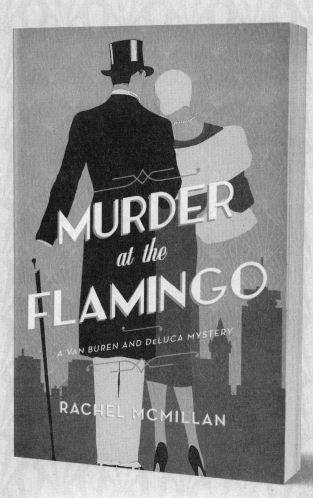

Available in print, e-book, and audio

ABOUT THE AUTHOR

Agnieszka Smyrska/Smyrska Photography

Rachel McMillan is a history enthusiast, lifelong bibliophile, and author of the Herringford and Watts series. When not reading (or writing), Rachel can be found at the theater, traveling near and far, and watching far too many British miniseries. Rachel lives in Toronto and is always planning her next trip to Boston.

Facebook: RachKMc1
Twitter: @RachKMc
Instagram: RachKMc